# GEORGE GREEN

# HOUND

## BANTAM PRESS

LONDON · NEW YORK · TORONTO · SYDNEY · AUCKLAND

**09501597**

TRANSWORLD PUBLISHERS
61–63 Uxbridge Road, London W5 5SA
a division of The Random House Group Ltd

RANDOM HOUSE AUSTRALIA (PTY) LTD
20 Alfred Street, Milsons Point, Sydney,
New South Wales 2061, Australia

RANDOM HOUSE NEW ZEALAND LTD
18 Poland Road, Glenfield, Auckland 10, New Zealand

RANDOM HOUSE SOUTH AFRICA (PTY) LTD
Endulini, 5a Jubilee Road, Parktown 2193, South Africa

Published 2003 by Bantam Press
a division of Transworld Publishers

A catalogue record for this book is available from the British Library.
ISBN 0593 051971

Typeset in 11/14pt Times by
Kestrel Data, Exeter, Devon

Printed in Great Britain by
Mackays of Chatham plc, Chatham, Kent

1 3 5 7 9 10 8 6 4 2

Papers used by Transworld Publishers are natural, recyclable products made
from wood grown in sustainable forests.

*To my mother, who always says that*
*things go at their own speed*

# ACKNOWLEDGEMENTS

Grateful thanks are due to Amy and Tim and the classes of '92 and '93; and to Ian Marchant and Saleel Nurbhai for much good sense. A deep debt of gratitude to Linda Anderson, without whom much would not have been possible. Lizzy Kremer for her enthusiasm and for showing me how to finish. Simon Taylor for understanding where I was coming from. Most especially to Adrienne, who kept the faith no matter how deep the darkness. And to the surveyor we met on Inishmore who, when I told him I was writing a story based on *The Tain*, threatened to beat the bejaysus out of me if I made a mess of it. If he cared that much, it had to be worthwhile.

# Note on Pronunciation

Irish is different to English, and Ancient Irish is more different still. It seems harsh to ask a reader to learn a new system of spelling and pronunciation in order to be able to follow a story. Where a name has a recognizable equivalent in English I have used it. Thus Derdriu in the original (pronounced **Der**-dru) is here given as Deirdre. Maeve is the English spelling of Medb, and pronounced much the same. Where a name has no obvious equivalent, such as Setanta (pronounced **Shay**-dan-da), I have tried to use a form that is memorable for the reader.

For those (like me) who like to know such things, the following rough guide to Irish pronunciation may be useful. Bold type indicates a stressed syllable.

| | |
|---|---|
| Ailill: | **Al**-il |
| Cathbad: | **Kaff**-a |
| Cuchullain: | Koo-h**ull**-in |
| Emer: | **Ay**-ver |
| Ferdia: | Fer-**di**-a |
| Laeg: | **Loy**gh |
| Naisi: | **Noy**-shu |
| Sualdam: | **Soo**-al-dav |
| | |
| Emain Macha: | **Ev**-in **Ma**-cha |
| Iraird Cuillenn: | **Ir**-ard **Kwil**-en |
| Sliab Fuait: | **Shlee**-av **Foo**-id |

There are a dozen different ways to spell Shakespeare, but there is only one *Hamlet*. The Irish Heroes wished their names and their deeds to live for all time. So long as we remember them and tell their stories, we honour them. Even if we don't say their names exactly right.

The story of Emain Macha, the palace of Conor the
Great King of Ulster and the home of the Heroes of
the Red Branch; and of Cuchullain, the Hound
of Cullan; and Leary, his charioteer.

Especially his charioteer, born Sigmund the German,
brought to Rome as a hostage by Tiberius, washed
up onto Ulster.

# 1

There was sand in my mouth, and a hundred gentle arms were pulling me downwards.

I opened my eyes. A wave broke at my feet and rushed around me, sending freezing fingers up my body. I breathed water, and lurched up onto one elbow, choking. The water hissed back again, pulling a myriad of rattling pebbles past me down the beach.

I was lying at the sea's edge, against a large rock covered with fat blue-black mussels. Rooted in the lee of the rock was a large clump of seaweed, lying in long greased-leather strips. They swirled round my legs like a witch's hair as the water broke and foamed up the beach.

I was covered in stinging cuts and bruises, which made livid purple leeches on my wrinkled skin. Every orifice seemed to be stuffed full of seaweed and sand. I was alive, but I didn't expect to be for much longer. I was a long way from home. If the cold didn't get me, the Anthropophagi probably would.

The storm had blown out, but the sea was still a dark slate, restless under a stiff breeze. Shipwreck debris surrounded me. Without sitting up I could see half a dozen bodies, some bundled back and forwards on the tide-line by the rolling waves, others thrown further up the beach, twisted into impossible shapes, faces down in pools of water.

The nearest was only a few feet away. I shuffled painfully across the sand and rolled him over. His face was shapeless and pulpy, the cheek framed by the outline of a dark bruise. The birds had already claimed his eyes. I turned aside and retched.

I struggled to my feet and saw a dozen more bodies. Some lay as if hurled from the Tarpeian cliff, huddled and broken. Others appeared unmarked, as if they rested, ready to sit up if I called. All of them were death-grey.

I left them to the gulls and walked up the beach to the dunes, where sharp-bladed rough-grass grew and the hard sand dried and turned to powder. The wind whipped it into stinging eddies around my feet. I picked up a rough length of driftwood for support, and used it to push myself upward as I waded through the sand to the top of the dunes.

The land behind the beach stretched flat for perhaps five stadia, and then great grey and purple mountains reared up on three sides of the valley. The plain was studded with bushes and trees and covered with rich dark grass. Not far away I could see a herd of cows were browsing. As I staggered over the top of the dune a few looked up at me, unconcerned, and went back to grazing. Their coats were thick and rough and their horns were cropped, as the Romans do to their animals, to avoid injury in the breeding season. My stomach ached at the sight of them. Domestic cows. Cows with milk.

I heard a noise behind me, the click of one pebble against another. I turned quickly, feeling every bruised muscle and frozen sinew protest at the sudden effort. A tremendous roar seemed to echo all around me. A human noise. Something cold and wet slapped into my face. I opened my mouth and then closed it again quickly, realizing that the thing that had hit me was an enormous cow-pat. I scraped frantically at the cowshit in my eyes. I managed to remove enough to see a couple of enormous figures descending upon me like rocks down a mountain. My flailing hands were brushed aside, a hand clamped onto

12

my neck, my leg and arm were seized, I was lifted as if I were a struggling puppy, carried for a few moments and then flung through the air. Dumb with fright and blinded by cowshit, I flew for a moment and then landed with a splash.

Freezing water mixed with the cowshit and filled my eyes, ears and nose. My enemies were behind me, still roaring that guttural foreign-sounding war-cry. Unable to see or even breathe, I whirled in the water for a few moments, hoping to land a lucky punch or two when they jumped in to finish me off.

The final blow failed to fall. Eventually it dawned on me that I was not under attack, that the water was only a few inches deep, and that the roaring that I had heard (and which I could still hear) was not a battle-cry, just the sound of the large men's coarse laughter. I stopped struggling, and sat miserably in my puddle, splashing water into my face to get the mess out of my eyes.

Three enormous men stood at the edge of the shallow pool into which they had hurled me. They could hardly stand for laughing. One of them – the largest one – was so overcome that he was doubled up, clutching at his midriff and gasping for air, pointing at me with a flapping hand. I found myself hoping that something painful and important was about to snap in his abdomen.

I could fall no lower. I could just accept that men are the Gods' playthings and that on a good day they sometimes decide to let us live. I started to laugh. I shook with laughter. Then a shaking overcame me, became me. I felt myself start to fall, and then lost all sensation. I heard a shout and the splashing of running feet through water, felt a hand upon me, then numb darkness.

# 2

When I arrived at Emain Macha, the castle of King Conor, Cuchullain was still called Setanta and he was far away and unknown. He was eight years old by then, but the story of his birth is part of it all, so I will tell it now.

His eyes were silver.

As Morag the midwife wiped the last clot of blood from his body with a soft cloth soaked in warm goatsmilk, he opened his eyes and looked up at her, unblinking. The midwife took a step backwards and held the child away from her body as if she feared infection. He looked back calmly, and then closed his eyes and seemed to fall asleep in her hands. His mother muttered softly in her sleep.

There was a pause, and then the midwife shook herself, as if she had dozed off in the heat of a summer's afternoon with work still left to do. It is imagination, she told herself. You have accompanied hundreds of women to the birthing stool, buried a few who could not be helped, saved a dozen more who would have died if not for you. This is just a child like any other.

She knew it was a lie. This was not just any child. This was the child of Dectera, sister of Conor the Great King, wife of

Sualdam, the chief of all his tribe. The blood of noblemen and Heroes ran in his veins. And there were rumours of more.

Morag looked around and shivered. The two women and the child were alone in the room. Would such a birth be so sparsely attended if this were just another child? The room should have been alive with women: virgins watching and learning; young mothers with the memory of their own deliveries fresh in their minds, full of sympathy and carrying warm towels; old women enjoying being past child-bearing age, sitting on wicker stools with folded hands and doling out endless advice; slaves carrying water and towels, and the whole adding up to a bright laughing time. Not like this, not alone, not in the half-light, not locked in with no help in a dark room as cold as a cave.

It was by order of the Great King himself that they were alone, and by his personal request that Morag stood by Dectera's chair when no-one else would do it for fear of what might happen. If he had ordered her to do it she might have found an excuse to avoid it, like the others had done. He did not try to order her, he asked her to do it for friendship.

Dectera stirred in her sleep and gave a soft cry. The birth had been hard. She had borne it silently, although her body had bent on the chair like a drawn bow with the pain. As soon as the child was born and she saw that he was healthy she had fallen asleep, exhausted. Morag washed the child in warm milk then placed him at her breast. Dectera's arms came up and looped around him in her sleep. The midwife gently massaged Dectera's soft belly until the afterbirth came, then inspected it carefully for signs of disease or unlucky marks. There were none.

The child coughed, and she picked him up to be sure that he was breathing properly. His silver eyes looked up at her again and she shivered. Perhaps the story was true.

She had heard the stories without paying attention. Conor and Dectera were, it was said by those with not enough to keep themselves busy, more like lovers than brother and sister. As children they preferred each other's company to anyone else's. Their father often joked that they would save him both time and dowry money, for he would have no need to look for marriage

15

partners for them so long as they had each other. Of course, there were some who read a darker meaning into their love, and there was a hint of recognition of this in their father's words. Few really believed the slanders, and certainly no-one dared face Conor with them, but it was nonetheless a relief when Dectera's engagement to Sualdam was announced. Those who had been cynical before remarked that the situation had hardly changed. Sualdam was Conor's closest friend and lived close by, so Conor and Dectera could still see each other almost whenever they wished. However, it was enough that Dectera would at last be married, Sualdam's wife, mistress of his castle, sharing his bed each night. The gossip would stop.

The day of the wedding was a bright spring morning. Conor had arranged to take Sualdam hunting, and a huge crowd rode with them, including every Champion in Ulster and every chief capable of throwing a leg over a horse. The hunt rode out noisily at high speed, leaving behind it a castle humming with preparations for the evening ceremony. Cooks, clothes-makers, carpenters, and a host of other necessary workers baked, sewed and sawed in a final frenzy of organization.

At the north-west corner of the castle stood a round tower. In time of war it was the central redoubt of the fort, but for the wedding it was Dectera's bridal place. Fifty women, her attendants and friends, were gathered from all over Ulster to help her prepare. They stood her naked in the centre of the room, and, slowly and with much laughter, they dressed her.

First they placed over her a shift of lambswool, spun so thin that it was almost translucent, soft as the underside of a day-old moorhen's wing and white as fresh sea-foam. Then they wrapped her in a sheet of the finest silk, all in one piece, and shot through with red, gold and green threads. The sheet was then pinned with a brooch of intricate silver wires which surrounded a great emerald at their centre, fastening it firm across her breast. The silk was the finest weave from Persia. It held her body kindly.

They then placed a head-dress on her head made of sheer samite, pinned to her black hair which rose high from her forehead and then fell back across one shoulder in a loose rope.

The samite was fastened to her hair at the back by a huge brooch made of shining gold, with seven emeralds gathered in a circle on it. The head-dress was held close to her head by seven threads of soft white gold which flowed from the brooch, passing around her hair and the head-dress to fall in twisted strands to the floor. The corners of the head-dress were attached to the bottom of the silk dress, holding it just off the floor so that the breeze would catch it and raise it behind her. Bracelets lined her forearms in rings of red gold, white gold and silver, each with emeralds and rubies set deep into them, and on each upper arm was a white-gold circle as wide as a woman's hand and with seven rubies around each edge.

On top of all this they placed a shawl made of Indian silk, light enough to fold up into a ball that could be hidden in a girl's hand, but unfolding into a square bigger than the main door to the tower. This shawl was pinned to one shoulder by a brooch of silver with seven emeralds in a circle on it. A heavy gold torc with Ogham letters inscribed on it was placed around her neck, and from it hung a ruby the size of a blackbird's egg which lay between her breasts like a live coal on a new linen pillow.

They brought her a sheet of polished metal, and she clapped her hands at her reflection and laughed. She reached for a cup of mead and drank a toast to her friends, not noticing that a mosquito lay on the surface of the mead. When she finished drinking, the insect was gone.

She put the cup on the window sill beside her and wiped the sweetness of the mead from her lips, then asked for her shoes. No sound answered her. Her friends all seemed to have fallen asleep. Those sitting had lain backwards and closed their eyes, those standing had just slipped silently to the floor. She was the only person in the room who moved or made any sound. She stood in confusion. A slight breeze moved a rich tapestry on one wall, making her step away from it nervously and then laugh at herself, and then the light through the window cast a shadow in front of her as if the sun had appeared from behind a black cloud. Dectera sensed that someone else stood in the room. She whirled around, and then uttered a cry, stepping backwards in surprise and upsetting a table. Metal goblets crashed to the floor, spilling wine, but none of her friends woke.

Before her, dressed in his full glory, shining with gold and silver embellishments from every part of his armour and with a woollen cloak that was so light that it floated out rippling behind his shoulders even though there was no wind, stood Laeg, the Father of the Gods, smiling at her. She knew it was him, it could be no-one else. Neither of them spoke for a moment. Then the God smiled and gestured at the goblet that she had just put down.

'You drank.' There was question and answer in his voice. She could only nod. She did not fear him, but she could not speak.

'Then you are mine,' said Laeg, 'for the fly in the wine was me.'

Conor and the rest of the wedding party returned from the hunt shortly before dusk. Conor was bad-tempered because a boar had given him a cut on one leg before he had managed to kill it. His temper was not improved when the party rounded the last corner in the road which led to Emain Macha to see that the whole castle was waiting for them at the gate in an uproar. Everyone spoke at once and Conor could get no sense from them. He asked for silence, then called for it, and finally roared it as an order, raising his hands for calm. The group gradually fell quiet. Conor listened to Cathbad the druid tell the story of how a light had shone from Dectera's tower window, and of how a flock of fifty swans had flown from it towards the setting sun, and how the men had rushed to the top of the tower to find the women all gone, and by that stage everyone had started talking again, but it made no difference because Sualdam was already galloping beside Conor in the direction that the swans had gone, with the rest of the wedding hunt party close behind them.

They searched the day away until it was dark, and the horses were tired, and they were forced to camp. In his sleep Conor had a dream. Laeg appeared to him and told him to turn back. Conor argued, unwilling to abandon his sister, but he had no choice. He returned the next morning, and it was said that he did not smile

18

for a year. Dectera's name was never mentioned in his presence. Sualdam went back to his castle and stayed there.

That winter it snowed hard, and food was short. Conor the King and Conall Gallowglass with Fergus and a dozen other warriors were out hunting. They were led far from the castle by a flock of swans flying in front of them, just out of range of their slings, slowing when they slowed, taunting the King and his Champions when they tried to stop so that the men plunged onwards after them without thought.

Conor at last looked up at the sky and saw it was getting dark. He called to Conall that they would have to camp, but the Champion pointed forward, and the King saw a light in the window of a cottage some distance in front of them. With a shock he realized that they stood at the edge of the valley of the Sidhe, the home of the Ancients. Both men were unsure of what to do, but at that moment a door opened, and a man standing there called to them to come in.

They rode up to the cottage, and saw that the man was crippled with age. He smiled, however, and invited them in. Fergus had taken an oath never to refuse hospitality, and it was a cold night and they were far from home, so the men overcame their fears and bent to enter through the low door.

Once inside the small house, they stood up and knew that they had entered the palace of the Sidhe. All around them the walls were ablaze with torches, the light from which was reflected from a thousand hanging shields, all polished and shining, made of rare metals and chased with wonderfully intricate designs, and each with a huge precious stone at the centre of the boss. These shields and torches were so numerous that it was almost as bright as day in the palace, although it was dark outside.

The King and his men turned to their host, only to find the old man gone, and in his place stood Laeg himself, dressed in his full triumph as he had appeared to Dectera in the tower. They knelt in front of him. Conor asked him what was to happen. The God laughed, and waved an arm, and fifty women appeared, each more lovely than the last and each with a perfect swan's feather in her hair. At the front of them was Dectera, most lovely of

19

them all, her face glowing and her baby plainly soon to be born, and she embraced her brother with many happy words, and there was a feast there that night that Conall Gallowglass spoke of every night for the rest of his life.

The next day, Conor and the other warriors brought Dectera and her women back to Emain Macha. That night she gave birth to a son.

Morag the midwife cleared her throat softly. She'd heard the stories, but she wasn't sure how much to believe. Conall Gallowglass was a drunkard and a windbag, and how did anyone know what happened in the tower when apparently everyone was asleep all the time through except Dectera and she was telling nothing? Morag tucked a blanket around the mother and child and suddenly felt weary. She knew her job was finished. She sat on a straight-backed chair and closed her eyes, knowing that the smallest sound would wake her. She fell asleep almost immediately.

She did not know how long she had been asleep, but it felt like only an instant. At the moment of waking, she knew that the child had not made a sound. There was someone else in the room.

She opened her eyes to see Conor standing next to the bed. He was looking down at the child, and he was smiling. Morag stood up and pressed her hands against her thighs, her head slightly bowed. Conor looked at her benignly and his lips said a silent 'Thank you'. Morag felt herself dismissed. She moved to the door. As she closed it behind her she looked back. Conor was sitting on the bed, leaning towards his sister. Dectera had woken. His head was resting on her breast, and her hand smoothed his hair.

The next morning, Morag went to tend the baby. It was gone. Dectera was alone in the bed. When the midwife asked where the baby was, she replied, 'Safe'. Further questions she answered with a weary smile. Then Conor appeared behind Morag and gently but firmly led her out of the bedchamber. When she stammered her surprise to him he looked stern, and with a shake of his head made his position and hers plain. The subject was not open for discussion.

# 3

I was washed up at Emain Macha eight years after the birth of Setanta. Conor was still King, and Dectera now lived outside the walls of Sualdam's castle. Sualdam and Dectera had married after her return, but now saw little of each other. There was perhaps too much of the past still between them to make a future together. Even if no-one was quite sure what the past contained. If Dectera knew she wasn't saying.

But for me, all that was to come. I lay on a pallet, half-drowned and exhausted. My mind was flooded with images, some from life, others from nightmares. I remembered my father, with my brothers beside him. I called to them but they turned away with blank faces. Then one of Tiberius's legionaries reared up between us and stabbed at them over and over again, his sword hacking great holes in their defenceless backs while I watched and did not move.

Then the images stopped, and there was nothing. The mist in my mind parted and honey-coloured sunlight flooded in. I was warm and comfortable. Without moving, I knew that I was lying flat on a soft pallet covered with animal skins. I was ravenously hungry. My eyes were still closed, but I was aware of something moving around near by.

I hoped that the something was not dangerous, because I felt utterly defenceless. I also hoped that the something was food, because whatever it was I planned to eat it.

With an effort I forced my eyes open. I lay still for a few moments, looking up at the woven rushes above me, enjoying the sound of rain outside. I felt that I had not truly known what properly warm and dry meant before that moment. I luxuriated in the warmth, smiling at the roof. Never have I stared at a roof with such reverence. Eventually, full of roof, I tried to turn and look around me. My muscles refused to help. It seemed an impossible effort just to roll over. I stopped trying to move my whole body and concentrated on moving just small bits of it in turn. That was more successful. I was apparently still in one piece, but I felt very weak and the smallest movement produced a wave of nausea.

A slim hand appeared in front of my face and smoothed my hair back. My heart almost stopped with fright. Had I not been so weak, I would have jumped ten feet in the air and landed with my sword upraised and ready for anything. As it was, I gave in gracefully and lay still. In my condition a couple of day-old kittens could probably have finished me off without trouble, so it seemed pointless trying to fight a whole human.

She leant over me with a silent smile and rearranged my blanket. Dark hair fell to just above my face. I could smell her skin, a tang of fresh sweet woodsmoke and new bread. She stood up and looked down into my face. Dark, humorous eyes met mine. I promised myself I would investigate those eyes further, in a hundred years or so when I felt better. She smiled and offered me a goblet. I took it and sipped at something disgusting. She propped my head up and I drank with difficulty. Most of it seemed to run out either side of my mouth. After managing a few small gulps I choked, and she took it from me with a satisfied sound. She lowered my head back to the pillow, and almost immediately dark clouds started whirling like campfire smoke in my mind.

The next day and night passed quickly. I would wake, the woman would be sitting beside me or working near by. She would smile, rise, feed me a little, then give me more of the disgusting drink, and I would fall asleep. For a while I would sleep soundly. Then the dreams started. I dreamt of wild battles, brutal orgies, howling charges, Caligulan perversions, the extremes and edges of experience. My mind seemed filled with blades and blood. Then I would wake, be fed, drink the bitter drink, and for a while I would sleep quietly. Then the dreams would begin again.

The following morning I woke and told her I felt better. She didn't understand what I said, but the meaning was clear enough. She didn't try to make me drink. (I suspect that the point of the remedy is to go on giving it until the patient is well enough to say it tastes like shit and he doesn't want it and is strong enough to insist.) I never found out exactly what herbs she had been giving me, but they seemed to have worked. I felt as if a herd of cattle had walked repeatedly over my body and that the strength in my muscles had been raked out by the claws of the Furies, but I could think clearly again. I had a pleasant feeling of well-being. I wondered if it was the medicine that was making me feel light-headed, suspected that it was, and hoped either its effects were permanent or else the plant that it was made from grew like grass throughout this country.

My nurse judged a patient's medical condition by the effect that brushing his face with her hair and letting him look down her dress had on him. Mind you, as a diagnostic tool I prefer that to attaching leeches to my backside or having the entrails of a chicken thrown at me, both of which I have experienced.

She was tall and graceful, and moved without disturbance. She wore a dress made of a dark green loose-woven material, with a thin gold thread woven into the fabric around the neck to make an intricate necklace pattern which looped down over her breasts. Thick dark hair hung in a heavy plait reaching down to the small of her back. Perhaps it was the medicine, or perhaps it was because I had not been with a woman for a long time, but I suddenly felt as if my body was filling with warm water very rapidly from the toes upward. I knew exactly the sensation of how it would feel to place my hand just where the dark plait

23

ended and hold her against me so that there was no ending or beginning to our bodies. I could feel the loose soft fabric of her dress. I knew the pliant muscles of her lower back on my palm, the strength of her hips as she pushed against me. I could smell her skin, touch her lips, see through her eyes into her heart. I shuddered involuntarily at the intensity of the feeling. I raised one knee to hide myself, but not before she noticed.

'Better?' she asked.

I understood. I sat up, startled, and repeated the word as a statement. It was her turn to look surprised. She said it again, and I replied 'Yes,' for I now knew what language she was speaking. She clapped her hands with delight and spoke several sentences very quickly. I understood almost none of it, but I knew that some of the words were familiar, that the sound was right. I have always been a quick learner of languages, and I knew this one. It was like Iberian and yet not like it. A dialect, perhaps. I stopped her in full flow, and signed for her to talk slowly. She did so, and I understood a word or two. I tried a few words in Iberian, speaking very slowly, trying to match her accent.

'Thank you for taking care of me.'

Her brow furrowed for a moment. I repeated it, slowly, and her face lightened. She understood, or thought she did. She smiled, indicated that I was to remain where I was, and left in a hurry. I assumed that she had gone to inform others of my recovery. I looked around me, and saw a little table with a rough bowl on it. The bowl contained something that looked a lot like food, although it felt like a lifetime since I had seen or tasted anything except my nurse's truly revolting drink, and I no longer felt sure of even recognizing food if it were put in front of me. However, acting on instinct I fell upon it, and in a few mouthfuls it was gone. Five minutes later, when the soldiers came to fetch me, I was outside the hut throwing up in a bush. Between heaves I grinned at them.

# 4

I remember the palace of Emain Macha well. A crowd of eager people watched Conall of the Victories and Buchal the Badger bring me in between them. Conall's sword-point trailed in the dust behind him as always, leaving a v-shaped trail between his footprints. Buchal looked equally businesslike, a studded club swinging loose in one hand.

Looking back, I now see that they were in a dilemma. They didn't know who or what I was. If I turned out to be a prince or a guest, they did not want to handle me roughly. However, if I was a commoner or an enemy, they did not want to show me too much respect. Conall in particular was in an agony of indecision, several times reaching for my arm to frogmarch me into the Great Hall and hurl me at the King's feet, then snatching his hand away at the last moment. Had it been his decision, Conall would no doubt have just knocked me on the head and been done with it for causing all this embarrassment. With his roaring temper, bristling red hair and majestically long beard, Conall put people in mind of a wild boar with a sore backside and a grudge and a headache. For connoisseurs of social unease the picture of Conall and Buchal – another man not renowned for his delicacy – bringing in the stranger from the sea was one to treasure. They both wanted to be in front of me and beside me and behind me all at the same time just in case, and competed with each other to make it seem like the other's fault if they'd guessed wrong. They were trying to guard, escort and march me simultaneously. They looked like two willing but not very bright dogs carrying home what they hope is a partridge but fear may be a chicken.

I was curiously unafraid, just a bit annoyed at being hauled about. The medicine left me feeling detached from the situation. I watched the crowd watching me, discussing me without any attempt to disguise the fact. I looked at them, and felt that I knew from the movements of their lips what they were saying. 'The stranger is tall, with fair straight hair, not one of us. He is the wrong colour, too fair. His facial bones are the wrong shape, softer, with low cheekbones supporting grey shadows of fatigue. His skin is unlined and youthful. He does not look afraid. He is strong, with the build of a warrior, but lacks the sort of battle-scars that one of our men of his age would have collected.' My medicine was a powerful aid to the imagination.

I was made to stand in front of Conor the Great King. I was respectful, but I didn't bow. Conall, finally coming to a decision, raised his arm to knock me to the ground, but Conor motioned him to stop.

'Peace, Conall.' Conor's quiet tones, as always, held more command than a dozen Hero shouts.

Conor looked at me and our eyes locked. There was a pause. Then Conor spoke. 'Who are you?'

I knew the words but not their meaning, like speech muffled by a closed door. I didn't know what to reply. I didn't yet know what their attitude to escaped slaves was, and I wasn't going to let them know how much I understood until I did. I announced in German that I had fallen off a ship and been washed ashore. Conor mulled over my reply. Not surprisingly, he didn't understand it.

I saw a man with a wispy red beard looking at me with a peculiar intensity, and I looked back at him steadily. He dropped his stare momentarily, then looked back again the same way. I winked at him, and after a moment's astonishment he smiled hugely and winked back. There were three young men close beside him. From their similar faces and builds – each one a slightly smaller replica of the other – I guessed they were brothers.

Conor looked around his court. He recognized the potential for embarrassment in this dialogue of the deaf and – as any sensible King would – decided to delegate the responsibility. He motioned a hand at an old man, who moved forward with a stately and rather self-important walk. He stood in front of me and pointed to his chest.

'Cathbad,' he said, and then pointed at me with a questioning look on his face.

'Sigmund,' I replied, after a pause. That seemed safe.

My name rustled through the assembly as the men and women tried the strange syllables on their tongues. Someone made a joke, and a section of the crowd laughed, then quieted suddenly. Some amused themselves and their friends by repeating the name behind their hands, contorting their mouths into unusual shapes.

Cathbad made an expansive gesture that took in the whole hall. 'Emain Macha,' he said, I'd never heard of it.

The druid began to speak simple words, enunciating every syllable clearly, much louder than would be normal and accompanying them with gestures that one might use to an idiot. I listened intently, feeling that I ought to be able to understand, but couldn't. Cathbad eventually stopped and shook his head helplessly. He turned to Conor, opening his hands in frustration.

Conall's heavy sword struck a spark off a flint in the floor as he stamped forward. He looked as if he had been given a body just slightly too small to contain all the vitality and aggression within it. I thought that he was about to explode. His tone was unmistakable.

'I think he's bluffing,' snarled Conall, shoving his face into mine. 'I think the thieving arsehole got left behind on a cattle-raid and is playing dumb so's we'll think he was shipwrecked and let him go. I say we kick the truth out of him and then nail him upside down to the front gate.'

I understood at least some of that. I looked at Conall with a grin on my face.

'Arsehole,' I said.

There was a moment's stunned silence. I repeated myself. Cathbad's jaw dropped open. The crowd in the Great Hall erupted with laughter. Conall looked at me sideways, his beard crackling with suspicion, unable to make up his mind if I was mocking him or not. He looked to be on the verge of hitting me just in case when Conor smiled and put his hand on Conall's shoulder, which calmed him – in so far as Conall was ever calm, naturally hovering as he did on the aggressive side of violent – but did not allay his suspicions.

Cathbad looked questioningly at the King, who nodded his assent. Cathbad rattled off a list of oaths. I knew some of them, and repeated them with a smile. Just to be on the safe side I used a few well-chosen gestures to show that I knew what he was talking about. The crowd roared encouragement. I was a success.

They were speaking a language much like the tongue of a soldier I had marched beside in the Tenth Legion. One of our diversions on the march had been to teach each other swear-words in each other's language. The rhythm of these people's speech – as well as their colouring and build – was similar to that of the man I had known.

Conor was much amused by the sight of the blond stranger from the sea who could speak only by swearing. He gestured to Cathbad to take me away. I saw a faint look of annoyance cross the old man's face as he agreed.

As we walked across the courtyard the young man with the red beard, who turned out to be Owen, trotted up to us and started to speak to Cathbad. I assumed – rightly – that he wanted to help look after me. Cathbad had just acquired a young wife in whom he was far more interested than in me, so Owen's offer came as a welcome relief. After a token hesitation by Cathbad, who never wanted to give up anything that might be of advantage, Owen became my tutor, reporting on my progress to Cathbad every time the old man emerged from his bedroom. They would confer, and Cathbad would nod magisterially to indicate that my progress was satisfactory, and then he would disappear again. I had nothing better to do, so I learnt the language from Owen and concentrated on eating and drinking myself well again. None of these tasks proved difficult.

My name changed a few times before we got it settled. Sigmund seemed to be a difficult word for them to pronounce, so I suggested Decius, the name I had been known by in Rome. That seemed to be easier for everyone and I was Decius for a month or so, until there was a banquet one night at which Conall rather bad-temperedly slurred that if the frogwit stranger was going to change his frogwit name every five minutes why didn't he change it to the sort of frogwit name that people would recognize, like Leary for example? I had drunk enough not to care about insulting him, and replied that Leary was indeed a fine name but if I was ever in need of the name of a frogwit I might just call myself Conall. My knowledge of the language was obviously coming along splendidly.

Everyone laughed. Conall bristled and started to climb across the table towards me, but Owen and several others jumped forward and managed to persuade him that he had mis-understood my execrable pronunciation. Conall was eventually pacified, and the two of us ended up falling asleep side by side under the table. After that night, whether they had called me Sigmund or Decius before, everyone now called me Leary. It started as a joke, but by the time the joke had worn off everyone had forgotten that I had ever been called anything else.

Until I was twelve I called myself a German. Then Germanicus took me as a hostage, and for fifteen years I was called a Roman. Now I was an Ulsterman, another life again. It wasn't surprising that Conall didn't know what to call me. I wasn't sure myself.

# 5

I was getting the guided tour. Again.

'There are four provinces in Ireland: Ulster, Munster, Leinster and Connaught.' Owen paused momentarily. 'There's Tara too, which is much smaller, not really a province at all, but the High King sits there so it's important I suppose. The Red Branch are the Champions who guard Ulster. They are the Ulster part of the Fianna, the bodyguard of the High King of Ireland. They were founded by Ross the Red, who married Maga, the same Ross who was – is – Aongus Og. He is the God of Love. Did I tell you that? Do Romans have a God of Love? Women pray to Aongus at Beltane, well, they pray to him all the time, but especially at Beltane. Did you once tell me that Apollo – no, was it Mars? – was your— no, I'm wrong, aren't I?'

I sighed. This could – usually did – go on all day.

It was about six months since the day of the shipwreck. The sun was shining, the birds were singing, and I had a hangover that made every whisper sound like a busy day in Vulcan's forge. Owen set out every day to show me everything. He drew my attention to anything of note in the court and much that was not of any consequence at all. He had a hunger for information, both given and received, and he talked. Zeus, how he talked! I despaired of exhausting him and took to hiding when I knew he would be looking for me. Eventually he realized what I was doing. He cornered me when I was snatching an hour's sleep after lunch.

'Leary?'

'What?' I immediately felt ungracious, and as immediately determined not to feel bad about it. Through the open door behind him I glimpsed the three brothers I had seen on the first day approach, see that Owen had me cornered, and retreat without saying anything. He didn't realize.

'May I speak to you?' This was progress. Today he was asking permission to speak. Normally it took a fist to the side of the head to stop him.

'Of course.'

'Have I offended you?'

'No.'

'Then can I ask why you are avoiding me?'

'I'm not avoiding you, not really, I . . .'

Damn, damn, damn. I looked up from my bed, and saw his stupid face with that stupid red hair, and I felt like a rat. He only wanted to help.

I had to tell him the truth, and he had the grace to laugh and told me that everyone said the same thing, and I must forgive his prattle and excitement for it was only because there was so much I could tell him and so much he wanted to tell me and I pointed out that he was doing it again, but I laughed, because I knew that he was good-hearted and that I had been selfish. He wanted to help and sometimes his enthusiasm ran away with him. He suggested that we do what I wanted, not what he suggested, and I agreed, knowing that it would not take long before he was chattering on again, but determined not to mind. I knew I had few enough friends to be able to afford to spend them so freely.

In order to shut him up I told him some stories of my own. I told him of how I was born in Germany, and lived there until I was given as a hostage by my tribe after the great defeat inflicted on them by Germanicus. He didn't seem to want to know about Germany. Perhaps the people were too much like his own. What really excited him was tales of Rome, both past and present. I told him of how I had been taken to Capri with Tiberius, how I escaped, of Caligula's purges, and how I made my living as a charioteer in the great games in the Circus Maximus, and he was politely interested, but he was most interested in tales of Rome's great past. The story he loved best was Hannibal crossing the Alps.

'Elephants?'

I smiled in a superior way. 'I don't suppose you've seen an elephant, have you?'

He looked slightly put out. 'I don't know, perhaps I have, perhaps I just don't know the name. What does it look like?'

'Big. Grey. More skin than it really needs. Oh, and a huge nose.'

'Sounds like Buchal.'

'No, better looking than that.'

'Like a very big pig?'

'No, more like . . .' I paused, stuck for a comparison. There isn't really anything that an elephant is much like. 'Imagine . . . let's do this one step at a time. Imagine a horse ten times normal size.'

Owen shut his eyes and screwed his face up in concentration like a child. 'Right.'

'Now give it legs like trees, turn it grey, make its skin slack like tar-cloth, and give it a dangling nose that almost reaches the ground and which it can use like an arm.'

He was already laughing. 'You are joking with me!' he said. 'There is no such animal!' He punched my shoulder play-fully. 'But there are some wonderful animals here, and some marvellous other animals that used to live here but have now gone away.' He had already shown me an enormous pair of antlers in the banqueting hall, which were more impressive than I was prepared to admit, and there were some ivory tusks, taller than a man, that I assumed came to Ulster off a Phoenician trader's boat.

'Oh, elephants have tusks too. Yes, like the ones you showed me.'

32

'Then perhaps there were once elephants here! Where did Hannibal get his elephants?'

'I don't know. Africa, I think.'

'Africa? Is that part of the Roman Empire too?'

I shrugged. Geography has never been my strong point. 'Some of it is. I've only seen a small part of the north. It's very hot, all the time. The people who come from there have black skin.'

He thought for a minute, stroking his ragged beard. 'Black skin? You mean they are burnt? By the sun?'

'I suppose so.'

'Black skin like a raven?'

'Some of them. Every colour from black to light brown. Depends where they come from.'

A thought struck him. 'Are ravens sacred to you?'

'No. They are just birds. Sometimes birds of ill omen, but not sacred.'

He fingered his beard. 'Ill omen, eh? We agree. Ravens are evil spirits.' He looked around. There weren't any birds near by. I watched his attention hurdle the subject and land somewhere else. 'Tell me again how big the Roman Empire is. Bigger than Ulster?'

'How long does it take to deliver a message from one side of Ulster to the other?'

'Four days.'

'That is nothing much.'

'And how long would it take for a man to get from one side of the Roman Empire to another?'

I nodded loftily. 'I know that it can take a messenger on horseback three months to deliver a message from Rome to the farthest reaches of the Empire.'

He tried very hard not to look impressed. 'What would be the point of an Empire that the King couldn't see all of? How would he enjoy it?'

'By bringing the best of the Empire to himself.' I described the exotic animals that died in the Colosseum, the foods that piled high on Roman tables, the slaves that made life pleasant.

He sniffed in a way that didn't suggest a running nose. 'So

anyone not a Roman in the Roman Empire is there to be killed, eaten or enslaved by Romans? I'm glad I'm not part of it.'

I wasn't sure if I'd won that exchange or not. His next action suggested I'd at least hit him in a soft area. He took me to the Trophy Hall. Again. I felt we had been there more than often enough, but Owen said that I could not possibly learn enough about the Heroes of Emain Macha to satisfy him or me, so off we went. His enthusiasm for my education was touching. I knew, of course, that his motives were not entirely unalloyed. He thought that I was a good story, and he meant to get it out of me. In Ulster, among a people who place power in words, in stories, and make the storyteller an inviolate person, then the man with the best stories is one to reckon with. I knew his ambition. He meant to be the best. He meant to compose songs that people would want to hear long after he had gone. By this means he would not die, he would live as long as people sang his song. (I think that dead is dead, once you're gone it makes no difference, but I didn't want to argue.) The song would be immortal, so he would be immortal. For it to be immortal, he reasoned, he needed two things. He needed a subject that people would never tire of, and he needed to tell it well. He already had faith in his ability to tell the story, but he had not yet found his subject. I know that he felt my arrival was propitious. There was a prophecy that the arrival of a stranger would herald the greatest hour of Emain Macha and its end. I was unconvinced – strangers arrive more often than once in a lifetime – but his faith was unquenchable. It didn't require me to actually do anything except let him spend time with me, so I was happy enough to let it go on.

It was strange to me – or the Roman part of me at any rate, the other parts didn't care – that they placed words so highly. They didn't write things down, except in a complicated script called Ogham, and they had no paper so the Ogham was chiselled onto stone, and then only the most important records such as the names of Kings and their victories and lineage. This made the storytellers into historians. If they made a mistake – deliberately or maliciously – it could not be undone by

34

consulting the library records, as a Roman would do. I smiled to think of the status that storytellers and actors enjoyed in Rome (somewhere below stray dogs, although usually just above cholera), and remembered the decay of subjects like rhetoric and oratory as well as storytelling. The Greek schools still taught the art of speaking, but no-one went there any more. Money speaks a language that no-one needs to study to understand.

I thought of Julius Caesar, and his books, particularly the *Campaigns in Gaul.* Tiberius always said that, notwithstanding their bombast and self-publicity, they were the finest military treatises ever written. I tried to tell Owen about them, but he wasn't really interested.

'Why write words when you can sing and play them?' he scoffed. 'Where is the pleasure in that? It is solitary, not social. Pleasure should be shared, don't you think?'

I snorted. 'I would expect that reaction from a member of a race that takes a day to write a single word by carving it onto stone.'

This produced an offended silence which lasted a few minutes. We did the tour of the Trophy Hall. Offence soon forgotten, he was throwing his arms about again as if he owned everything in it.

'This is the sword of the Great King, which no man may touch but him. This is the chariot given to the Great King by Queen Maeve of Connaught, who—'

'Ah, I've heard of her. I thought she was your enemy?'

'Indeed, she is Ulster's greatest enemy, and will never miss a chance to do us injury.'

'But his greatest enemy sends Conor chariots?'

He looked puzzled. 'Of course. Enmity grows and dies and grows again elsewhere. Alliances can be easily made and soon broken, but the laws of hospitality are eternal. Is it not the same with your people?'

'Not exactly,' I said. 'But please continue.' He beamed at me.

'This is the sword of Conall of the Victories, the one that he used to defeat King Oein of Munster, and there is the shield he threw away before the fight began, disdaining to use it against an enemy smaller than himself. There are enough helmets here for a thousand men, enough spears for an army, enough arrows to equip a hundred archers for a battle lasting five days. There is the shield of Conor, the Great King's grandfather . . .'

I was full to the top of his endless prattles of shields, helmets, spears and swords, and the ghoulish piles of brain-balls that littered the corners of the room. It was not enough for them just to kill their enemies, oh no. They then cut their dead heads off and tied them to the sides of their chariots by the hair. Then, later, when there was nothing better to do, they would lop the tops off the heads, scoop out the brain and put it to soak in lime. The lime soaked into the soft mush, and then it was taken out to dry in the sun. The result was a grey wrinkled rock about the size of a farmer's fist, which was piled up with the rest of the Hero's hoard to show what a ferocious fellow he was. The warriors carried them in linen bags at their sides and hurled the balls from slingshots at each other, finding a pleasing irony in using one enemy to attack another.

They did take prisoners, apparently, for ransom or as slaves, although it wasn't what a Roman would call slavery. Roman slaves were lucky if they got the same treatment as the house dog, and suicide was the most common form of death after maltreatment. I had been a galley-slave, fed on slop, another man's property, condemned to row under the lash until my heart burst. If the storm had not intervened and cast me up on the shore, I would still have been there. Ulster slaves were treated reasonably well and could be ransomed. And they could end their slavery by showing that they were useful soldiers in Ulster's defence. It would be more correct to call them hostages who worked without pay than slaves.

I looked around the Trophy Hall and shuddered at the piles of ossified brains. My father's tribe had practised human sacrifice within living memory, and I had attended enough Roman orgies to know better than to accuse anyone else of barbarism, but these wrinkled remains of men seemed to me to be symptomatic of a wildness at the heart of these people that the Romans had long bred out of themselves. Or perhaps just hidden. Perhaps it is circumstance that allows us to be civilized. In a society in which family and tribal feuds are common, what better way to strike at a man than the knowledge that you are not only going to try to kill him but are going to use his brother's brain to do it?

'Enough of this bone-shop,' I sighed. 'Let's do something that involves fresh air and nobody dying. Oh, and not too much effort.' The previous night had been a celebration, for I forget what, and I was still feeling brittle. I think most of Conor's men were.

Owen smiled, and patted my head. I swung at him with a fist. He sprang away, shaming me with words, or so he hoped. No-one may strike at a bard, not even a King. I growled that he wasn't a bard yet, and anyone patting me when my head hurt was going to get a fist on the ear. Owen contrived to look offended, and we were laughing as we went out of the hall into warm spring sunshine. I squinted against the light. From a distance came a high-pitched shouting.

'We'll go and watch the hurling,' he said.

'I don't understand it,' I replied.

'Come on then, I'll explain it to you.' He stood aside for me to precede him.

'If you can,' I said. 'I've watched it. There don't appear to be any rules.'

He smiled. 'I thought you said you didn't understand it?'

Hurling is practice for battle. Two teams hit a stone-hard ball up and down a field using flat sticks called hurleys half the length of themselves. The idea is – at least, they say the idea is – to hit the ball with the stick and make it go between two posts. If you prefer not to hit the ball but to run carrying it instead, that is allowed, but then everyone else is allowed to hit you repeatedly with their sticks until you get rid of it, and often they don't stop even then. I eventually learnt to play, and decided that on the whole I preferred fighting. True, a hurling stick is not as sharp as a sword, but a hurler does not wear armour, so the end result is similar. The major difference between this form of training for war and war itself is that they take war slightly less seriously

37

than they do hurling. Strong men had been killed while hurling, and no-one thought it strange.

The Boys' Troop were playing, watched by a couple of dozen Champions. The latter were lounging about, recovering from the previous night, calling out advice and instructions and bemoaning the falling standard of play since their own youthful days. Every province had a Boys' Troop. The Troop at Emain Macha was composed of about six times fifty boys, the sons of the Champions gathered around Conor, plus the sons of the chiefs who owed him allegiance, plus a sprinkling of boys who had no birthright to be there but who showed promise. These were few, and had to fight hard to keep their place. Ulstermen train their sons – and often their daughters – by making them fight as soon as they are old enough to lift a child's sword.

'Where is Fergus?' bellowed Conall as we approached. He was lying with a wineskin on the grass, watching the game.

'I haven't seen him,' I replied.

Conall lifted one leg and his backside let go a blast that would have extinguished a campfire. Several men lolling on the grass behind him staggered away, cursing and gasping for breath. Conall sighed with satisfaction. 'Well, he ought to be here. These boys play like babies. No-one has even started bleeding yet, and they've been playing for ages. What is the point of it all if they pad around each other like kittens?'

'If they can't do it on the hurling field,' agreed Buchal, 'they'll never be ready to do it in battle. Fergus needs to start banging their heads together, get some blood flowing. They'll never learn like this.'

Fergus. Now there was a man. Owen had told me his story at least three times already, and it still didn't make sense. Fergus had been King, but had voluntarily given up the crown! Why? Because he was tired of it, couldn't do what he wanted when he wanted. He liked the ceremonial and the admiration, but got tired of being everyone's final court of appeal. So, he asked young Conor to be his, well, his regent, I suppose. Conor was the son of a dead chief, and was trained and highly regarded, so Fergus knew that Conor could do it. In fact he suspected that

Conor might do a better job than he had, so he made Conor promise that he would step down after a year. Fergus was tired of the responsibility, but he didn't want to stop for ever, he just wanted a rest, go to a few parties, chase some women without being interrupted every time there was a dispute between two farmers. Some said that to do this he must have been under something called 'a glamour', which – as far as I could tell from Owen's description – wasn't quite the same as a magic charm or a spell. It was a bit like a trance as well. Having met Fergus I couldn't imagine him in a trance. He knew what he was doing. He just wanted a rest.

Conor made a good job of being King. Left to himself he might well just have given the crown back to Fergus after a year as he'd promised, but his mother, a fearful old witch by the sound of it who died shortly before I arrived, persuaded him to go round flattering everyone who mattered, bribing the various chiefs who would accept it, and telling the more principled ones that a King who was prepared to take a year off wasn't someone who was committed to the job. Why should Fergus have the glory if he wasn't prepared to do the work?

It was rumoured too that gold paid by the agents of Queen Maeve of Connaught may have encouraged some to acclaim the untried youngster against the old soldier. If so, it was probably a mistake.

Anyhow, when the chiefs met for the handing-back ceremony, at the moment Conor took the crown off and handed it to Fergus, a claque organized by the old witch set up a howling and a heckling, and all the bribed and flattered chiefs joined in with nodding and agreeing and criticizing, and by the time the dust had settled Fergus was placed in the dilemma of insisting on his rights and having no support among his chiefs or making as dignified a withdrawal as possible. He chose the latter, and apparently made rather a good speech that won him a lot of friends. Conor had the sense to make sure that Fergus was his right-hand man from that point onwards, partly because, although not a dedicated King, Fergus was a good general, and partly because being on Conor's right hand was a good place to keep an eye on him. As it turned out, Fergus was really rather relieved to have been let off being King, and took to his new post of chief trainer for the Boys' Troop and principal adviser to the new King rather well.

Of course, it did mean that Conall shouted at him a lot if the Boys' Troop showed any tendencies to what he considered to be effeminacy, such as coming back from a hurling game with any part of their bodies not covered in blood or asking for food or wanting to sleep occasionally. Fergus loved those boys more than his own life, and defended them against Conall's jibes with a will, to Conall's delight, who spent much of his time thinking of new insults to throw at them in order to rouse Fergus. It passed the time for us all.

# 6

The memory of the next part of the story is clear, but somehow faraway, as if it happened to someone else and was then told to me in exact detail.

We lay in the sun, enjoying the heat, listening to the men bantering with each other and yelling instructions and jibes at the hurlers. Occasionally arguments broke out but it was too hot for fighting. Naisi, Ardan and Ainle, the three sons of Usna, a great fighter in his day, or so he told me, sat beside me. They had seen me on the first day, and had made it their business to follow me around ever since, at least when Owen wasn't educating me. Conall sat a little way off, in the centre of a noisy group of men, throwing dice. The Ulstermen had never seen dice before I arrived. I whittled one for a carpenter to copy, and soon the whole place was sitting around in noisy disputatious groups, gambling their lives away. This idyllic state lasted for a week or so, and then things calmed down a bit. It was still a passion with Conall, however, and he usually managed to find someone to play with. Usually me, in fact, but with my sore head I wasn't available for being shouted at that morning.

I sprawled on a bank under a young apple tree with Usna's sons, watching the game with half a mind and resting the last of my headache while wondering if it was too soon for the first proper drink of the day, when I became aware that something was moving in the distance. I shaded my eyes against the glare. I could see a small boy coming along the road which led to the training ground. The road followed the contour of the hill on which we were sitting, and thus led away to our right before turning back on itself and heading up towards Emain Macha. He was hitting a ball into the air with his hurley, chasing to catch it before it hit the ground, then doing it again. He was too distant for me to tell properly, but he seemed to be hitting the ball impossibly far. I assumed that it was the effect of last night on my eyes. I blinked, and a shadow seemed to flicker across the sun. Blinded by the glare, I looked away. When I looked back, a large crow was circling just above the boy's head. He seemed not to have seen it, or I felt he could have reached out with his hurley and touched it. As I had that thought the crow gave a loud harsh cry and wheeled away.

He was small, with long dark hair, straight and shoulder-length. His clothes were good, but a different style to those worn at Emain. I nudged Owen and pointed. Owen looked startled.

'He isn't from here,' I said.

Owen looked at me appraisingly. 'An Ulsterman, though, by the direction he comes from.'

I got the feeling that the boy had not seen us, as if he had come a long way and was walking head down, using the rhythm of throw-hit-run-catch-hit-again to while away the journey. He did not look at the castle nor alter his stride until the ball rolled to within a spear-throw of where we lay. He picked it up and threw it into the air, pulled back his hurley to hit it and saw Emain and the game and us all at the same time.

The stick halted in mid-stroke and the ball fell to the ground. A look of astonishment appeared on his face. For a moment he stood absolutely still, then with a glad cry which I heard above the shouts of the Boys' Troop, he sprinted towards where they were playing and without pausing flung himself into the middle of the game.

For a few moments I lost sight of him in the dust. Then he

came hurtling out of the side of a melee of players, balancing the ball on his stick. I heard angry cries as the Troop took exception to having their game interrupted. Several of the larger boys ran to intercept him. With a flick of his wrist he lobbed the ball over their heads, dodged their attempts to knock him over and with a whoop of triumph he raced around them in time to catch the ball before it hit the ground. The whole Boys' Troop seemed to arrive there at the same moment he did. I saw one boy collide with him and go spinning to one side as the others jumped on him in a group. Two others reeled out of the scrum, blood streaming from their heads. For a heartbeat he was gone, covered in bodies, and then the struggling group seemed to erupt, flinging him out like a salmon over a dam. He landed just in front of us, rolled and stood up, still clutching his stick. I stared, and he looked at me, grinned, and tossed the ball in the air. He still had it! We applauded him lazily as he stood, waiting for them to realize that they were fighting only each other.

Eventually the Troop saw what was happening. They stood still, dusty and bleeding, as two of the largest boys went towards the small figure who tormented them. None of us lying at the side of the training ground moved to intervene. It was better sport than usual. Conall and Buchal started making bets. Out of the corner of my eye I saw Owen, leaning forward to catch what was said, his body tense with interest.

'My name is Setanta,' said the boy. His voice was light. He looked to be six or seven. His skin was darker than that of the Ulster boys around him, almost Egyptian in hue.

The bigger of the two boys from the Troop stepped forward. His name was Follomain and he was the King's son, a tall red-haired lad who would one day fill out into a real fighter but for the moment still had the gangling legs and erupting skin of a boy. Conor expected great things from him. He had his father's pride and demeanour. Whether he would ever have Conor's judgement I had my doubts. Right now he was furious because a boy five years younger than himself was taunting him.

'I did not ask your name, and I do not care what it is,' Follomain growled as he walked towards Setanta.

Setanta looked at him. 'You will,' he said.

Follomain stopped a yard short, trying not to watch the ball, bouncing tantalizingly in front of him on the end of the dark-haired boy's hurley.

'Don't you want your ball?' asked Setanta. Follomain snorted and made a dismissive gesture.

'I want you to go away,' he said, his face red. 'We are the Boys' Troop. We did not invite you.'

Setanta flicked the ball up, caught it, and stood with arms folded and legs wide apart.

'But I beat you.' It was said not as a provocation but as a statement of fact. The larger boy shook his head.

'No, you did not,' said Follomain. 'And even if you had done so it would not matter. You do not join the Boys' Troop by joining a game uninvited without asking for our protection first, and you do not earn our respect by doing a few tricks with a hurley.'

Setanta's eyebrows rose, and he patted the ground with his hurley. I felt myself tense involuntarily, as if someone had drawn back a fist to hit me. As I watched, the air around him appeared to whirl and dance wildly, as on a lake-shore on a hot day before a thunderstorm. He took two quick steps forward until their bodies almost touched. Follomain was well over a head taller than him. Follomain flinched, and his eyes squinted half-closed in puzzlement, looking around for a moment as if he too felt the air move, but he did not step back. There was a pause while their wills locked together like the antlers of young stags.

'How then should I earn your respect?' Setanta asked softly, looking Follomain steadily in the eye.

'The Boys' Troop is joined by birth or by arms,' said the other of the boys, a dark-faced good-looking lad called Niall who had been silent up until now. Setanta stepped back again, a smile on his face, and tossed the ball gently from hand to hand. He appeared to ponder the possibilities for a few moments.

'That is good,' he said. 'To join by birth is easy. I would not have it that way, at least not yet.' He nodded at Follomain. 'Are you the leader?' The Boys' Troop had no official captain, but

Follomain's birth gave him precedence. He drew himself up. Setanta smiled with grim satisfaction. He looked at the group of boys facing him, particularly at the boy that he had sent spinning earlier when first challenging for the ball, a sour-faced lad called Bricriu. He stood at the front of the group, fingering his hurley and looking at Setanta with a murderous expression. Blood streamed from the corner of his mouth. Setanta pointed at him with his stick.

'You. Will you fight me?'

'I will.'

'And you?' Setanta pointed to the largest boy in the Troop, an amiable, slow-witted lad named Coolard, who nodded. Setanta put down the ball and his hurley. Bricriu spat blood, and spoke.

'I'll go first.' He had not yet put down his hurley.

'I bet four to one on the little one,' muttered Conall, who was watching with huge enjoyment, as if the boys were squabbling bear cubs and he their proud father. Buchal spat and slapped his hand, and several other men took the bet as well. If I had owned any cows, I would have bet with Conall.

'No,' said Follomain, 'I claim the first blow.'

'No need for argument,' murmured Setanta. 'Why not all at once?' With that, he gave a shout that made my scalp tingle, and ran straight at the two boys in front of him. Niall was taken by surprise and was knocked up in the air to land flat on his face. Follomain was quicker, and grabbed the small boy's shoulder as they collided, expecting him to try to spin away. Instead, Setanta drove straight into him, pushing a shoulder hard into his midriff. I heard the wind come from Follomain's lungs like a gust through a flung-open window as he was lifted almost off his feet and went flying backwards into the group behind him. Using Follomain, as a battering-ram Setanta knocked over half a dozen of them, and the confusion allowed him to get a firm footing and charge again. Several of the Troop had looked unwilling to join a mass assault on just one small boy, but Setanta gave them little choice. With cries of anger they swarmed around him. His fists and feet seemed to be everywhere and the sheer fury of his assault worked for a few moments, but he could not fight them

45

all for ever. One grabbed a leg, another got his head, and he was swallowed up in a mass of heaving bodies.

We were debating lazily whether the boy needed rescuing (Owen's argument), or could look after himself and anyway it was too hot to move (Buchal's argument), or was getting what he deserved (Conall's contribution), when we realized that the King was standing beside us. We had been so involved in the events on the training field that we had not heard his approach. Instinctively I started to stand, but no-one else did, so I pretended that I was just sitting up to watch the boys better.

With Conor was Fergus mac Roth, the trainer of the Boys' Troop and quondam King of Ulster. They had come from playing chess. It was said by the poets that Conor spent a third of the day playing chess, a third of the day watching the Boys' Troop training, and a third of the day drinking beer to calm his restless energy so that he could sleep. None of these figures was accurate, but they are the sort of thing that bards like to say about Kings. It's more poetic than saying that they are like most men.

(In Rome poets usually make things up because they are liars and sycophants. I remember one story about Tiberius. A drunk woman at a party once asked him if it was true what they said, that he had a prick like a horse. There was an embarrassed silence, broken at last by Julia, Tiberius's wife, who said levelly that she knew it well and it looked nothing like a horse. Tiberius apparently laughed. It must have been early in his reign. Towards the end of his life he would have made the woman know a horse intimately for that comment before she died. At Emain Macha they make rude stories up about each other, and especially about Kings, because it makes life more interesting. A poet is inviolate so he has nothing to fear from a King's displeasure. The Kings of Ulster are more robust than Roman Emperors. Conor was amused, not angered, by his reputation.)

Conor looked at the writhing mass of small bodies in front of him with interest. After a few moments he lifted a quizzical eyebrow in Fergus's direction.

'Is this how the Boys' Troop trains now?' he asked mildly.

Fergus was horribly embarrassed. He marched over to the writhing heap of boys and started throwing them to either side like a terrier after a rat hiding in a pile of sticks. Setanta was at the very bottom of the pile. Fergus pulled him up onto his feet, shaking the boy in his anger, then stopping to look at him in confusion, not knowing who he was.

Setanta was covered in dust, and marked and bleeding from a score of cuts. He had probably been saved from worse injury by the sheer number of his opponents, who in their eagerness had got in each other's way. He himself had done good work, however. Half a dozen of the boys could not stand straight, and there was hardly one who did not have an injury of some sort.

'Since when does the entire Troop attack one small boy?' thundered Fergus. There was a silence, then Niall spoke up.

'When the Troop is itself attacked by that small boy,' he replied, and suddenly grinned at Setanta, who smiled back. I noticed that Setanta had grey eyes, almost silver, pale against his dark skin. Conor walked over to Setanta and looked down at him. He towered over the boy, who stood his ground.

'So. You attacked the Troop?' Fergus twitched visibly at the thought, and his face became redder.

Setanta nodded. 'They did not want me to play their game,' he said. 'So I attacked them. To gain their respect.' Fergus growled deep in his throat.

'He was not invited, and he did not ask our protection,' spat Bricriu. His nose was bleeding now as well.

'He was winning,' I murmured. I thought Fergus would have apoplexy. Conor looked at me quizzically. Naisi, Ardan and Ainle were standing beside me, all nodding in support. Conor turned back to the boys.

'One boy was beating all of you?' he asked mildly.

Niall nodded straight away. Follomain agreed after a pause and with a shrug to show he didn't care. Bricriu just glowered. Conor stroked his beard and looked sideways at Fergus. I got the feeling that he was trying not to smile.

'So, young Champion,' he said. 'Who are you?'

'My name is Setanta, son of Sualdam and your sister Dectera.

47

I came as a guest, to visit a kinsman. I did not expect such unfriendliness.'

Conor looked unsurprised, which made him the only one. The fate of the son of Sualdam and Dectera was something that interested everyone in Emain Macha.

'Well,' said Conor, 'we are kinsmen then. But should you not have asked the protection of the Troop before joining their game?'

Setanta shrugged. 'I know nothing of that.'

Conor looked stern. 'You must ask for protection from those who can give it to you, and give it to those who ask it of you.'

Setanta smiled. He had small, rounded teeth, very white. 'Very well,' he said, looking at Conor, 'I ask for your protection now.'

Conor made no attempt to hide his pleasure. 'You have it,' he said.

'That is good,' replied the boy. 'What shall I do now?'

Conor considered for a moment. 'It seems to me that either these boys must ask your protection, or the . . .' Conor glanced at Fergus '. . . the game you were playing must recommence.'

There was a pause. Setanta turned to face the boys. They shuffled their feet. Then Niall stepped forward. 'I ask your protection,' he said, smiling.

'Gladly,' replied Setanta.

Conor looked over their heads at his son. 'Follomain?'

Follomain looked back at his father, and then at his cousin. I felt sorry for him. His lips became thin. 'I ask your protection.' Setanta nodded. The other boys came forward. Bricriu was last. Conor stood with his arms folded, smiling like a man who has just been presented with a fine dog that already knows how to hunt without being taught. The Boys' Troop, freshly under Setanta's protection, went back to their game, harried by Fergus who was still in a rage. Setanta went to join them. Conor called to him.

'Will you not come with me, young nephew?' Setanta turned, but did not follow.

'After the game,' he replied, turning back and throwing himself at a seething mass of boys and hurleys.

We stood up to follow the King. As I watched, Setanta broke free with the ball. In one smooth movement he tossed the ball up, swung his hurley and hit the ball high and hard towards the goal. As my eyes followed it I saw a large black shape on top of one of the posts. As the ball flew past the raven it spread its wings with an angry screech and circled low away from the game.

# 7

The memory of what I saw that first day is as fresh as yesterday – in fact fresher, as lately my near memories seem to move away from me like dust in a breeze. I wasn't there a few months later when Setanta became Cuchullain. I was racing in a chariot – winning the race, I should emphasize – and as I rounded the final corner, the chariot wheel hit a rock and turned over. I was thrown sideways and landed hard. I couldn't get out of bed for three days, and so I missed the excitement. I had to ask Owen what had happened. He took a deep breath, which told me I was in for a long haul. He loved a captive audience.

'Yes, I'll tell it if you want. But I'll tell it my way.' He reached for his harp, which was resting against the leg of the bed.

I grimaced. 'Is that the only way I'm going to hear it?' He nodded. I winced. 'All right, but no genealogies. I know who everyone who matters is, and I don't care about the rest. And no lists of clothes either. I'll imagine all that for myself. All right?' Owen composed himself, and drew his fingers lightly across the harp's strings. I raised an eyebrow. 'No genealogies, agreed?' He looked pained, but agreed. 'You think the genealogies are the highlight of the show. They're just a long list of names.'

Owen plucked a discordant note loudly. 'You're a barbarian,

or you'd know better. I forgive you.' He plucked another string, sweetly this time, and his light voice became almost sonorous.

'It was the last day of winter. The morning sun was stripping a thin skin of frost from the earth as the King's Troop came out of the gate of Emain Macha at a fast trot. Conor called Setanta from the hurling game to accompany them to Cullan's castle, but he refused, for they were still playing. He said he would follow them when he had won the game. The boys laughed; it was said that Setanta always pursued a game to the finish.

' "How will you know where we have gone? Do you know the way?" asked Conor.

' "No," replied Setanta, pointing, "but even if I was blind I could follow tracks like yours." Conor looked behind his chariot and saw deep grooves where his heavy wheels had cut into the wet earth. The hill in front of Emain Macha was lined like an old man's face with the trenches made by the chariots that streamed to and from the castle every day.

' "Don't leave it too long," said the King with a smile, and pushed his horses forward. Setanta whooped and ran back to the game.

'The King's chariot travelled fast, but it was a long way to Cullan's castle. When they arrived it was nearly dusk, and the warriors were ready for the feast.

'Cullan the smith greeted them warmly. He provided water for washing, and then they fell to eating and drinking. Cullan's hospitality was famous and he didn't disappoint them.

'As evening drew in, Cullan turned to the King. "Are there any others expected?" he asked.

'The King looked around. His Troop were all present. "No," he replied. "We are all here."

' "Good," replied his host. "I would not like any man who was expecting a friendly welcome to arrive after this time."

' "Why is that?" asked Conor innocently, ripping a chicken apart and washing a hunk of its flesh down with a gulp of wine. Cullan looked pleased with himself.

' "I have a great hound which guards myself and my family and my property. It—"

51

'There was a roar from down the table where Conall sat. "Come on then, you old fart, tell us all about it! We've been here for an hour and you haven't once mentioned your wonderful dog yet! I was beginning to think we had come to the wrong place!"

'Cullan threw a shin-bone at Conall's head, who ducked with a laugh. Cullan turned back to Conor and smiled proudly. "I do often talk about him, for I am as proud of him as I am of my sons. He is as tall as my shoulder, and his chest is deeper than any man's, and the man or animal which can withstand him has not been born. He—"

'"Then we shall sleep safe tonight!" shouted Conor, forestalling any further bragging. Everyone roared approval of the dog and drank its health, and the feast continued.

'The hurling game finished not long after the King's Troop left. The other boys went back to Emain Macha, but Setanta set off after the King. He soon grew tired of running between the trenches left by the chariots, so he played a game of throwing his hurling ball high into the air and then hitting it with his hurley, and then running to catch it while balancing on the edge of the chariot tracks. He never once fell off, nor did he fail to hit whatever it was in the distance he aimed at, whether it was a bird on the wing or a twig on the end of a waving branch of oak.

'When Setanta arrived at the castle where the Great King stayed, it was almost dark. The boy heard distant shouts and the guttural sounds of feasting, and then all other sounds were lost behind the roaring of Cullan's huge dog as it galloped into the attack, pounding the earth as it ran towards him faster than any man could hope to run away. Conor heard the noise that the dog made and immediately jumped up with his food still in his hand, white with the shock of remembering that Setanta was outside. He shouted to his men and they jumped up and seized their arms at the thought that Setanta was alone and unarmed outside the walls. Cullan called out a warning and tried to prevent the King's men from crossing the walls, but the bravest of them brushed past him and leapt onto the battlements. Then they saw the dog, as tall as a man's shoulder and with paws as big as a two-year-old child's head, bounding across the dark grass towards the boy, and at that sight even Conall of the Victories hesitated for a moment, before he brushed aside fear and jumped down off the wall to help Setanta, bellowing a warning as he fell. He landed heavily and ran towards the boy like a swooping eagle, but he knew in his heart that the dog would reach Setanta before he did.

'Setanta stood still and watched as the dog bore down on him. When it was only a pulsebeat away, its great jaws open, its breath rank and hot in his face, Setanta drew back his hurley and, with a flick of his wrists, drove the hard ball down the dog's throat and deep into its vitals.

'The dog let out a strangled sound and the strength fled from its legs and body. As it crashed to the ground in front of him Setanta seized the dog by its hind legs and swung it around, dashing the great grey head against a rock, then threw it down, put his foot on its chest, reached deep into its mouth and tore out its still-beating heart.

'There was a moment of stunned silence, and then cheer after cheer rang from the walls of the castle as the men of the Red Branch applauded the boy's courage and skill.

'Cullan roared with grief and fury, and ran to where Setanta stood looking down at the hound, his hand steaming with its heartsblood. Cullan seized the unresisting boy, shaking him as a dog shakes a rat, and shouted into his face. "What have you done? What have you done?"

'Setanta saw that the smith was almost in tears. "I am sorry, but would you rather he had killed me?" the boy asked quietly. Cullan hesitated. The passion left him, and he released Setanta with an oath. Conor walked up to him and put a hand on his smith's shoulder.

'"What is it, old friend?"

'The smith gestured at the dead dog on the grass. "He protected us from enemies, defended our cattle from wolves, played with my children. I have lost a son. Where shall I find another like him? Who will guard us now?"

'There was an awkward silence. Setanta stepped forward. "I

killed your hound,'' he said, ''and I must therefore take on his responsibilities. Have you a whelp from him?'' Amazed, Cullan nodded. ''Then give him to me and I shall train him to do everything for you that this noble animal did, and until then I shall guard your walls and your cattle by night in his stead, and your children can play with the whelp as he grows. Is that a fair blood-price?''

'Cullan turned to Conor, his hands open in supplication. "Great King, he is only a boy . . .''

'Conor silenced him with a gesture. "A boy who killed your hound,'' he pointed out with a smile, "without even a sword.'' He gestured around him, including all the Champions who had come to Cullan's castle with him. "Is there anyone else here who could have done it? If so, that man is yours. Let the best of us guard your walls.''

'There was a silence. Then Cullan turned to Setanta. "I accept the price,'' he said. The men of the Red Branch set up a cheer, and Conor put a hand on Setanta's shoulder.

'"Well done,'' he said. "You are now Cuchullain, Cullan's hound.''

'"I like the name Setanta,'' replied the boy.

'"And you will still be Setanta, it is still your birth-name,'' replied the King, "but men will speak of the deeds of Cuchullain. May they be many and glorious.''

'At the King's words a spark of light seemed to flare up, burn wildly, and fall back to a deep smouldering in the boy's silver eyes. "Very well then. Cuchullain,'' he agreed.

'Conor turned to his host. "So, Cullan, you have your Hound. Can the feast now recommence?''

'Cullan knelt by the dog and touched the brindled hair on its still-warm side. "Of course,'' he said quietly. "I will be with you soon.''

'Setanta bowed to Cullan, picked up his hurley, walked over to the gate of the castle and stood beside it. Conor laughed at his serious face, and called for a spear and a shield to be brought. These were given to the boy, who weighed them carefully in his hands. He then leant backwards and threw the spear straight and

54

high into the air directly above him. He stood under it as it fell towards him, and then caught it as the point reached a hand's breadth from his chest.

'Cullan applauded the Feat with the other Champions. It was almost dark, and the spear was longer than the thrower.

'The men went back to their feast. Cullan followed a few minutes later, looking at Setanta without expression as he passed. A little later, Cullan's bard came out with food for the boy who guarded the gate. As he ate, the bard gave him a message. "My master forgives you the death of the Hound. Your blood-price is fair, and no more will be said. However, because of what you did today you are under a geis never to eat dog, or cook it, or handle it cooked, or help others to cook it."

'Setanta nodded his understanding. "I hear your words, and I accept the geis," he replied.

'The bard smiled. "Then have a peaceful night, Cuchullain," he said, and went back into the castle.

'The boy Setanta, now called Cuchullain, guarded Cullan's castle every night until the whelp of the great dog was trained to take its place. It is said that in that time he never slept.'

I looked at Owen sceptically. He looked more pleased with himself than is possible for one man to be without bursting.

'I hardly know what to say,' I said.

'Try.' His lips thinned slightly.

'Everything you relate took place yesterday, and yet at the end of the story you tell the future.'

Owen shrugged. It struck me how often he did that. 'The story needs an ending. I give it one, I predict what will happen. If it doesn't, I can change it.'

'And Cuchullain really didn't sleep?'

Owen looked at me. 'I don't know.'

'But you said he didn't, or wouldn't.'

'No. I said that it was said that he didn't sleep. Different.'

I tried another tack. 'Tore the poor dog's heart out with his bare hands?'

Owen looked pleased. 'Yes, I liked that bit too,' he said.

'But he couldn't have.'

Owen smiled. 'You're missing the point, as usual. Didn't you like the story?'

I was annoyed. 'Oh, as a story, fine, it's very fine, but as a description of what actually happened, well, isn't it a little, shall we say, unlikely?'

'Nothing is unlikely when Cuchullain is around.' Owen looked complacent.

I snorted. 'Nothing, except that you might keep a sense of proportion about what's going on around you! And what was that about playing games with spears? That was the silliest bit of all.'

Owen grinned. That was starting to annoy me as well. 'Oh, that.' He picked absently at a fingernail in a way that made me think he didn't want to look at me. 'That was real.'

# 8

After Owen told me the story of Setanta and the great dog, I lay awake for a long time. I remember feeling that I had to see Setanta, that it was important that I talked to him myself.

Early the next day I dressed myself with difficulty and limped to my chariot. For once neither Owen nor the sons of Usna were in attendance, and I was able to drive to Cullan's castle in a welcome solitude. The morning was bright, and the grass still sharp with frost. When I arrived at the castle gate the evidence of Owen's story was still there. A dust of clear crystals sparkled on the coat of the monster which lay dead on the grass in front of the gates. I watched as a group of men wrestled with the corpse to get it away from where its master would be able to see it when he looked out over his lands in the morning. Six of them could hardly shift it.

I thought about the geis the boy was under. A geis was absolute. An Ulsterman would rather die than have another man say that he broke it. There is no Roman equivalent. It isn't like taking an oath – you'd keep an oath because you swear in front of the Gods and they'd be personally offended if you didn't. It isn't like giving your word either. Some men's word is to be trusted, others' not. Giving your word depends on the giver, it isn't absolute. A geis is unbreakable, something that is utterly integrated with your self, becomes part of you, part of what defines you as a person. What's the most important thing to you, the one thing in the world you believe most strongly, the thing that names you, the thing you'd die for? Belief in a republic, love for your wife, a paralysing fear of spiders? That's like a geis. You'd no more break it than you'd vote for a dictator, sell your wife or go into a dark cave festooned with webs. It isn't about fear or power of the will, it's just unthinkable.

I walked over to where the boy stood. He watched my approach without curiosity. His right arm was encrusted with dark red blood. He had not left his post even to clean himself. He looked cold.

I motioned to a slave to bring him water. Cuchullain knelt to wash himself. Black hair fell straight and full to his shoulders and over his face, almost hiding it. When I say 'black', I do not mean just dark brown. His hair shone like polished ebony, a still forest pool flecked by a full moon.

He stood, and looked up as I stepped in front of him. The curtain of hair parted, showing me a thin face with high cheek-bones and silver-grey eyes. I was surprised. I had not seen much of him since the day he arrived and took on the entire Boys' Troop, and I had forgotten how strange his colouring was. His skin, hair, everything about him suggested that his eyes would be black, like an Iberian. Instead, he had eyes like a young rabbit's pelt, grey and soft. The effect was startling. He did not look tired, as an eight-year-old should after a night without sleep.

It was still cold. I offered him a cloak. He wrapped it around his thin shoulders without comment. We looked at each other for a few moments. I was struck by his dispassion, a lack of curiosity that suggested self-control beyond his years. He watched without wondering. He saluted me. I returned it.

'My name is Setanta.' His voice was soft. I smiled.

'Setanta? Not Cuchullain?' He looked serious.

'Men will know the deeds of Cuchullain, and poets will sing of them. That is for the future. Until then, my name is Setanta.' I managed not to smile in the way that patronizing adults do to precocious children that makes children want to start biting them.

'Then I shall call you Setanta now and Cuchullain then,' I said, and felt pompous. He looked at me, as if seeing me properly for the first time, and gave a little shrug.

'What you will.' He reached out his hand, and we clasped each other's wrist. His arm was slight, the skin soft and boyish. I wanted to go away and come back, start the meeting again, let him know I took him seriously. I started to introduce myself properly.

'My name is Leary, although—'

I stopped. The most extraordinary sensation seemed to flood up my arm and through my body. It was like nothing I have ever experienced, which is to say that it was like many things I have experienced, the best things, refined and fused together. It was the warm feeling in your gut that the touch of a beautiful woman's hand brings as she runs it across your chest for the first time; it contained the instant that you feel your opponent start to lose his balance after a long trial of strength; it brought back the joy of meeting an old friend unexpectedly; it held the warmth of watching a loved one go about some business of their own while unaware of your gaze; all of these things and a dozen others, brought together and joined. It raised the hairs on my arms and I wanted to laugh like a child.

I felt I wanted to ask him something, but I didn't know what it was.

His face was serious. I learnt later that he could laugh until tears ran from his eyes, and that the sound of it left you feeling as if warm sunlight had suddenly fallen on your skin in a cold forest. At that moment, however, he looked as if he had never smiled in his life. His eyes searched my face, not probing but absorbing, as if he would want to recall me in detail later.

He released my hand. The spell broke, but I still felt an odd elation. I wanted to find a woman and roll around with her on a bearskin for an hour or two. I wanted to stand on a mountain and watch the sun disappear. I wanted everything.

He was looking past me. We were not alone. Automatically my hand dropped to my sword as I turned. I paused, and smiled to myself at my reaction. I saw my father drop his hand to his sword by habit many times. Rome was fast receding from me. I was becoming a barbarian again.

Owen and a companion were walking towards us. They were similar men, both small and wiry, but Owen's red hair occasionally lay flat on his head, while his companion's shot up in the air as if he never combed it, like a sage bush in a hot summer. His name was Ulan. I remembered seeing him earlier, sitting with the bards. He had red hair like an Umbrian cow, exactly that colour, and his face never stopped moving. When I first met Owen I thought he was always looking, always enquiring, but Ulan made him look like a marble statue. He was like a nervous rabbit, sniffing the air, smelling the currents and sensing the waves that move amongst us. Of course, all the bards were alive to the shifting allegiances that flowed around Conor's table. Although the bards were theoretically safe from loss of status, and their lives sacred, it was still as well to know whose foot the heaviest boot was on. The courts of Tiberius and Conor had that in common. Tiberius's court may have been more Oriental in its intrigue, but Celts give no ground when it comes to protecting themselves and their position against threats and slights, real and imagined.

Ulan sat at the foot of the table, with the apprentices. As he strode – no, almost skipped – towards us, he carried no harp, but had no sword either. He played the part of a bard with a reputation, even if he was still a few years and an epic song or two off full recognition. He marched up to Cuchullain and saluted him, then stepped back and watched as Owen did the same. Owen and Cuchullain clasped hands. I remembered my feeling as I held the boy's hand; I wondered if the poet's face would show a similar reaction to mine. A fleeting change danced across his mouth, and was gone. He broke grip with the boy, and saluted me. Then Ulan walked up to me.

'Leary, is it not?'

I was not surprised at his knowing my name – many knew of

the blond man who came from the sea and fell into the cowshit – but was irritated by his informality. Feeling a little priggish, I nodded. At that time, as an honorary Gael I was probably keener on proper solemnity than most. Those who had been Ulstermen all their lives could afford to let formality slip sometimes. For me, manners and codes were the only way I had of defining myself. I was, I suspect, over-formal.

He grinned, not at all put off by my stiffness.

'Call me Ulan,' he said, grinning and showing off good teeth.

Cuchullain looked at him with interest. I felt a twinge of jealousy, and found myself scowling at the young bard.

'You won the prize last month,' said Cuchullain.

He was referring to the prize awarded each full-moon day to the young bard who most impresses his teachers. Ulan nodded, gave a little shrug (a characteristic movement, I was to learn), grinned again, and clasped my arm in a friendly gesture. For a moment I almost snatched it away, then realized the absurdity of my feelings. Ulan gave me a brilliant smile, and made a wide gesture aimed at Cuchullain which took in most of Ulster.

'Do you know who this young man is, Leary?' I nodded, but was given no time to reply. 'He is to be the greatest Hero our people have ever known.' Ulan looked at Cuchullain with enormous satisfaction, as if a favourite son had lived up to expectations and beyond. Then he grinned at me again, and clapped me on both shoulders. 'And you and Owen are to be his keepers, and his guides, and his friends, and the spreaders of his fame. Well, I suppose Owen will have to do most of the fame-spreading on his own, but then he doesn't drive a chariot, so you'll share the load evenly in the end.' (He grinned again. I was getting a little tired of this meaningless cheerfulness.) 'What do you think of that?'

I thought he was talking patronizing horseshit and was taking liberties that had not been earned or asked for, and I was about to tell him so but Cuchullain spoke first, his face serious. 'Who told you this?' he said, quietly. Owen smiled at him and opened his mouth to speak, but Ulan jumped in first.

'Cathbad,' he said. I could hear the excitement in his voice.

'He had a dream. He told us all about it. First thing this morning.' On the word 'all' he made another broad gesture, and I caught his outflung hand just short of my nose. I growled at him, and backed off a little in disgust. Owen made pacifying movements with his hands at me behind Ulan's back while Ulan chattered on without pausing.

'Our destinies are one. Cuchullain' (and here a gesture to the boy) 'is to be a Hero, you' (a nod to me) 'are to drive him to where he will do his heroism, and the bards' (a sweep of the arm for Owen and himself) 'will appear from behind a safe bush once he has done it and tell everyone the story. Suitably embellished with the poetic refinements, of course.' (The bards both smirked.) 'We are a perfect combination. Without Cuchullain, there is nothing to tell, without Leary, Cuchullain would not arrive to do the tellable thing, and without a bard or two to tell it no-one would know it had happened and thus needed telling.' He smiled. I thought his words were warm mist from piss-wet straw, but Cuchullain seemed amused.

'Did Cathbad say all that?' he said. Owen was suddenly serious, and hushed Ulan, who was trying to speak.

'Yes, he did,' he said. Owen's eyes became brighter and his voice changed.

Bards have a way of talking which they put on when they are at their most inspired and also when they are at their most pretentious. The two cannot usually be told apart. I tend to assume the latter until proved wrong. Owen's voice had that tone now. It is a peculiar earnest sing-song tone that is either risible or inspirational, depending on your viewpoint.

'You will be the brightest star in the galaxy of Ireland's Heroes.' (Owen's voice became slightly husky as it dipped and swooped over Cuchullain. I stood clear, watching as the little man got more and more excited.) 'Your deeds will live long after you. Your prowess as a warrior will be held up high as an example to all men and an encouragement to those who follow. A time will come when you will defend Ulster alone, with only Leary and myself to accompany you.' (Ulan tried to interrupt but Owen snarled at him and he shut up.) 'Your deeds will outstrip all the Champions of Ireland, both those who have been and those who are to come. From now on, all Champions will be measured against you but none will take your place. Whenever people gather to talk and sing of great men, your song will be the first to be sung, and the last.'

Ulan turned to me. His eyes shone, his excitement spilt over into his voice, making it shake. I thought that he was about to have some form of seizure. 'You are the greatest charioteer that ever took up reins. He is to be the greatest Hero Ulster has ever known. His deeds will take him where no man has been, and his horses shall be born of fire and the wind, such that only your skill can drive them.'

That sounded a bit more like it. I looked at him. Perhaps he was onto something. Even allowing for exaggeration by the raving poet, it sounded as though the young lad was going to need a good charioteer. In about ten years' time.

Cuchullain looked at Owen calmly. I supposed that he thought as I did of what the poet had said. I was wrong. 'And you? What did Cathbad prophesy for you?' I was struck, as I was often to be, by his directness. I was also struck by Cathbad's industry. Normally you couldn't get 'Good day' out of him, but he must have spent the better part of the morning throwing chicken entrails at people to get the effect that he had obviously had on Owen and Ulan.

Owen looked at the boy as if he were a barrel of beer at the end of a long dry journey. 'I am your storyteller! I will tell the world of your exploits, of the Hero and his charioteer! Queen Maeve will hear of us and tremble. I will compose the greatest song ever heard, and men will sing it for all time, and all our names will be immortal!'

His eyes shone, his voice was raised, his colour was high. I wondered if he was drunk.

'Cathbad dreamt all this?'

Ulan nodded vigorously. His red hair flopped over his eyes, and he pushed it back on his forehead, where it stood up like a horse's poll. 'Cathbad said it was the clearest dream he had ever had. The Gods have sent a message.'

Cuchullain looked up at me through his curtain of hair. His eyes were twinkling. 'Well,' he said, 'we wouldn't dream of not doing what the Gods told us to, would we, Leary?'

I looked at him, and saw that he was laughing at Ulan too, but without malice, and felt a little ashamed. Cuchullain always had that effect on me, of making me feel that I was a cynical old fart. I tried to match his mood. 'Ignore the Gods?' I said seriously. 'Indeed not. That would be inviting trouble.'

The four of us stood in a small circle, and I felt a bond between us. Well, between the three of us. It was becoming obvious that Ulan was just along for the ride, Cathbad hadn't said anything about him. Not that I took a syllable of any of it seriously, of course, but Owen's enthusiasm, while it seemed unlikely, was uplifting, contagious. The boy was . . . unusual. I felt that I wanted to be near him, to see what he would do. So the four of us stood in a group, Owen grinning like an idiot, me trying to look as though I knew what to think, and the boy smiling his sideways smile at both of us. Ulan was in the group but not part of it, but that didn't seem to matter to him and I didn't care. Then Cuchullain broke the spell by stepping backwards, and a voice came from the castle wall behind him to call us for supper.

# 9

I stayed at Cullan's castle and watched Cuchullain for the next few months. It wasn't entirely altruism or curiosity that made me do it. When I asked Cullan if I could stay at his home until my leg was mended, he smiled his agreement and said that he would send his doctor to me. I would have preferred to just stay in bed until my leg stopped hurting, but I knew that the smearing of entrails and the application of mouse-dropping and garlic poultices was part of the price one would have to pay, so I agreed with a good grace. Politeness pays. Instead of the bearded dotard that I expected, the doctor was young, humorous and female. Before coming to Ulster I had never known women to take much interest in medicine, but here it seemed to be quite common. We talked while she probed my injured knee with long fingers. Within minutes the knee felt better. She must have sensed the improvement, for as I was about to move towards her she pushed deep into the soft part of the joint with a sharp knife disguised as a finger. A bolt of pain ripped through me.

'Oww!' I threw my head back and whacked it against the wall behind the bed.

'Did that hurt?'

'Why, did you think it wouldn't?' She smiled, and stroked the outraged knee. The pain began to subside. My head still hurt though.

'I know what's wrong,' she said.

'Can you fix it?'

She nodded, looking at my leg seriously. 'Yes, but it will take time, and you will have to stay in bed and do exactly what I say.'

I folded my arms and smiled.

I was in bed for a week, while she pushed and pulled at my leg for what seemed like hours every morning. Then she pronounced herself satisfied, and I was ordered to walk several hours every day without shoes on the soft grass outside the castle. Back and forth I went, to the initial amusement and eventual boredom of the guards. I had nothing else to do, so I watched Cuchullain.

I watched as he practised his skills to while away the day, then kept vigil outside Cullan's walls at night. Sometimes, when I didn't feel like walking and knew that my doctor of the iron fingers wasn't watching, I kept him company. Once he realized that I neither doubted him nor was laughing at him, he accepted me as part of his surroundings. I was reminded of a jaguar that Helena told me Tiberius kept on Capri. It wasn't a pet – no-one told it what to do, and it came and went as it chose – but it never hurt anyone who left it alone. So long as you did nothing that made any difference to it, you could do anything you liked and remain quite safe. Most of the day it dozed in the shade. However, if you made a sudden loud noise near by, or threw a spear too close whether deliberately or by accident, then a yellow eye would flick open and not blink again until the situation was clear. Helena said that it made you feel like a very small and helpless animal. Tiberius was devoted to it, and it slept outside his quarters every night. If the jaguar had not died of poison shortly beforehand, I do not think that Macro would have even got into Tiberius's bedroom the night he died.

Cuchullain had the jaguar's detachment. I was no threat to him, and so he tolerated me, but he was not interested in me for myself, and would probably not have noticed if one day I was no longer there.

Almost every morning I was woken by the first rays of the sun. I would get up and walk out of the gate. Cuchullain would be standing near by, watchful, awake. During all the time I stayed with him, I never saw him asleep while he was supposed to be on guard, unless he knew how to sleep standing up with his eyes open.

After a few nights Cullan relented, offering to release the boy from his bond, but Cuchullain refused, and continued to stand guard until the puppy was old enough to take his place. All this time he kept up his own regime of practice and training. Sometimes he slept briefly in the middle of the day, but always woke instantly if anyone approached.

The evening of the day when the dog was finally grown and ready to take over the guarding of the castle, he came to see me.

I looked again into his eyes. They were still the same calm grey-silver colour, but his expression was strained.

'May I rest here?'

I realized that he had no room of his own. I waved him in. He smiled, and walked to my bed, where he lay down, stretched out his limbs once, breathed out and fell instantly asleep.

For three days and nights I sat and watched him while he slept, occasionally dozing myself, mostly just watching him, thinking. He slept almost soundlessly. Every so often, he would stretch like a cat until the bones cracked, and then settle again.

Except for the very poorest, all Ulster children are taken from their mothers immediately after weaning, and given to the women who look after the communal nursery. Mothers only see their children if they want to, fathers usually not at all until they are old enough to hold a sword. Then fathers choose whether or not to take an interest. I have never had children, never had someone to look after. I do not know what it means to be a real father. I do not know what it feels like, but I can guess. It feels like Cuchullain sleeping soundly on my bed while I watch over him.

We rode back to Emain Macha together. Over the next few months, I saw him often. Each time we met, I was reminded of Owen's words. It was true, I felt a bond, as if there was

67

something between the boy and myself, something we had already shared. Owen I saw often. He was amusing for a short time, but I found his dogged optimism and relentless good spirits too much to take for long. I preferred to sit with Conall and the older men, and get maudlin drunk, talking about the good old days, days of better battles, more frequent cattle-raids, harder swords, more respectful children, warmer sun, stronger beer, greater Heroes. They were simple men, and yet they were worldly, and perhaps most importantly they had a love for life. I spent most of my time with them. Owen on the other hand found them dull company, and tried to get me away from them. I suspect that he wanted to pick my brain and couldn't do it when I was befuddled with drink and distracted by the roaring that passed for conversation amongst Conall and my other cronies. Owen could not leave me alone. He was determined that I should be happy. He could not see that I was happy already, I was just not happy in the way he was. I was content, which Owen never was.

Meanwhile, despite the Owen problem – which was really no problem, because he was basically good-hearted and I bore him no ill-will – I passed the time pleasantly enough, amusing myself by learning more bad words, going on minor cattle-getting excursions, drinking myself insensible, encouraging the spread of rumours about the fabulous sexual potency of people of my race, that sort of thing. Waiting for Cuchullain to grow up, while suspecting that he already had.

# 10

I have to work hard to remember the next part of the story. It pains me to bring it to mind. I have pushed the memory of their laughter away from me for so long, hidden Deirdre's face behind the dark skirts of time, left Naisi's smile in a dark place where it will not haunt me every time I glance towards it. But the memory is only quiet, it does not fade. I do remember.

Cuchullain joined the Boys' Troop and I didn't see him for a while. I carried on with my education. A few months passed. There were rumours that the Connaughtmen were gathering their forces together, but I had never known a time since my arrival when similar rumours were not around, so, like everyone else, I paid no attention. I remember being bored, so when Naisi and his brothers suggested a short hunting trip, leaving at a sensible time of day, I agreed happily. The weather was beautiful, the drive pleasant, the game plentiful. I did little actual killing, but contented myself with impressing my friends with a display of driving skills. Naisi and Ardan amused themselves by throwing the tiny javelins they called 'tooth-picks' at any rabbits that came within range and insulting each other's marksmanship, while Ainle, as the youngest, rode beside me and did his best to look above such childish behaviour.

It was not long before we came to the edge of the forest, where we had to leave the chariots and mount the horses in order to be able to manoeuvre between the trees. Within minutes, Ardan had roused a good-sized boar. With whoops of delight we chased the animal through bracken and round thick furze bushes until we got it cornered between an impenetrable thorn brake on one side and a sheer drop into a small defile with a stream at the bottom on the other. The boar realized it was trapped, and turned to face us, bristling with aggression. I immediately thought of Conall. Our horses stamped and started at its fierce eyes and the tusks that curled up from its jaw. Conall had that effect on animals too.

'Better all get off,' I said. 'Don't want the horses to end up at the bottom of the gully with us underneath them.'

We dismounted, and Ardan led the horses back into the trees. Then the four of us stood in a semicircle, blocking the boar's escape. I looked at Naisi. His pale face was flushed with excitement. He looked very young. I wondered for the first time if this was his first boar hunt. His brothers were even younger than he was. I swallowed hard. I was in charge of three children, and a vicious animal that could easily kill a grown man was about to attack us. It was too late to back away, and the brothers would not have obeyed me if I had suggested it.

'Ground the butt ends of your spears,' I said urgently, 'and aim for his throat. Don't try to thrust, just hold the spear steady.'

The wild pig took exception to my voice, and charged. It feinted towards Naisi, then changed direction at the last moment and came at me instead. I felt the shock as it collided with my spear-point, and then the metal flew sideways off its breastbone and I was on the ground with the pig on top of me. I twisted away as a tusk the length of my hand and as sharp as a strigil came past my face. I could smell the animal's acrid sweat, felt the harshness of its bristles as my hands pushed frantically against it. A tusk ripped at my forearm and then slashed down towards my face again before pulling back for the kill. I closed my eyes. I felt a weight thump against my chest, as if the boar

70

had jumped up and crashed down onto me again. I couldn't breathe. I was dead.

Time stopped. I waited. More time passed. The pain did not come. I was not torn to shreds, although the boar pressed heavily down on me, pinning me to the earth. I heard a shout, and then the weight lifted. I suddenly felt lighter than the air. I turned sideways and gasped for breath, sucking great shuddering lungfuls in like a man drowning. A water skin was thrust into my hand, and I drank a little while I waited for the world to settle around me.

When everything had calmed down, I opened my eyes to see the boar lying beside me, twitching as it died, its lips rolled back to show the full length of its tusks. A spear was through its throat from side to side, and another stood vertical between its ribs. I looked up at Naisi's face, framed with black hair, held close to mine as he took me by the shoulders. He looked concerned. 'Are you all right?'

I had a nasty cut on my left cheek, which bled far more than it hurt and eventually left an interesting scar without doing any real harm. My only genuine injury was to my arm. Naisi examined it with a serious face and pronounced it a flesh wound. 'Come down to the stream and I'll wash it.'

By the time he had dressed the wound, and I had stuck my head into the cold water to clear it, the boys had told me the story a couple of dozen times, and I had a fair idea what had happened. The boar's sudden change of direction meant that my spear missed the vital spot where the neck met the chest. It bowled me over and landed on top of me. Naisi had his own spear knocked away in the confusion, so he drew his dagger and flung himself onto the boar's back, stabbing at its throat. That had been the sudden weight I had felt. His action had delayed the boar's killing thrust just enough to give Ardan and Ainle time to use their spears. I looked at them all. Naisi was covered in the boar's blood, but was unharmed. The three of them had saved me. A lump came to my throat. I spoke gruffly to cover it up.

'Get yourself into the stream and wash that blood off, or they will think I've let you be mortally wounded.'

Naisi pulled off his leather jerkin to reveal a hairless chest and a flat stomach ridged like a turtle's back. He splashed into the middle of the stream. He stood with his legs wide apart and bent forward, putting his head in the water and then straightening himself like the arm of a siege-catapult so that the water flew back towards us in a wide sparkling arc. Under his white skin the sharply defined back muscles were long and smooth. He pushed his long black hair back from his face with both palms, shaking himself like a dog and laughing as he ducked the sticks we threw at him for splashing us.

I think that we all saw her at the same time. It was as if she was not there and we were laughing at Naisi, then we blinked, and she was standing on the opposite side of the stream, her bare feet just touching the edge of the water.

As soon as I saw her I felt two things. The first was that she was the most beautiful thing that I had ever seen. The second was that sadness hung around her like a veil. Even though her smile cut through my heart like sunlight through darkness, I felt sadness cloak it.

We were all startled into immobility for a second, but Naisi looked as though he had been turned to stone. He looked at her without speaking or moving for what seemed a month. We might all still be there now, but eventually Ardan decided that enough was enough and ran into the stream, lifting his knees high so as not to fall, and crashed into Naisi, sending him tumbling. Everyone laughed at them wrestling in the water, and the stone-spell was broken. Naisi eventually beat off Ardan and grinned sheepishly at her. She smiled back, and Naisi smiled again so hugely that it looked as if the top of his head might fall off backwards. It seemed quite natural that she should cross the stream and join us for our meal, if only to stop him making an even bigger idiot of himself.

Her name was Deirdre. She had watched the fight with the boar, and her voice trembled as she told of Naisi's bravery. He listened to her with the eyes of a starving man who has seen a table piled to the roof with every kind of food. If I hadn't believed in love at first sight before, then looking at Naisi I had no choice.

72

The hunt was over. Ardan and Ainle went off to do some desultory bird-shooting. I dozed in the shade, half-listening to Deirdre and Naisi talking all afternoon, sometimes without pausing to draw breath, sometimes without words but staring at each other with an intensity that I felt surely could not be healthy. They sat together on the stream bank, as close as two eyes in one face but never touching. When it was time for us to leave, she looked at him in a way that would have stopped the heart of an old man like myself and made him promise to come back the next day. Naisi sat fourteen feet tall in his saddle. He looked at her directly, and said, 'I will come.' I believed then that the end of the world would not have stopped him.

We rode home in silence. Owen listened to the story of the boar with great enjoyment, and laughed uncontrollably in a particularly inane way as I told him how I had been almost killed. Then I told him about Deirdre. The name stopped his laughter like a slap across the cheek. 'What's the matter?'

He looked serious. 'Haven't I told you the story of Deirdre?' I groaned inwardly, then decided to be honest and groaned out loud as well. I shook my head.

'My arm hurts and I need a drink,' I said. 'Can you keep it short?' Owen couldn't. It was a story that he had told before around the fires, and he knew no other way to tell it. For once, however, I think he tried, and so for once I tried not to interrupt.

'Sixteen summers before Setanta arrived at Emain Macha, the child of Felim, son of Dall, was born. Conor and Cathbad and all the Champions of the court came to see her, for the table of Felim was famed as one of the finest in Ulster.

'Conor held the child in his arms and smiled. The baby was unusually small, with black hair and green eyes, and her nurse said that she had never once cried since the day she was born.

'Conor turned to Cathbad. "Prophesy her future!" he shouted. "And make it a good one!" Cathbad laughed in a strained sort of way and went off to light his fire and prepare a sacrifice. The King and his men went off to begin the celebration feast, calling back to Cathbad to bring them good news soon.

'The banquet had been planned since the day that the pregnancy of Dergara, wife of Felim, was known, and the country had been crossed and recrossed by messengers in search of special foods until their tracks resembled the weave of a rich woman's shawl. The King and his men fell to feasting and quite forgot Cathbad, who was gone far longer than was usual, and it was with surprise much later that the King turned to find Cathbad behind him. The druid was silent, his face grave.

'Conor welcomed him with a shout, offered him wine and food, and told him to prophesy to them. Cathbad at first refused, asking for a private audience with the King, but Conor would have none of it, insisting that he shout the news out to everyone.

'The druid stood beside the King and began to speak. His voice was quiet, but those nearest him realized the tone of his words and hushed their neighbours, and in moments his soft but clear voice carried right across the silent hall, like the footsteps of a hangman on prison flagstones.

'"The child will be called Deirdre, and she will be the fairest woman in Ireland."

'"There's good news!" shouted the King, and a few others drank and cheered, but most of the guests could see the tears that ran silently down the druid's cheek, and they were quiet, knowing that good news can be bad fortune. Cathbad continued his prophecy without looking at the King.

'"Her beauty will be beyond compare, beyond the memory of any living man. Flowers will wilt in envy as she passes by, and all animals will sit at her feet in peace together. Her accomplishments will be many. She will be fair of speech, quick of wit, even of temper, strong of will. All women will wish her as a friend. All men will envy her husband, for she will be faithful until she dies to one man alone."

'Cathbad paused. His voice seemed to fail him for a moment. A ribald remark from the bottom of the table failed to get a response and the speaker subsided into maudlin silence. Cathbad lifted his head up and looked over the heads of the seated men, up to the roof and the stars beyond.

' "The story of Deirdre will be the greatest love story ever told in Ireland."

'Conor banged his cup onto the table. "Then we are blessed!" he cried, "for Ulster has the greatest Champions already, and now we have the greatest lovers too! It is a good time to be alive!" This did not raise a sound from the men, who sensed a weight about to descend on them. Cathbad's voice became hoarse and fell even softer.

' "She will wed a great King. Her beauty will be spoken of for all time, but not her happiness. Her life will be short, although her love will be great. Men will split a great kingdom for love of her, and she will bring death and ruin to Ulster."

'There was a terrible silence. Conor the King stood up slowly and looked angrily at his druid. The evening was spoilt and his men were disheartened. A black shadow fell across his face, and he shouted his words.

' "You are a fool, old man! Go and play with your chicken bones somewhere else and do not bother honest fighting men with your silly stories! This is another of your foolishnesses, like the time you told us that the sun would shine for a year and a day, and it immediately rained for a month!" The King gestured to his men, and his tone became more reasonable, warning the druid instead of threatening him. "It is a happy day that you spoil, and a good meal and fine wine. Go from us now, and do not come back until you have some good news!" He spread his hands wide. "We are accustomed to your foolishness, and it pleases us to let you amuse us with your stories, but do not think that we take them seriously." Conor looked around. The faces that surrounded him were unconvinced. He laughed at them.

' "You are old men without teeth who fear shadows! Very well then, I shall ensure that this girl is well taken care of. I place her under my protection. She will be taken far away, to where no man will see her, and she will live there until she is seventeen. Seventeen summers from now, we shall have a great wedding feast – which we will begin planning for now! – and I shall marry this girl. It is best this way. If she is beautiful and two Champions fall out over her, then the peace will be lost. I am the

King! No man will question my right, no matter how beautiful she is. Is this not the best way?"

'"She must be put to death!" said a voice from the back of the hall. There was a murmur of agreement.

'Conor was on his feet in an instant. "If you believe the prophecy, then hear me! She is to marry a King. Very well, I am that King. She will love one man alone, and that man will be me, and she will be faithful to me. All men will know the prophecy and know that there is no point in trying to alter matters. That is, if you believe in this foolishness. If you do not, then trust me that I will keep her from mischief, and there is an end to it."'

Owen paused in his story. I looked at him for a moment. 'I suppose they trusted him?' I asked.

'They didn't have much choice. Conor was even stronger then than he is now. Not many people would cross him once he'd made his mind up.'

'But did they really believe the prophecy?'

Owen shrugged. 'You've seen the way people treat Cathbad's prophecies. Mostly they cheer when he predicts sunshine and scoff when he predicts rain. I think he was so obviously affected by what he thought that for once they were a bit shaken by it.'

'So why didn't they accept it?'

'They don't like the idea of allowing themselves to be controlled by star-gazers. And they weren't too taken with the idea of slaughtering a baby on the strength of a prophecy. Conor offered them a way out and a way back to the party. It wasn't a difficult decision.'

I nodded. 'I suppose so. They didn't have to decide whether to accept or reject the prophecy. Conor let them off the hook.'

'Quite. The nurse took away the baby, Conor announced another drinking contest with a jewelled cup as the prize, and everyone was glad to forget about her.'

A thought struck me. 'How long ago was this?'

Owen grimaced. 'Seventeen summers ago.'

'Ah. So Conor is expecting a young wife to arrive any day now.' Owen nodded.

'And you say she is beautiful?'

It was my turn to nod. 'What can we do?'

Owen looked serious, and started calling off the options on his fingers. 'We can't tell Conor, that's certain. He won't take kindly to someone poaching his property. Anyhow, after Naisi saved your backside today you won't want to hand him over to the King for skinning, will you?' I shook my head. Owen ticked off another finger. 'In fact we can't tell anyone, because they will gossip and the King will hear. I only hope those three will have the sense to keep their mouths closed.'

I nodded. I had a feeling that the brothers would not be telling anyone about Deirdre.

'Good. Then I think the only possibility is to find Naisi as quickly as possible and remind him of what he's getting into. Unless, of course, you think it might just be an infatuation which will blow over?' I shook my head.

'You haven't seen them together,' I said. 'Nor have you met her, or you would not say that.'

'Then we must find Naisi and hope he will see sense.'

'I fear he only sees one thing, and that is Deirdre,' I said, following him.

As we walked, Owen took up the story again.

'Once Conor had placed the infant Deirdre under his protection and vowed to marry her, she was taken away and lodged with Levarcam, Conor's old nurse, and her husband, in a secure castle at the heart of the great forest near Quelgny, in a hidden house without mirrors or shining surfaces, and no man knew where she was but the old couple and the King. When Deirdre was ten, the old man died, and she was brought to womanhood by his widow. She reached the moon before her seventeenth birthday without ever having seen her own face, or that of anyone of her own age, or knowing any person apart from the old couple. Occasionally, at night, she had been aware that a tall man would visit, coming into her room and holding a lamp up to see her face. She did not know who he was, but she knew that she was supposed to be asleep, and so she lay still, but she could smell the leather and sweat from him, and she once heard his deep voice talking to the old widow over the sound of coins being put on the low deal table, followed by a soft laugh. Her heart ached to know who he was, but when she plucked up the courage to ask the widow she denied that it had happened, said that Deirdre had dreamt it all.

'One evening, when the day for her marriage grew near, Deirdre and Levarcam looked over the rampart of their castle, at a world lit by a full moon and covered by winter. Snow lay as deep as a man's thigh in every direction, and was piled up in thin fingers on branches, waiting for the day's first wind to pull it silently to earth. The trees stood as though wrought from old silver, shining in the snow's reflected light. The usual green in front of the castle was a deep carpet of white, save for a dark patch where a scullion had killed a calf for that night's supper and the animal's blood lay scarlet and black on the snow. As they watched, a raven flew silently down from one of the trees and began to sip at the blood. Deirdre felt a rush of feeling come over her, and she exclaimed to Levarcam in a sorrowful voice:

'"Oh nurse, such would be the colours of the man I would love! His hair would be the colour of a raven's wing, his cheek the hue of blood and his skin like fresh-fallen snow."

'The old nurse looked troubled, and Deirdre seized on it.

'"Oh, do not tell me that Conor who will be my husband is not such a man, I have already guessed it! But, tell me truthfully, is there such a man in Ireland as I have described?"

'The old nurse answered truthfully, but with a heavy heart.

'"There is, child. You have described Naisi, son of Usna, a Champion of the Red Branch."

'Deirdre turned from her in sorrow. "Then I shall never be happy with Conor, nor shall I consent to be his wife, not while Naisi lives." Then Deirdre fell on her knees before Levarcam and clutched at her skirts. Levarcam tried to look stern, but she loved Deirdre and had no desire to see her unhappily married to the King.

'"You must."

'"I shall not, I cannot. I would rather die. Naisi will prevent it, and we will be together for ever."

'The old nurse turned away from the beautiful face that looked up at her, and silent tears fell from her cheeks like snow melting off the dark branches of the trees.'

Owen fell silent. We split up to look separately for the sons of Usna.

As I searched I remembered Deirdre, her dark hair surrounding her face, telling Naisi of her childhood. Behind her words I could imagine truths that she could not know.

# 11

I woke with a start. My head was pounding.

Naisi was sitting on the edge of my bed. He looked at me with a strange expression on his face, a sort of burning sheepishness.

'What is it?' I asked.

'I want to talk to you.'

I sighed. 'Can't it wait until morning?'

'It is morning. Almost.'

I looked out of the window. The first signs of dawn were, it was true, perhaps less than three hours into the future. The fire that warmed the room still burnt brightly. I had been asleep for about an hour. It wasn't enough.

'You're crazy. It isn't morning, and it's too early for talk. Go away, come back later.'

'It'll be too late then.'

I didn't like the way he said that. 'Why, what will happen?'

He looked sheepish again. A muscle twitched in his face. 'That's what I need to talk to you about.'

I could see that I was not going to get out of this without doing as I was asked, so I sat up in bed. 'Go on then.'

He sat on the end of my bed, fidgeting as if he would never be comfortable ever again. He seemed to be hovering above it, wound up so tight that he would surely burst. I got out of bed and crossed the room to where I kept a goatskin of wine. I poured some into a goblet and returned to the bed. 'Here,' I said. 'Drink this.'

He hesitated, then threw it down his throat. I feared that it might be like spitting on a fire, but it seemed to work. He stopped twitching quite so obviously, but I noticed that he kept glancing towards the door and then back to me. He looked almost embarrassed by my bare skin. As if I— A beam of light seemed to enter my clouded mind, and I knew what was wrong.

'Oh, Zeus, no,' I breathed. 'She's here, isn't she? You've brought her here?'

He looked like a pleased puppy for a moment, then like a scared little boy. 'You won't tell anyone?'

I shook my head, whether in agreement or wonderment I wasn't sure. I reached for my trousers and put them on. He visibly relaxed, and went to the door. A hand came round the doorpost, and he brought Deirdre into my room.

She looked very young. They both did. They were just children that night, even though she was seventeen and Naisi a year older and already earning a reputation as a warrior. I looked at them for a while. They stood, silently, hand in hand, waiting for me to say something. The love shone out of both of them; it was not something even worth arguing about, there was no point in trying to persuade them against it, might as well tell the sun not to rise. I had to think of what to do, and I didn't feel up to it.

'How did she . . . how did Deirdre get here?' I asked.

'She walked,' said Naisi, proudly. 'I was going to get her, and we met halfway. She knew I was coming.'

'I didn't want to wait for you,' said Deirdre. Her voice was a Pan-pipe on a spring dawn. They were in terrible trouble.

As if sensing my thoughts, Naisi turned to me. 'Can you help us?' he asked.

I tried to force my brain to work. It was obvious that they had to go away, far far away. They needed transport, food, luck, money, weapons, a destination, protection, more luck, a cloak of invisibility, a winged horse . . . They were as good as dead when Conor found out. He'd cross the Styx to catch them. I cudgelled my brains into movement.

'Where are Ardan and Ainle?'

'Waiting at home.'

Action was needed, any sort of action rather than standing in my room half-dressed in front of Hero and Leander. I pulled on my cloak.

'Stay here. I will arrange things. Don't go out.'

I slipped out of my room and went to arrange things. What things they were, I didn't yet know.

It was actually easier than I thought, once I got going. I stole food from the kitchen, gathered blankets from an unused room that I had once marked down as a place that would make a useful meeting-place if ever I needed a place to meet someone, and I chose some good weapons from amongst the sleeping men in the Banqueting Hall. The horses were the hard part. I had to walk to the pen and bring them out one by one. I could control them and keep them quiet on their own, but I couldn't be sure that I would be able to do it leading more than one at a time, so I crept past the sleeping guards four times, dying a little with each journey, sure that they would wake and put my welcome at Emain Macha to an end.

I tied the horses to a tree, loaded them with the supplies, and went back to my room to collect the children, hoping that they would have had the sense not to leave.

They were still there all right. Something made me stop and listen at the door before I went in. Then I went silently to the window, and looked through.

They had not been able to sit quietly and wait for me to return. Their clothes lay on the floor beside my bed, and in the soft dying firelight I could see their naked bodies, golden in the hearth-light.

He lay on my bed, and she moved above him. Her long dark hair fell onto his face as she bent forward to kiss him, and his hands moved slowly up her sides to cup her breasts. I watched as he brushed them with his lips, then lay down and arched his back as she moved her hips onto him.

I am usually bored by watching people make love. Perhaps I am too keen on doing it myself to want to watch others do it. But I was transfixed. I stood at the window and watched them, listening to every soft cry, feeling every movement. I wanted Deirdre more than I have ever wanted any woman, and the wanting was especially keen knowing that it would never happen. So I watched, and for a short while I was Naisi. When she let her head go back and a cry escaped from between her lips, it was my body that brought her to it. When her body shook with pleasure and her legs clasped him like a wrestler's, it was my hands that gave her everything she felt. I felt as though I was there with an impossible intensity. At the end I was lost. I didn't know what to do. They fell against each other, slick with sweat, and there was no place for me. I slid down the outside wall, feeling like an intruder.

I waited for five minutes, and then coughed quietly. Immediately there was a scuffling sound inside. I stood outside for a minute, then went in, not looking at them. They were dressed, holding hands and ready to leave.

We got on the horses without a word and rode for a day and half the night. I pointed them towards the coast and rode back to Emain Macha. Twice I saw riders coming towards me in the distance and I rode wide around their path to avoid them. I spent a couple of hours looking for a deer and eventually found an old doe who wasn't fast enough to escape my limited skills. It was nearly dark when I arrived back. The palace was in uproar. The old nurse had told Conor of the elopement. Conor had sent armed horsemen along every road to intercept them, but they were not caught. The guards at the gate looked at me suspiciously but they saw the deer, and my hunting skills were notoriously bad. My alibi was accepted. I looked suitably surprised when they told me about Deirdre and Naisi. No-one thought to tell Conor I'd not been around for two days, and Owen and I didn't dare speak of it. The men Conor sent out to catch the fugitives returned empty-handed. For a while Conor was in a black temper, but things cooled down eventually and life returned to normal. For a while.

# 12

My head hurt again. It was my own fault. I had been to enough banquets with Conall to know that what starts as a few drinks becomes a round of toasts, proceeds inexorably to a competition and ends up as a fight. Conall's latest enthusiasm was to persuade visiting traders from the Mediterranean to bring him ever-stronger wines, which he would then inflict on us without warning. His newest acquisition was from Cyprus, a thick, sweet, resinous mixture that wrapped iron bands around a man's vital organs and then squeezed. I liked the idea of drinking like a Hero, but I doubted if drinking with Conall would let me live long enough to die like one.

Just as I was trying to go to sleep again, after turning myself almost inside out over the night-bucket, Owen came into my room with no more fuss than a flock of pigeons landing on a cornfield full of starving cats, and tried to get me up by pushing me out of bed.

'Leary, come quickly! Here, put your clothes on, quick, come on, don't just lie there!'

'I have warned you before,' I growled, very softly, without moving. 'Carry on prodding me like that and I shall kill you without a shred of remorse.'

Owen had the sense to stop trying to roll me out of bed, but carried on fluttering around the room and talking in an excited voice until I could stand it no longer.

'Go away,' I snarled. 'Go away before I turn you into dog food. Or if threats do not touch you, go away for friendship, or for pity, or for any reason you can find, but leave me alone!'

Owen flew across the room, ignoring the venom in my voice, and knelt beside my bed. His face was a hand's breadth from mine, an error that he realized as soon as I breathed on him, which blew his eyes in opposite directions and turned his skin pale green. He gulped, swallowed, and withdrew to a safe distance.

'You must come!' he said excitedly, once he got his breath back. 'Cathbad is prophesying!'

I groaned, partly at the prospect of Cathbad blathering on about his friends in Hades, partly because I felt that an elephant had just landed on my stomach.

'Cathbad prophesying,' I murmured. 'How fascinating.'

Owen would not give up. He moved towards me and then remembered and backed away again.

'No, no, you must come! A druid prophesying is something that only happens once in a year, or less!'

'Too often,' I muttered through closed teeth. There was a silence. It went on for a while. With a sinking heart I gave in and opened one eye. He was sitting across the room from me, waiting. As soon as he saw me looking, he pounced.

'You always say that you want to learn about us, and then when something happens that could teach you more about our way of living in an hour than in a month of normal life, you turn it down!'

I could bear it no longer. I propped myself up on one elbow and snarled softly at him.

'That, idiot, is because I am dying. Cathbad could prophesy the end of the world, and I would still lie here, quite happy. Cathbad could turn into an eagle and fly up the Great King's bottom and I would not come out to see it. I want to be left alone, not to come out and hear some half-crazed old man

86

blather on about how he mixed a badger's brain with a dozen larks' tongues and smeared the result on his wife's head left-handed using an ocelot's ear, whereupon a message became clearly visible telling him that the harvest would be good, that the King would be healthy, and that it would rain on my birthday.' My voice rose. 'Do you understand? I don't care. I don't believe in prophecy, and I'm not interested in watching a lot of gullible half-wits being taken in by an old swindler. I am glad it makes you all happy, but leave me alone.'

I sank back onto my bed. My head boomed like a sea cave in a storm. A drop of oily sweat ran from my forehead onto my lip. It tasted of salt wine.

Owen was silent, for almost the time it takes to think. 'Come on,' he said, in the way that an adult speaks to a recalcitrant child, and he grabbed my arm. I realized what he meant to do.

'Oh no, no, not that,' I said firmly, and prepared to sell my life dearly.

Unfortunately my stomach chose that moment to turn traitor on me, and for a minute I was incapable of caring what happened to me. When I eventually looked up from the bucket, several pairs of legs were standing around me. I tried to resist, but the owners of the legs picked me up and carried me off without letting my feeble cries trouble them.

There is a saying that there is no cure for what drinking does to you, except more drinking. This saying is not true. The Ulstermen have a cure. There is another saying, which is that sometimes a remedy can be worse than the disease. This saying is true.

In Rome there are bath houses, in fact in every town in the Empire there are bath houses, civilized places where people go to meet other people, to talk, shave, have something to eat, to wash and get warm, to sweat out in a civilized and gentle fashion the previous evening's enjoyments. In Ulster there are no bath houses. At the northernmost edge of Emain Macha, against the corner of the wall, is a small hut, built of thin sheets of wood and covered with large sods of the soft black earth that surrounds Emain. The floor is made of square flat stones. The victim is put into the hut, and then his persecutors light a fire in a pit underneath the stones. It is not long before the stones become hot. Then the persecutors drop water onto the stones, thus producing enormous amounts of steam which very nearly kills anyone inside. This is supposed to cure his illness. It is true that, in the unlikely event of his surviving the ordeal, the victim comes out somewhat restored, but he must spend a miserable hour before any sort of benefit is felt.

On this occasion, I was in there for a lifetime or two, and I came out looking like one of Augustus's famous beetroots. Owen enquired jovially if I felt better. If I had had the strength I would have torn him limb from limb and fed him to the crows. As I did not, I simply nodded and glared at him as best I could. He looked pleased. He put his arm through mine and led me to the courtyard.

In the centre of the yard sat Cathbad, looking even more than usual like one of those venal corrupt parasites who packed the Senate when the Emperor was present and cheered him to the rafters, then cursed him as soon as he left and they could get back to the serious business of parcelling up the honour of Rome and selling it off to the highest bidder. Cathbad's beard was impressive by any standards, his demeanour equally so to the credulous. I found his solemnity amusing and his certainties facile. He was a proud man, and yet he did not resent me for my disbelief. I liked him. He had been kind to me, and only smiled sadly when I told him what I thought of his religion. We eventually tacitly agreed to allow each other to live in our separate follies.

Around the old fraud sat the Boys' Troop, arranged in a becoming semicircle. For some reason the Ulstermen felt it most appropriate that questions for someone prophesying should come forth from children. Something to do with innocence, I suppose. Or gullibility. Children like fairy stories almost as much as adults.

As Owen and I arrived, it seemed that the session was coming to an end. Cathbad was finishing an involved answer to a question from Follomain, Conor's eldest. His voice was suitably sonorous and slow-paced, and those present were nodding to the rhythm of his speech (or possibly falling asleep). Everyone was smiling. Cathbad appeared to have given satisfaction. People seemed to forget that giving satisfaction was his job.

As we stood at the back of the group, young Niall asked the traditional final question of the druid.

'Father, what is today a good day for?'

Owen whispered that this question was the traditional final question asked of the druid. I nodded. I already knew, but I wasn't going to tell Owen that and have him start a discussion.

The old man leant his head back, as if the weight of his knowledge was too heavy to bear. He paused, for just the right length of time, and then opened his mouth to speak.

Nothing happened. There was a frozen moment, during which the druid seemed incapable of movement or speech. Then he relaxed, and he spoke.

His voice was normal, in contrast to the portentous and artificial sound that most druids, including Cathbad – no, especially Cathbad – normally used on even social occasions.

'Today is a good day for taking arms,' he said. 'The boy who takes arms today and becomes a man will be the greatest Hero that Ulster has ever known. But his life will be short.'

Another pause. Cathbad blinked and shook his head, as if dazed or dazzled by a bright light, although there was no such light, then smiled and extended his hands for the boys to help him up.

Owen nudged my ribs, and indicated with his eyes for me to look across the courtyard. Cuchullain was standing in a shadow. His body was absolutely rigid, almost as if he was having a fit of some sort. Then he seemed to relax, and he looked at us, his eyes meeting mine. He loped across to where Owen and I stood.

'Will you come with me?' he asked. 'I shall need help.' Without waiting for our reply he moved away, towards the King's rooms. I was so surprised that I stood with my mouth open. Owen, his nose for a good tale quivering, grabbed my elbow and propelled me in front of him and in the boy's wake.

The King was at his table. He had finished eating, and was

talking in an undertone to an exceptionally pretty serving-girl. She was responding in a way that left me in no doubt that this was a bad moment to approach the King with anything less than news of a full-scale invasion of his kingdom. I tried to pull back so that he would not see us, but Cuchullain looked fiercely at me as if I had betrayed him, so I set my shoulders and waded up to the table as apologetically as I could. Cuchullain walked in my shadow, Owen in his. I felt very exposed. The King turned, and the smile set like lime on his lips as he saw us.

'So,' he said. 'What's this? A deputation?' He waved a hand in blessing. 'Your request is granted.' He turned back to the girl. We were dismissed. She was really very pretty, I didn't blame him. I was at a loss. Conor didn't want us there, but my friends were pressing up behind me so that I couldn't leave. I stood still and waited. I didn't want to just stand there doing nothing at all, so I stood there with my mouth open. For variety I made an 'um' sort of noise just once, but it sounded wrong, so I stopped that and went back to the open mouth.

Conor gradually realized that we had not gone away. He tried to pretend that we had for a while, but it didn't work and we were clearly putting him off. He gave up, and turned to me with an irritated sigh.

'Leary,' he said. I tried to reply, but my voice had gone. He sighed. 'I have said yes, without even hearing your request.' He used a low tone of voice which mixed great courtesy with a terrible threat. 'What more can I say?' The serving-girl simpered, in a way that in most people would have been irritating, but somehow wasn't when she did it. Conor looked at me as if expecting a reply. Cuchullain kicked my ankle. I realized that my problem was that not only was I standing with a suddenly sore ankle and a foolishly open mouth in front of a very annoyed King, but I was a spokesman who had not been given a script. I did not know why we had come.

'I . . . Owen and I . . . that is, we . . . we have brought Cuchullain. To see you.' I tried to smile, as if I had just ex-plained everything.

Conor looked at me, then at Cuchullain, then back at me, and then nodded slowly, as an adult nods when a harmless but rather stupid child brings a carefully gathered muddy stick collection for him to admire. 'Yes, I can see that you have brought Cuchullain,' he said with slow menace. 'What I am wondering, and you must forgive my lack of perception, is exactly why you have brought him to see me, especially when you can see that I am busy?'

I was wondering myself, and reckoned that it was time that Cuchullain stepped forward to explain himself or else time we left. I stepped aside to give the boy an uninterrupted view of the King.

Cuchullain looked at his uncle. Or his father. Or both. 'I want to take up arms,' he said.

Conor looked munificent. 'And so you shall, one day.'

'No, it must be today, I want . . . it needs . . . I need to do it today, now. I must . . . it is the day. Today . . . today . . . is the day that Cathbad says is the day to do it.'

It was a day for firsts. I had never known Cuchullain ask for help from me, nor look as if he were frightened, nor look beholden to anyone, nor lose his usual assurance in speaking. Today he had done all four. He looked very young. Conor saw only a nine-year-old boy demanding rather inarticulately to be allowed to take arms so that he could fight grown men, at a time when Conor was busy with adult matters. Cuchullain looked desperate. Perhaps for the first time since arriving at Emain Macha, something that he wanted to do could not be got by fighting better or playing harder than the next person. His wish was in another's gift. It is a frustration that most people learn young, even Princes.

Conor sighed and looked serious, very like a King. 'Your request is not possible. You are too young.'

'I am not,' cried Cuchullain. 'Today is a day for Heroes to take arms. Cathbad said so.'

Conor let the impertinence go, but was plainly irritated. 'That is as may be, but that does not mean that you are the one to do it.'

Cuchullain was twitching with anxiety and tension. I watched, feeling for him. He knew that he could not insist, that an outburst of anger would not help his cause, but in his eagerness and frustration he could not completely control himself. His muscles seemed to be writhing independently just under his skin.

They both looked at me, Cuchullain with desperation written all over him, Conor with exasperation. I was obviously expected to take part in the discussion. 'Cathbad also said that the Hero's life would be short,' I said, for something to say.

'Short in days, perhaps, but longer than the world in deeds,' said Cuchullain.

Conor nodded slowly. 'A good reply.'

'Taken from a good poem,' murmured Owen.

Cuchullain rounded on him, his face furious, and then the King laughed.

Conor was the only person who was allowed to laugh at Cuchullain. Other boys felt the strength of his arm if they made fun of him, which they were mainly too sensible to do, and adults usually found the boy's intensity too much trouble to bother making fun of. (In fact, many of them found him boring. They admired him, but had no wish to share time with him.) Only Conor refused to take Cuchullain at his own measure. He made no attempt to hide his affection for the boy, but treated him like a slightly dim country cousin. Cuchullain blushed and worshipped him for it. Perhaps more of us should have tried the same treatment.

Conor continued to smile as the boy spun back and glowered at him.

'Why do you mock me?'

Conor composed his face slightly. 'I do not mock you. But what is your hurry? Stay another year or so with your friends in the Boys' Troop.'

Cuchullain looked serious. 'If I am to be a Hero, I do not want to wait. If I am to die young, I want to start my life as a man as soon as possible.' We exchanged knowing adult glances, but were unable to fault his logic. Conor stood up decisively.

'Very well, young cousin. Let us get you some arms.' He bent down, whispered something in the serving-girl's ear that made her blush becomingly and walk towards the King's quarters, and then he turned away from her with a wistful look and set off briskly towards the armoury. Cuchullain bounded behind him for a few steps like a young dog on a spring morning hunt. Then he remembered that he was about to become a man, looked serious, stopped gambolling, and fell into step just behind the King.

'Um . . . who will stand for his father?'

Owen's voice was tentative, as if he was merely musing on the subject, or as if he were merely voicing something that Conor would certainly have already been thinking about. He used exactly the same tone that I remembered Tiberius's secretary using whenever Tiberius was on the verge of making a decision that might not be possible to implement in practice. It was intended to signal an error, without giving offence, which was no less difficult a balance for an underling to maintain in Ulster than it was in the Emperor's palace on the Capitoline Hill. Cuchullain's paternity was not a subject that sensible people talked about in front of Conor. There was no way of bringing up the subject without calling the boy a bastard, or Conor a committer of incest, or Dectera a liar, or even Sualdam a cuckold, or possibly all of these at the same time and a few others besides. The subject could not be safely discussed. Owen was right though. The boy needed a man to hand him his new weapons. The man would usually be his father. If he had no father, his chief would normally take the job.

Conor hesitated for the briefest of moments. 'I shall stand for his father,' he said without turning round, and walked on to the armoury.

# 13

I told Conall these events, and I remember how his eyes widened as I told him what Conor had said.

'So Conor actually admitted that he was Cuchullain's father?'

I flinched. 'Not necessarily, not necessarily at all. Conor stood for him because he had no father. That is all we need assume.'

Conall looked sly. 'Is that what you think?'

'I think it is always safer to assume the more likely of any two conflicting ideas. If you ask me to choose between the possibility that Conor was Cuchullain's incestuous father and so stood by him, or that he was just doing what any honourable man would for a boy under his protection, I prefer to think that he was honourable.'

Conall smiled and looked at his feet and shook his head, then glanced briefly up at me. He didn't believe a word of it.

The armoury was dark, with only thin bars of sunlight coming in through the narrow windows high in the walls. Some fell on armour lying on the floor, spinning off the jewels and burnished metal in knives of light that made you blink and wish your head didn't still hurt so.

Conor walked across to the far wall, where a huge bundle of

94

spears stood in the corner. He took one, glanced at it, and tossed it butt-first to Cuchullain, who caught it one-handed, spun it through a half-circle and banged its end down hard against the stone floor. The spear shivered visibly, and then split along its length in his hand. He looked at the shattered wood and then dropped it without a word.

I remembered how a young man outside Cullan's castle threw a spear in the air and caught it an inch from his chest.

Conor and Cuchullain looked at each other without speaking for a long moment. Then Conor reached for another spear, which he threw properly, aiming to miss him by perhaps a couple of feet. Cuchullain stood his ground. The point of the spear hissed over his shoulder, and then his hand came up fast and grabbed the shaft halfway along its length. He hefted it to the end and brought the spear round in a wide circle, striking sparks from the ground with the metal tip, which buckled and flew off.

The King threw up his hands and laughed, this time at himself. 'Enough!' he chuckled. 'We shall have no weapons left by the time this ends.' He walked across the floor amongst the broken spears to an anteroom, and re-emerged a moment later with a huge spear, his own. (When the bards sang of Conor's fighting skill they called his spear 'Brain-cleaver'. Roman soldiers too give names to weapons, especially to their siege engines. The Seventh Legion in Gaul had a giant catapult they called 'The Celtfucker'.) Conor's spear was taller than a full-grown man and as thick as my wrist at the base. The shaft was polished ash, chased with white gold along its length and inlaid in Ogham with the King's name. He offered the spear to Cuchullain, who took it with a smile, then raised it up, and dashed it against the floor. Owen and I both winced and held our breath, but the wood hummed a deep note and sprang back, whole in his hand. Cuchullain grinned.

'This is a spear!' he said.

Conor nodded, smiling. 'Indeed it is,' he said. 'May many Connaughtmen fall before it.' He looked around. 'Now, let us find you a chariot.'

Conor led Cuchullain out to near the stables, where the chariots stood in a row. The King waved along the line.

'Choose,' he said.

Cuchullain handed me the spear without looking, so natural in the movement that I took it without really thinking. He walked to the nearest chariot, and stepped up onto the shaft.

'What do you think?' asked Conor, watching him examine the chariot with interest.

Cuchullain moved his weight around the chariot, concentrating intently. Then he paused, tensed himself, and brought all the weight of his small body down on one part of the floor. There was a splintering crack, and the chariot broke across its centre.

We all stood for a moment, open-mouthed. Cuchullain got off the wreck of the chariot and made purposefully for the one beside it. Conor stepped forward.

'Nephew,' he called, and, when the boy looked round, motioned Cuchullain towards his own chariot. We were impressed by the grace of his gift, as well as feeling that he had probably saved most of the other chariots from destruction.

The King's chariot was the biggest at Emain. The shaft was a solid trunk, and the floor was cut from a single oak. The sides were bent from a single bark, and three lines of red gold traced its circumference. The handles at each side were shining bronze, and bright precious stones studded the reins and bridles. Cuchullain's face shone. He stepped into the chariot and moved around, testing how it moved, how it felt to him. Then he turned to the King, beaming with pleasure.

'Your permission?'

The King smiled. 'Of course,' he said, 'it is yours.' Both Owen and I knew that Conor valued his spear and chariot as the finest in Ulster, which made the gift the finer. I once watched Owen give his cup away because a man admired it. I saw the wistful expression on his face, and asked him why he had given away his favourite cup, when he had a dozen in his room which he would not have missed. Owen looked surprised. 'Where is the point of giving something that you do not value?' he asked. I could see what he meant, but it seemed a sure way of losing everything you liked. It didn't pay for Ulstermen to get too fond of things.

Conor shouted for servants to fetch his horses. They were brought and fitted into the yoke of the chariot. They were both magnificent animals, one huge, known as the Grey of Macha, and one smaller but deceptively strong, dark as ebony, called the Black Sanglain. Cuchullain called out to me, 'Leary, will you drive me?' I paused for a moment. My head had nearly stopped hurting. The sun was shining, and I had nothing else planned.

'Of course. I would be proud to drive you on your first day as a warrior,' I declaimed, wasting my time. Cuchullain had no sense of irony. Besides, if Conor could accept him as a warrior, I was not going to disagree.

Conor held a sword in a scabbard out to Cuchullain. In contrast to the spear, both the weapon and its sheath were entirely plain. I thought I heard a wistful note in Conor's voice as he said, 'It was my father's. You will bring Ulster honour with it, as he did.'

Cuchullain pulled it slowly out of the scabbard. The handle was a simple hard wood, but the blade shone in the sun. He lifted it and watched the light play on the metal.

Conor came up and clapped me on the shoulder, whispering to me from the corner of his mouth so that Cuchullain could not see or hear him. 'Well said. Now keep an eye on him for Laeg's sake, and don't let him kill my horses.'

I clambered into the chariot. The reins fell into my hands like a woman's hair onto my pillow. I was never so much at home as at that moment.

Cuchullain stood in front of me, a boy-warrior, grinning like a marmoset on heat. We set off to slay dragons.

# 14

The curtains of the past part and I remember a hot day. A small boy, too small even for the Boys' Troop, his fists tight with wanting, begs Owen for the story of Cuchullain's first day as a warrior. His eyes are alight with possibility. He sees himself as Cuchullain, sees how a boy can be the centre of attention, even be a Hero.

'What happened then? Did you meet the enemy? Did he fight anyone?'

He'd like that. He wants Cuchullain to succeed.

Then Owen speaks without opening his eyes, his voice a slow drawl. I hear the tone in his words, I understand him. He knows the expression on the boy's face even though he can't see it, can tell it from the tone of his voice. He knows that voice, lives through it, thrives on it. A willing audience. It's all he's ever wanted from life.

'Fight someone? Oh yes, he fought someone.'

Cuchullain let out a shout that startled the horses, and they raced halfway around the castle before I had them properly controlled. Owen galloped after us on a pony, whooping with excitement. I would have hit him if I'd had an arm free and a moment to spare. I cursed him anyway, just so he'd know how I felt. I eventually got the horses calmed down enough to slow to a trot, although their coats still flickered as if stinging flies tormented them and their heads pumped up and down like a victorious boxer's arm.

'Where to now, oh great knight?' I asked sarcastically. Wasted. Cuchullain didn't know what a knight was, and wouldn't have cared anyhow.

'Onward to glory!' screeched Owen from behind us with a laugh, and I nearly lost the horses again.

'Have you lost all sense?' I snarled, hauling at the reins. 'Just because he's decided to turn into a little Emperor there's no need for you to be his herald.'

'Drive west,' Cuchullain said, his voice unusually deep.

I turned to him incredulously, but he was looking at the horizon as if he were posing for a statue of Alexander the Great. I turned back to Owen, who grinned, shrugged, and mouthed Cuchullain's command silently back at me.

'Yes sir,' I growled, and moved the horses warily on. My sarcasm bounced off Cuchullain like an inflated pig's bladder off a rock.

We drove to the province boundary at Slieb Fuait, near Loch Echtra. Cuchullain posed at the chariot side and contemplated his destiny in silence, Owen sang and I seethed and wondered how long I was going to have to put up with it all.

Conall Chernach was on guard. I was always amused at the idea that one person was enough to guard a province's borders, but wouldn't have said so out loud. Conall Chernach did not have a sense of humour about things like that. Or, indeed, about anything else. Conall Chernach always spoke in the formal way, rather than the colloquial register that people normally used. This meant that everyone had to do the same back to him. It made me uncomfortable. It was like talking to a priest, and I've never had much taste for that.

'Greetings,' said Conall. 'I wish you victory.' His voice moved ponderously, the better to keep pace with his thoughts.

'Conall,' said Cuchullain, stretching and looking around as if to suggest that he had just happened to be passing by on a whim, 'go back to Emain, the drinking will be starting soon. I have no taste for it. Let me watch for a while.'

'You are perhaps enough to look after the men who ride with you,' said Conall, 'but Ulster needs a warrior at its gate.' He'd insulted all three of us in one sentence. Cuchullain didn't reply, but looked sideways across at Loch Echtra, as if distracted by something. Conall's gaze followed Cuchullain's like a dog watching a chicken leg travel to its master's mouth, and so he didn't notice Cuchullain fitting a stone to his sling and swinging it lazily. I said nothing, but I got ready for something to happen. I felt as if I was back in the crowd at a play in one of Carthage's reeking theatres, about to yell to the rich old cuckold that his young wife was kissing her lover behind his back. Cuchullain suddenly whirled his arm and hurled the stone at Conall's chariot shaft. The pin that held the shaft in place shattered into two separate pieces. The horses started forward and pulled the shaft away from the chariot, which pitched forward and sent Conall Chernach and his dignity toppling out over the front as if diving after the horses. He hit the ground with a clang of armour against stones.

'Why did you do that?' asked Conall furiously, jumping to his feet and stamping in the dust. I kept my face absolutely expressionless, watching Conall's horses disappear into the distance.

'To test my aim,' said Cuchullain. 'You'll agree now it's good enough to preserve me if I meet any invaders.'

Conall's shoulders slumped. The loss of his chariot seemed to deflate him. I was amazed. Nothing else ever had. I almost felt sorry for him. 'How shall I get back to Emain Macha, now that the new Guardian of Ulster has broken my chariot? I can't very well be expected to walk,' he said grumpily.

'Of course not. The bard will lend you his horse,' said Cuchullain. The bard was delighted to do so. He rode in the cramped chariot with us and so got in the way, and Conall returned home.

'I don't see why he couldn't have walked,' I said, trying to drive with my elbows in Owen's ribs. 'It isn't so very far.'

100

Owen looked surprised, and quoted me back at myself. 'Why walk when you can ride?' he said.

Cuchullain spoke without looking round. 'Why should a warrior ever have to walk?' he said.

His tone was insufferable. It was time to make a stand. 'You're turning into a pompous little bore,' I said, with feeling. 'If you get any more puffed up you'll explode. If I have to listen to one more of your overblown remarks I shall turn us around and go home.'

There was a silence. For a moment I thought that I had gone too far, then felt righteous about it and didn't care. Then, after the silence had gone on too long for it to be embarrassment, I realized that they were only silent because they hadn't been listening to me. Cuchullain was gazing as if far out to sea and searching for land. Owen was leaning against the chariot rim, singing happily under his breath. I kicked him on the ankle. He grimaced momentarily and then went back to smiling. 'I don't know why you encourage him,' I muttered.

Owen smiled wider, and folded his arms in a way that made it look as if he was hugging himself. He had an insufferably pleased look on his face. Half to me, half to the wind, he murmured dreamily, 'Did you see what he did? Did you see the way he smashed that chariot shaft?'

I blinked exasperatedly at him. 'It was a stone from a sling, not a bolt from heaven,' I said, as if he were mentally deficient. Owen looked vague. 'And he smashed the pin, not the shaft. The pin is smaller than my hand. The shaft, unlike most things, is thicker than your head. Never mind using a pebble from a sling to break it, he couldn't have smashed that shaft by rolling it over a cliff.'

Owen smiled at me and nodded, and carried on murmuring to himself. 'Smashed it. Smashed the shaft like a twig, with one stone from his sling.'

I gave up. As the chariot travelled across Slieb Fuait, Owen told Cuchullain the name of every mountain that they could see, and every river and every valley, every house and farm and every place of any sort of note, and the name of every port between Temair and Cenannos. And balls-achingly dull it was too. Last of all he pointed out an ugly but solid-looking fortress about a mile to our left. This apparently was the castle of the three sons of Nectha Scene. These were called: Foill, which, he said over his shoulder to me in a patronizing sort of a way, meant 'Deceitful', Fanall 'the Swallow' and Tuachell 'the Cunning'.

'And I am Leary, the Utterly Indifferent,' I growled. 'Except to wonder why a mother would name her son "Deceitful" and think it a good start in life.'

'Let's go and visit them,' said Cuchullain.

'There is a bitter feud between Conor's kinsmen and the sons of Nectha Scene,' said Owen.

'Fair enough,' I said, and started to turn the horses around.

'Keep going,' said Cuchullain. I caught Owen's eye. Cuchullain had finally gone crazy. Owen frowned theatrically and gestured me to turn back and be quick about it, and then positively beamed at Cuchullain. Whatever dream-mushrooms Cuchullain had been eating, Owen had clearly shared them too. I took a deep breath. I was sane and on my own with two lunatics, and that's lonelier than Ariadne on Naxos.

'There are three of them, you say,' I said in my best cajoling tones. 'It's a lovely day. Let's live a little longer.'

Owen looked as though he was about to burst from a surfeit of drama. 'Laegaid their father died at the hands of Ulstermen, and there has been bitter enmity between the sons of Nectha Scene and the men of the Red Branch since that day!' he intoned.

'Hardly surprising, when you think about it,' I said. 'Still, no reason for us to get involved, eh?'

Cuchullain jumped down off the chariot, and Owen watched him with a thrilled expression. 'Take me to them,' said Cuchullain.

'That will be dangerous,' said Owen, with a roguish look at Cuchullain that said that a little danger couldn't possibly be even the slightest bit of a problem for someone as bold, courageous, well-armed and skilful as him. Thereby completely ignoring

102

Cuchullain's total inexperience, extreme youth, small size and utterly outnumbered condition. Cuchullain smiled benevolently at Owen.

'That is why we came.'

It definitely wasn't the reason I came, but they weren't listening to me. I might have been able to deal with Cuchullain if Owen hadn't been feeding his self-esteem, but had no chance while the two of them were making love to the boy's sense of his place in history. Cuchullain was going to get killed so that Owen could write a sad song about it. If I didn't throttle him first.

We drove to the corner of the field, where a shallow river drained from a dark bog that stretched to the horizon. Planted in the ground at the river's source was one of the challenge posts that seemed to be as plentiful in Ulster as thistles. Usually the posts were no higher than a man, but this one was twice that. The spancel hoop, the wooden ring etched in Ogham with fearful insults to any challenger, hung from the top of the pole on a hook. Cuchullain made me drive the chariot up to it, then seized the hoop and threw it into the river.

'Will they see it?' I asked. There is no Ulster equivalent of the Latin interrogative 'expecting-the-answer-yes', or I would have used it. A participle meaning 'desperately-hoping-to-Zeus-for-the-answer-no' would have been even better.

'Oh, yes,' smiled Owen. 'They'll notice. It'll float right past their castle.'

'I thought you'd say that.' I didn't hit him. I just looked glum. Cuchullain jumped down from the chariot and stretched out to rest on a grassy bank.

'Don't wake me unless they all come,' he said, and went to sleep.

'Heavens no,' I muttered. 'The Gods forbid that anything but overwhelming odds should be sufficient.' We settled down to wait, lulled by Cuchullain's snores.

It was not long before the sons of Nectha Scene came galloping to meet their challenger. I looked at them and wished I had brought a wineskin with me. All three men were dressed in the skins of very large and fierce animals that had no doubt taken one look at them and died of fright; they had hair the exact rust colour of Munster oxen springing upwards from their heads as thick as ivy on a great oak, and all three were as ugly as the Minotaur's backside. It was time for me to assert myself.

'Grab Cuchullain, quick, while I get the horses,' I hissed casually out of the corner of my mouth to Owen as they thundered towards us. 'Get the silly little bugger, stuff him in the chariot and we'll make a run for it.' Stupid of me to even think about it, really. Owen didn't move. Then it was too late.

'Who has thrown our challenge hoop in the river?' one of the monsters asked Owen in a voice deep enough to make my teeth ache.

'It is the warrior Cuchullain, on his arms day!' declaimed Owen, as if he were a herald. I winced. 'Idiot,' I muttered. He struck what he took to be a heroic pose and ignored me. Fine for him, he wasn't the one who was going to get killed.

The largest of the three men drew himself up in his saddle and made a dismissive gesture. 'We have not got time to waste playing with babies. Take him to win his spurs elsewhere.'

'Excellent thought,' I said, and jumped into the chariot, pushing Owen to go and wake Cuchullain. The boy bounced up, sword in hand. He wasn't asleep – he'd been listening.

'I have come to fight, not to leave!' shouted Cuchullain.

Nectha Scene's sons looked at him carefully, and then at us two again. One of them made a sound in his throat that might have been a chuckle. It sounded like a bull getting ready to charge.

'Ulstermen,' said the biggest one ponderously. It seemed pointless to argue, but I was prepared to try anyway.

'No,' I said.

'Yes,' said Cuchullain. Another good idea gone.

'Very well,' said one of the three. 'If you do not kill the whelp in the spring then you only have to kill the cur come the summer. In the ford, then.' He drove into the shallows and jumped down from his chariot. I fancied the ground shook. The other two kicked their horses up a slight hill in order to get a good view, and, pulling food and a wineskin from a saddlebag, settled down to watch.

'Be careful,' said Owen softly to Cuchullain. 'That is Foill. They say that if you do not get him with your first blow you may strike all day without hope of hitting him.'

'A good trick,' said Cuchullain, 'but the last time he plays it on an Ulsterman.' With that Cuchullain heaved Conor's spear at Foill with all his strength.

The tall man was looking down to check his footing as he waded across the ford and he didn't even see the spear that killed him. He fell forward without a sound and the water foamed red around him. I stood with an open mouth as Cuchullain sprinted across the ford and leapt up into Foill's chariot. He slapped the reins on the horse's back so that it leapt forward and crossed back over to our side, sending a wave of water up around its chest towards us. Cuchullain jumped out again halfway across and seized his spear, which ripped out of Foill's body with a sickening grinding sound, like breaking a rabbit's neck in your hands. Owen stopped the horse as it came out of the water, and frantically started to pile Foill's trophy heads into our chariot while laughing like a maniac. I watched him for a moment, then heard another butcher's shop noise from the stream and looked up just in time to see Cuchullain sever Foill's head with two swipes of his sword and hurl it at us like a discus thrower. It flew towards us with its long red hair streaming out behind it like Greek fire, bounced once on the bank and landed at my feet. I looked at it and was promptly sick.

Cuchullain splashed up the bank towards us with an enormous grin on his face. Owen picked up Foill's head and threw it on the pile.

Foill's two brothers were running towards the ford, shouting angrily, their heavy arms clashing. As my stomach emptied and I lifted my head, I heard Owen whisper to Cuchullain, 'The next is Fanall, who skims the water like a marsh-fly, and he will be followed by Tuachell, the greatest of the three, who has never fallen to any weapon.'

As Cuchullain trotted back to the edge of the ford and into the water, I heard Owen singing under his breath. I decided to die, and reached for my sword.

'Help him, you stupid sod!' I shouted, and stumbled towards the river. Owen didn't move.

As I ran towards Cuchullain, I could only watch as the two men attacked him together and pressed him back. Then Fanall stumbled in his eagerness and fell forward between Cuchullain and Tuachell, and Tuachell held back for a moment for fear of hurting his brother. As Fanall floundered in the water, trying to regain his footing, Cuchullain stepped away slightly and slashed downwards, ripping his sword across the side of Fanall's throat. Fanall's hands clawed at the sword, and then he spun round so that his face was turned up to the sky as he fell. A terrible gurgling cry came from a gaping hole below his chin, and a fountain of blood sprayed up into Tuachell's face as he bent to help him. Tuachell stepped back, blinded for a moment. Cuchullain was as swift as a snake. In the time it took Tuachell to scoop a handful of water from the stream to wash the blood away, Cuchullain had vaulted over Fanall and plunged his sword deep into Tuachell's neck. There was a paralysed moment as Tuachell stood, not believing what had happened, and then he crumpled like a dropped cloak. The two brothers lay side by side in the muddied water. I was still only halfway across the river by the time it was over.

I was dumbfounded. Owen set up a cheering. Cuchullain just grinned.

We helped him hack off his victims' heads, or, more accurately, I watched him do it. I knew that this was one custom I wouldn't get used to. As we drove away from the ford I was looking down into Fanall's dead eyes, tied by his hair to the chariot rim, next to the reins attached to the horses of the three sons of Nectha Scene.

Owen braced himself against the side of the chariot rim and sang the same thing over and over. I realized that he was composing a song, trying different words to the tune he'd chosen. Having nothing else to do but drive the chariot and gaze back at Fanall and his brothers, I listened. It was nine parts fantasy to one part exaggeration, with a shadow of the truth thrown in for glue.

'Then a change came upon him
and his body grew
and became twisted and contorted
like an old blackthorn bush.
His hair stood out from his brow
and blood gushed from under it
Into the air, blinding his opponent.
His eyes separated and moved around his face
and his body changed.
His limbs exchanged places
and his teeth ground together with a sound like clashing stones
and his voice was that of a wild beast
and he flung himself upon his enemies like a wolf upon sheep.
It was not long before all three heads
were together in blood against the side of Cuchullain's chariot
and the sound of Nectha Scene crying for her sons filled the valley.'

I remember once hearing an Armenian poet perform a grotesquely flattering account of Tiberius's virtues, and Tiberius exclaiming that not even Apollo could lay claim to the perfection that the man ascribed to him. It must have been around the time that Tiberius's mind was starting to turn; the shout of laughter that the courtiers sent up at the Emperor's witticism could have been heard a mile away.

'Balls,' I said, flicking the reins in annoyance.

Owen looked surprised. 'It's true.'

'It isn't.'

'Well, it's true on the facts. I've done a bit of colouring-in.'

'Colouring-in? You've thrown the whole paint-pot at him!'

Owen took me by the arm. I showed my teeth at him until he let me go. 'You have to understand how we do things here,' he said. 'This is my purpose, it is what I am here for.'

'And you call it honourable?'

I could see that I had deeply offended him. He drew himself up and looked at me along the ridge of his long nose.

'Only someone totally ignorant of the honourable way of doing things could ask such a question.'

I had never heard his voice so cold. I had managed to hurt him. I had often offended him before, frequently annoyed him, but I had never hurt him. I apologized, pleaded my ignorance, the heat of the moment, drink, stupidity, anything, everything. He calmed down. I smiled. He smiled back and returned to composing his fairy tale. I could wait. We would have the disagreement later. A two-man chariot with three men and a barrow-load of heads in it is no place for arguing.

On the way home as we passed back through Slieb Fuait, Cuchullain saw a herd of deer. They were plentiful that year. Every man at Emain had brought home a deer across the front of his chariot – it was rumoured that even Owen had managed to kill a particularly old and stupid doe – but Cuchullain wasn't likely to be happy with just killing one. He wanted history written about him, and his accomplice was beside him, watching him as an eager girl watches her Hero. 'Run the chariot behind them, make them go towards the bog,' Cuchullain shouted. His colour was high, and his eyes absolutely clear. I knew we weren't going to get home quietly. The fight had given him strength, a sense of his own potency.

'Now I'm a bloody dog, driving deer like cattle,' I growled, urging the horses on.

'Why are you so determined to pretend you aren't enjoying yourself?' said Owen. I opened my mouth like a fish accepting a crumb, then shut it again. He slapped me on the shoulder. 'Go on and catch them!' he shouted.

The deer ran from us in a roughly circular pack, led by a huge stag. He tried to lead them away from the bog, but by concentrating on him, knowing the others would follow where he led, I kept his nose pointed towards it. The ground started to become heavy. The chariot wheels made a dark, sucking noise as they rolled across the soft peat. Then, suddenly, the bog began. One moment the stag was skimming the surface of the earth, the next he was plunging forward up to his chest in black water. I pulled the horses up sharply to avoid following him in. The deer herd milled around us, their eyes rolling as they shied away from us and plunged back again in confusion.

'Now what?' I asked Cuchullain, but he was already pushing past me and climbing over the front of the chariot with a rope in one hand. He ran along the chariot shaft and jumped off it, landing almost beside the trapped deer. It saw him approach and slashed at him with a sharp horn. Cuchullain was too eager, and had got too close. He leapt up to avoid it, but the deer flicked its head as he jumped and caught his foot with the broad middle of the antler, turning him over and landing him on his backside. I burst out laughing. For a moment he looked furious, then, backing away from the deer until he was out of range, he started to smile himself.

'Now you've got him, what are you going to do with him?' I shouted, leaning forward in the chariot and resting on folded arms. He looked at me with an expression of amusement.

'I thought we'd give the horses some rest,' he said. 'Hold this.'

I'll never know how we managed to avoid being trampled or gored or both. We tied the rope to the chariot, looped the end around the stag's neck, and pulled him out. As he stood there, legs numb and quivering with shock, roaring at his herd to stay away, Cuchullain dropped another rope over his antlers. Cuchullain and I stood on opposite sides of him, legs braced and ropes held tight, each of us preventing the stag from putting an antler through the other. We spoke softly to him and he seemed to become calmer, although I wouldn't have dared approach him. Owen unhitched the horses from the chariot and led them away. We manoeuvred the stag, slowly and with many retreats and changes of heart, up to the chariot, and somehow got him on one side of the shaft. Then Owen brought the Grey of Macha back and placed him on the other side. We yoked them together, and I got into the chariot and picked up the reins. The stag looked back at me, his eyes huge.

'This isn't possible,' I said. Cuchullain didn't answer, but jumped into the chariot, leant forward and brought the flat of his sword down hard on the deer's rump. It jumped forward, the Grey followed, and we were off. It was useless to try and drive them. I concentrated on staying in the chariot. The Grey was too strong. We were being pulled like a crab walks, almost sideways. I thought that the chariot would turn over. I hauled on the reins to slow us down. As I fought for control, Owen shot past us, bareback on the Sanglain. At that point I knew the world had gone mad.

Cuchullain whooped a war-cry as Owen overtook us, and then fired a slingshot almost absent-mindedly at a swan flying overhead. We were going one way, the swan another, and I don't know if he seriously aimed at it, but the stone hit the bird where its neck joined its chest and brought it crashing to the ground. It wasn't dead, but it was obviously stunned, and its great wings brushed along the ground like long white brooms as it staggered in circles trying to get its bearings. Cuchullain grabbed the reins, pulled the horse and stag around in a wide circle and charged straight at it. When the animals realized that they were going to collide with the bird, they stumbled to a halt, sending a cloud of dust over it, and shied and bucked so that the chariot felt like a coracle on rough water. We were in a narrow part of the road with deep ditches on both sides.

We stood in the chariot and looked at the swan. It arched its neck and hissed at us.

'Go and get it then!' said Cuchullain eagerly. I looked at him. He was obviously insane. I pointed at the ditch beside me.

'How?'

'Run along the shaft, of course. Grab it, tie it to the back and we can go home.'

'I can't.'

'Why not?'

I had had enough. I spoke slowly, wanting him to understand. 'There are ditches on both sides, if I fall into them I'll not get out again without a rope. I cannot get past the horse because he is maddened by the stag and irritated by the swan, as well as being disappointed with me for driving so badly and cross with

110

you for cracking the whip at him, which he thinks is insulting. I cannot get past the stag, because it is terrified of me and hates the horse and the swan, and doesn't like you much either. I can't go around the wheels because there isn't room and I can't squeeze past because the edges are like razors from the way we've been driving. And even if none of this were true, the swan hates us more than the horse and the stag put together, because you threw a stone at it, making it crash, and then tried to run it over.' I folded my arms. 'That is why I can't do it.'

Cuchullain shrugged. 'Very well.'

Owen flurried to a halt behind us. 'What is it?' he asked. He sounded breathless, and he wrestled with bits of rein as the Sanglain showed him what it thought of his horsemanship.

'He wants to tie the swan to the chariot,' I said, saw Owen's eyes light up, and wished I hadn't. 'No,' I said.

Five minutes later the swan was flying behind us at the end of the longest rope we had, and I was nursing an arm that was probably broken.

'I told you if I looked into its eyes it would obey me,' said Cuchullain airily.

'Oh, so you told it to attack me, did you?' I snarled. Owen galloped past white-faced, trying to look as if he was racing us home, when in fact it was obvious that the horse wanted its dinner and was going whether or not he wanted to go too.

Cuchullain and I drove the rest of the way home in silence. We didn't speak until we arrived outside the walls of Emain Macha, where the women were washing, taking turns to immerse themselves in a deep tub of warm water. The women of Ulster believed in washing properly, and no nonsense about modesty or keeping your clothes on. I forgot the pain in my arm and stood straight. I tried to look heroic as we drove past, as Heroes seemed to have most success with the women, but it didn't seem to have much impact. I wondered if perhaps I should have got Owen to write a song about me. A few liberties with the truth might make some of the women look more interested. Most of them looked at Cuchullain, who blushed like a rose and looked down, a little too coyly, I thought. He was still young enough to be embarrassed by bare breasts, but old enough to know what was attractive to their owners.

I heard Owen tell our story that night at supper. I still think of it as part of my education.

He started with the story of Cuchullain smashing the spears and the chariot. That wasn't too bad, although to hear Owen tell it he had reduced them to splinters, whereas he had really just cracked them so that they couldn't be used. But, fair enough. Then he told the story of Cuchullain fighting the sons of Nectha Scene, with all the exaggerations that I had heard in the chariot, plus a few more he'd obviously just thought of. Cuchullain was sounding like a cross between Hercules and Apollo. I kept my peace. It wasn't for me to stand up and say, 'Actually, it wasn't quite like that.' The Champions were hammering their swords on the great oak tables with pleasure at Owen's story, and cheering loudly at every Feat he described. I wasn't going to spoil the party, and no-one was asking me anyway, apart from a small dark-haired woman who seemed to find me of some interest as an accessory to the expedition Owen was describing. As Owen warmed to his theme, she warmed to me, and I warmed to Owen. As her hand slipped into my shirt, I began to think that perhaps this form of history had something to commend it after all.

Then Owen went too far. He described how he rode back to the palace on the Sanglain, told of rushing into the throne room, out of breath and dusty. He told how he gasped out the story of the day's great deeds, and how the boy Champion was, even now, bearing down on Emain Macha in a berserk frenzy, unable to stop himself, filled with the lust to kill anyone he met. Then Owen told how Mugain, Conor's mother, rose grimly to her feet. 'Let him come,' she said, 'we will be waiting,' and she took her women to the gate of Emain. There they waited for Cuchullain, and he came roaring over the hill, with a flock of wild swans tied to his chariot and flying overhead and almost lifting it off the ground, with a rearing grey horse pulling at one side and a maddened antlered stag at the other, and Leary driving like a madman, and Cuchullain in the chariot

112

with his battle frenzy upon him which made the wind blow from every direction at once and forced fire from the earth as they passed, while a spout of blood flew up from his forehead and his body writhed like a knot of mating snakes. Owen told how the men and women of Emain trembled, but they were ready. When Cuchullain reached forward past Leary and pulled the reins in a frenzy, turning the left side of the chariot in insult to Emain Macha, crying, 'I swear by the blood of your fathers that if a man is not sent out to fight me I will spill the blood of every man and woman inside!', Conor looked steadily down at them from the battlements and then motioned the men of Emain to open the gate. When Cuchullain rushed forward to fight, his body twisting into the terrible shapes of his battle rage and his mouth howling his awful war-cry, instead of the great warrior that he expected to see galloping towards him, he saw fifty women of the court, led by Mugain the mother of Conor. Some were young virgins, others were older women who bore the marks of giving life and living on their skin. All were unarmed and naked. They stood before him without speaking or moving.

Owen told a rapt audience how, at this, Cuchullain's will to fight flew from him, and he hid his face for shame, for he was still a boy in his heart and innocent of women, and he dropped his sword and his rage left him. However, no man could stand near to him for long because of the heat of his body, and a barrel was brought full of freezing water which had been prepared in readiness, and he was plunged into it, but the barrel boiled over and burst its bands, and a second was brought and suffered the same fate, and it was not until the third barrel that his fury was fully contained. Then they took him from the barrel, and his body was limp although his eyes were alive, and he was given a blue cloak with a great silver buckle, and he sat at Conor's right hand that evening.

It didn't happen. A story with just a nodding acquaintance with the truth, in places just barely recognizable. Owen had made a fantasy out of the whole day. As he spoke, my mouth opened wider and wider until I got cramp in my jaw and was forced to close it. By the end of it all I was spluttering incomprehensibly. I turned to my neighbours.

'It isn't true. He's made almost all of it up. He wasn't . . .'

I stopped, and stared at those around me. No-one was listening. They were hammering on the tables, they were banging their cups, pounding each other on the back, and above all, shouting, yelling, bawling for more. They loved it. I was dumbstruck, and then I realized something else. For the last part at least, the arrival home, most of the men who were pounding and shouting had been present. They had pretended not to watch the women, just as I had. They had seen it. They knew what Owen said wasn't true. They didn't want it to be true, they liked it as a story. They liked Owen's story better than the facts, which they themselves had witnessed.

I realized that this was a new form of history. It was like Aesop's *Fables*, instructive rather than accurate. I looked at the cheering crowd all around me. Whatever I felt about it, I wasn't going to get anyone to listen to my version of the story while they were like this. Conall was near by. He saw the look on my face.

'What's the matter?'

I shrugged. 'It didn't happen that way.'

Conall looked perplexed. 'And so? Bards don't exaggerate where you come from?'

I was determined to say it at least once, no matter how pompous it sounded. 'It isn't history, it's . . . doggerel. It's a lie. Bards tell lies. Owen is a liar.'

Conall thought about that for a moment. Then he said, 'Perhaps. But his lies have more truth in them than your history.' Then he turned away from me and applauded even louder.

Owen came up to me, flushed and grinning. I clasped his hand.

'Congratulations.'

He almost simpered. 'Did you like it?'

'It was a great story.'

He missed the irony, or perhaps didn't care.

'He is but nine years old,' said Fiacha mac Fir Febe with

more portentousness than could be good for anyone. 'What will happen when he is a man?'

So it was that Cuchullain was disarmed in the height of his first battle-fury by the strategy of Mugain and the nakedness of the women of Conor's court.

Or so they said.

# 15

The story of Macha. Cathbad's favourite story. I heard him tell it a few times. To be fair, no more than thirty or so. I never thought I would wish he was here to tell it again, but I do.

I still remember how he looked in the firelight, the narrow planes of his face rearranging the shadows, and I remember how he told the story to me, and I repeat it as close to the way he spoke as I can.

Crunniuc, son of Agnoman, a wealthy merchant, had four sons but no wife. She died bearing their last child. The sons had grown up tall and strong and were old enough to fight, but a combination of a solitary disposition, a lonely situation and a melancholy for his lost wife kept Crunniuc from marrying again. He had settled into a comfortable bachelorhood, by default rather than by design, without many cares but without many joys either.

He was walking through his castle one spring morning, thinking about a boar hunt. He didn't much enjoy hunting, but the day and his status demanded that he at least think about it. He turned a corner, and thoughts of hunting vanished. In front of him was a stranger. She was tall and fair-skinned, with shining dark hair and green eyes into which a man could fall deeper than the sea floor. She smiled at him, introduced herself simply as Macha, embraced him in a way that made him remember how much he missed his wife without making him feel that he was betraying her memory, and then took upon herself all the duties of the mistress of the house. Crunniuc felt that he ought to object, but decided just to watch instead, while she put his life in order.

At the end of a confusing day, Crunniuc had watched his comfortably disordered home tidied out of all recognition, and had listened without paying any attention to the horrified complaints of his servants, exhausted at being made to work properly for the first time in years. He was then fed a splendid meal. A voice like quicksilver made him laugh and let him feel clever (no mean feat) and encouraged him to enjoy himself, while a smile full of promise fogged his mind with enchanted mist and made his heart pound. Crunniuc went to bed with his head entirely confused, so much so that he completely forgot to allocate his stranger a bed. It didn't matter. She came to his room, smiled, slipped out of her clothes and allocated herself half of his.

His new wife turned out to be a paragon of domestic efficiency, and turned her new stepsons' initial suspicion into unhidden adoration in less than a week. Crunniuc's castle vibrated with cheerful activity. She played the harp like a spirit, sang with a purity that charmed all who heard her, and was an organizer of children's games without equal. She could also run like a deer, and often kept pace with Crunniuc's horse for the first mile when he set out hunting, both of them laughing at the ease with which her silent feet flew across the turf beside the pounding hooves.

They were happy, and loved each other. Then Macha announced her pregnancy and their happiness was complete.

Shortly before Macha was due to be delivered, Crunniuc was bidden to a great meeting of the Ulster chiefs. She begged him not to go. He insisted that he had no choice, although the prospect of great feasting and improbable boasting sessions with old friends long unseen was perhaps not altogether unpleasant to him. Eventually, with much lamenting, she let him go, but begged him not to tell anyone of her existence, reminding him of how she had come and telling him that she would only be allowed to stay if no-one outside Crunniuc's household knew of her. He laughed at her, but gave his promise, joking that he would be sad not to be able to boast of the great treasure he had in her, but that he would obey for her sake.

He arrived at the festival, to the surprise of all his friends, who hardly recognized the cheerful and convivial newcomer who looked a bit like a glum man they had once known. They drank his health and set to feasting with a will.

The chief cause of interest that day was the horse racing, and the greatest admiration of all was reserved for the King's horses, a grey and a roan, who carried all before them. It was a perfect day for racing, warm sunshine after a day's rain. The turf was dry underfoot and the horses had flown across it like swans over a river. Eoin the King was exultant. 'There is nothing in all Ireland swifter than my horses!' he shouted, his face flushed and his voice thick with wine.

Crunniuc heard the boast, and his pride was stung. His own horses had been beaten out of sight by the grey and the roan, and he had no love for the King. He was a simple man, unused to looking beyond the moment. He was as proud of his exceptional wife as an unexceptional man must be. Besides, he was drunk.

'You are wrong,' he said. 'My wife could outrun them, and be home for supper too.' He toasted the crowd, who cheered lustily, and he swigged from his cup.

Eoin heard him, and swung round, his face mottled with anger. Crunniuc felt Eoin's look rest on his face like the first winter breeze and stopped in mid-swallow.

'Then they shall race,' said Eoin, his voice hard as stone, 'and we shall see. Fetch your wife.'

Crunniuc tried to pretend that he hadn't said anything, called out to a complete stranger some distance away as if he were a brother and set off towards him. Eoin's handsome face took on a cruel expression. 'Hold him until she arrives!'

Crunniuc's brain cleared and he realized what he had done. He protested, tried to laugh it off, scoffed at himself for a fool and a drunkard, denied he even had a wife, only to see the King's anger deepen. Eoin was black drunk and meant evil to someone. Crunniuc's wife would serve very well. Real fear then swept over Crunniuc, and he fell at the King's feet, told of his wife's condition and begged him for mercy, offered his lands, his house, his life, if Eoin would only relent.

The King looked at him with a dead eye, said nothing, drank more wine. A great black bird circled overhead.

Macha was brought to the festival the next morning. She looked sorrowfully at her husband. Crunniuc bowed and shook his head in shame and confusion, his face shining with tears. She gave him the shadow of her normal smile, whispered her forgiveness, and touched his face with a soft hand. Then she turned away from her husband, lifted her head and went proudly to the King.

He looked at her through red-rimmed eyes. She stood, waiting for him to speak. All who were there that day remarked on her bearing and beauty, and on how the King looked at her and then at Crunniuc, asking him scornfully what magic he had used to find such a one and keep her secret. Crunniuc burst out with fresh pleading, but the King was unforgiving and cursed at him to be quiet. He looked at her proud face shining defiance and he turned his eyes away and waved his hand to his grooms, reached for more wine and gruffly told her to prepare to race.

Her face went white at his words, and she pulled her cloak aside with a sweeping gesture so that everyone saw her swollen belly and none could say they did not know.

If she had begged for mercy even then perhaps he might have relented, but her voice was quiet and reasonable, though trembling with emotion. She spoke to him as an equal, not as if he was the King and she a supplicant. She spoke to him as a man who happened to be wearing a crown, but that day Eoin was a King who happened to look like a man. He made a dismissive gesture at her with the hand that held his cup, making wine fly in an arc from it which stained the hem of her cloak like a row of bloody tears.

'I am close to my hour,' she said.

'That is no concern of mine,' replied Eoin, sitting back in his chair and stroking his beard. 'Your husband has insulted my horses, and so insults me. You must run.'

'I will not. It will be the death of my child and of myself.'

'And of your husband if you do not.' The King turned to his Captain and gestured at Crunniuc, who struggled to free himself from the grip of two soldiers. 'Hew the fool to pieces,' he said. The soldiers grinned and threw Crunniuc to the ground.

Macha went pale. 'No!' she cried. 'Give me a little time, until I am delivered. Then I will gladly run.'

'No,' said the King. Macha turned desperately to the men who watched, the flower of Ulster's Heroes, men all bound by honour to protect her.

'Will you not help me?' she cried. 'You see how I am. A mother bore each of you. Would you see her here, in my place?'

Some men looked at the ground, others screwed up their faces in anger and guilt, but none would be the first to step forward, and there were enough drunkards baying for sport to make their shame a force for silence. Macha saw that she was alone. Her face set hard against them. 'You will not help me, and you will not help my husband. Is that the way you will have it?' There was no reply. 'Very well.' She looked at the King and nodded her acceptance of the situation. Some say that even at that moment a shadow of pain crossed her brow. She gestured at Crunniuc, her face strong and proud.

'He shall not die while I live to help him. Bring up your horses. I will run.'

The King clapped his hands at her words. 'Your wife has spirit!' he said to Crunniuc. 'What is her name?' Crunniuc could not speak, but looked at her as if his happiness was walking away from him, never to return. She touched his face again, and smiled her full smile for him, then turned back to the King.

'My name is Macha, daughter of Sainraith mac Imbaith, and my name will be given to this place.' The King's mouth smiled, but his eyes were black. She swept an arm around her like an orator, flinging off her cloak disdainfully, including them all in her rejection.

The horses were brought with difficulty. They had arrived at the start of every previous race snorting and pawing at the ground, eager to run. Now they dragged their feet and lowered their heads, trying to turn away, so that the grooms had great difficulty getting them to the start line. As they finally got them to the start, the sun went behind a cloud so suddenly that the abrupt darkness made the horses pull away again, their eyes glaring. Macha watched the King silently as his impatience with the grooms grew. Eventually he lost his temper and shouted at them. His voice made her tremble, and she drew herself up to her full height. She cursed him then, her voice ringing with anger and hopelessness.

'Loose your horses! Let what will happen, happen! But know this, that a greater misfortune than mine shall befall you all from this!'

Her words struck to the hearts of some of the men watching. Their eyes and minds became clear as if the sun rose to dispel night, and they understood what was happening. It was too late. A few men tried to speak up, but they were swept aside. The horses and the woman lined up together. Tears darkened the cheeks of the huge animals, who bowed their heads before her and pushed their soft muzzles into her hands. Even then it might have been halted, for when the King called the start the horses refused to move, but an Ulsterman who had bet loud and long on Macha losing gave a drunken shout and laid the flat of his sword across the horses' backs. The animals reared up in fear, and it seemed that the woman who stood looking contemptuously at the men of Ulster must surely be crushed under them. More than one voice shouted, 'Enough!', but then Macha looked up fearlessly at the horses' great hooves, and as they crashed to earth she sprang aside and was away down the track with the horses chasing her like a thundercloud following a bird.

Misgivings forgotten, the men of Ulster let out a cheer, swigged from their cups and ran across the centre of the course to see the end of the race at the other side. Only Crunniuc remained. He stood alone, watching the horses pursue his wife round the first bend, while silent tears flowed down his face and his body shook with the misery of what he had done and what he had not done.

The race was almost over. The competition pitted earth against air. The horses were sculpted flesh, solid-muscled and clear-sinewed with effort, throats flecked with ivory foam, flared nostrils sucking desperately at the dry wind, their harness ornaments clashing like armour, their hooves booming against the dry turf like a distant waterfall, sending up a spray of dust and clods; and Macha, silent, feet skimming the grass without touching the earth, her body balanced and moving in rhythm despite her pregnancy, alive with movement. Only her face told the full story. Long tears splashed into her hair and pain pulled her mouth sideways.

Fifty paces from the finish her waters broke. She fell to the ground with a cry that cut to stooping Crunniuc's heart and made him turn and run towards where she lay, bursting through the crowd to get to her like a wave through sand. Someone shouted that Macha had won the race, and the men of Ulster knew through shame and confusion that the horses would not have caught her. Then they knew something else. As the first pain of her labour lashed her body into an arch a terrible agony burnt through them, pulling them to the ground where they lay, groaning with pain.

Macha writhed and then lay still on the ground, looking up at Crunniuc who knelt beside her, holding her hand in his, his face contorted with sorrow and loss. Her fingernails cut half-moons in his palms as she fought for breath. 'I am a fool,' he whispered. 'I have lost you.'

She nodded. 'Yes,' she whispered, 'you have lost me for now. But the men of Ulster shall not forget me.' Her voice rose so that those near by could hear. 'For nine nights, at the time of their greatest peril, nine generations of the men who defend Ulster shall suffer as I suffer now.' She gasped with pain, and pulled him closer to her. 'Never forget me, my husband.' Then she felt the child tear free of her, and her life's blood flowed from her as if her body was a spilt jug of wine, knocked over by a careless suitor. Crunniuc saw and knew she could not live beyond it, and the light went from his eyes and he never spoke again.

She gave birth to twins, from which comes the name 'Emain Macha', the Twins of Macha. When the delivery was complete she turned to the King and cursed him and his men, repeating her prophecy that for nine generations, at the time of their greatest need, they would be struck down for nine days and nights with the pain of a woman in her labour.

The twins were wrapped in wool blankets and given to her. As she held them, her face white as hawthorn and her lips pale as dawn, a great black bird flew down and landed at her feet, making the woman who sat there jump aside with surprise. The bird pecked at the ground, picking up earth mixed with her blood, throwing back its head to swallow. Macha screamed at it, and the bird fell sideways as if buffeted by a great wind, and then flew away. When the women looked again, Macha was dead.

The pains lasted nine days and nights as Macha had promised. So it was that the fighting men of Ulster lived in fear of great danger, not for themselves, but for what could be done to Ulster while they were unable to defend her.

So it is that Ulster has been afflicted from the time of Crunniuc, son of Agnoman, for five generations so far, and four more to come.

Part of me scoffed as Cathbad's rolling portentous tones finished the story, but another part looked uncertainly into the room's dark corners and I moved closer to the fire. I once saw a man in Carthage cursed by an old witch-woman whom he refused money to. She railed at him, called on her ancestors. He was superstitious, she looked the part. He looked into her eyes and went white as she screeched a prophecy of doom at him. He became ill and we thought he would die. We went to the witch's house, hoping to persuade her to lift the curse. She wasn't there, but a soldier was, slouching on guard, who told us all about how she had taken an officer to bed, went to rob him while he was asleep, and then tried to stab him when he caught her with her hand in his pockets. She had cursed him and he laughed at her. The guard knew the woman from his childhood, and told us how she pretended to be a witch to frighten people into giving her money. I wanted to tell our stricken friend to get up and stop faking, but a wiser companion told him instead that we had gone to the witch at great personal risk and bought the curse from her for a small fortune, and that he was now free as a result of our bravery and generosity. By that evening he was sitting up and eating soup. By the weekend he was reinstalled in the wine shop and buying us all the wine of thanks that we could drink, so at the back of it all everyone was happy. Perhaps curses don't need magic to work, they just need men to believe in them. Perhaps that's the magic, making men believe.

But I still saw how the shadows moved on the wall, and I still came close to the fire.

# 16

'I want to go and see my mother.'

I was used to Cuchullain's directness, but I was not ready for this. Emain Macha was an open court, anything could be discussed – well, anything except Fergus mac Roth's appalling flatulence, and Conall's astonishingly unfaithful wife, and perhaps one or two other small things, but even they could be discussed if the discussers were prepared to take the consequences – but one subject that everyone left well alone was the subject of Conor's half-sister. That subject was taboo. It was not that the King had exactly forbidden discussion of Dectera, it was just that it was plain to all that this was a subject best avoided.

I looked at Cuchullain. He was on fire with his latest idea, as always. He vibrated with the intensity of his thoughts. (I laughed at him once and told him he lived life twice as fast as anyone else. He replied, 'That is because I have only half the time that other people do.' He could be annoying like that.)

'Will you take me to see my mother?'

I pondered a moment. I didn't want to go against the King. On the other hand, visiting Dectera was not actually forbidden, and Conor need never know. Besides, if we got there and Dectera didn't want to see us, then we would just leave and no harm would be done. On the other hand, if she invited us in, then we would be welcome and Conor could have no real complaint. Truth be told, I was bored. A long chariot ride would blow the cobwebs away.

I was harnessing the horses when Owen came out of the castle towards me running, something I had never seen him do before. I fell back against the side of the chariot and held my hand to my heart in exaggerated surprise.

'Is the castle on fire?' I gasped.

'Cuchullain says you two are going to see Dectera,' he puffed.

'True,' I said, stopping my pretence. 'Coming?'

He flapped a hand in breathless agitation. 'Are you mad? Conor will have your ears!'

'No he won't,' I said. 'Cuchullain is Dectera's son, she's bound to want to see him. Besides, I am merely a lowly chariot driver from the sea who just does what he is told. Talk to the tiny Champion, it was his idea.'

Owen slapped his thigh in exasperation. I think he was mainly concerned that there wasn't enough room for him to come in the chariot as well. He might have argued for a place anyhow, but at that moment Cuchullain appeared, wearing every bit of armour, jewellery and ornament that he possessed, and carrying all his weapons and trophies so that he clanked with every step and kept tripping over his spear-ends. He looked at Owen as if he were a stranger, and then rolled past him towards our chariot like a metal sailor just off the boat. He could hardly lift his leg high enough to get in with the weight.

'Be careful,' Owen called, but we were already thundering out of the gate with the wind and the warm earth smell of horses flowing sweetly past my face. Cuchullain stood silent beside me, his face pinched and strained. We drove half a day's journey to Dectera's castle and he did not speak once.

I could understand the way Cuchullain felt. My parents were dead, but I had at least known who my father and mother were.

126

I had seen my father die, in battle, fighting bravely against the Roman invader as he would have wished, and my mother had died peacefully not long after. Cuchullain had had a different life altogether. He had been given to the foster-mothers by Dectera as early as possible. They had taken him far away from Emain, to no-one knew where, and Dectera was sent away to her castle, presumably both at Conor's order. Only Dectera knew for certain whose child Cuchullain was. If Conor's, then it was not surprising that Conor her brother sent them away, to hide their shame. If Cuchullain was Sualdam's son, then it made less sense. The Ulstermen did not have the taboo of illegitimacy nor even a word for 'bastard' (nor any word for 'prostitute', having no need of either). However, if Laeg was Cuchullain's father . . . well, the God of the Sun was always going to be a hard act to follow.

We arrived at Dectera's home in the heat of the day. Cuchullain was still determinedly wearing his armour. The sweat ran down his body in a hundred thin streams, cutting fingertip-thin roads through the dust of the journey and making his skin shine like wet sandstone.

A groom came out and took our horses. Another brought us water, and we drank and washed off the dust. Then we presented ourselves to the guard at the gate. He brought us inside and told us to wait.

The castle was medium size, but well appointed. Arms hung on the wall, and the table was large enough for fifty men. Cuchullain looked around with seeming indifference – unusual for him, who always wanted to know everything.

'Have you been here before?' I asked. Cuchullain shook his head. I was starting to feel uncomfortable. I had assumed that I would let Cuchullain go and talk to his mother while I went to the kitchens and talked to the serving-women; I hadn't planned on being part of the visit. However, the castle was quiet, and there was no obvious way for me to slip away. A soldier appeared and indicated a passage for us to go down.

'This way.'

I turned to Cuchullain. 'I'll wait here, you go on,' I said. He looked at me blankly and pulled me along after him without replying. We walked down a dark passage until we came to an open door. Dull ochre firelight spilt onto the floor from inside. Cuchullain hesitated, and I stopped beside him, waiting for him to decide what to do. He took a breath, set his shoulders, and rounded the corner into her room.

Dectera sat on a blue-silk-covered cushion in a large chair shaped like a cup. Her dress was long, low-cut, of the same deep blue as her eyes. She was very beautiful. Her hair was her gift to Cuchullain, the same thick dark mane, running sleek to her waist. Her most obvious quality was stillness. Cuchullain had it sometimes too, when he wasn't seized by some pressing idea, but Dectera made him look like a nervous greyhound left out on a cold night. She was totally relaxed, her face calm and unlined. I had never seen anyone like her before. It was as if there was nothing she needed, nothing she wanted from us, nothing in the world that she didn't have.

'You are welcome in my house. Please, come in.'

Cuchullain walked towards her as if to embrace her, then stopped just short instead and bowed awkwardly. They looked at each other silently for what seemed a long time, and then she motioned him with a graceful gesture to sit beside her. He sat as if the chair was likely to bite him, and there was more silence. I perched quietly on a stool in a corner of the room and tried to pretend I wasn't there.

'Leary, please come and sit with us.' She smiled at me and a smooth hand glided across my stomach. I swallowed, and walked across the room to the seat she indicated. As I settled myself she turned back to Cuchullain. 'How are you, my son?'

Cuchullain paused before speaking, as if ensuring that his voice was under control first. 'Well, thank you. And you?'

She smiled. 'Oh yes.' She reached out and touched his hand. He stared at her fingers as if he had never seen anything like them before. 'Well,' she added. A pause. 'And my brother, the same?'

'Well also.' Another, longer pause. I began to worry that we

128

wouldn't be home for supper. Cuchullain fidgeted. His mouth opened and shut a few times. Then the reason for our visit tumbled out of him.

'Who is my father?'

Cuchullain's approach to any problem was always the approach of Alexander to the Gordian Knot. Dectera did not flinch, although her eyes opened a little wider at Cuchullain's directness. Then she smiled again. 'You are to the point.'

Having said the thing that he wanted to say, Cuchullain was left dumb. He could not have repeated the question to save his life, but he would never have withdrawn it. He sat by her, looking very young and full of ill-concealed tension, not speaking, chewing his bottom lip. She looked straight at him. 'Who would you like your father to be?'

It was not the answer either of us had expected. She waited to see if Cuchullain would say something, but he looked more likely to burst. She gave a little shrug.

'You can have Conor. Or Sualdam. Or Laeg. Or there are those who will provide you with a list of other suspects. The possibilities are wide. Who would you prefer?' Cuchullain clenched his fist and beat it on his knee. I suspect I just sat there with my mouth open.

'But I want to know the truth. I want to know from *you*, so that I will know without doubt,' he said, his voice cracking with emotion.

'Why?'

'Because . . . I . . .' He could not say it, or did not know the answer. He swallowed, and his eyes looked upwards. Then it came, slowly, softly, like a prayer. 'Because knowing my father tells me who I am.'

'Is it not enough that you will be the greatest Champion that Ulster will ever have?' Cathbad's prophecy had wings, even to here.

'No, it is not enough,' Cuchullain said, his knuckles white with tension. 'Not without knowing who I am. When they sing of me, they will say "Cuchullain, son of Conor", or Laeg, or some other, and I do not mind who they say it is or if they are right or

129

wrong, but I must know the truth for myself.' He looked intently at her. 'I want to know where I came from.'

She shook her head. 'It is better that you do not.'

'You must trust me to know for myself if that is true.'

Dectera looked at him for a moment that seemed to become an hour. Then her face set as she came to a decision.

'I tell you this, and it must suffice. When the foster-mothers took you from me, they took you to the Tuatha. It was with them that you grew up. It was there that you learnt everything that you know, and it is through their teaching that you know more than a boy of your age should. Time also passes more slowly there, so although you are only eight years old in the time that men count by, your heart and mind are aged twice that. That is why you are a Champion now, and that is how you fight and beat men twice your size. That is all I will say. You must draw your own conclusions.'

'But . . .'

She would not be drawn further. Cuchullain badgered her, questioned her, even tried to trick her, but she would say no more about it. She took me by the arm and led us to her hall for supper. We ate an awkward meal, with Dectera speaking to Cuchullain when he stayed off the subject of his father, and speaking to me as if Cuchullain didn't exist when he tried to push her in that direction. I thought her charming, and found myself wishing that Cuchullain would shut up and go away for a while so that we might get to know each other better. Then I felt ashamed, then I decided I didn't need to, then gave up thinking and got drunk instead. Dectera encouraged me, laughing at my jokes and making me feel an altogether excellent fellow, and eventually we enraged Cuchullain to the extent that he went outside for a walk in disgust.

Dectera turned from silently watching him leave, and dropped her voice so that I had to lean towards her to catch what she said. Her breath smelt sweet.

'You are his friend. You will look after him for me, as I cannot.'

'Yes.' I would have faced Cullan's hound at that moment and ripped its balls off if she asked me to.

She looked grave. 'There are many things that he will never know, and many other things that he will know but not know why. He thinks that this matters, but he will realize eventually that it does not. One day he will cease wondering why, and just wonder. I would like you to help him see it.'

I had not the faintest idea what she was talking about. 'I am yours to command.' Even if I'd no idea what that command was. Her head was close to mine. Her lips were moist and within reach.

She laughed at me. 'You are a good man,' she said, 'even though you do your best to hide it.' She looked into my eyes and I felt my heart kick like the tiller of a boat hitting a rock. Cuchullain came back into the room. I suppose we looked a bit suspicious. I may even have been leering drunkenly at his mother. He scowled, and jerked his head.

'Come. It will soon be dark. We must go.'

'Will you not stay? There are beds ready for you.'

I nodded like an idiot, and then saw the look on Cuchullain's face, and started scratching the back of my neck to pretend that the nodding was verminous in origin rather than any sort of agreement. Dectera gave a little shrug, and walked up close to Cuchullain. 'Go well, my son.' He stood at attention in front of her.

'I thank you. Go well too.'

She leant forward and brushed her cheek gently against his. For a moment I was sure that Cuchullain was going to fall into her arms, but he caught himself just in time and his hands stayed by his sides.

'You will come again,' she said. I was not sure if this was an invitation or a statement.

As we drove away, I looked back, to see her standing in the arch of the entrance to her castle, waving with one arm. I raised a hand in farewell, almost falling out of the chariot. Cuchullain snorted at me, and did not turn round.

'She is saying good speed and farewell,' I said. He looked forward into the falling gloom ahead.

131

'It is well,' he said. 'I should not have come. We shall not meet again. Whoever my father may be, he is a great man, everyone agrees with that. I should let that be enough.'

I wanted to say something, in fact I wanted to say a lot, but I had the sense to keep quiet. He never mentioned his mother again.

# 17

Owen wasn't the greatest singer ever born, even by his own account – and he was not a modest man. Those who knew about such things assured me that his harp-playing was notable more for its enthusiasm than its delicacy, and I can vouch for the fact that a harp is a not an instrument to be played with gusto. People who listened to him did so for other reasons. He had an excellent memory, which is essential if your songs can last up to several hours and are not written down, and he loved telling stories. People responded to this. Some bards told stories because they loved to hear the sound of their own voices. Others liked the cheering and attention that they received. Owen did it because he was incurably curious and loved gossip. He remembered things that people told him and wove them around other things he knew, then added a few things that he had made up, until he ended up with a story that was worth telling.

It came as a shock to me to realize that the Ulstermen didn't have historians, at least not in the sense that I understood the word, recorders of the truth as far as was possible. They didn't write things down, except when they wrote royal records in Ogham, and the difference between writing in Latin and writing Ogham is the difference between buying vegetables and waiting for them to grow. Owen and his ilk were about the closest to historians that they had. Which meant that Owen was recording history, but not as it happened, rather as he thought it should have happened. The facts were the bones on which he built his stories, but he saw them as things to be included, distorted or ignored to serve his purposes. After a few drinks, I could get quite upset about it.

'It is wrong, it's immoral, it's a lie, it's . . .'

'Why are you being so pompous?'

'Because . . .'

I didn't know. I had to be honest and admit that I knew that many Roman chroniclers had made up or judiciously improved stories. Homer himself invented stories. I suppose that having nothing written down made me feel that truth was somehow more sacred. I often resolved to be more patient with Owen, but occasionally the thought of someone I knew being in charge of writing the story of his people became too much for me. On those occasions I would shout for a while and Owen would look on tolerantly. I suspect it was good for both of us. He thought that I was a little bit mad anyway, and it was obvious to him that I just didn't understand. Which I didn't.

He asked me what we did in Rome instead of listening to bards.

'Well, we do listen to them, up to a point, we do have them, but they don't tell stories. They used to, mind you, but not any more.'

'So who tells your stories?' I thought for a minute.

'I suppose our writers do. We get our stories from books.' I had told him about books. He couldn't see the point. I think he thought that books were cheating.

'And your bards don't sing?'

'Oh, they sing, but not about battles and Champions and great feats. Historians and playwrights do that. Bards are more concerned with love and how sad it is to be away from home.'

Owen clearly didn't think much of this sort of bardery. 'And people listen to this?'

'Well, not really listen, not in the way that people here do.

More often they just play in the background while the dinner guests tell stories.'

His eyes flickered. 'You mean that one man plays while another sings?'

'Sometimes, although usually not. It isn't a bad idea, given that it's by no means certain that the best harpists are good singers, or vice versa. No, they just play music while people brag about their victories and tell dirty jokes. It makes things more civilized to have a bit of music in the background.'

It was plain that the idea of playing to a lot of drunks who shouted throughout his songs was not Owen's idea of civilization. I remembered something else. 'Then, if there was something good to see, we might go to the theatre.'

'What's that?'

I let myself feel superior, for once. It wasn't often that I got the chance to talk about something of which I knew Owen knew nothing. 'People dress up as other people and pretend to be them while they act out stories.'

'Why?'

I thought about that for a moment. 'Because it can be amusing, or entertaining, or instructive. Or all three.' Owen looked unconvinced. I felt bound to embark on a defence of the theatre. 'Look, it's not really different from what you do. You sing a song about a great King from the past, and you tell of his betrayal and horrible death and the great love he had for his Queen, and how what happened to him was an inspiration to us all, yes?' (It was obvious from his pained expression that he felt that I had missed some of the subtler nuances of his songs.) 'Anyway, in the theatre, men pretend to be that King and Queen, and they act out the story, and other people pretend to be their murderers, and people can actually see what happens. You can be a part of it.'

Owen frowned. 'But where is the listener in all this?'

'Booing, or cheering, or crying, doing whatever the play makes him feel like doing.'

'People do those things when I sing.'

'I know, but . . .' I felt exasperation approaching. 'Don't you see that if you can see it as well as hear it, then the effect is multiplied?'

He shook his head. 'I see that the hearer, who should be listening to the words and letting them run through his mind creating pictures, is fed his thoughts from a spoon like a child. Where is a man's imagination to go, if everything is given to him?'

I was nonplussed. 'But the theatre is the most highly creative art that exists!'

He shrugged. 'For the man who creates it, perhaps. The man who listens to it is a man who drinks his thoughts from a cup instead of a running stream. Your theatre tells people what to think. My songs tell people to use their imagination. I wouldn't want to be part of your theatre.'

I wanted very much to explain how theatre worked, but the words didn't seem to get it across. 'Imagine,' I said, 'imagine the wife of a great Champion on stage, keening over his dead body. Can't you see the drama in that?'

'My songs do that anyway.'

'No they don't. It's you, they know it's you, Owen the singer, it's you saying, "I will now tell you what the Queen said." On stage, the actor actually is the Queen for a while, it's like being there, hearing her actual words spoken by her.'

That was when his expression changed. 'The actor says her words?' he asked slowly. 'Her actual words, spoken by someone who is impersonating her?'

I was getting through to him at last. I didn't want to complicate matters by telling him about boys playing women's parts. I nodded with relief. He turned away slightly, smiling, his face excited, ending the discussion. I tried to get him to tell me what he had thought of, but he wouldn't.

'Wait and see,' he said. I shrugged in a way that was intended to indicate that I didn't really want to know anyway and left him to whatever it was.

A couple of nights later, Owen unveiled his idea. Supper was almost over. He came in, holding his harp, sat on a stool and cleared his throat. Most people turned to listen. It was one of those ruminative, thoughtful evenings that often follow a period of celebration. We had been celebrating something – I think everyone had forgotten what – for what seemed like for ever, and by unspoken agreement people seemed to feel that the time was right for a quiet night without any serious roistering. It was a perfect opportunity for Owen to get everyone's attention, while they were, for once, restrained. Conall, who was never restrained, was doing his noisy best to kick some life into the company, but his efforts were becoming mechanical, because no-one was interested. Most people just wanted to listen to Owen and fall asleep with full bellies.

'Play us a song, bard,' someone called.

Owen waited until the chorus of agreement died down, then paused a few moments longer. For a man who knew nothing of being an actor, he knew how to time his speeches.

'I will tell a new story,' he said. This was a risk. People generally tended to prefer the old stories, the ones that they knew so well they didn't have to think about what was being said, where they could even go to sleep for a while in the middle without losing the thread. 'I will tell the story of the first time Emer met Cuchullain.' That got a better response. Owen looked around and held the silence for a few beats again. 'I hope you will enjoy the way the story is told,' he said softly.

No-one understood what he meant, and they paid no attention. The harpist played a familiar chord, and everyone settled themselves down. Then he began. His voice became softer, higher than usual.

'The very first sight that I had of his solemn face, his charioteer was lashing his chariot towards my sitting friends and me sitting outside the walls of my father's castle, coming at us through a huge cloud of dust and horse-spume, as if the chariot were runaway and we were to be crushed under his terrible wheels. Then, at the last moment, when it seemed that our deaths were inevitable and all around me women were scrambling for safety, the charioteer pulled the horses to one side and stopped in front of us. A haze obscured him, pebbles danced across our feet and away. I could see his shadow and the plume of his helmet, no more. There was a long silence while we waited for the dust and the gravel storm to settle, broken only by the curses and spitting of my dearest friend Grainne, who had taken the worst of it.'

(I looked around. People were sitting up and listening, many with expressions of puzzlement. Romans wouldn't have thought it strange for a storyteller to adopt someone else's voice and point of view, but to Ulstermen this was a new idea. Owen looked up from his harp at me, just for an instant, then down again. He knew he had their attention.)

'I have been courted by Champions before. They all arrive this way. It seems to be compulsory. I hate it. Grainne, I felt, didn't like it much either. Covered from head to foot in grey-brown dust, she looked even more like a plump mouse than usual.

'I glowered at him through the cloud as best I could, trying not to blink or sneeze, waiting for it to clear. I could see him standing, motionless in the chariot. Even though his charioteer was with him, I felt that he was alone. He was dark, slight, almost a boy. His horses were magnificent. One was a fine-boned grey, the other black as a Fomorian's heart, their rectangular heads like Ogham stones tossing high above us and their nostrils flaring like the mouths of great fish. Their sweating flanks gleamed like wet rock, steaming under the harness. A King's horses.

'A Hero's horses.

'The dust finally settled. His eyes met mine. I drew myself up fully. The fine green cloth of my dress, my favourite, with the thin gold thread all around the border and cut low at the neck, rustled around me. The bright morning sun was behind him, shining full into my face. I resisted the temptation to shake my hair over my shoulders to catch the light. He had come to me without invitation. Let him take as he found.

'I have always loved men's eyes. They are by far the most attractive part of a man, for they are the only part of him that cannot lie to you. Sometimes his eyes look you up and down as if they were parched and you the only water for a hundred miles

138

around. Sometimes they dismiss you as above or beneath them, or too much trouble, or not their preference. Sometimes they look at you with the slight smile of a love reserved for another. And sometimes they watch you, swallowing every detail, as if you were the only thing in Ireland worth looking at. I look at a man's eyes and I know him.

'But not this one. His eyes were silver, bright flecks in his dark face, but they told me nothing. I could not read him.

'He looked at me as if . . . I do not know what. I have often asked myself what he saw. His look was . . . perhaps, an acknow-ledgement. As if he said quietly, with a slow nod, "So, there you are." Not as if he had been searching for me, but as though I had gone out of the room for a moment and he had been waiting patiently for me to return so that a journey could start. As if something had already passed between us, although we had only just met. As if this moment of meeting had already happened, long before.

'Which it had not. I have never liked being taken for granted. Stronger men than this had raced their chariots up to my walls to disturb a fine morning's embroidery. One had even raced a bit further, with a pair of horses that did not respond to his instructions, raced right into the walls without stopping, and as a result was a house guest for a month while we waited for him to wake up. This small dark man was nothing new to me. I had seen men before. Great Heroes had come to woo me and discovered that covering the womenfolk in dust does not count as an introduction in my house. He was no different, except that he was almost a boy. A beautiful boy, but a boy nonetheless.

'I saluted him. After the smallest of pauses he saluted back.

'"Greetings. What is your name, and what brings you to our house?"

'He nodded. "You do."

'His voice was light, like a boy's, and yet rounded like a man's. My companions and I had many discussions on what makes a man. When it came to voices, we were divided. Some liked deep, growling tones that come from the chest. Others preferred a lighter music. My friends were gathered behind me like so

139

many ducklings behind their mother. I did not look round. A whisper and some laughter from behind hands told me that the old trick with the chariot had worked on more than one of them. It was indeed a wonder how one so frail-looking had won the dozen severed heads that surrounded the sides of his chariot. He must have hidden strengths, the sort it might be fun to uncover. If one were not Emer, the daughter of Forgall Monach. Besides, the heads might have been borrowed or stolen. His beard was not yet grown – I exaggerate, his beard was not yet more than a figment of his imagination. It was hard to take him seriously.

'He stood in his chariot like a young prize bull, letting the women look him over. Well, I was not on the market for bulls of any size. It was time to show him the way home.

'"Do you not have a name at all, or is it not the custom where you are from to give it?"

'I think he smiled. "My name is Setanta, but men call me Cuchullain."

'"What should a woman call you then?"

'"That depends."

'"On whether she minds you arriving uninvited at her door like the west wind?"

'"She should always welcome the wind on a hot day."

'"Only when it cools her down, not when it brings the storm with it."

'Cuchullain looked puzzled for a moment. I shook my hair back and dust flew from it, catching the sunlight. He took the hint and looked serious. "I apologize. In my haste, I am ill-mannered. Would you rather I left you?"

'I waited for a moment, to see if he meant it. He carried on looking at me earnestly, and I realized that he did. I walked up to his chariot and beckoned him down to the ground. He stepped off the platform and landed lightly beside me. He was hardly taller than me, and as dark as I am fair. I felt as if everyone else present held their breath to see what would happen. I bent down and picked up a handful of dry earth. I held it over his head and allowed it to trickle through my fingers, running in tiny streams onto his head and down his black hair.

140

He stood still, waiting for me to finish. When my hand was empty, I placed it on his head and rubbed it as if he were a favourite dog. Dust flew up in a cloud.

'"Now we are even," I said.

'There was a pause, then someone – probably Grainne – laughed. His face did not change expression, but I saw amusement in his eyes. He bent over and picked up two handfuls of earth, throwing them high in the air so that they landed on everyone. We all laughed, except Grainne, who glowered and looked around for a fist-sized rock, and the tension broke. He moved closer to me, to arm's length, and put his hands on my shoulders.

'"You are indeed the one I have come for," he said softly.

'I let him look for a few moments, then I smiled and stepped back.

'"It will take more than two handfuls of dust for you to win me."

'He set his shoulders. "What then?"

'"Many men have tried, every one of them a Champion. None has succeeded."

'"I shall not fail."

'"You are very sure of yourself." I was used to men's bluster. Yet he was different. His words were the same, but they sounded different. He did not seem boastful and vainglorious, like most of those who came for me. Something moved in his eyes that I liked. There was something else as well, a feeling of indefinable sadness, a sense of melancholy that surrounded him without being of him. It was not depressing, it was like salt to meat, but I found myself wanting to touch his cheek and whisper that all would be well. He glowed with life, yet I felt a pang as I looked at him, as if a handful of long dry grass had been brushed gently across the strings of an old harp next to my heart.

'He looked over my shoulder at my friends. "There are too many people here," he said. "We should go elsewhere to talk."

'I smiled. "There is no need for that," I said. "We both know why you are here. We can talk in a language that we will both

141

understand." This was a game I could play well. "We shall speak as the poets do. Why do you come to this place?"

'"I see a fair country," he said, looking at me steadily. He knew the game too. "In such a country a man might lay his sword."

'"No man will walk this country or lie in its valleys or lay down his sword here until he has killed a hundred men at every ford between Scenemenn on the River Albine and Banchuling where the River Brea froths into its mouth."

'"I will, and then I'll rest my sword in this fair country."

'"No man shall rest his sword here until he has performed the Feat of the Salmon-Leap, carrying twice his weight in gold. Then he must strike down three groups of nine men with a single stroke, leaving the man at the middle of each group unharmed."

'"I will do it, and then I shall come to your fair country and lay my sword there."

'"No man will travel this country until he has gone sleepless from Samhain, when the summer goes to its rest, until Imbolc, when ewes give milk and spring begins, from Imbolc to Beltane whose fire sets light to summer, and from Beltane to Samhain again, when the earth droops with sorrow into the chill of winter."

'"I shall not sleep until you are content."

'"Do all these things, and I shall be."

'"It is done," said Cuchullain.

'I desperately wanted something to happen, I just didn't know what.

'Cuchullain and his charioteer stayed at our castle that night. We fed him well. My father was away, but his brother sat between us, trying I suspect both to keep us apart and to interrogate Cuchullain to find out his prospects. However I kept filling up my uncle's cup, and in a few hours the slaves carried him off to bed and Cuchullain and I could talk without interruption. We sat up talking all night. He told me about coming to Emain, how he was the King's nephew, and how he had taken arms. He told me about the prophecy, about glory and dying young. I didn't believe it. There was strength in him, but I could see the blood moving beneath his pale skin, I saw a pulse at the root of his neck as he spoke of his plans, I smelt the sweet sweat on him as he pushed my hair from my face. He was alive, so he would die one day, as would we all. I hoped the good part of the prophecy was true, felt it could be, but I didn't care. He was special, but he was the same as me. And I wanted him like no other.

'The next day Cuchullain left, looking back at me as his charioteer drove him away. My mother looked troubled as we stood at the gate watching his chariot disappear over the horizon, and my father was still not home to see him go. I wondered why this was so, but my thoughts were full of Cuchullain. Before that day I had known men that I admired, that I wanted, even men I might have married, but until that day I had not met one that made me feel incomplete when he was not there. Already I ached for his return and the touch of his hand.'

The story was over. Owen stopped plucking at his harp and put it on the floor. Then he got up and came over to me, took my full cup from me and emptied it in one swig. He looked around the Hall. Everyone who was still there appeared to be asleep.

'Was that like your theatre? Telling the story in her words?'

I nodded. 'Yes, in many ways it was, very like it. How did you know all those things about how Emer felt?'

He shrugged. 'I spoke to her afterwards, and made up the bits myself that she couldn't explain.'

'Including all that stuff about the other women, and all those conditions that Cuchullain had to meet if he was serious about her?'

He shook his head. 'No, that bit she told me herself. She's got the gift. If she was a man she'd make a good bard.' He waved the cup in a gesture around the room. 'It seems that our friends here aren't quite ready for your new ways of telling stories. They like the old ways best.'

I looked around. A more complete picture of snoring in-difference it would have been hard to imagine. 'So it seems.'

# 18

Owen and the other bards took their role as guardians of the social narrative very seriously, but the part that gave them most pleasure was their privileged position when it came to old-fashioned gossiping. Everyone was talking about Cuchullain and Emer, and all the stories and all the embellishments eventually got back to Owen. I wasn't sure if he ever made things up or if he stuck to the facts when he could, but I do know he was enjoying himself enormously. He was full of how Emer's friends told their fathers about Cuchullain's visit to Forgall's castle and everything that had happened there, and their fathers rushed to tell Forgall about his daughter and the strange boy who had promised himself to her, adding the sort of embellishments and ribald remarks that no father wants to hear. Furthermore, Forgall's wife was still disturbed by a bad dream from three days before that she could not forget, a dream that told her of bad things that would arise from Emer's meeting with Cuchullain. Forgall sat and thought for a day and a half about what he should do. Then he harnessed the horses to his chariot. He rode to Cuchullain's castle and asked to see him.

Cuchullain received him graciously without knowing who he was. Forgall had disguised himself as a Gaulish trader, and gave

Cuchullain tribute of wine, gold, cloth, and other valuables, and traded him much more. A great feast was held on the third night of his visit, the night before he was due to leave. He treated Cuchullain as a man, which made the reception from his host all the warmer. Although the other Ulster Heroes were in awe of Cuchullain's achievements, it was still difficult sometimes for them not to treat him like a ten-year-old boy.

Forgall pretended to drink Cuchullain's wine, and then started to tell stories about Ulster's warriors. He praised Cuchullain, Conall Chernach, Conall of the Victories, and half a dozen others, exaggerating the extent of their reputations and the stories of their deeds, many of which (he said) had reached to Gaul and beyond. Mostly, however, he flattered his host. Cuchullain seemed immune to the worst effects of such praise, but did not discourage it either.

'And it is known,' enthused the Gaulish trader, 'throughout Gaul, that Cuchullain can move mountains, knock them down with the edge of his hand. Many Gauls wish to ally themselves with such a warrior, and the other warriors of the Red Branch, to fight against the Romans, or to protect themselves should Ulster ever decide to come and take Gaul for its playground!'

'We are all warriors of the Red Branch,' said Cuchullain, laughing at his guest's enthusiasm. 'We seek to outdo each other in reputation only, for our own glory and that of Ulster.'

Forgall looked at him and smiled. He turned his cup between his finger and thumb.

'But is it not prophesied that Cuchullain will be the greatest of them, although his life will be short?'

There was a short pause while everyone waited for Cuchullain to reply. He spoke without looking up. 'Both those things are prophesied.'

Forgall pressed him. 'And yet, at this moment Cuchullain is one great warrior amongst many in the Red Branch. Is it not time that your training became equal to your station, equal to your ambition?'

'I am still young. There is time.'

Cuchullain kept calm, but Forgall could see that his words had struck a willing chord. Cuchullain had plainly had the same thoughts himself. Forgall pressed on.

'There is surely not any warrior left in Ulster that you can still learn from.' Forgall turned to the rest of the guests, talking about Cuchullain as if he were not there. 'If only Cuchullain were to train with Domnall Mildemail in Alba, he would become twice the warrior he is now – and if he were to train with Skiatha, away from distractions on her island, why, no warrior in Europe could stand against him!'

Forgall said these words with a smile on his face to the company at large, but they were aimed at Cuchullain like a stone from a slingshot and they struck home. Cuchullain leant across the table, his face flushed with excitement and decision.

'By Laeg, you have said what I have been thinking for these last six months, that there is not a man in Ulster left who has anything to teach me! I will go to these men you speak of, and I will learn all they can show me!'

Forgall grinned at him. 'Be careful then, for at least one of them is a woman. But Skiatha is the greatest warrior in these islands for all that.'

'Man or woman, I will go!'

'It would be a shame if you did not. But you will wake up tomorrow and forget your resolve.'

'I shall not. I swear it!'

Thus did Forgall trick Cuchullain into leaving Ulster and going to Alba, where many hazards waited for him.

That next day, Forgall returned to his castle, where his wife and daughter waited for him. His wife, who knew his plan, took him to one side.

'Did he agree to leave?' she asked. Forgall nodded. She smiled for the first time in days. 'Then my dream perhaps may not be true?'

Forgall's wife's dream had kept her awake since the night she had it, for fear that it might come again. She dreamt that Cuchullain killed Forgall, stole Emer, and burnt their castle to the ground, killing many of their warriors. She had given Forgall no peace until he had agreed to try and get Cuchullain to leave

Ireland and try his fortune abroad. Neither she nor Forgall had any reason to hate Cuchullain, but she feared him and what he might do to her family and home. She knew that no man in her castle could hope to beat him in a fair fight. The best chance seemed to be to get him as far away as possible, in a place where he might be killed in battle or by the treachery of the Albans.

Cuchullain went first to where Emer and her friends were together, outside in the sunshine, near where they had first met. Her friends were clustered around her, watching her embroidery, and some tried to copy how her fingers wound through the cloth like smoke passing through dry sticks, but they could not match her speed or dexterity. He paused for a short while to watch her; to see how her hair fell across her face, how her white skin made her dark eyes look into the deepest place within him. He wanted to carry the memory of her inside him while he travelled.

When Cuchullain approached, her friends called to him happily, and some looked at him again and then enviously at Emer, for they knew that he was promised to her, and he made a fine sight striding towards them through the long summer grass. His long black hair fell around his shoulders and framed his thin face, putting it in shadow so that his silver eyes shone from dark into light. His limbs were slim, yet he moved with the grace of a powerful hunting animal, and any woman who saw him felt the power that surrounded him. His cloak flowed behind him when he walked as if held up by invisible attendants, and his clothes were the finest cloth, inset with rubies, with a deep red-gold band at his throat to hold the cloak around his shoulders.

Emer looked up into his eyes and saw that he was leaving. She touched his beardless face with a fingertip. 'You will not forget me?'

'I will remember.'

'You will do the things I have asked?'

'I have said that they are as done already.'

'I wish that they were done now, and that Cuchullain was returning, not leaving.'

'I leave my heart here in your hands.'

147

'And you take mine away with you. May the Gods smooth your path.'

'And straighten it to speed my return to you.' He kissed her for the first time, and then turned, calling for his chariot.

And of course, his faithful charioteer.

# 19

Emer filled my thoughts in those days, waking and sleeping. Her face had not left my mind since the day we drove away from her castle. I remembered every detail of how her hair fell straight and golden down her back, the stillness that surrounded her, the way her lips never fully closed, the dancing behind her eyes. I knew what her skin would feel like to touch though I had never even been close enough to her to try it. She moved me in a way that made sense of the world, and I would never have her.

My friend loved her, and I suspected she loved him. I would never hurt either of them, never allow myself to interrupt what they were creating together. I knew that I was going to have to stop thinking about her in this way, but I wasn't quite ready to do it. So, I got drunk and distracted myself as best I could.

I was lying on the grass half asleep one day soon afterwards. The sun was pleasantly warm on my face, and I had nothing to do. It was one of those perfect moments that arrive every so often, when one wishes that time would stop, or that the world would go on and leave one behind. Such moments are short, and too good to last.

I became aware that I was not alone. I lifted up the glove covering my eyes. Cuchullain was standing by my feet. The sun shone from behind him, giving his dark head a shining halo. His expression was serious, as usual.

'Hello,' I said.

'I have to go.' To the point, as usual.

'You've only just got here.' His smile was as bright as sunlight between two clouds in a thunderstorm, and as quickly gone.

'No. I have to go away.'

As so often, his manner took me aback. It never seemed to occur to Cuchullain that there were other ways of saying something than just to say it. He was absolutely honest and totally tactless. He never prepared you for surprises, or played games or wondered how you might take what he said. It was so, so he said it. 'Where to?' I asked. He looked pleased.

'To become a warrior.'

I was surprised. 'But you already are a warrior,' I said. 'Your enemies' heads hang in the Hall of Trophies beside those won by Conall and the greatest of the other Champions of the Red Branch. You are still just a boy. What more do you have to prove?' I was rather pleased with that speech. He looked at me and smiled. I knew that smile. It reminded me how little I really knew him.

'I must learn to fight like a real Champion,' he said, 'and then I must learn how to fight better than any Champion. I will learn every Feat, every Art, every Movement, and when I return no-one will be able to stand against me and live.'

'If you are going to be so fierce I would rather be by your side than facing you,' I said. 'Can I drive your chariot?' I threw a small stick at him. He smiled back.

'I must go alone.'

'When you return, may I drive you then?'

'Of course. Was there any doubt?' He had not heard the irony. He seldom did. 'I have learnt everything that Ulster can teach me. I shall go and train with Skiatha. She will give me the Gae Bolga. Then I must go to Alba, to finish my education. Then I will range across Ireland to kill my Hundreds.'

I shivered. The sight of this slight, intense boy talking seriously and matter-of-factly about slinging hundreds of heads

150

around the sides of his chariot made me feel old and soft. The Celt in me admired him, but the Roman part saw the waste. He was a killing machine, bred to slaughter. It was glorious and honourable, it had rules to be kept and broken, it had shame and chivalry, but it was still slaughter. A Roman would say that soldiering was a job, no different in essence from being a carpenter or a farmer. A job in which glory, fame and fortune could be won, a job in which you sometimes lived more intensely than at any other time in your life, a job which could kill you or leave you in pain until you died, all these were true, but at bottom, it was just a job. The purpose of the job was to capture land and resources that would be useful to Rome, and to defend everything belonging to the Empire against anyone outside who wanted to take it. Simple. The Celts saw it otherwise. Farmers farmed because they could not fight well enough. Anyone who could fight should and would. Fighting, including training for fighting and resting between fights, was man's natural condition. The tangible rewards – comfort, riches, admiration – were enjoyable but short-lived. What was important was glory, because glory meant story, it meant memory, it meant the bards singing your name every night long after you died. A Roman Emperor could become a God, and in so doing become immortal. A Roman soldier did not aspire to immortality. At best, the men who knew him might murmur his name sometimes after he was gone. Every Celt, no matter what his station, knew that he could become a Hero by his deeds, and that the bards would sing his name around the fires and make his deeds ring down the years.

The Celtic women were different too. Many fought beside their men or when their men were injured or helpless, but not for the joy of fighting. Women seldom went on cattle-raids or invasions, but those who did were met by many women fighting ferociously to defend their homes and friends. Roman women did not fight at all, not with weapons a soldier would recognize.

I looked again at Cuchullain. He believed he would die young, and that his life would be glorious. No wonder he was in a hurry. And what else should the boy do? Farm? Be a fisherman? Let those who can, fish, and let those who can fight, do so. The boy had a talent, that talent had a value, and there were all too many ready to test their skill against his. I saw waste and destruction in what he intended, but I was always a foreigner, no matter where I went. What right had I to look down at him?

'What about Emer?' I asked.

'She will be here when I return.'

'No doubt, but will she still be yours when you do?'

'She is mine now, as I am hers. She understands why I must go.' No doubt, no doubt, I thought, but she was beautiful, rich, and had a smile that would turn the thoughts of a standing stone to lechery. I did not think she would lack for suitors while he was gone. If I did not find sufficient distraction I was likely to be one of them myself. I had the sudden sensation that he could read my thoughts on my face.

'Shall I mention to any persistent visitors that Cuchullain's shoes are behind the door already?'

He smiled again, a happy smile. 'Get to know her better, Leary. She would like you, although I think you'll soon see that she doesn't need much help from you or any man. She is frightened of nothing.'

He hadn't seen how I felt. There was nothing else to say. I raised my hand in farewell. He surprised me. He bent over, grasped my arm and pulled me to my feet. I seemed to tower over him, but he did not step back. As well as being tactless, Cuchullain had no sense of social proprieties. It was up to me to move, either to retreat and wave or advance and embrace him. I chose to advance, and he held himself tight against me for a moment before turning and walking away without looking back. I thought perhaps that he was crying, but more likely he was planning his departure.

I turned, and saw Conor coming towards me. He looked agitated. He waved me to come to meet him, and then started talking before he was close enough to be heard properly. I walked quickly towards him to catch what he said. '. . . and don't let him do anything stupid.'

'What do you want me to do?'

He looked at me as if I were stupid, whereas I am only a little deaf. 'As I said, take Cuchullain to Skiatha.'

I looked at Cuchullain's retreating back. 'He told me he has to go alone.'

'What does he know about it?' growled Conor. 'He's a child. I don't expect you to stay with him once he's arrived and you've tucked him up in bed, but make sure he gets there without getting lost or falling off a cliff or being eaten by wolves or killed by Connaughtmen. Deliver him to the coast at least, then come back again, all right?'

I went after Cuchullain.

# 20

The journey took two weeks. We stayed in cottages on the way, stopping wherever we happened to be at dusk and knocking on the nearest door. Owen had often told me that the Ulstermen regarded hospitality as more sacred than marriage or property, and (not surprisingly) I didn't believe him. I was wrong. Instead of being sent on our way with a few suspicious arrows whizzing past our ears, as would have been the case in, say, Carthage or Tuscany, we were never made less than welcome. Sometimes the cottages were empty. These houses had bread and beer placed outside for the hungry traveller. When the cottages were occupied we were welcomed like long-lost children, and on more than one occasion the name that the Ulstermen have for their country, 'the land of the friendly thighs', came true for me. Maybe the road from Emain Macha to Skiatha's island is dotted with little fair-haired Gael-Romans, I don't know. If the same thing happened to Cuchullain he didn't speak of it. Women were not a subject for discussion with him. Besides, he had Emer, and once he had her he seemed to lose interest in others.

Owen had been upset when he learnt that Cuchullain was going away, and furious when he found out that I was going too and that he was not. He appealed directly to Conor, who told him to stop wasting his time. Owen was not yet prominent enough to tell the King that he would do what he felt like doing, and so contented himself with telling me anything that he could think of about Skiatha, her island, and everything possible that we were likely to meet on the way. By the time that Cuchullain and I left Emain Macha I was the best-informed chariot driver ever.

We arrived at the cliff-top in the middle of the morning. The sun had burnt the dew off the grass and felt warm on my back. I watched the waves roll lazily onto the shore below me, breaking into handfuls of white foam that the rocks at the cliff-foot then tossed up towards us. A bowshot away, Skiatha's dark island pushed up out of the water, looming above the cliff where we stood. It rose up away from us, in the shape of a giant slipper of which we were approaching the heel. At the top of the heel, a great stone fort rose up above the ocean, protected on three sides by the sea and approachable only by the hill that we looked up. It was practically impossible to approach unseen, and absolutely impossible to attack unless the attacking force could fly or were indifferent to their losses, which would have been crippling. It was said by the local people (and Owen, endlessly, once he knew I was going there) that Skiatha's fort had been the last redoubt of the Fomorians in Ireland before they were finally driven into the sea after the battle at Moytura, where the Great God Laeg came back from across the sea and led the Tuatha De Danann to victory.

(This was the same Laeg with whom Dectera had her wedding-day experience, or didn't, depending where you stand on that issue. The Tuatha were his people, warlike nymphs and so on. Fomorians seemed to be some sort of ugly amphibious demon, a cross between a contrary octopus and a bad-tempered Minotaur with no sense of hygiene. I once served under a centurion who was one.)

If Fomorians actually existed and Skiatha's island had really been theirs, then I felt that they must have decided to leave of their own accord, or else they were overthrown by treachery or magic, for the island could only otherwise be taken by a frontal assault. I would not have followed a King who would ask his warriors to attack such a fort, even to defeat Fomorians. Death with glory is one thing. Waste is entirely another. Attacking Skiatha's island would have been just a noisy form of suicide.

As Cuchullain and I stood at the cliff edge, looking across at the island, we heard footsteps behind us. We both turned, to see a tall, red-haired boy coming towards us. He was armed with a businesslike sword, and looked well able to use it. My hand was on my sword pommel when I felt Cuchullain touch my arm. He walked forward to the newcomer and saluted him.

'I am Cuchullain. My companion is Leary. We have come to learn from Skiatha.'

The red-head saluted back and looked at us appraisingly. 'I am Ferdia of Leinster. I am a pupil of Skiatha's.'

He had a ready smile, and he saluted us again before walking past us to look at the bridge.

The channel between the island and the mainland was perhaps half a spear-throw. The only way of crossing over was an old and narrow rope-and-plank bridge. I have seen more impressive crotchet-work in the hands of old women.

'Is it strong enough?' I asked. Ferdia grinned.

'Oh yes,' he said. 'It won't break. That isn't the problem.'

'It isn't?' It certainly looked like a problem to me.

He gestured towards the bridge. 'Watch,' he said.

I watched. He was right. The bridge never stayed in one position for any length of time. One moment it was still, then it would sway wildly among the gusts coming up off the sea. The high cliffs so close together seemed to funnel the wind so that it became stronger, in the way that water flows faster through a narrow channel than through a broad one, and the bridge undulated like a drunken dancer's arm as the wind pushed it up, sideways and then down again. I watched it carefully, to see if I could work out a pattern to its movements. After a few minutes I realized it didn't have one, that it was as random as it was malevolent.

I saw some boys on the far side and heard a noise that sounded like jeering. Ferdia smiled as he waved back at them in an insulting way. 'More of Skiatha's pupils,' he said. 'We always come down to watch people crossing.'

'There can't be much for you to do around here then,' I said.

Ferdia grunted with amusement. 'Oh, there's plenty to do all right. But we drop everything when someone is crossing. It's good sport. If I was on the island, I'd be with them.' He cupped his hands and shouted across the gorge. 'Cormac Tinyprick! Come to watch how a man does it?'

'Ferdia! I thought it was a girl come to visit us! Learnt to fly while you were away?'

'Like a bird. Stay and see how it's done!'

'That should be useful when you fall off! We wouldn't miss it!'

'When I get over there it'll be you who needs the wings!' Ferdia bawled offhandedly above the wind. I wasn't sure if it was just bravado or if he genuinely wasn't afraid. I didn't feel offhand at all.

'I wonder how many people have died trying,' I murmured, and then cursed myself. If it was that dangerous, I couldn't very well let Cuchullain try it alone.

'Has anyone ever failed to cross?' asked Cuchullain.

Ferdia told us what he knew. Crossings were usually good value to watch. No-one had actually died attempting the bridge in the three months since he arrived on the island, but several had come close, and there were any number of stories from the past telling of the unwary and the inept and the plain stupid who had tried it without proper respect and gone spinning into the water. I lay on my stomach and looked down over the crumbling edge. Rocks like black teeth stuck up from the swirling green sea immediately below. You might survive such a fall, if you were lucky, and you missed the rocks, and you were a good swimmer, and the tide was with you, but I wouldn't have bet my bed on my chances.

'Hey! Ferdia you big ox! Watch those great flat feet! Mind you don't trip!'

Ferdia waved back with a wan smile and looked at the bridge, heaving a deep sigh. He wasn't hurrying to get to it. I started to feel a bit better about the churning in my stomach. I wasn't the only one.

'He's having a good think about it, he must be going to jump the whole thing in one go!' Some more boys arrived, skidding down the rocks in their haste. We heard their shouts. 'Has he fallen in yet?' 'We came as fast as we could.' 'Let's throw rocks at him when he's halfway!'

'They wouldn't do that, would they?' I asked.

Ferdia shrugged. 'They know how difficult the crossing is. They wouldn't throw rocks at us.' He looked thoughtful. 'Probably not, anyway.'

The time arrived when we could no longer say to ourselves that our hesitation was merely judicious preparation, a point which coincided with the start of loud organized jeering from the island. I was about to suggest to Ferdia that he went first, on the grounds that he had done it before and could show us the method, and was nerving myself to march at the bridge, full of outward confidence and an inward sinking feeling, when Cuchullain walked past me. I wondered if I should try to stop him, and then didn't.

Ferdia called after him. 'Be careful. It plays tricks.' Cuchullain paid no attention. He started to trot towards the bridge. As he reached it and took a couple of steps onto the narrow planks, the wind caught the end that he was on and made it snake wildly from side to side. He almost lost his footing, and only just steadied himself. I was quietly pleased, while being a little concerned for his safety.

He turned back to Ferdia. 'Thank you for trying to warn me,' he said. 'I was hasty. I should have had the courtesy to listen to your advice more closely.'

Ferdia made a dismissive gesture. 'It looks all right the first time you see it. It's only once you get to know it that you begin to see how tricky it is.'

Cuchullain nodded to him, and then looked at the bridge seriously. He took a few steps backwards, braced himself, and took off at a run. I realized what he was trying to do and moved forward to stop him, but it was far too late. He ran swiftly to the edge and sprinted along the planks. The wind stirred the section just in front of him, and he bounded above it like a hurdler in the Colosseum. His feet landed square in the centre of the bridge. As he landed he glanced back at us and opened his lips to let out a whoop of triumph. Ferdia stepped forward and began to shout a warning, but it was too late. Before the sound was out of his mouth the wind cracked the bridge like a whip and the centre flew upwards, catapulting Cuchullain back the way he had come. He rolled back along the bridge length almost all the way towards us to where it met the cliff and then fell over the side head-first. Ferdia and I ran to catch him but we were too late. I threw myself forward onto the cliff edge at the point where he had vanished. Lying face down in the dirt, I looked over the side. He was hanging from the bridge support a man's length beneath me.

'Are you all right?' I called.

He answered with a sound that was more animal than human, and then swung himself lithely over the beam and jumped up beside me. He was covered in brown dust. Blood trickled down his pale face from a cut high on his forehead, and he looked furious. This was not helped by a chorus of jeering and laughter carried on the wind from those on the island, by now grown to a crowd of about twenty.

'Ferdia! Who's your friend? Should you be letting him try this before he's old enough to walk properly?'

'He's even more of a useless cow-pat than you are!'

'Maybe if the two of you held hands you'd manage it better! Shall I send out my little sister to show you how it's done?' Cuchullain looked at me, daring me to laugh. I didn't mean to, but I suspect that the sight of his fierce expression at the taunts from across the water made me smile.

Something strange happened. I noticed for the first time in a while that his eyes were silver-grey, and at the moment of my noticing they darkened, as though the sun had shifted, moving from the colour of wood-fire ashes to the shade of charcoal, and a dull red point glowed deep at the centre of them as if a wind passed over embers in the night. The muscles in his face and

159

neck twisted so that his face became ugly and deep red with anger. He stepped away from me, holding one palm out as if forbidding me to come closer, and I heard his breathing, which whistled harsh and shrill through his throat like winter through a narrow stone doorway. He turned, and the sun caught his hair in a peculiar way which made it seem for a moment as if a line of fire burnt around his head.

In the bubbling marsh near Emain Macha I have sometimes seen devils dancing above humps of grass, shining purple and white flames. The same flickering fire seemed to dance around him.

He ran back a spear-throw's distance from the bridge, and then flung himself at it. He looked as if he intended to clear the whole chasm in one leap. Those on the island shouted insults, and began to laugh in preparation for when the boy would get bounced back to where he'd come from, or, better still, take an unexpected bath. I called out, but it was too late. His feet left the ground and he seemed to fly, impossibly far, so that he landed at the exact centre of the bridge. As he landed he bent his legs and leapt again, so that the bucking bridge, instead of flinging him backwards, threw him forwards, somersaulting him through the air to land safely on the other side with room to spare. There was a heartbeat's pause, and then everyone burst out cheering. The crowd ran to congratulate him, but something about the way he looked at them made them stop a yard short and mumble their admiration from a distance.

Then someone remembered Ferdia and me, and shouted so that they all turned to watch us. Ferdia had been here before, he had seen what the bridge could do, and he knew how he was going to deal with it. Advance a few steps, cling on tight while the bridge tried to throw him off, wait for it to calm down, then advance a little more until the next time. It wasn't heroic, it took time and effort, it drew roars of derision from the crowd on the island, but he knew that he could do it. I followed him, imitating his movements. Like him, I knew that I could not do what Cuchullain had done.

Once on solid ground, drenched with sweat from the effort of hanging on while the wind tried to wrestle us into the sea, I watched as Ferdia half-heartedly tried to wreak revenge on our tormentors, but they were not fools enough to stay around for him to catch them. He smiled and shrugged. 'It does not matter – anyway, we will all be on the hurling field this afternoon. My hurley will make friends with their shins and heads in that game or I am not Ferdia mac Damain of Leinster. Where is your friend?' I looked around, but Cuchullain was gone. Ferdia shrugged and picked up my pack. 'Don't worry, they'll have taken him to meet Skiatha. We'll soon see him again, the island isn't big enough to hide on for long. Come and wash off the journey.'

I went with him and we sluiced the dust off ourselves. We shared a frugal meal and talked about Cuchullain, and then I watched Ferdia ready himself for the game. He wrapped rough cloth strips around his right hand, to give better grip, he said. He tied a longer strip around his forehead. He gestured to it. 'Before I learnt this trick, no matter what I did, I had what seemed like a river running down my face. Skiatha laughed at me and said that red-heads always sweated the most, and then tied the cloth round my head. Since then I have learnt more in three months than in the previous three years, just through being able to see properly!' His open face smiled happily.

I smiled encouragingly. One should always applaud discovery. 'I find that seeing properly helps in most things.' We set off towards the hurling field. Other boys called to Ferdia as small groups converged on the field. I sat on a grass bank, and Ferdia joined a rowdy knot of boys, their skin browned darker than the ash of their hurleys. I didn't see Skiatha.

'May I watch with you?' asked a respectful voice. I looked down. A small boy was standing beside me. His arm was tied across his chest in a rough sling.

'What happened to you?' He shrugged. His face was like one of those stern unsmiling sculptures that Romans put up in front of their public buildings in order to inspire virtue. I straightened my shoulders.

'I broke it.'

'When?'

'This morning.'

'Does it hurt?'

He shrugged again and said nothing. He made me feel that I was the child and he the man. I asked him about Skiatha. The stone profile crumbled and he pointed with his undamaged arm. I looked, and saw a heavy-set woman coming around the side of the castle. Cuchullain was with her, carrying his hurley in his hand, still with his pack over one shoulder. They walked towards us without looking at each other.

'She permits him to walk at her side on the first day,' said the small voice beside me respectfully. 'Who is he?' I didn't answer.

She was as tall as me, and broader across the shoulders. Under the thick jerkin which was all she wore to protect her torso, she was heavily scarred from a hundred sword-cuts, and her arms were cross-laced white with them. She wore a flat metal cap which had a thin nose piece that continued in a deep scar running from the edge of her nostril down the side of her chin. Across her back, she wore two crossed swords, sharpened to an edge that would cut silk, arranged so that a handle protruded over each shoulder. When she fought she reached backwards with both arms and pulled out both swords at once. The blades slashed across each other as they flew forward, and then she would attack, using each sword as well as most men use one, so that facing her was like trying to fight a wheel spinning in front of you with a dozen blades tied to its rim. She was the fastest, strongest woman I have ever seen, and the most frightening. Only Maeve, the Queen of Connaught, was perhaps her equal. All her students would have died willingly in a moment for a flicker of her approval. She was, of course, no beauty. Her children had grown children of their own, and the sun and men's swords had weathered and cut her skin so that it looked like old polished leather. It was oiled to prevent an enemy getting a hold on her, and her face was always watchful. She was frightened of no-one and no thing. I never saw her smile.

'This is a new comrade come to stay with us,' she said, indicating Cuchullain. Her voice was deep, rough like water flowing over gravel. A sword pommel had once been driven into her throat, crushing the voice-pipe. A second later she had killed her attacker, hurrying to do it because she could hardly breathe. The wound had healed, but her voice was left a ruin. She stepped back, to allow the new arrival to introduce himself.

'My name is Cuchullain, and I ask your protection.'

The others in the group seemed to be waiting for Ferdia to say something. Ferdia saluted him. 'Welcome then, Cuchullain.' Other boys turned to watch. 'I am Ferdia. You have my protection. We shall be friends.' Ferdia gestured with his stick at the playing field. 'Do you play?'

It was an unnecessary question. All boys played, some better than others. Besides, Cuchullain carried his hurley in his hand. Ferdia was asking Cuchullain if he wanted to match skills with him. Perhaps the business at the bridge had hurt his pride more than he let show.

'I play,' said Cuchullain, dropping his pack and hefting the hurley from his left into his right hand.

'Then we shall indeed be friends!' Ferdia shouted. I found myself liking the big red-head enormously for no reason that I could think of straight away. He took Cuchullain by the arm and dragged him unresisting to the edge of the field. They held their hurleys up, ready for the ball to be thrown onto the pitch.

Skiatha's cracked voice rasped beside me. As she spoke, she stepped in front of me. She had come directly from the training field. I could smell fresh sweat from her, and her skin, smooth between the scars, glistened with oil and a fine sheen of dust.

'I am sorry that Ferdia has forgotten his manners,' she said, her ruined voice carrying to the boys across the field in the still warm air. 'It is customary, even in these benighted parts, to offer a new arrival water to wash off the dust and food for his stomach before dragging him into a game.'

She looked at Ferdia with what was obviously meant to be anger, and he grinned back. I could see that he took pride in being her favourite. Not that this entailed easier treatment for him. Quite the opposite: it meant she demanded higher standards of him than of anyone else. However, it also meant

163

that she found it difficult to be angry with him. On this occasion anger was justified. Ferdia had let his enthusiasm overcome his manners. He looked ruefully at Cuchullain.

'Skiatha is right. I am forgetting my obligations as your host. Please come and wash and eat first.'

Cuchullain looked up at him, and then over to Skiatha. 'You are indeed hospitable, and I thank you for it,' he said calmly. 'I am quite comfortable. Shall we now play the game?'

There was a few moments' startled silence while Skiatha looked at Cuchullain and the two boys looked at each other, and then Ferdia let out a roar of approval and clapped Cuchullain on the back so hard that it sent him flying forward onto the grass. He picked himself up, jogged to the centre of the field and picked up the ball. He flicked it onto the end of his hurley, drew the stick back and then hit the ball vertically upwards in one smooth, effortless motion. It flew up until it was almost out of sight, so that Skiatha and I had to squint to see it, and then it came down to land without a bounce on the end of Cuchullain's hurley. He looked up and saw that a tall boy was leaning against one of the goalposts, perhaps two spear-throws away. Again Cuchullain hit the ball, this time parallel to the ground and straight at the goal. The boy held out his hurley to prevent the ball crossing the line, but the force of the shot made him yelp with surprise and pain as it knocked the stick out of his hand.

There was a moment of stunned silence, then Ferdia let out a cheer which most of the other boys echoed. Several of the older boys, who had not seen what Cuchullain did at the bridge and who had wandered off, bored at the thought of the arrival of another small boy, trotted back to see what was happening. One of them collected a ball on his way and tossed it towards us. Cuchullain danced forward and caught it. He flicked the ball over the head of the first challenger and sidestepped round him, trapping it with his hurley at the moment that two much larger boys arrived at the same point. Anyone else would have been sent sprawling, but he feinted one way and then ran forward, sending one boy spinning sideways with a roll of his hip and colliding shoulder to shoulder with the other. Instead of being flattened Cuchullain appeared to take the bigger boy's weight and ride the impact so that the boy seemed to go over him without knocking him down and then crashed to the ground. It was a repeat of the scene that I had watched the first time I saw him, the day he arrived at Emain Macha. He turned to the goal and hit the ball clean between the posts without looking up.

Ferdia let out a glad whoop of excitement. 'He's on my team!' Skiatha shook her head.

'No,' she said, 'never on your team. No number of opponents could stand against you together. You must always be opposed, or there is no point to it.'

'Always opposed then. So be it.' Ferdia looked at Cuchullain appraisingly. Cuchullain looked straight back. 'Do you think you could do that again?' Ferdia said quietly.

Cuchullain smiled. 'Which bit?'

'Any of it. More, if you have it.'

'Of course.'

A red-headed boy called Maine, one of the seven Maines of Maeve and Ailell, jogged past with a ball. Ferdia whistled, and Maine hit the ball over to him. Ferdia bounced the ball three times on the end of his hurley. Then he pushed it forward, so that it landed in front of him and came to rest against Cuchullain's foot.

'Now try and score again,' Ferdia said softly. 'This time while I am in your way.'

Skiatha picked up the ball, stepped back, and threw it. The ball flew up and Cuchullain and Ferdia met where it landed, both of them yelling defiance at each other and the other boys who joined them there. The game dissolved into a mirage of shining dust. Skiatha watched them for a few minutes, and then turned away, smiling. As she did so I saw a raven settle on the ground beside her, watching the game intently, its head turned slightly to one side as if listening. Skiatha stood still, waiting to see what the bird would do. Each time Ferdia and Cuchullain clashed, it shifted from foot to foot in a way that in a human would have looked like excitement. Skiatha shrugged and was about to leave it and walk away when Ferdia called her back.

She waited as he came running across. He had taken a stick across his brow. Blood streamed down his forehead, soaking his sweatband and running into his eyes, making it difficult for him to see. Skiatha inspected the cut while he exclaimed impatiently for her to hurry so that he might rejoin the game. She took her time, growling at him to be patient, but she could see that it was only a scalp wound. She ripped some cloth from her skirt and tied it round his head, over the sweatband that was already there, to keep the blood out of his eyes.

As he ran back to the game Skiatha looked for the raven. It was still there. It made two or three hops towards the game, and then took off. It flew silently with slow beats of its wings towards where the action was hottest. Skiatha watched as the bird dipped low over Ferdia, easily distinguishable by his height and his golden head at the centre of the melee. It grabbed at him with its claws and Skiatha's makeshift bandage came off. The raven wheeled in the air and then beat its wings twice, which carried it to where Cuchullain ran with the ball on his hurley. As he drew back to hit the ball, the raven opened its claws and the bloodstained rag landed in Cuchullain's face.

I felt a cold shiver trickle down my back as I heard the boys laughing at the bird. I saw Cuchullain exclaim in surprise as he pulled the cloth off his face, and heard him join in the laughter. Then he looked up for the raven, bouncing the ball on the end of his hurley, shouting to Ferdia to watch. Skiatha saw that he meant to knock the raven out of the sky. She opened her lips to shout, but the bird was quicker. It spun above his head with the flick of a wingtip and flew straight at Skiatha. Cuchullain hesitated. He could not hit the ball at the bird for fear of hitting Skiatha too. It let out a screech and its wingtips brushed her cheek as it flew past. Her hand went up instinctively to touch where she had felt the feathers, and her fingers came away stained with Ferdia's blood.

She looked at her reddened fingertips, and then at the still-laughing boys. Ferdia said something which made Cuchullain throw the bloody rag at him. Ferdia threw it back, and they wrestled, trying to force it into each other's face. Then they tired of that, and separated, laughing and gasping for breath. The blood flowed freely again down Ferdia's broad cheek from the cut in his scalp, carmine against his fair skin. All the boys laughed at Cuchullain, smiling as he held the bandage, while Ferdia's blood stained his hands and dried black under his nails.

# 21

I stayed at Skiatha's island for a week, watching Cuchullain find out, for the first time, what it is like to be tested. None of the boys at Emain Macha had been anything like his equal. The boys on Skiatha's island didn't know his reputation and feared no-one. Ferdia especially could match him in almost every respect, and others came close. It was obviously good for him. Being beaten is character-forming, or so my father always said, and returning to beat your conqueror is the sweetest feeling that a man can have with his clothes on. (The Ulstermen usually fought naked – 'sky-clad', they called it – like Greeks. Anyway, Cuchullain enjoyed coming back at Ferdia and beating him, clothed or not.)

The boys came from all over Ireland. It seemed that the rivalries between the provinces didn't matter at Skiatha's. Boys became fast friends who would certainly meet in battle soon as men. Ferdia was from Leinster, was apparently a kinsman of Queen Maeve, but saw no difficulty in befriending Cuchullain, who was kin to Maeve's greatest enemy. It wouldn't happen in Rome.

I was out of place, as I didn't train with the boys and my only accomplishment was with horses, of which there were none on the island as they weren't keen on crossing the bridge, so I was really just wasting my time and the boys'. I felt I had to watch Cuchullain for a while, to make sure he really didn't need me. After a week even I had to admit that, not only did he not need me, he had forgotten that I existed. I took my leave of Skiatha and went back to Emain Macha, making sure to stop at the same cottages we had visited on the way out, in the hope that they might still think of me fondly.

A year passed. There was no word from Cuchullain, no message. I didn't miss him exactly, because we had never really talked very much. I just felt as though I was walking in circles rather than from or to somewhere. I stayed away from Emer as well. The court went to Forgall's castle a couple of times and I went with them because Conor told me to. While we drank with her father, Emer sent messages to me, asking me to see her in her rooms. I knew she wanted to ask about Cuchullain and I knew I didn't want to discuss anything with her, especially not Cuchullain and especially not in her bedroom. I pleaded drunkenness and illness and anything else I could think of and sent messages back instead, telling her the little I knew. I felt like a boy, afraid to talk to the girl he secretly likes best, but I knew that the best way for me to get her out of my mind was not to see her. She was Cuchullain's. That was an end to it. The requests to visit her stopped, so I supposed she was satisfied or understood.

Then, one winter day when the everlasting rain was at its most sodden and chilly, a horseman arrived at Emain Macha. It was in the aftermath of one of Conall's parties, the calm after the storm. I was sitting drinking with Ulinn, a tall red-haired woman who had befriended me soon after I arrived in Ulster. We had briefly tried being lovers, but it hadn't worked very well. Fortunately being failed lovers had made us better friends. She could arm-wrestle better than I could and drank me under the table two nights out of three, so we suited each other very well. Talking to Ulinn, I noticed the horseman arrive, but didn't recognize him until he came close to me and said my name. It was Ferdia. He was exhausted and I should have let him sleep, but I was hungry for news.

He humoured me and found strength from somewhere to join in the party Ulinn and I put on to celebrate his visit. We sat up most of the night, defying a goatskin of Conall's latest paralysing medicine and talking about Cuchullain. Ferdia had filled out considerably since the last time I saw him, and was now broad-chested and had a fine scar on his cheek (which Cuchullain put there), and the beginnings of an impressive beard. His laugh was as loud and as infectious as before, and there was a charm in his eyes and his manner that brought people near to him. Most of these people were now lying in a ragged heap on the floor around us, thanks to Conall's hospitality.

Ulinn had gone to bed, allowing us to talk over old times without feeling self-conscious. Ferdia turned his cup slowly between his scarred, freckled hands. 'We trained or played every day until after sundown. Most of the others gave up or got bored or collapsed with the heat, but we kept going.' He tapped a fingernail against the goblet. 'It was always too easy for me till I met Cuchullain. I am bigger and stronger than him, but Cuchullain is faster, and we cancel each other out.' Ferdia smiled. 'We ran around the field until we couldn't breathe, then we stood in the centre and tried to turn each other around by using the ends of our sticks with the ball on the ground, then we fought for high balls hit by Maine, then we stood buckle to buckle and battered at each other using our sticks like swords, then we hit the ball at each other standing still, just twenty steps apart, then we—'

He stopped, shrugging his shoulders, inviting me to under-stand. I felt a curious jealousy.

'Sounds like a perfect relationship,' I said. Ferdia laughed. I don't think the edge of bitterness reached him.

'Better than that,' he laughed. 'It was . . . exhilarating.' He touched the scar on his face. 'Painful as well. He always seemed to know what I was going to do, and yet I could anticipate him too, and so we chased each other like a dog after his tail until we were both exhausted. Those nights after Cuchullain first arrived, I slept as though I were dead.'

'He has that effect on everyone,' I said. Ferdia smiled.

'The day he arrived, I knew I had found what I came to Skiatha's island for,' he said. He arranged himself more comfortably.

Conall, sleeping stertorously beside me, let go a fart that would have stopped a charging Minotaur in its tracks. The man immediately behind him woke up choking and, not sure what had happened but determined that he wanted no part of it, rolled awkwardly away while breathing as though there was a scarf wrapped too tight around his throat. Ferdia and I got up more steadily and went to get some fresh air. As we stood, Ferdia's armour creaked like two dry flints rubbed together. The night outside was clear and cold. We pulled our clothes tight around us and walked. 'Go on,' I said. Ferdia's voice was low and serious but I could hear the intensity of his memories.

'We trained endlessly, harder than I would have believed possible. I could feel my strength grow and my speed increasing, and I knew that I was gaining in skill every day. Cuchullain matched me blow for blow and skill for skill, so that sometimes I wanted to shout with frustration.'

'I know that feeling too,' I said with a wry smile, which Ferdia returned.

'But more often I just laughed and ran back to the game again. Soon Skiatha took to handicapping us to slow us down, tying one hand behind our backs, loading stones on our backs, but each time she found something new to do to us we would find new ways of getting round it. Eventually she gave the other boys to her sergeant to watch while they played, and took us off to the war field.'

I remembered the scarred woman with the broken voice, sword-handles over each shoulder like antlers. Ferdia did a recognizable imitation of Skiatha speaking. '"Now you stop playing,"' he rasped. '"So far you have fought each other with sticks. Now you will fight with swords."' He returned to his own voice. 'She had to let us train with real weapons. The only concessions she insisted on were that we wore helmets and that the swords were blunt. Apart from that, she encouraged us to do everything as if we were enemies on a battlefield. We hacked at each other as if our honour depended upon it.' He absently touched the scar on his cheek. 'I sometimes practised on my own, trying out new ideas to surprise him, and I know he did the same. We watched each one of us trying to outwit the other.'

Ferdia seemed to become distant, withdrawn, remembering. His past, Cuchullain's past. A past I had no part of. 'We became like brothers. The other boys, my friends from before he came, they drifted away from us. We had no need of them. None of them could stand up to us, and we needed no opponent but each other, so there was not much contact. I was sometimes sad at this, and would go and try to be friends with them, but they would smile and ask how Cuchullain was, and I knew that they knew that I had moved away from them. They were still friends to me, but Cuchullain was more than a friend.'

He was silent for a few moments. 'Then what?' I asked. He laughed.

'Skiatha finally thought we were ready to start learning the Hero-Feats. First, she made us show her everything we could do. We both showed off everything we knew and a few we didn't, making a hash of them and hurting ourselves in the process. She laughed at us. From anyone else, I think that laughter would have been wounding, but from Skiatha it was inspiring, for we knew that soon she would teach us everything she knew.'

'What are Feats?' I asked.

'Things on the end of your legs,' he said, and smiled. I cuffed him round the head. He ducked, and carried on. 'First, she showed us the Apple Feats.' I must have looked blank. 'Spinning an apple into the air,' he explained, 'and putting three arrows into it before it lands, then spinning it in the air on the blade of a knife so that the peel falls to the ground but the apple stays on the knife.' I tried not to look sceptical. His expression seemed to challenge me not to believe him. 'She showed us the Feat of Running On Sharpened Spear-points, starting with bundles of small blunt spears, like sharp pebbles underfoot, progressing to men's throwing spears, and so on up the scale, until we could jump from sharpened spear to sharpened spear without falling or drawing blood. She made us practise the Salmon-Leap until

172

we could do it blindfold; the Blinding Shout until our ears rang and our throats were raw; the Throw Around Corners; the Rope of Feats, where we had to balance on our toes practising our sword-strokes while she tried to knock us off with javelins; the Pierced Flagstones, where we danced for hours over the fire until our feet wept tears of blood and water through skin cracked and blistered black by the heat; and she showed us the thousand thrusts and cuts and throws that a warrior needs to know if he is to stay alive long enough to become a Champion, to win not just every time but well, too.'

I waited for him to go on. He seemed to be waiting to see what I'd say. 'I'd like to see those things,' I said finally, as neutrally as possible. He nodded.

'You will,' he said. He carried on. 'It is tradition that Skiatha always gives each of her pupils a gift when they are ready to leave. Cuchullain and I spent the last day fighting with staves, until we were both covered in dust and bruises. Skiatha left us to it for the afternoon. As the heat started to go out of the day she returned.' His voice became hoarse again. '"Ferdia,"' he croaked. 'I limped up to her and took what she offered me. It was this jerkin.' I looked at it. I hadn't really taken it in before. 'It is made of horn. The pieces interlock, as if woven, and when I took it from Skiatha it was supple and hung limp from my hand. I put it on. It was comfortable, but as I moved the armour creaked as the horn moved against itself. Cuchullain laughed, and slapped me on the shoulder. "You'll never creep up on anyone unnoticed again!" he said.'

Ferdia paused again. I felt that he wasn't waiting for me to speak, but was remembering. I said nothing. 'We admired my horns for a while. Then Skiatha held out a spear to Cuchullain. I recognized it at once, even though I had never seen it before. It was the Gae Bolga. Cuchullain recognized it too. We both looked at it like idiots, as if we were afraid of it.'

'Everyone is afraid of it,' I said. 'Owen told me the story.' I watched Ferdia, wondering how he must have felt. The Gae Bolga is the trophy reserved for the greatest Champion, and Skiatha gave it to Cuchullain. Losing it must have been hard for

Ferdia to swallow. There was distance around him like smoke as he talked.

'It is as thick as my arm, and the shaft is taller than I am. It is made from the bones of a sea-monster that was cast up on the island shores. The point is covered with hundreds of sharp barbs, which, if thrust into a man, reach out and fill his whole body and make it impossible to remove. The spear can only be freed by pushing it right through the body in which it is trapped.' Exactly as Owen had described it. 'It sings as it enters a man.' He took another drink and a cloak of tiredness settled on his broad shoulders. 'Cuchullain tested it in his hand. Skiatha shook her head, and handed him a leather thong. "The spear is thrown with the foot," she said. For the rest of the day we practised separately, me getting used to my new armour, Cuchullain learning the ankle-throw for the Gae Bolga.' He looked wistful. 'That was the first time since the day he arrived that we did not train together. I stood for a while and watched him. This was one thing which we could not share. I watched as the spear was hurled back and forth, over and over again, until Cuchullain could hardly stand with tiredness. I will never forget the sound that the spear sang to me as it passed through the air, a single high note that became more shrill as it passed by and then faded as it hit the straw target. The next day I left to go home, without saying goodbye.'

His story was finished. We had walked all around the castle and were by the gate again. A sleepy sentry looked at us and grunted something that might have been a greeting from under his blanket. I was cold and I wanted a drink. I pulled Ferdia back towards the Hall. He shook his head. 'I need to rest.'

He walked towards his room, and I watched his back until he turned the corner and was out of sight.

# 22

Owen said to me more than once that there is more than
one way to tell a story. He meant different oratorical styles,
different levels of address, depending on audience and situation.
At the time I thought he meant different degrees of truth, and
disagreed with him. Now, I'm not so sure. Two men who witness
the same event may have different views of it, and so tell
different stories of it. If they have different purposes in telling
the story, it may be more different still.

The bards tell how, when Cuchullain returned from Skiatha's
island and his time in Alba, clutching the Gae Bolga, full
of stories and with a fistful of tricks and Feats to show off, he
first had to rest for a while to recover from his wounds and to
prepare himself for the test that winning Emer was sure
to be. When he had rested sufficiently he armed himself and
went to Forgall's castle to ask for Emer for his wife. He was sent
away without Emer's hand or tasting her father's hospitality.
Cuchullain swore in front of the castle walls that men had tried
to assassinate him on Skiatha's island, and that before the last
one died he had confessed that Forgall had paid them to do
it. Cuchullain's duty to the father of his intended bride was
therefore void. He would take her by force. The bards say that

he stood in his chariot outside the walls of Forgall's castle and spoke to him at length across the fortifications. At the end, Forgall challenged Cuchullain to take Emer or give up asking for her, for he would never surrender her. For a year and a day, Cuchullain tried to get past the defences, but they were too strong. Then he told Leary that he would attack Forgall's castle as a Champion and drive Forgall and his men before him as a herdsman drives goats. Leary harnessed Cuchullain's horses and dressed him in his armour, and the sickle chariot was prepared, and Cuchullain attacked the castle as the sun rose. He drove around the castle with the left side to the wall until the men inside could bear the insult no more and some of them jumped out to do battle with him, but Cuchullain did a mighty Thunder-Feat and of the three hundred who left the castle to fight him only three came back. Then Cuchullain made his Salmon-Leap from the chariot rim, clearing the walls and the three inner enclosures. He dealt three strokes at three groups of nine men each, killing eight with each stroke and leaving the middle man untouched. These three were Forgall's sons. Forgall ran across the rampart to get away from Cuchullain, but fell and broke his neck. Cuchullain broke down the door of the room where Forgall had hidden Emer and her sister, scooped them up along with their weight in gold and silver, and leapt out over the triple ramparts again. They raced the chariot away from the castle, pursued by all the remaining men. Leary slowed the chariot so that they would catch up one at a time, and as they did so Cuchullain killed them. At the ford at Glondath a group of a hundred caught them, and Cuchullain killed them all by luring the armoured men into a deep part of the river and killing with his slingshot those who managed to escape the current, including Calatin, a kinsman of Forgall's from Connaught. Then he did the same at the fords at Crufoit, at Ath Imfoit, and at Albine, just as he had said that he would to Emer at their first meeting.

That's how the bards tell it, but of course, that isn't exactly how it was. The bards never let their lack of knowledge get in the way of the story. They weren't there. I was.

The day Cuchullain arrived back from Alba he demanded that I take him to see Emer. I drove the chariot up to Forgall's castle. A hundred truculent-looking spearmen looked down at us from within easy throwing distance, and so I was naturally delighted when Cuchullain bellowed a courtly greeting.

'Forgall, you miserable pig-fucker! Where are your assassins? Where are the men you sent to kill me now?'

Forgall appeared on his ramparts and looked down at Cuchullain and me. A lot more of his men were beside him.

'It was not me who sent those men, Hound. You cannot blame me for every man who attacks you.'

'Not for every man, fake Gaulish trader, just for the ones paid by you to do it!'

Forgall didn't speak for a few seconds. 'What do you want?'

'To marry your daughter, or no-one!'

Forgall drew himself up. 'Then you will die a bachelor, because Emer will not marry you while she is my daughter.'

Cuchullain grinned up at him, but his eyes were hard stones.

'It could be arranged for Emer not to have a father. It could be arranged for her father to be stuffed up a pig's arse in a hundred separate bits!'

'Would his daughter still love you then?' asked Forgall mildly, as if Cuchullain wasn't really insulting him but making a suggestion. I murmured from Cuchullain's side that Forgall had a point. Slaughtering the intended bride's father isn't the preferred wedding gift for every bride. Cuchullain brushed me aside.

'If Emer knew that her father had arranged to have Cuchullain murdered, then yes, I think she might understand my anger. I will take that chance. Anyway, she is promised to me, when I have fulfilled all the conditions she set me.'

I wondered if it was a good time to suggest to Cuchullain that his ideas about what women will and will not do, particularly when men tell them that they must do something, most particularly so in Ulster, were perhaps somewhat optimistic. I decided not to. Forgall's men were gathering on the battlements and growling at us while hefting spears and notching their arrows. It wasn't discussion time. It was time to retire with as much grace as extreme haste would allow.

Besieging the castle a year and a day, hogwash. A couple of hot and dusty afternoons, more like. We spent a couple of nights trying to sneak into the castle, hoping to be able to grab Emer and take her with us. The second night Forgall's men almost caught up with us, and we went back out over the wall again with no Emer and a barrow-load of arrows hissing towards our backsides.

'Enough of this tiptoeing about in the night,' said Cuchullain. 'Tomorrow we go in and get her.'

'Oh good,' I said. 'Hundreds of them against two of us. That should be an interesting and swift and painful way to get killed. Can't we just go home?'

Cuchullain looked at me. Lights were dancing in his eyes. 'Always finish the game, my friend,' he said. 'Always finish the game.'

'Horseshit,' I said, and got ready to die.

It wasn't the left side of the chariot that bothered Forgall's men, it was our bare arses pointing at them. But I suppose that was too obvious for bards to tell, far better to have something really offensive, like the wrong side of a chariot. The chariot looked like a ball of knives by the time I'd finished preparing it, and the shields tied to the sides made a noise like the heavens colliding, so that the poor buggers who tried to fight him were so deafened and confused that half of them just ran onto the wheels without realizing what was happening. The horses stamped on the ones who managed to avoid the wheels and Cuchullain ran round the chariot behind me and slashed at anyone left alive. Then he galloped up to the walls, jumped onto the horses' backs and then jumped off them again, over the walls like a monkey. I scrambled up after him a lot less quickly, swiped at a couple of soldiers that he'd forgotten to kill and ran after him as fast as I could, knowing that we were trapped and almost certain to die, and cursing him for a fool. Ahead of me I saw men charge up to him and then lose their nerve, pausing while they remembered the stories, so that he killed them while they tried to make up

178

their minds whether he was human or not. Every one he killed made it harder for the next to succeed. He wasn't entirely stupid though. He killed a lot of men, but he didn't kill Emer's brothers.

Then every man left in the fort rallied and ran at us in a body, and he yelled at me to jump down off the walls, and we ran across the bloody grass back to the chariot and I was driving like a lunatic, and spears and arrows were going past us like angry wasps, and Cuchullain was picking off the leading pursuers with his bow from the back of the chariot, laughing like a madman and calling to Emer to admire his skill. The major skill as far as I could see was in not falling off the chariot, which was bucking like a heat-maddened bull-calf as we drove as fast as the horses could gallop on the bumpy road, but he did appear to be hitting a lot of them, as the numbers after us seemed to decrease every time I looked back. They had to stop to let some of the others catch up and then charge after us again. Then some of them pulled level with us, and Cuchullain stood on the rim of our chariot and jumped across the gap with a roar of excitement, knocked them out of the chariot, turned it round and raced straight back at our pursuers. Sensibly enough they parted to let him through, hacking at him as he went past. Then he let out that shout again, the one that means he's about to do something really stupid such as charge a vastly superior force head on and unarmed, and meanwhile I was wrestling with the horses to stop the chariot being pulled into a ravine, and by the time I looked round everyone seemed to be dead or dying except him. Not hundreds, it's true, but many more than one. I then saw Emer by the gate. Her hands were clenched into tight fists and her bitten lips stood out against her bloodless cheeks like spilt wine on marble. Cuchullain took her hand and they went together to the castle at Muirthemne given to him by Conor. We heard that they were married, but we did not see him again for a long while. Then he brought her to Emain Macha, and they were married properly, and we floated their happiness on islands of food and a sea of wine.

I asked Emer on her wedding day if Cuchullain had fulfilled

her list of impossible conditions. She only smiled. I think I understood. I saw the way she looked at him. Anyone who saw that look would know that he had done everything that was necessary.

I remember her face, and the way they drank the sight of each other like parched animals. Her face turned to Cuchullain and not to me left me feeling as if something precious had been torn slowly from deep within my chest. I feel the ache of its absence still.

Oh yes, there's more than one way to tell a story.

And there was something else too. Cathbad sent for me a few weeks later. I had not been in his house before. Somehow I expected it to be dark and slightly damp, and festooned with bits of dried animal and all the paraphernalia of wizardry. It wasn't. It was dry, warm and cheerful, and there wasn't anything to tell a visitor Cathbad's occupation. I sat opposite the old druid with no great sense of expectation – I felt like a rather dim schoolboy who was about to get the 'disappointed in you' lecture. His young wife brought us something to drink, smiled at her husband in a way that any man would welcome, and withdrew.

Cathbad was unusually thin, but he held himself erect both sitting and standing. His brow was heavily wrinkled at the best of times. As he looked at me now I felt it was even more creased than usual.

'You don't have an awful lot of time for me, do you?' he said. His voice was a dry whisper. It wasn't a question, but it wasn't an accusation either. I fancied he smiled as he spoke. He gestured my insincere protests aside. 'Don't worry,' he said. 'I don't mind. It makes no difference.' I began to pay attention. This was new – I had never heard a priest say that his religion didn't matter.

He paused, as if counting his words in advance.

'Cuchullain killed a man at the ford, a man named Calatin.'

I shrugged. 'Maybe. He kills a lot of men, often at fords.'

Cathbad nodded. I got the impression he was smiling even though his face didn't alter. 'Calatin's wife was pregnant. She went into labour at the news of her husband's death. The delivery was difficult. There were three children, but they were

180

born all at once, joined at the hip and back. The birth killed her. She died cursing Cuchullain.'

I almost shrugged again, then didn't. 'That's sad.'

Cathbad looked out the window, as if hearing a distant voice. 'The child, or the children, whichever you call it, was taken away by the midwife, and has not been seen since. The midwife is known to me. She is said to have power, and she holds me in no esteem. The child was born of a dead father and a dying mother. It has three minds in one body, and the only thing its mother left it was a curse on Cuchullain. They will do great harm to Ulster, I have seen it.' He paused. I waited. He seemed to have gone into some sort of distant trance. I cleared my throat. He blinked, and was back with me again.

'Should I be concerned?' I said.

He looked at me. 'You may not think so.' He smiled. 'I had a dream. The dream told me that the Daughters of Calatin would come to you soon.' He raised an amused eyebrow. 'I see from your expression that you do not put much store in dreams.'

I didn't say anything. He stood up and put a hand on my shoulder as I rose too and stood in front of him.

'I have been wrong in the past, and doubtless will be again. I hope I am on this occasion. But if I had not told you, my mind would not have been easy.' His hand squeezed my shoulder with surprising strength. 'Forgive an old man for bothering you.'

I mumbled something about being grateful and left.

I met Ulinn just outside his doorway and within a few heart-beats I had forgotten what the druid had said.

I would remember it again, soon.

# 23

The King woke up one morning after another feast and looked around through red-rimmed and bleary eyes. I had been awake for just a few minutes, and was lying very still while concentrating on not moving. The King moved his boot off the oak table with a crash that made me open my eyes the width of a hair, a precaution against stray light creeping in and shoving a stiletto into my head. It was obvious even to my dulled brain that Conor saw nothing that pleased him. The sight of a hundred sleeping, crapulous, farting warriors slumped amongst the remains of last night's banquet had never troubled him before, but power has strange effects on men. Ask Caligula. Ask Tiberius.

The King was in bad temper but excellent voice.

'Get up!'

A dozen men immediately cried out in distress, cursing and begging him not to shout. Conor scowled at them and shouted again, louder.

'Get up! You stinking unwashed pile of cowardly bog-dwellers! Am I just talking to myself here? Is there anyone even vaguely like a man in this Hall, because Laeg himself knows that there isn't anyone here who looks anything at all like a

Champion! Wall-eyed squint-faced sons of prolapsed hag-crones and cretinous senile pig-keepers! Worthless cowardly ignorant shit-bucket dwellers! Wake up!'

Conor undeniably had a way with a figure of speech, but the last bit was unnecessary. He stood on the long main table and walked along it bellowing like Stentor, kicking out hard at anyone within reach. Those revellers who had fallen asleep across the table suffered terribly, while those who had had the foresight to slide under it were relatively safe. However, as the men above them swore and jumped painfully away from his flying boots, some whimpering for Conor to talk quietly, others roaring back at him, those underneath the table were trodden on and had cups of rancid wine upset on them and lumps of greasy meat dropped on them and in one unlucky case got pissed on, so within moments the Hall was a cacophony of cursing, dripping, still half-drunk men trying to work out if they were being attacked and if so where the enemy was and where in Hades is my sword and what's all the noise for anyway can't a man get some sleep?

I rolled away from trouble and sat propped up against the wall. My head hurt very much and I was going to sit very still and quiet (if I was permitted) until it calmed down. The King was still in a fury and his every shout hummed and scraped in my head like the clash of swords on metal shields, but at least I was out of range.

'You fat capons!' raged the King. 'Drunken slack-mouthed feeble-brained weak-armed shit-beetles! Any of the Boys' Troop has more dignity, more balls, is more use to Ulster on his own than the lot of you put together! I wouldn't put you in a pigsty for fear of offending the fleas that live in the straw, let alone the upset and embarrassment it would cause the pigs to have to associate with you! Fomorian gut-worms! What use are you? The rest of Ireland laughs at the Red Branch. Its so-called Champions have grown complacent and slobbish! They no longer drink for valour, they drink to forget that they are a shadow of what they once were!'

His words were starting to penetrate into men's brains, and I began to wonder what Conor was up to. A Caligula or a Nero may swear and curse his captains with impunity, knowing that they would have no choice but to listen silently and shake in their shoes, but a Celtic King is no Roman Emperor. He is first amongst equals. He owes his position to respect and honour alone, and depends on his Champions for support, which is honour-given but can be withdrawn. Conor was insulting his warriors' manhood, which was good grounds for a fight in most countries, and the men in the Hall of the Red Branch that morning had proved many times that they needed no grounds at all for a fight but would do it just for the fun of it. I had thought the King to be a clever man. I hoped he knew what he was doing.

'You are all drunken pigs, worthless cowards! Scavengers, leeches, maggots, parasites!' screamed the King, who was losing his voice. 'Who last killed an enemy of Ulster? Which is not to ask which of you last killed one of his fellow drunks in a brawl. Which of you has defended Ulster's honour within living memory?'

There was a pause. The sound of angry muttering and drawn swords rasping through metal scabbards filled the space which the King left. After a few moments he spoke again more quietly with a withering sarcasm that made even my skin seem to fit badly, and I wasn't a Champion and it wasn't particularly aimed at me.

'I don't hear any reply. Perhaps you've forgotten how to speak as well as how to fight. I asked, who last killed a man for any reason that mattered?' He was almost whispering. 'Why do you hesitate? Is it so long ago that you did something useful that you have forgotten when it was? Or have I been asleep, and while I slept my brave Champions killed all Ulster's enemies, so now there is no longer any need to go and seek out those who steal our cattle, hunt our deer, kill our sheep, burn our fields, take our women? Is that it? Is that why you are all here?' His voice rose again in an exaggerated formality and his sweeping arm included them all. And me. His foot stamped on the table, like a dancer. 'Then I am glad! Come, let us fill our cups and begin to feast again, for Ulster has no enemies and we can enjoy ourselves in peace and security.'

Conall of the Victories slammed the flat of his sword down on the broad wooden table, a sound like a great brass-bound door thrown shut. 'You are unjust!' he cried, his voice filled with anger and resentment. The Champion's eyes blazed, and a huge blood vessel writhed in his forehead like a snake pinned under-foot. Ever since I had felt the weight of his hand on the day I arrived in Ulster, I had walked carefully around Conall. He was generous with his hospitality – which was a given for any self-respecting Champion – and he could be amiable enough, if you played his game and played it his way, but he always reminded me of a bear with a grudge and a hangover and a boil in an inconvenient place. Conall had half-killed men who thought themselves his friends for presuming to suggest that he was perhaps not the greatest Champion that Ulster had ever known. I feared for Conor's safety. I saw several men pick up their swords ready to defend him as Conall advanced threateningly up the side of the table.

'It is true that we are all here now.' Conall swept his sword in an arc to include everyone, hitting a burly man near by across the face with the flat of the sword. The man dropped like an empty sack. Conall didn't notice. 'We are here now, but at your bidding. Many of us have come from the borders only in the last few days, and every man here has killed his Hundreds. I'll not take such criticism from anyone. What man mocks me? I'll have his head for my chariot and the head of his wife for my dogs to play with!'

There was a murmur of resentful agreement. The King stood with his fists on his hips and gave them all a withering look. 'Oh. I see. Everything is all right, is it? Nothing needs to be done?' He waited a moment, then his arm shot out with a pointing finger at the end of it. Those who were in the area that he indicated visibly flinched. 'Calum! Calum MacDonagh! How is your father?'

A red-faced man at the back of the group bridled and threw his head back defiantly. 'Dead. As you know.' The King looked at him.

'Aye. I know well enough. And how are his killers?'

'Alive, as you know! Which is more than you will be!' Calum MacDonagh tugged at his sword and plunged forward towards Conor. Startled, the crowd began to part to let him through, then realized what he intended and rushed to stop him. They held him a spear-length short of the King and took his sword from him. Calum stood, held firmly, screaming insults. 'You do not have the right, you do not have the right! No man has the right to accuse me . . .' The King appeared not to notice what was said. He jumped down from the table and stood in front of Calum. His hand went out and rested gently on the shouting man's shoulder. Conor shook his head and he placed a quieting finger in front of Calum's mouth. Calum subsided into maudlin tears, chewing his bottom lip until it bled. Conor signed for him to be released, and put his arm around the weeping man.

The King turned and addressed them all. His voice was low, reasonable, the words of a man who speaks an unarguable truth. 'I do not choose Calum because he is the only one, or to embarrass him alone. He is just one man who has tasks to perform, like us all. Who among you can say that there is not a single slight against his honour, an unavenged death, a duty left undone, an honour price unpaid?'

I started to smile to myself. Conor had got them. They were on fire at his taunts, and yet had to admit that he was right. Each knew that if he tried to assert his case the others would remind him of some long-forgotten slight, or some wearisome geis that had fallen out of use, or a death that needed avenging even though the victim was no loss to the man who should avenge him. Conor had them caught by their shortest hairs. They lived to a principle, and the principle was absolute. Either it was observed totally, or it was worthless.

Conall huffed and grumbled and looked around from under low brows to see if anyone would oblige by fighting him, and a few of the others looked around with a wary pride (not at Conall), as if daring anyone to question their honour, but the anger was gone. There was a lot of looking at the

186

ground, some shuffling of feet, and an amount of soft whistling. The crowd dispersed. There was no more to say. Conor saw me watching him, and perhaps saw the smile on my face. He indicated with a small movement of his hand that I should stay behind.

The King went back to his seat, sat in it, lifted up a foot and put it against the table. He pushed hard, and watched the table go over with a crash, spilling cold scraps of last night's food and greasy plates far across the rush-covered floor.

'That's better,' he said, stretching out his legs contentedly. I sat near to him and watched. He arranged himself comfortably, poured himself a cup of last night's beer, gulped it down, made a face and spat most of it out again, roared for fresh drink to no-one in particular, eased himself, folded his arms across his chest and looked at me.

'So, my friend from the sea,' he said, 'what will you do, while my Champions go off to consider their duty?' He spoke in the demotic style, not the courtly. I smiled.

'Weren't you speaking to me too just then?'

'Not really. You aren't an Ulsterman.'

'No, but I am not anything else much either, and I have eaten your food and slept in your castle. I live by the same rules as they do.'

Conor shook his head. 'No you don't. You have your own rules. You may become one of us, but you can never be of us. We can never take you for granted like we can our own. You are a German without a tribe and a Roman who isn't welcome in Rome. You will always have a home in Ulster while I live, but I wonder sometimes what you have planned for the future.'

'Now that you have reminded everyone of their obligations?'

He shrugged amiably. 'These are stirring times.'

'Especially when the King does the stirring?'

'If you like. Come, what are you going to do?'

'You mean, what will I do, now that you have incited the Red Branch so much that by tomorrow there won't be a worthwhile drinking companion left in Emain Macha, while Ulster's enemies will be lying in bloody heaps all around its borders, wondering what has hit them?'

He showed his teeth like a wolf. 'I thought you probably realized what was going on.' He turned serious, and looked down the table for something to drink. There was nothing, and he yelled again for more beer. A hand appeared from behind him and placed a large jug in front of him. It was Ulinn. I probably looked surprised, for she was no serving-girl. She winked at me and was gone.

Conor crossed his legs again. I was impressed as always by the easy fluidity of his movements. His face was still blotched red and white from last night's drinking and there were the first signs of broken veins in his cheeks, but his eyes were clear and his attention sharp. He grinned. He was being friendly, taking me into his confidence, treating me as the only sane man at his court. It was a gift he had. Even when you know that someone you admire is flattering you for a purpose it is still difficult to resist.

'You bring fresh eyes, you see what I have to deal with. Was it like this in your country?'

I paused, considering before replying. 'Quite different, as the sun differs from the moon. Your men are not afraid of you. Romans fear losing position and influence, they fear being out of favour.'

Conor snorted scornfully. 'What use is any of that?' he growled. I spread my hands, and shrugged. What do you say to a King who asks you what power is for? Conor frowned, then brightened. 'So. As you say, all your cronies are off to the wars for a while. What will you do?'

I pondered for a moment. I really had no idea. For months, since Cuchullain left for Muirthemne with Emer, I had not thought much beyond getting rid of a hangover in order to be able to start drinking again. I wondered what Conor wanted to hear. 'I shall go and fight Ulster's enemies,' I said, pleased with my reply. He smiled.

'Good of you to offer, but none of Ulster's Champions want

or need any aid. Ulster's enemies will be sorry enough in a day or so without your help.'

I opened my hands to him. 'What would you have me do, then?'

That was the right thing to say. 'Owen leaves tomorrow for Connaught.'

'Why?' I asked. Owen had not told me. Why had he not told me that, when Zeus knew that he told me everything else twelve times over?

'To finish his training. To learn. To frighten Maeve – if that's possible – with tales of the massive balls of our terrible fighting men. To watch, listen and remember. And then come back and tell me what he knows.'

I was horrified. From what I had heard of Maeve and knew of Owen it sounded as though Owen's painful death was only a matter of days away. 'But will Maeve let him in? And if she does, will she let him look? And if she does, and he sees more than she intended, will she let him back?'

Conor sat back in his chair with a self-satisfied smile. 'Oh yes. He will see only what she wants him to see, of course. He will see the best she has, and that is all I need to know. I am not very interested in how many hundreds of men she has, although I wouldn't mind if she chooses to let the number drop into my lap. You might have a good look at that King of hers too. I want to know what sort of man Ailell is. Will he control her or will he obey her? How does he hold onto her? What is the mood of her court? Has she kept the fealty of her chiefs? Are they willing or coerced? Do Mordach and Raurai still march with her, or are the rumours that they have thrown in their lot with Leinster true? Come to that, do Leinster's men march with Connaught? And are Maeve's halls still full of armour and do men's heads still hang from the walls like grapes, or has she taken up baby-minding and a quiet life?' He laughed, a deep barking sound. 'And no, I don't seriously expect her to have done that.' He smiled at the thought. 'But if she has, I definitely feel I should know about it.'

I was thinking as fast as I could, wondering what the odds

were of Owen getting me killed. Far higher than if I went on my own, that was certain. 'I see. And you want me to go with Owen?'

'Yes. They do not know you. They may try to impress you. Certainly they will be interested in you, you will probably be allowed into places and told things forbidden to Ulstermen. And, who knows, Maeve may take a fancy to you.' He laughed raucously. 'Don't let her bewitch you. She is a spider who eats her mate.'

I smiled grimly. 'So I have heard, and more besides.' I paused, choosing my words carefully. The King raised an eyebrow. I plunged forward. 'Aren't you afraid that I may tell her of Emain Macha? Or that they might try to persuade me to stay with them?'

Conor shrugged. 'They will certainly try. They might succeed. Maeve can if anyone can. But Cathbad says not, and he has spoken to a fearsome pile of chickens' guts on the matter, so he should know if anyone does.' He looked at me in a way that suggested that his opinion and mine on Cathbad might not be all that far apart. 'Don't think you're indispensable. Besides, you could leave any time and I wouldn't know until you were long gone. I don't want to lose you, but I can't force you to stay. And there is Cuchullain to think of. I don't think you'd want to lose touch with him. No, you're safe enough.' Conor smiled at me. His smile pulled me towards him. I felt as though I had gained a brother. His voice became confiding, confident in my good sense. 'Besides, I trust you. As you said yourself, you have eaten our bread, stayed under our roof, slept with most of our women. It really would be a monstrous ingratitude to go to our enemy now. No, I think you'll stay with us. Anyhow, don't flatter yourself. What could you tell the witch of Connaught except the truth, that Ulster is full of massive and hugely endowed fighting men who fuck like cats and whose taste for ale is equalled only by their liking for blood-letting and their scorn for Connaught-men? If Maeve were stupid enough to make war on us we would send her home crying like a scalded puppy, and you can tell her I said that if you want, although I advise against it, and of course

190

I shall deny it completely if Maeve and I ever cross paths socially again, which I doubt.'

I chuckled, and thought about it for a moment, but there was no real doubt in my mind. I was going. Conor read my face, as he did all men's, and grinned again.

His famous grin. Like a wolf looking up from the ribcage of a fresh kill.

# 24

Nowadays Maeve is legend. Every legend has a dawn, and every dawn needs a herald. Owen was that harbinger for me.

The disadvantage of being in a moving chariot with someone is that you cannot get away from them. The journey to Connaught took several days, and Owen talked at me for all of them. He stood just behind me, which meant that much of the time I couldn't hear him properly, thank Zeus. His mouth was permanently open. I hoped a bee would fly into it and shut him up. He felt it his duty to tell me everything he knew about Maeve and Ailell and everyone else he could think of and every random detail that came to mind, until I was heartily sick of the whole crew, felt I knew them better than they knew themselves, and wanted just to turn round, go back, and forget the whole thing.

'Was the study of Maeve part of your education, or have you used your own spare time to become so well acquainted with her?'

I hadn't meant to show my irritation, but I obviously had, because his expression became hurt and turned red like his hair, and he looked as though he might retort just as rudely, but just then we hit a pot-hole that was more like a well and he had to concentrate on clinging on tight to prevent himself being catapulted out of the chariot. He satisfied himself with cursing me for driving too fast. When the ground became even again – or at any rate less mountainous – I spoke to him more softly.

'Tell me something about her that not everyone knows.'

'What do you mean?' he replied sullenly, looking anywhere but at me. Other people sulking always makes me laugh, but I looked out over the horses and tried to control myself. We were stuck on the same chariot, which is not the place to have an argument.

'You've told me everything I will ever need to know about the court and its rituals, not to mention the people, but there's nothing new about any of it – don't get me wrong, it will all be very useful, I'm sure – but if I were an Ulsterman I'd know it all anyway. But you are a bard. You know things that are denied to ordinary men; bards and druids hold secrets and pass them amongst themselves. Everyone knows you do. Share a little of your great knowledge with a simple foreigner cast up on your shores.' He looked at me warily. Quite well put, I thought, a judicious mix of challenge and flattery, but with the badinage he'd expect. If I didn't insult him he'd think I was trying to get round him, which of course I was. I waited a second or two, watching out of the corner of my eye. His face softened. Got him.

'It is true that we have knowledge that is not in common circulation, but it is a trust, I . . .'

'But in the service of the King? If it helps me to understand, if it helps me get to our goal more quickly? What could be wrong with that?'

I was becoming slightly ashamed of myself, but had no need to go further, for he turned back to face me with an irritatingly superior smile and smoothed his hair with one hand, which he always did when called upon to do something that appealed to his vanity. The breeze promptly blew it back up again.

'Very well. I will tell you the secret of Maeve's heart.'

That sounded interesting. 'Please do,' I said, with genuine enthusiasm. Owen hesitated, enjoying the moment. It was not often he had my full attention. The moment stretched into the plural and I growled at him to get on with it.

'When Maeve was eighteen, she was already a ferocious warrior.'

(He had already dropped into the bardic language that he – and all the other bards – used when telling stories. It had its own rhythm, and a slightly formal choice of words. It usually sent me to sleep, but I had a remedy to hand and whipped the horses to go faster. Driving a chariot like a maniac keeps one awake under even the most soporific of influences. Fortunately.)

'She fought at her father's side at the Battle of Glenarbrough and took as many heads as any of his Champions, as well as saving his life on at least one occasion. She was also a great hunter, and not only went with the men on their hunting but led them from the front, so that they had trouble keeping up with her. She was always first to the kill and sometimes beat the hounds too. She once killed a boar that had maimed two Champions with her bare hands.' (I hid a smile.) 'She was wild, strong in battle, the finest horse-soldier in the army, and beautiful too. When she rode, her hair flew about her like a golden-threaded shawl in the breeze. Men died admiring her beauty as she rushed towards them. Her legs and arms were strong and shapely, her breasts deep and her back straight. She knew many men but allowed none to be her master.'

He paused. I waited, not allowing myself the luxury of comment. It would only make him get cross and refuse to continue. He licked his lips and took a bardly deep breath.

'One day Maeve and a group of Champions hunted deep into the forest, and she and three others became separated from the main body, and it grew dark before they could find the way home. They were tired, and the horses could not continue, so when they came upon a house in a small clearing they asked for hospitality, and a woodcutter and his son fed them and gave them shelter. After they had eaten, the four visitors soon fell asleep, for they were tired from the hunt, and the hut was warm, and they had drunk well of the woodcutter's ale.' He paused again.

194

I forgot my resolution. It was getting annoying. 'Get on with it, what happened?' I said crossly. He was letting his enjoyment of a captive audience spoil the rhythm of his story. He looked a little piqued, but smiled as if I could not possibly be expected to understand, and continued.

'In the middle of the night Maeve woke to find cold sharp steel at her throat. The woodcutter's face was inches from hers. Behind him crouched his son. She opened her mouth to cry out, but he pushed the sword hard against her skin.

'"Call all you like, it won't make any difference," the wood-cutter said, "they can't help you now." He moved aside, and Maeve saw her companions lying still, surrounded by pools of their own blood, their throats cut with a heavy knife so deep that their heads were nearly severed. Their positions had not changed since they fell asleep, so Maeve knew that they had been killed without being given a chance to defend themselves. She sat up and cursed the woodcutters for murderers who had broken the sacred trust of hospitality.

'"Why have you done this?" she asked. "You are outside the society of honourable men, outside the King's protection. Every man's hand will be against you. Brothers will seek a blood-price from you that only your lives will repay. Why?"

'"Because your father banished me from his court, stripped me of my honour and called me coward," replied the wood-cutter.

'"If he did so, then so you must be," said Maeve.

'The man pushed her backwards onto the floor. "If I am so, then I have nothing to lose," he snarled. "I have killed his Champions, and now I shall have his daughter, and my son will have her too. If you resist, you will die." He smiled, and his teeth showed black in the firelight. His voice cajoled her, soft like a poisoner offering a cup, but the knife stayed at her throat. "Submit, and I may let you live."

'"This is wrong," she said. "You cannot touch me. If you had asked, I might have thanked you for your hospitality, even though my father is a King, even though he banished you. Instead, you offer us hospitality, then kill my friends and force me. You have broken the trust that binds us together. You are not a man!''

'The woodcutter chuckled. "Not a man, eh? We'll see about that!" He ripped at her shirt, uncovering her breasts.

'She did not prevent him, or speak again. She did not make a sound. She listened for help without expecting it, but the forest was like an empty place. Not even the night-time creatures moved. Their calls stopped, as if a great hand had risen up and commanded quiet. Even the beasts were still for shame of what men did. She lay on the ground surrounded by bitter silence while the man and his son forced her legs open. The son held the knife at her throat while his father pulled at her clothes until she was exposed. He grinned and loosened his breeches.

'"You'll not forget me in a long year," he said.

'"Nor you me," she said softly, and there was something in her voice and expression that made the younger man hesitate and pull away, looking at his father, as if it were still not too late to rectify a terrible mistake. But his father saw the indecision in his face and laughed.

'"Don't you want her, boy? Take a good look, and tell me you don't want her!" He reached out and tore her remaining clothing from her with hands like a badger's paws scratching at earth. There was a long silence as they both looked at her lying naked at their feet, defenceless but unafraid. The younger man drew the back of his hand across his mouth, and his father could see the desire in his eyes. He laughed loudly, and roared at his son to hold her down.

'The woodcutter lowered himself over her and tried to kiss her. She bit hard, driving her teeth through his lower lip. He pulled away in surprise and pain, leaving a bloody gobbet of his flesh between her lips.

'"Bitch!"

'Her arms were held aside as the woodcutter's fists smashed into the side of her head, first left then right. He wiped his lip with his sleeve.

'"No kisses then," he said quietly. "Very well. We will do this the simple way."

196

'He pinned her thighs down with his knees and hands and pushed himself roughly into her. At his first thrust she fought down the scream rising in her throat, forced it down and made no sound, then thought that her mouth had betrayed her and she had let it out anyway as a single piercing shriek seemed to come from all around the hut, coming at them as if they were surrounded by pain, making the woodcutter's son jump in fear and move his hand so that the knife pricked her throat. Blood dripped slowly down and gathered in the soft hollow where her neck met her chest.

'"What was that noise?" he stammered.

'"It was only wolves or foxes doing the same as us," grunted the woodcutter. "Hold her down."

'She did not make a sound from then until the time that they had both finished. Then they tied her up while they disposed of the three bodies, and then they came back and took turns again. They tied her over a fallen tree, spreadeagled naked and open across the sharp branches. The son was the leader this time, laughing wildly as he attacked her as if his guilt made him plunge deeper into the wrong. When they had done with her for the second time, they left her on the tree while they finished the bottle, laughing at her helplessness and promising more of their attentions in the morning. They mocked her silence, then they fell into a drunken sleep.'

Owen paused. I hit him on the shoulder, making him wince. 'What happened?' I asked. 'Obviously they didn't kill her or she wouldn't be here now, but what did they do? Did they just let her go?' Owen's eyes grew huge, and I glanced back at where we were going. The edge of the chariot was about to collide with a blackened tree stump. I hauled frantically at the reins. Instead of crashing into it we glanced off it. Owen was thrown sideways, and I reached out to grab him. He swung angrily at my hand as if it were a wasp and nearly fell out backwards as the chariot rolled over the mud at the side of the track. I started to laugh, then stopped when I saw his expression. Some people have no sense of what is ridiculous, especially when it's them.

'Under control,' I said. He looked unconvinced. 'Carry on.'

'I will continue if you keep looking where we are going, but only if,' he quavered, trying to rescue his dignity, which as far as I was concerned had fallen off the chariot even if he hadn't.

'Get on with it then.'

Owen looked serious. 'The story is a warning to all those who would cross Maeve,' he said. 'When the search party arrived at the hut the next afternoon, drawn by the smell of smoke, they found two men tied naked on the ground like starfish. They were pegged out beside the fire with stakes and ropes, like animal skins stretched out to dry in the sun, unable to move. The younger man was already dead. Red weals surrounded his wrists and ankles where the rough narrow ropes had bitten deep into his flesh as he had writhed to free himself. The earth was stained deep red with a skirt of his blood.

'As the hunters arrived, they saw her kneeling by the fire, her clothes torn to rags, her hair wild and uncombed. Maeve looked up from what she was doing, and the force of her expression alone was enough to make them halt at the edge of the clearing and not interfere. She advanced slowly on the woodcutter, carrying a knife and a flat sword, both glowing red-hot from the fire. She bent down and cut off his testicles with one slash of the knife, ignoring his cries and the blood that spurted over her torn clothes. She tossed the dripping handful carelessly into a steaming pot on the fire behind her. Then in almost the same movement she put the flat of the glowing sword against his groin as if patting fresh butter, staunching the flow of blood in a cloud of steam and filling the clearing with a smell of burning fat. His screams rang through the forest and made startled birds leap shrieking from their trees for miles around. Then Maeve picked up a bag of salt and emptied it onto the still-smoking wound. She took her sharp knife and sliced him from tip to root, so that the two halves of his manhood fell away from each other like peeled bark off a tree. Then she walked back to the fire and kicked over the bubbling pot, spilling the water onto the ground. There were small lumps of something left in it. Maeve carried them over to where the screaming man lay, unable to get free but thrashing his limbs on the ground in pain. As she approached, he saw her and was still, and his screams became sobs as he watched her. She knelt beside him and opened her hand to show him what it held. His eyes became huge, and he cried for help and mercy. She reached forward and took a little of the salt that was piled on his groin, and sprinkled it onto the meat on her outstretched palm. Then she picked one up and ate it, chewing slowly. He screamed as he watched. When she had finished, she spoke. The watching soldiers said that her voice was like that of a lover cajoling her mate to another sweetmeat.

'"You had me first, and now I have had you. You see that I am fair to you. It is your turn once more. Eat." She smiled and pinched his jaw, blocking his nose and forcing his mouth open and then she pushed his own manhood and that of his son into his mouth, holding it shut so that he could not spit. She leant forward and whispered into his ear as he choked on himself. "Swallow," she said softly. "Remember? Submit, and I may let you live."'

I did it for him. My throat was dry. 'So, did he?' Owen shrugged.

'Does it matter? She left him for the crows and they rode home.'

'But how did she escape? How did it end? What happened?' Owen looked at me as if I were stupid.

'She broke her bonds while they slept. She cut their heel-tendons so they couldn't run away, using the same knife that they had held to her throat while they forced her, and then she tied them up with the same rope that they had used on her. She cut their balls off, boiled them up, ate them, forced their owners to share the meal and then left them for dead. Clear on the details now? That's the woman that Conor thinks we are going to persuade to tell us her innermost secrets using only our masculine charm.'

We were both silent for a time. I felt a bit sick. My balls were hiding up around my lungs somewhere and I suspected they wouldn't come down until we were safely back in Ulster.

'What is the penalty for rape in Ulster?'

'What is rape?' He didn't know the term. I explained. He

199

looked affronted at the idea. 'It sounds as if you are punishing a man because he has diminished the value of something that belongs to another man.'

The Ulstermen didn't really have an idea of property as a right. If something was yours and another man admired it, you gave it to him. Nor did they have the same ideas of marriage or marital fidelity. If a man and woman decided to restrict themselves to each other, that was respected, but many marriages merely indicated a preference, not a commitment. Infidelity was, at worst, a joking matter, only a matter of concern when one partner expected a fidelity that the other was not prepared to provide.

'So if a man forces a woman—'

Owen didn't let me finish. 'No man would do that.'

I was incredulous. 'It happened to Maeve. Are you telling me that it never happens to anyone else?' He opened his mouth to deny it and then closed it again. He fidgeted for a few moments and frowned to himself. Finally he was forced to be truthful.

'Yes, it happens. But any man proved to have . . . done that would be killed instantly, or at least banished and his lands forfeit.' I noticed that he couldn't even bring himself to speak it.

'So it is important.'

He glared at me. 'Not in the way you imply. The physical forcing would not be the point, nor would any husband feel that his wife was devalued by it.'

'What then?'

He looked at me as if I was a stranger. 'Have you been here so long and understood nothing? A man who did that would have violated the law of hospitality.'

We had had this discussion before. There was no centrally enforceable authority in Ulster, such as an Augustus sitting like a great spider at the centre of a web of mutually supporting systems. The King – even Conor – was elected, and could be removed at any time. His position rested upon his fighting prowess, his strength of personality and his decisions being acceptable to most of those who received them. The druids declared upon points of law, but had no sanctions except what the people agreed to accept. Thus the community depended upon a contract between those who formed it, an agreement that certain forms of behaviour were anathema and thus did not – could not – happen, not because of fear of punishment but because such behaviour was not part of how they wished to live and conduct themselves. The law of hospitality was central to this, and applied to castles and cottages alike. In a sparsely populated country like Ulster, where the weather was usually cold and always unpredictable, if people appeared at your door and asked for refuge, to refuse might be a matter of life and death. It was a simple system, but it worked for the Ulstermen. At least it meant that the corruption and politics which plagued the Capitoline Hill had no place in Ulster. There was no need for it because there was nothing to be gained. I assumed that Maeve held a similar position in Connaught to that which Conor held in Ulster.

'She sounds a formidable woman. That is, you make her sound one.' He looked up at me.

'She is,' he said. 'Maeve is one subject that bards do not need to embellish. There is enough there for anyone.'

I remembered the fate of the children of Sejanus. Tiberius had trusted Sejanus as his regent and then found that he was plotting to take the Empire away from him. Tiberius's rage was awesome, and his revenge terrible. Sejanus perhaps deserved all he got and more, but neither my tribe in Germany nor the Ulstermen – both of whom would have been called barbarians by the Romans – would have treated his family as Tiberius treated them. Sejanus's son was old enough to realize what would happen to him, and why. He got his crying over with in the prison, and died bravely on the scaffold. His sister was only six. She was bewildered, and asked to be forgiven, begging uncomprehendingly to be beaten as a child for whatever childish thing it was she had done wrong. They condemned her like her brother, but there was a brief hiatus when it was pointed out by the lawyers that there was no precedent for the execution of a virgin. The Senate judges took precedent seriously, yet there was no doubt that Tiberius expected the sentence to be carried out.

After a serious debate involving much legal muttering and citing of examples, the learned Senators decreed that they had found an answer to this ticklish problem. The jailer was instructed by the judges to rape her first. Then he could legally kill her. Their mutilated bodies were thrown naked on the Gemonian steps for the crows.

I never told Owen about Sejanus's children. I would have been too ashamed to answer if he had asked how Romans dared call Maeve a barbarian. The day Sejanus and his family died was the first time I felt ashamed of my association with Rome. Tiberius relished the punishment, and the degradation of the name of the house of Sejanus. Much as we all hated Sejanus, I had no ill-will for his family. Perhaps I was too close to being a child myself not to know their pain.

And yet, I knew why Tiberius did it. How could an Emperor kill a father and expect the children to accept their father's death and not seek vengeance? By avoiding violence now he would ensure it later, and perhaps the deaths of many others in civil war. Better perhaps to annihilate a family and let the matter die?

'Look!' I said. 'That must be it!'

Owen looked where I was pointing. His face was grim under the dust as he hung on against the swaying of the chariot. 'I never thought I would want to see Maeve's castle more than anything else, even my own death,' he said, 'but after driving in a chariot with you I now know I was wrong.'

Owen and I arrived at Maeve's court in the middle of the afternoon. The sun was shining, and a hundred warriors were practising their arts on the field outside the main gate. They were not doing anything that I had not seen the warriors of Emain Macha do already, but they were doing it equally well. The Feats that Heroes do were not confined to Ulster alone.

Although I assumed as a matter of course that scouts would have reported our approach, and that therefore there might be a welcome of some sort prepared for us, I did not expect what actually happened. As our chariot pulled up by the gate, a burly sentry came forward and took the horses' bridles without a word. I didn't protest as he led us into the castle courtyard. Nor did anyone say anything to us beyond grunts as we were invited with polite and open-handed gestures (but no words) to leave the chariot and follow another man, lightly armed like a courtier not a soldier. He led us to two small rooms, one a living area, one with two sleeping pallets. He said, 'For you,' indicating that these rooms were for our use, pointed out the large jugs of wine ('Connaught's finest') and a couple of chickens ('Fresh cooked') that stood on a table in the corner, smiled, and withdrew. Silently.

I turned to Owen, puzzled and exasperated. 'What's going on? Doesn't anyone here speak complete sentences?'

Owen smiled. 'Oh yes,' he said. 'The men of Connaught speak when they have to.'

'And when is that?'

'When calling a cow, or calling a woman if they cannot catch the cow, or calling a boy if the woman and the cow will not come. Like the people you call Greeks.' I smiled at him. I had told him the Roman saying about the Athenians: 'A woman for duty, a boy for pleasure, but a goat for ecstasy.'

'Not my Greeks, I assure you,' I said, and looked around the room. A knock came at the door, which was half-open, and a woman came in, pulling a metal bath into the room. Behind her were several other women, all carrying large earthenware jugs of hot water. These were placed on the floor beside the bath, and we were left alone again, though not before a few knowing glances had been exchanged, particularly with a black-eyed woman who met my admiring gaze with one just as appraising. I was cheered to think that Connaught's women might be more forward than her men.

Something bothered me. 'How was it that they are so unsurprised to see us, that rooms are prepared for us and water boiled ready for us to use?'

Owen grunted in reply (it was obviously contagious) and took advantage of my slowness to start washing first. I persisted.

'I mean, I didn't expect them not to know about us at all, but they must have known when we would arrive to the nearest

203

minute to get all this ready. Unless they plan on receiving visitors at all times of the day and night? Very hospitable.'

He refused to answer my question beyond a few banalities about 'being prepared for anything' and then tried to change the subject. I knew he was hiding something, but he wouldn't tell me anything else, other than that Maeve was a special kind of Queen and that I would understand more when I met her.

We washed and had a drink or two, and then decided that we felt well enough to demolish the chickens, washed down with a few more drinks and some theorizing about our chances with the women who had brought the water. Owen was a bit stuffy about it, saying that we were at Maeve's castle for finding out about what went on there, not to chase women, but I pointed out that – done right – the two were essentially the same thing and anyway I wasn't about to turn down any offers and I knew damn well he wouldn't either. After the chickens were gone I was for exploring, but Owen felt that we should stay until we were sent for. Owen knew more about that sort of thing than I did, so we stayed, and got some sleep. I had a full stomach and a pleasant sense of anticipation. As long as Maeve didn't decide to kill us, staying at her castle seemed like a good way to be.

As the sun began to set, an elegant young man appeared at our door. He said 'Follow me please' pleasantly enough, but ignored our requests for details. Owen and I shambled along behind him, very conscious of our clothes and feeling slightly at a disadvantage. I have always felt awkward beside good-looking, poised and self-confident people, and this man was all three. He walked smoothly, gliding across the floor like a dancer, yet he had the scars and the muscles of a warrior. I was looking enviously at his broad shoulders and erect posture, hoping he would bump into something sharp, when I became aware that Owen was nudging my arm to get my attention. When I looked at the bard he mouthed the Queen's name and then made a surreptitious gesture with his fingers. We had had this con-versation in the chariot. I understood. Owen was telling me that this was one of Maeve's . . . what? The thing that Sejanus had said I was for Tiberius? A pet, a toy? I had heard stories of

Maeve's sexual voracity from more than one source, even to the extent of taking a lot of ribbing at Emain Macha at the news that I was to come to her court. 'You'll need to eat a lot more good red meat before you're ready for Maeve!' Conall had roared, and much more in the same vein. Mind you, if a Queen were to keep a harem, this would surely be the sort of young bull she would keep in it. The rumours said she liked to have a ready supply of handsome young men close to hand. Or whatever. In case the urge came upon her.

I wondered how much of the rumour was true, and what sort of man was Ailell, to marry such a woman?

Young Adonis motioned to us to wait under an arch which led at a right angle into the Hall. Light from many braziers flooded into the entrance. We were looking sideways across the Hall. The table was piled high with food and I could smell roast meat, but there was no-one at the table. I leant to look, but Owen pulled me back. Then the young guide-God reappeared, and gestured us inwards.

He led us towards the top of the table. A woman sat there on her own. I assumed this to be the Queen. The banquet was laid out, but no-one had yet been called. It seemed that we were to be first to be invited to sit with her. I supposed this an honour. I became sure that it was when I looked at Owen. His face was turning somersaults with the effort of struggling not to let his pleasure at the privilege overcome his determination to stay unblinded by flattery.

She looked at us, dismissing the young Adonis with the smallest of smiles and then ignoring him. I wondered if the habit throughout her castle of holding conversations with the minimum – or even without any – words stretched as far as the Queen.

The first thing you noticed was her thick hair, which fell – no, it flowed, spreading like bound silk – to her waist, in summer-corn yellow waves from beneath a white-gold band that encircled her forehead. It looked as if she had freed it from tight braids just before we had entered, and it seemed to surround her in a circle of shining gold. Her face was strong, not beautiful in

205

any obvious way, but attractive, magnetic. Her skin shone with energy and the strength underneath it. She was taller than most men, and in her prime at an age where most women were thinking of giving up. She was the centre of attention and she knew it, and she held your eye by force of will, a thing almost palpable that seemed to make the air glow all around her. A woman who would fight beside you, not one to die for while she sat at home. This was not a woman who would tolerate weakness. Any man who wanted her would have to be unusual himself if he wished to hold onto her.

She raised a hand in greeting, and a dozen solid gold bands slipped from her wrist to her elbow with the sound of far-off swords clashing.

'Welcome, men of Ulster,' she said. 'We have been expecting you.' I wondered again how she knew, but said nothing. Not that I was becoming a Connaughtman, but we had agreed that Owen would do most of the talking. He at once launched into a speech that he had obviously been rehearsing since Jupiter was a boy. Maeve watched and listened without comment, but I was sure that her eyes were missing nothing, probing us both all the time Owen was making the most of his chance. When he finally stopped, she smiled gracefully and indicated that we were to sit at the table just down from her, at the place of honour. We were both impressed.

I was dazzled by Maeve, but I made a little time to look at Ailell while I had the chance. The husband of Maeve was not a man to be lightly ignored. His position was similar to that of the man who jumps over the edge of the Colosseum arena and dodges the chariots as they race round – he attracted admiration and some praise, he was in a lot of danger and while some men envied him few would have taken his place.

He was a good-looking and solidly built man who liked his people and they liked him. The laughter from his end of the table was much the loudest. He and Maeve were King and Queen of Connaught by virtue of the fact that their union had brought together two neighbouring kingdoms of equal strength and wealth, and their alliance had quickly, brutally and efficiently flattened any resistance to the idea that the province was theirs to rule. I also knew that he had become King of his tribe not through inheritance but because he was their finest warrior.

He would have been a worrying man to have opposing Ulster on his own. And he was married to Maeve. I decided not to think about it any more.

It was a good party. I discovered that Connaughtmen make up for their laconic sober hours by talking non-stop when they are drunk. They were also just as quick to pick a fight (and as quick to forget it) as the Ulstermen. The food and wine were as good as I have tasted, and there were plenty of women about who had obviously received instructions to flatter and be pleasant, so the evening passed pleasantly enough. Within an hour or so I felt myself to be a very fine fellow indeed. Even so, every so often I remembered to glance at the Queen. She ate moderately, drank sparingly, and she never stopped watching. Her eyes moved from face to face, from speaker to listener, missing nothing, weighing every man, what he said and what he didn't say. I did my best not to give too much away, although I suspect that the wine and her women probably got most out of me that they wanted. (I am not so vain or so stupid as to suppose that the women who hung around my neck and sat on my lap were there entirely for my charm and good looks. Nor was I so stupid as to send them away just because their motives were perhaps not entirely pure.)

Only once did I catch Maeve looking directly at me. She smiled as our gazes met. Her face was warm, but the eyes were a glacial green. I smiled back falteringly, and looked away.

That night as I slept, Maeve's wine sent me a powerful dream. First, I knew that Emer lay beside me. Her hair was on my pillow, I felt it brush against my lip. I didn't dare move in case she disappeared. I felt her hand soft on mine. Then there were three women in my bed, none of them Emer. I felt drained, slow, drugged. One kissed my lips, one stroked my chest, the other worked at my groin. I was the centre of an enthusiastic tangle of limbs and heads, yet somehow I felt that something was wrong. I could not quite grasp what, as if the wine-fumes obscured all but a corner of the picture I was trying to see.

When they were finished with me the smoke in my mind cleared and I saw them truly. I saw three heads on one mis-shapen body, thin lank hair, faces with eyes set deep and glowing with a malevolent life, and I saw them grin at me and I knew who they were. The Daughters of Calatin, the same Calatin killed by Cuchullain at the ford when he was busy collecting heads to fulfil Emer's impossible quest, had visited me. As they rose from my bed I heard their serpent's voice, a hoarse sibilance that time does not dull the memory of.

'You have entertained usss well, Leary from across the water.' I felt them looking down at me and my skin felt cold and wet under their gaze. 'You are sent by Conor to know the Queen's mind. We will help you in your undertaking. We will visssit you again, seven times in all. Seven times we will visit your dreams, seven times we will ssshare with you what we know, seven times will we ssshare your bed.' They were silent, and I knew myself to be on the verge of waking. Then I saw the Queen, as if I looked into a highly polished shield and she were behind me, asleep in her bed, her hair a golden fan on her pillow. The sibilance faded, leaving me with a faint 'We will ssshare . . .'

When I woke, I felt embarrassed. I had had too much to drink, and dreamt a foolish dream.

Except that my lips were bruised red and cut in several places, as if I had been held by strong hands and kissed by a mouth with sharp teeth, and my back was raked bloody with scratches from long hard nails. And that was not all. My body smelt of something else. Another person, but not the warm salt smell of a young woman, more like old milk, a stale and sour odour that made my gorge rise every time I caught it. I washed myself three times, but did not feel properly clean until I went out and found a stream falling down a hillside. I stood for a long time under the fresh tumbling water, rubbing myself raw with a rough stone until the smell was gone.

# 25

Owen and I had been at the court of Maeve and Ailell for just over two months. Our original plan had been to spend only a couple of weeks at most there, but we found ourselves invited to stay. I say 'invited'. There was no compulsion, but we knew that we were not leaving. Maeve sent word to Conor that we would not be returning home for a while, and we settled down to wait.

'It's a marvellous opportunity,' said Owen, lounging on his bed. He didn't want to leave. I suspected his motives. I suspected that his main motive was short, plump and noisy, had red hair and green eyes, and an engaging way of looking up from under her hair that made you think of warm summer evenings. She was called Gollia, and Owen, who had not bothered much with women at Emain, was making up for lost time.

'I'm not sure,' I said, made defensive by his enthusiasm over our position, not quite sure why I felt uneasy. I felt ridiculous.

'You are ridiculous,' he said. 'We are honoured guests here, we have our own rooms, everything that we could want, the women are under instructions to be especially nice to us, and while all this is being shoved towards us we can still legitimately say that we are doing the job we were sent to do.' He made an exasperated motion of his hand. 'What more do you want?'

'We came here for a serious purpose, not to roll around with Maeve's women and drink her beer.'

Owen rolled onto his stomach and looked up at me with wonder. 'Is it Leary talking to me, or has an impostor taken his place?' I shrugged. He was right. We seemed to have exchanged places. I, who always lived for the moment, was worried about what was going to happen, while Owen, who normally saw problems around every corner, was having a wonderful time by closing his eyes and ears to everything about him. I was angry at myself for not being able to relax and feel the way he did, the way that I usually did. I felt like a prig. A part of me listened to my voice and laughed.

'I just don't feel comfortable, that's all. And I don't like having to stay here. We are prisoners here. Just because we came willingly and have an invitation to stay doesn't mean we are any less trapped.'

'We aren't trapped.'

'Have you tried to leave?'

'Why in the name of the Gods would I want to try?'

There was no talking to him, so I threw a goblet at him instead. He caught it with annoying deftness. Filling it with wine, he laughed and drank my health. Then he turned serious for a moment.

'Look. We are sent here to find out what we can. Everyone knows that, especially Maeve. She doesn't mind, she thinks she's more impressive than what we're used to, so it's all to the good for her. She's intent on keeping us to be witnesses to her fabulous wealth and power. Meanwhile, she can hardly complain if we wander about and talk to people, can she? We should have a good idea of how things really are here by the time we leave. You'll see, we'll become part of the furniture, it'll be easy to talk to people once they've got used to seeing us around for a while. We'll applaud when we see what they want us to see, and we'll try and get a look at anything they want to keep hidden. And then when she's done with us we'll look suitably impressed, assure the Queen of our undying allegiance and then piss off home to tell Conor our good news.' He glanced at me. 'Well, I am anyway.' He lay back on the bed luxuriously. 'Meanwhile, we are here at the Queen's behest, which is something with which no sensible man argues. All we can do is wait. So why not enjoy it while it's here, eh? And stop being such a pain in the back-side.'

It was exactly the speech that I would have expected myself to make to him. For a moment I hesitated, then we both burst out laughing.

He was right. The Connaughtmen were laconic with us, but then they were laconic with each other and everyone else. However, in their cups they were as garrulous as Greeks. Not that there was an enormous amount to learn from their talk. They were amused by the quarrelling between Maeve and Ailell, and could be persuaded to make jokes about them. And yet, they plainly had a deep respect for the two of them. Maeve they regarded with almost superstitious awe. They respected her abilities as a leader and were twice as amazed to see such qualities in a woman. One man spoke bitterly of her as being a man in disguise, but he was mocked by the others, who spoke in low voices of their envy of Ailell. I noticed that some men did not join in these conversations. One of the Connaughtmen told me later that these men were those who had shared her favours. Those who had been bedded by Maeve did not brag about it, it seemed. They had no need to. I spoke to one myself, tried to encourage him to boast, but, while he smiled at the memory and acknowledged readily enough that it had taken place, he would not be drawn on details. Owen reported a similar conversation with another. It was strange that men who were ready enough to bellow their every accomplishment to the roof-joists at any occasion where there was someone to listen were unwilling to speak of being bedded by the Queen. They smiled, nodded, and said nothing. It was not fear of her that held them back. They were proud of her. Because of that, they were proud of themselves.

211

# 26

The following night was the second time the Daughters of Calatin visited me. They took their pleasures slowly. I lay unable to move while they wrapped their cold limbs around me, put their dry lips against my skin, dragged their ragged black nails through my hair.

Several lifetimes later, when they were done, they sat on the bed around me and the air moved beside the bed as it does on a hot day above bare rock. Through the haze I saw Maeve and Ailell in their bedroom. The Queen lay naked on the bed, Ailell stood by a low table holding a flagon of wine. I saw them, I heard their voices, I knew their thoughts. I could not move, but the Daughters smiled to each other as they saw me watching and listening.

'We keep our bargainsss.'

Maeve and Ailell's lovemaking was just completed, the sweat not yet dry on Ailell's forehead. The Queen's pale skin and yellow hair formed a pool of light in the centre of the bed, reflecting the fires that burnt around the room.

Maeve smiled. Ailell knew that it would not be long before the glow would wear off and any smile would have to be watched and read carefully for what it signified, but he could relax for the moment. She was always Maeve the Queen, but sometimes it mattered less. Ailell sat upon the bed, poured himself a goblet of wine and drank almost all of it straight off. Like many men without a head for drink he drank often, in the belief both that he could hold it well and that he could train himself to tolerate it even better, as a recruit soldier learns to tolerate marching. On a number of occasions he had been proved wrong in this belief, but he assumed that this was because he had not tried hard enough.

Maeve stretched luxuriously.

'You are very good,' she said. Ailell smiled back, and did not deny it.

'I have to be,' he replied. 'There are plenty waiting to take my place if I were not.'

'True,' she replied, pulling a wolfskin up under her chin in a way that made her look fifteen years old. 'But you are.' She looked at him with an arch expression. 'A perfect mate.'

Ailell grinned. He poured himself another large goblet of wine, as a reward for his exertions. 'Mate? Am I one of your horses?' She looked at him sharply, then relaxed.

'You could do worse,' she said. 'No, I meant that you are a bull in bed. Added to that, you aren't bad-looking— ow! don't ... All right, you are handsome, peerlessly handsome, stop that. Thank you. You are tall, a bit dull sometimes but usually fair company, you don't get in my way too often, you are nearly as rich as me, you are a fair warrior, even I have to give you that ...'

'... very gracious ...'

'... no, you are not very gracious and if you put your finger in my ribs again I shall make you very sorry indeed.' She smiled at him as he stopped prodding at her. 'Yes, all in all I think I chose fairly well.'

Ailell was dazzled by this unaccustomed praise. Which is probably why he went too far. He understood Maeve intuitively, and could handle her on ground of his own choosing. Unfortunately, here he was far from home. He took a large draught of wine – a mistake – and disagreed with her, which was another. He must have forgotten who he was talking to. Poking her in the ribs as a lover may was one thing. Contradicting her on a matter that touched her pride was quite another.

'You didn't,' he said. 'And you aren't.'

Her eyes narrowed and her smile became thin. 'What?' Ailell grinned at her and spilt wine down his chin.

'You didn't choose me. You just thought you did, and I let you think it. I chose you, really. And you aren't richer than me.'

Maeve's eyes went cold. She sat up, pulling her shawl around her. 'You. Chose. Me?' she asked deliberately.

He grinned again and nodded slackly. Like the village idiot, she thought. She let out a long measured breath, and spoke with sarcasm that could strip bronze off a shield.

'Then I must be wrong. Of course. That's it! I must be wrong! Never mind that I am married to a clodpoll who thinks with his prick if he thinks at all and can only get it up once a year! Never mind that I run this province while he gets drunk and rolls around farting in slave girls' beds, never mind that I brought riches to this marriage while he brought only himself and a couple of dying sheep long past any hope of lambing, never mind that I do all the work while he gets all the credit, never mind all that, the Great King Ailell says that Maeve is wrong, why then she must be!' Maeve waved a hand at the ceiling and looked amazed. 'There I was, thinking I knew how things were, and all the time I just had to ask you and you'd have put me right.' She clapped her hand extravagantly to her forehead. 'Here I am, a mere woman trying to sort my unimportant thoughts out in my silly way and there was a man to hand all the time. What an idiot I am not to have seen it before!'

Ailell realized that the post-coital honeymoon was to be short, even by their abbreviated standards. He noted her slip about the slave girls for future reference, surmised that it was too late to save the situation, and so attacked.

'I did choose you. And I am richer than you.'

'I have more slaves.' Her words were a whiplash from a voice cold with anger.

'I have more land.'

'Not much more, and most of it is sodden bog, unfit even to walk on, let alone to graze those starving bone-bags you call cattle.'

Ailell was affronted. His cattle were his pride. Which Maeve knew. Which is why she had insulted them.

'I'll match my wealth against yours any day you care to contest!' he cried. 'And I especially will back my cattle against the best you can gather!'

He tried to stand, but the wine swam round his brain and made him dizzy so he sat down again a bit too quickly, hoping she hadn't noticed. She had. The sight of the man she had just been praising, drunk, the alcoholic stubbornness with which he argued, and above all his resemblance to the man who had only a short while ago been mingling his cries of pleasure with her own, all of these things suddenly maddened her. Someone, everyone, especially Ailell, would pay. She swung her bare legs round and off the bed, making Ailell suffer a pang of memory which he hurriedly crushed as he realized that he needed to start defending himself, and she strode to the door, throwing it open with a crash and roaring at the guards to attend her.

Within fifteen minutes the castle was in a ferment. Not a bed was still being slept in. Servants, slaves, chamberlains, bards, all were saddling horses or setting out on foot, mounting carts, anything to get away from the Queen. They were off to the far corners of Connaught without breakfast, but that was preferable to standing up to the tempest that raged inside the walls of the castle.

Maeve meant to have proof. She intended to count the value of her possessions, to match them against Ailell's, and to win the argument. For a little time her temper had borne her on wings around the castle, and she had thoroughly enjoyed stirring everyone up, but now she had cooled. She stood in the centre of her Great Hall, arms folded on her breast, relishing the bustle around her. Her thoughts were already working far ahead. She was still angry, and she meant to have her victory, but she was clear in her mind. She watched Ailell giving slurred orders to his sleepy men, trying to organize them not to set out all in the same direction. She hid a smile. Everything was well, there was advantage to be gained from what she knew was a petty quarrel. She would win the argument, the enormous pile of Ailell's and her own wealth combined would impress their vassals greatly, the servants would be given some much-needed exercise, and the chiefs who came to enumerate their possessions for each side would form a great assembly the like of which had not been seen for a decade. Time to recreate and relive another time, a future that harked back to the glorious past. Ulster was weak, it might fall apart without even a push and the pieces could be picked up without a fight. Even if not, a strong Connaught could march in and take whatever she wanted. It was time. Time for Maeve and Ailell to be seen at the head of their forces, to be seen commanding others. She would hold games, banquets, judgements. Maeve would lead. There was too much content, not enough contest. She would repair that omission.

There was a harsh noise, and Maeve looked up involuntarily. A large crow sat on a beam twenty feet above her head. It was looking down at her. She felt something land on her shoulder. She scowled and reached for a bow and a quiver of arrows. She notched the arrow in moments, but when she raised the bow the bird was gone. She brushed at the soiled shoulder of her gown in disgust. Her fingers met nothing. She looked and saw a large red spot on her shoulder, spreading across the fine fabric of her shawl. She searched again for the vanished bird. It was gone. She drew the shawl about her, feeling cold.

Suddenly the Daughters were gone and I could move again. I walked around the room, their smell still on me and the blood hardly dry from half a hundred scratches. I knew with an absolute certainty that what I had seen was real, that Maeve and Ailell had quarrelled and that the consequences would be far-reaching. I threw on a cloak and left the room. The whole castle was pandemonium. I walked towards the only group of men I could see who seemed unaffected. Owen was there, talking to the men from Leinster. They were Maeve's allies, not her vassals. She did not command them and they did not fear her. The Connaughtmen, on the other hand, were riding from the castle on every road that offered relief from Maeve's terrible energy. We Ulstermen and Leinstermen had nothing to do but wait. So we discussed women.

The Leinstermen said that the stories of Maeve and Ailell's quarrels showed the terrible consequences that inevitably followed if women were allowed to give orders to anyone but their slaves. They were convinced that the worst man could run almost anything – except perhaps a domestic household – better than the best woman. I didn't agree. The world watched Livia, Augustus's wife, run the largest empire ever known better than any man – without ever being officially in charge or even possessing official rank – and then watched Caligula throw the same Empire away more casually than any noblewoman would have dropped a soiled cloth. Besides, for me the story of Maeve and Ailell was not about that. Ailell's dilemma was simple. He was hopelessly in love with Maeve. She liked him well enough, but would only have him for a husband if he agreed to her terms. These terms were little things to her, such as the freedom to take any man she fancied to her bed and also the right to have her way over the running of Ailell's kingdom as well as her own. Not an enviable choice. They were King and Queen, each with their own lands and possessions, ostensibly equals, but she was the stronger partner. I respected him for choosing the way he did. Besides, Ailell was no innocent himself, and Maeve was not a hypocrite. She was not demanding the right to rub his nose in her affairs, only the right to take other men if she felt like it, as he would sometimes feel like taking other women. It was nothing personal. She had every intention of taking her fill of him too. He was tall, handsome, rich, not terribly clever but not at all arrogant about the lack of it, which made it less of a handicap. He was a leader to his men and a King to his people, and he had always succeeded in everything he had attempted. He aimed to make Maeve love him alone. He failed in that, but came closer to success than any other man had done, and

217

perhaps closer than any other man could have done. There were some who scorned his choice, but more who respected and envied him for it.

He was also no coward, which was a prerequisite for the husband of the Queen. The court was always full of stories of their latest battle. Maeve would rage around the Hall, still in her night shawl and careless of what showed under or over it, her corn-yellow hair streaming out around her shoulders to her waist, her green eyes flashing out of her long face, standing as tall as most men and shouting like some thunder-goddess. And Ailell, meeting her fury with his own weapons, sometimes head on so that their wills collided and their voices clashed like cymbals through the castle and sent servants and soldiers alike scurrying for cover, sometimes drawing her into an ambush, watching and waiting, countering her wild attacks with measured defence, attacking when she relaxed, giving her no respite. Those who watched and understood what was happening nodded their approval. Ailell knew what he was doing. Maeve would let no man bore her. Ailell might not have all of her all of the time, but he could hold her, which was more than any other man had done. She always came back. Ailell was clever enough to see that peace was not her way, and that if it went on too long the eruption that followed would be all the more terrible, and he was brave enough to start a fight if she did not do so first. She would then storm and strike at him, and for a day or a month he would stand his ground while imprecations and insults to his honour, his manhood, his valour, his beard and every other thing would rain down around him like rocks down a steep hillside at the start of the spring thaw. Then, suddenly and without warning, she would stop, and she would look at him and smile, then laugh, and she would put her hand on the back of his neck and pull his head against hers, and soon the castle would resound with the sounds of their lovemaking, and then peace would descend, until the next time Maeve grew angry or Ailell saw the signs of boredom on her.

No-one could say that he had an easy task. Ailell was as good at dealing with Maeve as any man could be, but even he could not always keep her under control. She could be wilful and cruel. If she saw a man she liked then she made no secret of it. She would not seek out Ailell to show him his replacement in her bed that night, but nor would she trouble to avoid him. More than once she had sent him backing hurriedly out of her room with missiles crashing round his ears and rage in his heart at the sight of another man in his place. He knew that the next day she would smile at him, and he would smile back. He might seethe inwardly, but he was too wise to let her see into his heart. He knew what was happening. She needed to see if he still wanted to keep their agreement, and her, more than he wanted to kill his rival. He sometimes growled his discontent into his cup when she was not listening, but generally he kept his peace, and so Maeve always came back. She did not have a double standard. She only demanded for herself what every man took as his right. She did not expect Ailell to be faithful to her, and knew he thought no less of her if he took a slave girl to bed. Why then should she think any less of him because she chose to spend the night with another?

The Leinstermen around the campfires disagreed with each other as well as with me. On the one hand they thought Ailell to be too lax in controlling his wife. On the other hand, most of them were prepared to admit that Maeve was probably un-controllable. They asked me what women were like where I came from. (I was tempted, I admit. I could have told them anything at all, and they'd have known no different. I thought about spinning them Homer's tales of Penthesilea, Queen of the Amazons, killed by Achilles the hero and bloody idiot, or tales of the Gods as if they were human, but it wasn't really worth it. I decided to stick to what I knew.) I told them of how Livia ran the Empire while letting Augustus think it was him who was doing it; about Cleopatra, who seduced an Emperor and his chief rival simultaneously – well, almost – while still a girl; and the story of Boudica, who fought the great Julius and whose fame had spread even to Ireland. Boudica they applauded, but they weren't sure about Livia. I suspect that to them she sounded like an even more terrifying version of Maeve. (There was some truth in this. Both were powerful and magnetic women, but Maeve had a spirit like the west wind and lived her life like a child running headlong down a hillside, whereas Livia had a stone with a snake living under it where her heart should have been, and loved only power.) The Leinstermen had no difficulty enjoying stories about female warriors. They just weren't keen on the idea of women telling them what to do. But then they thought most Roman ideas about women were crazy. I told them of temple prostitutes and the whores of Carthage, and they laughed. Why should someone pay for what is freely given and freely exchanged? To them it was like charging for smiling. I could not explain why things were the way they were in Rome. My language did not have power for them, and their language lacked the words for me to express what I wanted to say.

# 27

I remember the day that Tiberius heard that the Germans had crossed the Rhine. Rome was a giant barrel full of rats and he dropped a lighted rag into it. Messengers hurtled out from the Capitol in every direction. Favourites and hangers-on either had the sense to pack up and go to ground, or were dumped without ceremony out of whatever place or position they were in so that the system could move faster. It was as if we lived on top of a huge sleeping animal. Tiberius stirred it into action, and it moved beneath us all. Those who knew it and were ready could ride it and make it serve them. Those who were parasites on its body, tolerated in quiet times, were caught unprepared and slid off its back as it stood up and shook itself. There were those who thought that Rome was decadent and inefficient, a shadow of its former greatness. When I saw Rome get ready to go to war, I knew they were wrong.

I remembered that same feeling the day that Maeve and Ailell quarrelled. Maeve stood on the steps of her castle and gave her people three months to prepare. From the look on their faces it was obvious that they did not feel that this time was even nearly long enough. They had a choice: argue, or run. They ran.

Men scattered like swallows at the sound of a battle-horn,

riding their strongest horses across Connaught to spread Maeve's commands, but it still took a month for the messengers to reach every corner of the province, and another month for those who owed fealty to Maeve or Ailell to count their belongings and to organize themselves to come to the Great Meeting that Maeve had called. There had not been a day like it in ten years, and Maeve knew that no-one would want to miss it, partly for the spectacle and the feasting, partly because to miss it and incur her displeasure was not a road that many would willingly follow. Time was short. Within a week messengers were already returning and going out again. The first chiefs arrived not long after, eager to get a start on their rivals. As the day approached it seemed that the whole province shook with the hooves of horses carrying messages and commands concerned with the three days of feasting and games at Maeve's court.

Every so often, Maeve would see Owen and me and call us over to tell us about the feast to come, promising us a display of magnificence that would make Conor's wealth look like a child's jewel box. We made polite noises.

The Counting (by the end of three months of fevered preparation 'the Counting' was all anyone called it) was to be held on the third day, after two days of games and contests. Most of Maeve's and Ailell's men arrived several days before the games were due to begin, joining those who were already camped in front of the walls, swelling every day into a mass of tents, horses, equipment and followers, covered over at meal times with a thick pall of smoke. I wandered amongst them, finding agreeable drinking partners at every turn. It was half celebration and half military operation, flavoured with competition and with an undercurrent of blood-feud. Only a madman could enjoy it. Fortunately for the party there seemed to be a lot of those around.

Maeve's men and Ailell's men camped indiscriminately together. The lords may have been at odds but their vassals were not, and old friends met every day with shouts of welcome and much beer. I had supposed that Maeve would have wished Ailell's bondsmen to stay away, but this was obviously not so. In a relatively sober moment of reflection, I began to appreciate her political acumen. She knew that the quarrel was only a temporary spat, whereas her rule with Ailell was to be seen over the long term. She wished their strength to be seen and acknowledged. She wished the spectacle of their displayed wealth to be a marvel to all who saw it. The only qualification she had concerning this display of their joint magnificence was that her portion of it should be somewhat larger than Ailell's in every respect.

The games and contests were impressive, and Maeve made sure that if there was a warrior who could throw a spear unfeasibly far or use a sword well or was stronger than a bull then Owen and I were well placed to see it happen. We refused all attempts to get us to join in, except the chariot race, which I thought I could win but diplomatically decided to lose. Which was fortunate, because the winner would have beaten me easily anyhow.

Maeve listened with obvious enjoyment to the rapturous acclaim of her people, both those who owed allegiance to her and those who paid it to Ailell. The cheering went on for what seemed like hours, and was equally strong for both of them. Despite their arguments, everyone knew that in all important matters Maeve and Ailell moved with one body and spoke with one voice, and their possessions were one kingdom, not two. Those who owed fealty to either one knew that the other was a source of strength to their own protector, and so there was little reason for the supporters of each not to cheer the other.

For two days the guests ate, drank, fought, played, and tried to outdo each other in every kind of contest. I wasn't a very good spy, because I wasn't very often sober, but I had no trouble watching Maeve. Despite the tension she must have felt about the Counting that was to come, I never saw her mask slip. She was gracious to every man she met, no matter how unwashed or drunk he might be. She didn't have the common touch, but she was always unquestionably a Queen. She smiled and gave prizes to the winners, and praised her own men and Ailell's equally lavishly. Owen and I nodded sagely as we watched her making yet another speech, praising the virtues of the fat chief of a few square miles of rancid bog-land in the far north of the province, making it sound as if only his sword stood between the Queen's virtue and the ravening hordes from Ulster. The fat chief swelled like a pig's bladder and would no doubt have died for her at that moment.

'She's good, isn't she?' I murmured, taking a deep swallow from my cup.

'Praise costs nothing, and goes a long way,' said Owen. 'That fat prick thinks Maeve will be sitting on his face tonight, but she's made the same speech to a dozen others since breakfast.'

'Going to be a busy night for her then,' I said, chuckling. 'I wonder what I have to do to get on the list?'

Owen turned to me in surprise. 'You want her?'

I looked at him in the same way. 'You mean you don't?'

He blushed. 'Well, I . . . I mean, not that she's . . . you know, but . . . or anything, but . . .'

I pushed him hard on the chest, and he staggered and fell backwards over a saddle. I laughed loudly. 'Don't pretend to me,' I said, 'you'd join the queue if you knew where it started.'

He got up, furious, and swung a fist at me. It came from behind his back, so wide that I had time to take a drink from my cup and put it down safely before putting up a hand and stopping his arm.

'Don't be silly, you'll only hurt me, and neither of us want that.'

He glowered at me. 'Don't be so sure.' I offered him a drink. He thought about it, but when I poked him in the ribs he grinned and poured his drink over my head, so I knew he'd forgiven me.

Behind Maeve's travels around the camp, Owen and I gradually realized that a more serious inquisition was taking place in her wake, as agents of both Maeve and Ailell spoke to each man, ascertaining his allegiance and his possessions. On one occasion a particularly myopic and out-of-touch old courtier tried to interrogate me. He obviously had no idea who I was. He liked a drink, and in no time we were the best of friends. Owen and I worked as a team. I kept the old man happy and matched him drink for drink, Owen stayed fairly sober and remembered what he said. It seemed a good enough arrangement to me. He explained why Maeve and Ailell were so eager to find out the mood of the gathering. Both wished to know the result in advance; the Queen because she was impatient to know; the King because he feared that either result would damage his kingdom, and wished to prepare against both in advance. However, their agents had no clear message for them. By the beginning of the third day, our new friend told us, the King and Queen would know only one thing for certain: that it would be desperately close.

Excitement and tension ran through the crowd gathered on the plain in front of the Royal Castle on the third morning. Owen and I hid at the back, partly because we were not dressed for the occasion, partly because we didn't want to attract attention, partly because we were supposed to be spies. The chiefs and the Champions and all their cohorts gathered in a group, dressed in every fine garment that they could muster, so that the earth was covered in emerald green, red bronze and white gold, shot through with blues, whites and brilliant red. From the platform on which the King and Queen sat, together but separate, it must have seemed that the whole plain was a swirling cloak of colour.

The method of counting was simple. The Champions were first to be called. Each marched forward without looking to either side, paused for as long as it took for the men and women around him properly to admire his armour, weapons, cloak and bearing, then announced his allegiance clearly, followed by a declaration of his possessions.

There were men standing on the platform behind the King and Queen, listening keenly to what was said. I went back to find our myopic friend, who was snoring behind a pile of saddlery. Despite my friendly questioning, he didn't want to help as much as he had the previous evening, but eventually I persuaded him to stand on the saddles and tell me what was going on.

'Ow! Stop, you're hurting.'

'Sorry, I was just trying to hold you up. There, better?'

'Ow! Let me go!'

'Now don't be silly, I'll let go when you've told me what those people standing behind Maeve and Ailell are doing. And if you go on wriggling like that I'll break this arm.'

'All right, all right, no need to be so – ow! – unfriendly.'

'Who are they?'

He squinted against the bright morning light with red-shot eyes.

'They listen to every declaration, checking what the man says against what their informants have told them. If they can tell their patron that the amount declared is inflated, then they will obviously earn gratitude. In this way the declarations are kept accurate.'

'Thank you,' I said, freeing his arm but not letting him go. 'Why not stay and share the rest of the day with me here? There may be other things you can tell me.' He moaned, rubbed his arm with a long-suffering expression on his wizened face, and looked at me suspiciously.

'Only if you promise not to hurt me again.'

'I promise.'

He looked at me uncertainly for a few moments, then made up his mind. 'Can I have a drink, then?'

The Champions each approached, their swords dragging in the dust behind them, and made their declarations. Then there was a pause while they were persuaded to withdraw to one side to allow others to come forward, something that Champions tended to be unwilling to do. Then men from all other levels of Connaught society were called and stepped forward in their turn in the same way. Druids kept the official score, and unofficial counts were also made all around them. Bets had been laid everywhere on the outcome of the day, and no-one wanted to miss out on the final tally.

It took all day. It all had to be counted. It's extraordinary how many things one accumulates when one is running a province. Swords, spears, cattle, lands, slaves, jewels, fine cloth, everything that had value went into the Counting.

By the end of it, most people were sitting down, eating and drinking. We weren't keeping a tally, but it was obvious that the two sides were closely balanced. The druids were assessing both quantity and quality, so although Ailell controlled more lands, it was agreed that Maeve's were more fertile. Maeve had more cattle, but Ailell's were finer bred. This long tallying process obviously made Maeve angry, although she tried not to show it. The mask that she had worn for the two previous days was plainly starting to chafe her. She wasn't very good at hiding her impatience. Being polite to people she considered fools for political ends was something she could manage. Waiting was not.

Around us, people were remarking on Ailell's frowning face, shook their heads, and muttered their concern that no good would come of it all. Owen and I exchanged frequent glances. I was sobering up. Things were getting interesting.

At last, the chief druid stood up and held his hands high for attention.

'You have seen the might and wealth spread before you. The glory of Maeve and Ailell is displayed here for all to see.'

He paused. Everyone cheered, but it died down abruptly. Ailell looked sombre. The colour rose in Maeve's face. The druid took a deep breath, and the crowd took one with him.

'We have deliberated long with the King and Queen, and our advice to them has always been for them to resolve their . . .' (the druid chose his words carefully) '. . . their disagreement, without arriving at this point, where one must win and another lose. However, they are determined to finish the matter in this way.' (Ailell's face fell, as if he had hoped that the druid might announce that, even at this late stage, the matter would be allowed to rest.) 'Therefore we will pronounce a winner, against our better judgement.' A murmur ran amongst the watching people. The druid was on dangerous ground. Maeve's eyes were flashing fire. (I whispered a question to Owen about the life expectancy of the average druid at Maeve's court. Owen took me seriously, and told me that she could not harm a druid, but she did not take kindly to criticism, and that the druid courted trouble even speaking as carefully as he did. Then he realized I wasn't serious, and threw a cup at me. Everyone hissed at us to be quiet.) The druid paused. He savoured the attention, probably knowing that it was the only satisfaction he was likely to get from the day's work. We could see his dilemma. The druid knew that his position meant that whatever he said would be unpopular with half the crowd, and as there was nothing he could do to alter that he was determined to extract the maximum status for himself at least. He paused for further emphasis. The silence goaded Maeve into action. She stood and shouted at him to hurry, her voice cracking with tension. He nodded, and spread his arms to the crowd. There was absolute silence, broken only by the harsh croak of a raven in the distance.

'After due deliberation, we find that Maeve and Ailell are equal in all things, except one.'

Maeve leant forward towards him, like a bird of prey looking down a rock face at a rabbit. The druid looked at her, swallowed, and spoke, his resolve undermined by his high voice, carried by the wind to every point of the natural amphitheatre in front of the castle.

'The White-horned Bull Finnbennach is the only beast, thing or item that separates the possessions of Maeve and Ailell. In every other aspect are they evenly matched. So judge we, and hope that there is an end to the matter.'

Silence.

Pandemonium.

'Who in Hades is Finnbinwhatever?' I asked Owen, almost shouting to make him hear me above the excited discussions that had broken out all around us.

Owen looked grim. 'Finnbennach is a bull who used to belong to Maeve. Worse, he was produced by one of Maeve's cows, but refused to live in her herd. The first time Maeve inspected her herd after his birth he broke past her stockmen, tried to run Maeve down, then broke a fence and joined Ailell's cows, refusing all attempts to get him back. The stockmen said it was because he refused to belong to a woman.'

'I imagine Maeve took kindly to that,' I said. Owen nodded.

228

'Whatever the reason, he's now enormous, and a valuable sire. They tried to get him back to Maeve's cows, during which several stockmen were trampled, gored or worse. Maeve eventually just said he wasn't worth the trouble and gave him to Ailell.'

I understood. That open-handedness was now costing her the wager.

The noise slowly died down as people realized that Maeve had lost and became a low murmur. Everyone looked at the Queen. She was motionless for a dozen heartbeats, then stood up from her throne, white-faced with emotion. She did not look at Ailell. He stood as well, and lifted his hand for attention. There was absolute silence as he spoke.

'I give the White-horned Bull Finnbennach to Maeve my wife, freely and without hesitation. That which was once hers I now return.'

There was a scattering of shouts from some of the crowd at Ailell's generosity, which froze in their throats as Maeve turned to him. Her face twisted with anger. The force of her gaze seemed to push him a step backwards. She did not speak, but turned on one heel and swept off the platform, her cloak sweeping a wide circle on the boards. Ailell stood alone, his face and body sagging like a man suddenly made old. It was as if she had struck him with all her strength. Then he looked around and saw the crowd watching him, regained some of his composure and turned to follow her.

After that, matters began to move very quickly indeed.

# 28

I pulled Owen to one side, away from where the crowd around us could hear.

'Now we should leave,' I hissed, 'slip away while they are distracted.'

Owen looked at me as though my senses had melted and run from my head. 'Are you mad?' he said, too loud, and I motioned him to quiet as several heads turned towards us.

'Are you mad?' he asked, slightly more quietly. 'This is exactly what Conor sent us here for, to gather information. For the first time since we arrived here, these Connaught peasants are actually more or less sober, talking about something other than beer, women or horses, and aren't worrying whether or not we hear what they say. And now you want to leave?'

I could see his point, although the sensible part of me was still all for making a run for it. Owen grinned slyly. 'Besides,' he said, 'isn't this fun?'

I realized that Owen had discovered politics. Romans take politics for granted, but intrigue and speculation, guesswork, information-gathering, favour-seeking, influence-peddling, back-door back-slapping back-stabbing, all the excesses and inversions that make a court a place both fascinating and terrible, all this was new to Owen. Of course, he had some way to go before all those possibilities opened up to him. But he was getting the idea. He could see shapes and angles that he had not thought of before. I knew them of old and wanted little to do with them. I who had known complexity wanted only peace and simplicity. Owen, blessed with what I wanted, wanted what I knew well and had rejected. Like a child, he had to make his own mistakes, he would not take my word for it. Besides, he was a grown man, and what did it matter to me? I felt closer to my old self than I had done since we arrived, and shrugged.

'All right. We won't go yet, and I hope I won't have to say I told you so. You stay and listen here. I'm going to get a drink. It's going to be a long day.'

I was right. Armed with a goblet and a goatskin of beer, I wandered amongst the crowd, listening to what they were saying, amiably smiling my best vacant drunkard's smile if anyone turned to look at me suspiciously, offering them a drink if they looked too long. This made them either my friend or made them turn away in disgust. Both were fine by me. The drunkard's grin became less and less of an act as the afternoon wore on, and I was in a large company. Maeve knew that the secret of a good party is to keep the drink flowing and all else will follow. I saw Owen several times in our travels, but we avoided each other. Separate, we meant nothing. Together, we were spies.

Late that night, footsore and tired (I think politics was suddenly no longer quite as much fun as he had thought), Owen and I found ourselves sitting on opposite sides of a crowd of men lounging around one of several large fires which had been built in front of the castle to keep Maeve and Ailell's guests warm during the night before they made for their homes the next morning. We made no sign of recognition, nor did we join in the conversation, in case our voices were recognized as foreign.

'She won't take losing, not without a fight.' The speaker was a burly man, of medium height and with a large wart on one cheek that spoilt an otherwise pleasant face. He spoke as one who was prepared for anything that life – or his Queen – might throw at him. A gloomy-looking soldier with an old sword-cut deep into one forearm answered him.

'You're right, and it won't be pretty. She'll make us all dance a few times around the forest before she's done with us.' There was a pause. Someone else spoke from the back. It was too dark for me to make him out under a hooded cloak.

'It's Ailell I feel sorry for.' Some grunts of assent followed this.

'Why?' said Wart. 'He got himself into this – he gets the smooth of her as well, unlike us who only get the rough. Mind you, to be fair, I don't think there's much smooth to be had.' Everyone laughed. 'It seems she spends most of her time yelling at him, and only stops when she's yelling at someone else.' More laughter. This was interesting to me – I had never seen it before. I was trying to imagine a group of Romans sitting around discussing the Emperor as these men discussed their King and Queen. It was inconceivable. Sneaks and informers would have had the words into the Emperor's ears before the echo had died away. The Connaughtmen spoke their minds and had no fear of informers, and no fear of the King or Queen either. Their terror of Maeve was from her fearsome temper and redoubtable personality, not because she was the Queen. The man in the hood spoke again.

'If it comes to war, would you follow her?' Wart's friend Gloomy – the one with the cut arm – laughed bitterly, which allowed him to make the sound without changing his morose expression.

'Don't be stupid. Maeve and Ailell aren't going to go to war over a personal quarrel. It's only a bull, after all.' Several voices murmured agreement. I heard a voice behind me mutter that Maeve was capable of anything if she thought she was in danger of losing – an argument, a slave, a drinking bowl, anything at all. The others behind me agreed. She was open-handed with those she felt were deserving, but she was suspicious of cheats and thieves. Her pride demanded that she was never beaten.

'If she isn't going to go to war with Ailell, what will she do then?' asked the hooded man.

A round man beside Wart dressed in what looked like borrowed clothes, with a choleric face and a goblet, both of which he kept refilling from a large goatskin, belched loudly. 'She'll have to produce a fine bull from somewhere, one that is at least as good as Ailell's. And we all know that Finnbennach is the finest bull in Connaught.'

For a fat scruffy drunk he spoke sense. There was a pause while everyone digested this thought. The conclusion wasn't difficult. If there were no better bulls in Connaught, then she would have to look elsewhere. I stared down into my cup, and then raised it to my lips. Over the rim I could see Owen, signalling frantically at me while trying not to attract attention. He resembled a dog pretending not to look at a bone that he hadn't yet been promised. I looked at him stupidly for a moment before realizing what he was doing, then inclined my head in the direction of a rendezvous and shambled from my place as if I needed to relieve myself. Owen set off at the same time, but in the other direction. I assumed that this was a clever move and that he was going to double back, otherwise we weren't going to have much of a conversation.

I was pouring out the last drop when he appeared, uncoiling through the shadows and looking exactly like a very bad paid informer from Tiberius's secret service. If it had not been dark, every man near by would have wondered what he was up to. As it was, only a few hundred of those not entirely blind drunk were likely to have noticed. He was enjoying the intrigue hugely until I cuffed him for an idiot and made him walk properly.

'The essence of secrecy is normality,' I said, quoting Sejanus, who may have been a duplicitous treasonous cut-throat, but knew what he was talking about when it came to sneaking up on people who wanted to hurt you and getting your knife between their ribs first. 'Try to look inconspicuous and men will look at you as if your hair is on fire. Just be yourself, only less so.' I thought this was all rather apt and good advice. Owen seemed to take my point, although he obviously felt that it was a lot less fun than creeping about in the shadows trying to move silently by lifting his knees and pointing his toes like— it took

me a while to think what he reminded me of, then I remembered. Tiberius had flamingos around his pool in Capri. Owen
walked like one of them, an old, cautious, probably arthritic
flamingo.

'So. What do you think is going to happen?' His excited
whisper would have carried across the Seven Hills. I shushed
him as best I could.

'How the hell do I know?' I gulped the last of my beer in
order to arrange my thoughts into orderly lines. It didn't seem
to help much. 'The woman is capable of anything. She's also
obviously half-demented, but that's no obstacle. In fact, in Rome
it's almost a prerequisite for high office.'

'I think the problem is worse than that.' He sounded worried.

'Why?'

'They say that there is only one bull in Ireland that can match
Ailell's. He is known as the Brown Bull of Cooley, part of the
estate of Daire mac Fiachna's house.' He looked at me. I looked
back blankly. He gave me what was obviously a punchline.
'Cooley is in Ulster.' He stopped again. It didn't work. I was
clearly still not giving him the response he wanted. He spelt
things out for me with the emphasis one would use to a very dim
child. 'The power to make Maeve altogether happy or else very
angry indeed lies in an Ulsterman's hands. She will go after the
Bull of Cooley, and she'll get him one way or the other.' I was
still trying to see what the problem was.

'Can't the Ulsterman just let her have the blessed bull and
avoid the fuss? At least let her borrow him, if it means that
much to her?' Owen looked serious. 'The man who will have to
make that decision has met Maeve before, and has no love for
Connaught.' He sounded ominous.

'Why?'

'Daire mac Fiachna and Maeve have crossed paths before.
Before she met Ailell or became Queen. Two of Daire's
sons were killed by Firg, a brother of Maeve's, while failing to
prevent him carrying off a hundred of Daire's best cattle. In
revenge, Daire burnt one of Firg's houses to the ground.'

'And?' I felt there was another punchline coming. There was.

'The house had Maeve in it at the time. She only just got out. A lover of hers wasn't fast enough.'

I looked at Owen, seeing the worry in his face. 'So you think he may refuse to lend the Brown Bull?'

Owen shrugged. 'No way of knowing,' he said. 'It was all a long time ago, and the druids sorted it out in a way that meant that no-one was entirely happy, as usual, but Firg paid the blood-price in the end and it stopped a full-scale war. A lot depends on how she goes about it, on who she sends to ask for the Bull. We'll just have to see.'

I put on my best thoughtful expression. 'If I were Maeve, I'd use her two tame Ulstermen to conduct the negotiations.' Owen joined in my laughter.

'She's hardly likely—'

A large hand landed on my shoulder, making me bend at the knees. The hand had the weight and appearance of a full-grown badger dropped by a high-flying eagle.

'Leary of Ulster?'

I whirled like the battle-trained warrior that I was, one hand raised, the other reaching for my sword, ready to fight. I then paused, gulped, nodded, and used the raised hand to scratch my head as unthreateningly as I could. It was pointless to deny the question, especially as it was true and the questioner was the size of the Colosseum, only taller. He was easily the biggest man I had ever seen. He grinned at me in a way that made my toes curl like frightened hedgehogs, and then twisted me around to face the other way using just his fingers, as if I were a chess-piece.

'The Queen asks the privilege of seeing you and your bum-friend here, right now. Would you be so kind as to accompany me to her quarters?' This was not a question. Owen bridled at the insult, but had the sense to fall silently into line even so. This messenger was not a man to argue with. This messenger was a man to agree with now and save your disagreements to be sorted out later in different circumstances, such as for example the circumstances of him being alone and drunk and asleep and you being in possession of a heavy club and a free shot at his head.

\*　　\*　　\*

'But I don't want to go!'

I looked at him in disgust. 'Fine, I don't want to stay! Let's both defy the Queen and see how long we last!'

Our visit to Maeve's quarters was over. The mountain with legs that she had sent to fetch us had steered us to her with enormous tenderness for her feelings and none at all for ours. We arrived in a swearing and shuffling heap, trying not to let him hurry us along while knowing that there wasn't an awful lot we could do to prevent him.

The Queen's message was brief and to the point. Owen was to go with a party of warriors to beg, borrow or hire the Brown Bull of Cooley. She loomed at us from her throne as she spoke.

'You and mac Roth will speak to him.' (Mac Roth was Maeve's herald, and a bard of wide fame. Owen detested him on professional grounds. I liked him.) 'Ask Daire, in the name of the peace between us, to lend me the Brown Bull for a year. At the end of the year I will send him fifty good heifers back with the Bull. And if he gets upset at the thought of losing the jewel in his crown, tell him that if he accompanies you himself with the Bull I'll give him a piece of the Plain of Ail as big as his own lands, and a chariot to take home worth three times seven bondmaids, and if he has a mood for it he and I might even spend a few hours together on a feather bed. Assure him of my friendship if he does this for me. He will already know that to refuse will earn him my hatred, and what that will mean.'

Owen was to go. I was to stay. The word 'hostage' was not used, but none of us was naive enough to think that it was anything else. Maeve called me her guest, but guests get to go home. If Owen did not return, I supposed that I would be food for Maeve's dogs.

'But what if Daire won't co-operate?'

'Then you tell him how important this is, and you keep on hitting him until he agrees with you, understand?' I was terrified that Owen was going to do something principled which would get me killed. 'Just do what she wants, grab that bloody bull and come back to get me, all right?'

'Couldn't you escape?'

I took three calming deep breaths and then answered. 'From this castle? Possibly. I would then have to find my chariot which is Zeus knows where in order to be able to travel across Connaught on a road I don't know and frequently won't even be able to see while being chased by an angry mob of people carrying sharp swords who grew up here and know every inch of it.' I glowered in a pleading sort of way. 'If you can't be clever, at least try to be sensible. This is my life we're talking about.'

He rested a comforting hand upon my arm. 'Don't worry, old friend. I will return, with the Bull.'

He was half right.


'What in the Gods' names went wrong?'

He looked awful. He had come straight to see me, without even stopping to wash. Normally Owen was as fastidious as a Roman tribune about washing, so I knew that things were serious. He sat on the bed looking like a man who had not slept for three nights – which he soon told me was in fact the case – and every time he moved tiny plumes of dustsmoke flew off his clothes. He had ridden hard and long to get here, which was good of him, but now that he had arrived he was sitting still and not talking, which was useless.

I walked up to him and pulled him into a standing position. I frogmarched him across to the deep bowl of water in the corner and, before he realized what was about to happen, plunged his head into it. I held him there for a second and then dragged him back up again. He spluttered spray at me and swung a clumsy fist.

'Ungrateful . . . !'

I blocked the fist without trouble, grabbed his wrist, spun him round, marched him back to the bed, plumped him down, crossed the room, threw a towel at him, poured us both a large drink, crossed back, gave him his drink and knelt in front of him.

'Owen, you're a bard, I am your perfect audience, I won't interrupt, but either you talk or with regret but no alternative I shall have to kill you here and now. Will you for Zeus's sake tell me what happened?'

He scowled, dripping into his beer. Then a slow smile crept across his face, in which I joined, and he started to towel his hair. Then he told me the story, and both our smiles faded, although I did keep my promise not to interrupt.

'We got to Cooley without trouble. I persuaded the Connaught idiots to let me have first go at Daire, who I have met once or twice, so they sat me beside him at the banquet and I worked on him, and although he wasn't too keen at first, once I had dangled Maeve's favours in front of him a few times he was coming round to the idea. Of course, he spoke a lot about his honour and the pride of his people, and the price he was asking was quite exorbitant, but I knew that Maeve's men were authorized to pay it, so I smiled and kept him going.'

I was right. Owen had discovered politics and his vocation at the same time.

'We agreed a price, and Daire gave us a great banquet to celebrate, and of course those knuckleheads had too much to drink, and things got out of hand, and all my work was wasted.' He had an expression that I knew. I had seen it before, back in Germany, on the exquisitely coiffed and oiled face of a Greek whom Tiberius used for his negotiations with difficult tribes, when one of Tiberius's generals decided to take part in a discussion which was at a critical point. Owen's sour expression was exactly that of a seasoned diplomat who practises his art with all the finesse at his disposal and then sees some (usually military) clod undo days of delicate negotiations with a few ill-chosen words.

'Before I could stop them, a dozen of Daire's men were bumping heads with some of these Connaught bullocks who were with me, and everyone was shouting, and it was about to become full-scale when Daire let out a roar that stopped everyone for a moment – he's impressive, you have to admit – and demanded to know what was going on. Everyone starts shouting at once, so he strides round the table, grabs one of his own men and one of the idiots from Connaught and he shakes both of them until the story comes out.'

He paused. I said nothing. He had a drink. A big one.

'You can guess what had happened.' I shook my head. 'The Cooley men had been telling Maeve's lot how lucky they were that Daire was such a forgiving man, and how lending them his precious bull – for an exorbitant fee – was more than they deserved. They went on a bit too much about it, and eventually one of the Connaughtmen decides that he has been patronized for long enough and replies that it was fortunate that Daire had given them the Bull because if he hadn't they'd have just taken it anyway. You can imagine how that went down. Everyone grabs everyone else by the throat and only Daire stops a slaughter. We were outnumbered four to one. Daire can hardly speak, he's so angry, but he's still just about in control and shouts to them not to foul the laws of hospitality. We are driven to our beds like cattle put in stalls, breakfast is thrown at us at dawn the next day, and we are made very aware that we have to leave as soon as we've eaten it. That was three days ago; here I am.'

I opened my mouth to ask questions, and then shut it without speaking. There wasn't much to ask. Then I thought of something. 'What will happen now?'

Owen looked serious. 'I don't know. The men I rode back with think she'll do what they threatened to do.' I was startled.

'Take it? But that means invading Ulster! She wouldn't start a war over a bull? Would she?'

Owen looked very tired. 'She might anyway, even if she didn't know about the curse of Macha.' I looked at him in disbelief.

'The what? You don't believe in that, surely?'

He nodded, his head almost falling forward with tiredness. 'It doesn't matter whether I do or not,' he said. 'Everyone else does. All of the warriors will take to their beds and roll about in pain. Only men not of Ulster blood will be unaffected.' He managed a wry smile. 'And women, of course. Children. Very old men. And bards, of course.' I couldn't see the point.

'But everyone in Ulster is of Ulster blood!'

Owen leant forward slightly. 'Not Cuchullain, my friend,' he said, his voice sliding into sleep, 'not the Hound.'

# 29

A messenger arrived from Conor, asking for us. We went to a private room and he drew every piece of information he could from us. Conor already knew about the Counting. We were to stay in Connaught until it was clear what was going to happen, then come home as swiftly as possible. Conor wanted to know what Ulster was up against. I could see the sense in that, I just wasn't sure that I was the man to find it out, but Owen stood beside me with a worldly expression and agreed with everything, so I didn't have much choice. We said our goodbyes and the messenger rode back to Ulster. The fact that Maeve had not killed him or blocked his mission was sobering. She let him go; she wanted Conor to know what was happening.

The messenger brought news of Cuchullain too. He lived at his castle at Muirthemne and spent his days hunting and being with his wife. It was said that they hardly spoke together in public, but everyone knew that they understood each other's wishes better than any other man and woman in Ulster.

I wondered if Cuchullain would bring Emer with him to Emain Macha when Maeve was at Ulster's gates. I felt the need to see her in my chest like the ache of an old wound on a cold day.

We stayed in Connaught for about two more weeks. We tried hard to find out as much as we could, but there wasn't much to find out beyond what we already knew or what anyone could see without trying. We went to pack our things, wondering if we would be allowed to leave.

A knock came at the door, and a muscular youth opened it without waiting for a reply. It was our guide from the first day. He looked at us arrogantly.

'My lords,' he said sarcastically, 'the Queen requests your company.'

Owen and I looked at each other and then followed him without speaking.

Maeve sat on her throne, flanked by Ailell. He looked wary. She had a smile on her face that I didn't much like the look of. A big man, covered in the dust of a long journey, was sitting near to her. He looked familiar. A large group of rough and equally travel-stained men were eating along both sides of the main table.

Men that I knew. Ulstermen.

I turned to Owen. His eyes were as round as Roman coins. His mouth hung open like a lobster trap. He was as flabbergasted as I was.

We walked across the straw-covered floor to where they sat. The big man at Maeve's table was Fergus, the trainer of the Boys' Troop. He was soaking wet from the rain. He had a fresh cut on his forehead that had recently bled freely, and he had only managed to wash some of it off. Dried blood speckled his forehead, mixing with the dust that covered him. There were sword marks on his forearms. Blood spattered his clothes. I looked past him. Every man near him was an Ulsterman, all bore the marks of recent fighting, all had obviously travelled a long way and were as wet and as dirty as Fergus.

'Fergus? What in Zeus's name are you doing here?' I blurted out.

Maeve chuckled. 'Tell your friends what has happened,' she said, 'I could bear to hear it again.'

Fergus looked at me without speaking. Great emotions were

241

obviously playing inside him; he looked as if he might collapse with the strain or burst into tears or start a fight or all three at any moment. Ailell intervened, speaking in his most formal kingly voice.

'Our friends from Ulster are, of course, welcome. They have travelled a long way. We will arrange rooms for them, and they can rest. We will all meet here in the morning, to discuss what has happened and what is to be done.'

Maeve looked at him with annoyance. She obviously felt that whatever was going on was too good to miss, but Ailell looked stern, and she gave a little shrug. (I noticed her do this more than once, preparatory to giving way on a small thing. She never gave way on big things, and she didn't shrug all that often either.) Ailell and Maeve swept away, leaving the dusty Ulstermen to be sorted out by the court chamberlain, a job he had obviously been preparing for all his life. Slaves scuttled, blankets were brought, rooms were readied, bedpans provided, more wine and food were produced in an amount of time that suggested that visitors had been expected imminently, and within what seemed like a few minutes the whole thing had been organized. Owen and I would have been impressed if we had been paying attention. We couldn't find out what had happened. The Ulstermen were mostly too tired or too angry to talk or else made no sense. We grabbed Fergus and some dry blankets, two bottles of wine and a haunch of beef and dragged the whole lot off to the largest room. We splashed Fergus down, wrapped him in clean blankets, sat him comfortably, shoved wine into one hand and meat into the other and demanded to be told what was going on.

Fergus looked at us for a long time without speaking, eating or drinking. Owen and I glanced at each other with the same thought. Whatever had happened, it was serious. Neither of us could remember a time when Fergus had been awake and had not been doing at least one of those three things, usually more. We let him think for a bit, then, tentatively, I raised his cup to his lips. The wine-fumes went up his nose, which twitched visibly, and he drained the cup in one go. Owen refilled it, and he swallowed it all again. The third time he only drank half of it, and we felt he was ready to talk.

His voice was hoarse from recent shouting and the dust of the journey, and his words came slowly through a heavy mist of emotion. We had to lean in close to hear him.

'Deirdre,' he said. Owen and I exchanged wary glances. 'Deirdre and Usna's sons. They came home.'

This sounded like good news, but obviously wasn't, so we sat quietly and listened, as Fergus mac Roth told us about the death of the sons of Usna, the taking of Deirdre, and how the Red Branch was split in two.

# 30

Fergus told us the story back to front, punctuated with curses and gulps of wine, and with frequent 'Oh, I forgot to tell you's and 'Did I mention?'s. The next morning he told it again to the court. It wasn't much less confused. Owen and I talked to Fergus and the other Ulstermen for a full day. Their words burn in my mind.

After they eloped, Conor pursued Deirdre and the sons of Usna for over a year. Realizing that they had escaped him, he sent agents to every corner of Ulster, offering money and his favour for fresh information. The agents came back only with rumours and guesswork. Those who had actually seen Deirdre and the sons were not disposed to speak of it. Even the poorest, who might have been forgiven for taking the opportunity of escaping their condition, when Deirdre and the sons of Usna came to them for hospitality, they gave it gladly and asked for nothing in return. Deirdre's beauty and gentleness, the love that shone between her and Naisi like sunlight reflecting off rainwater, the fierce devotion of the brothers to each other, their determination to stand together despite the odds against them, all this touched people's hearts. When asked by Conor's agents if they had seen the fugitives, people usually denied having seen them at all. If Conor's men were hard on their heels then people would mislead the pursuers or even waylay them. On the rare occasions that accurate information was offered, it was almost impossible to disentangle from the mass of false trails that had been laid around it.

After two winters, Conor gave up the chase. The sons of Usna had escaped him, at least for the present, and although Deirdre fled from him through all his dreams and thoughts of her distracted his every waking moment, Conor was King enough to know that he must return to his life at Emain Macha and Ulster. However, he kept his agents moving around the province, he increased the reward, and he drank deeply as he waited. Soon no woman wanted to be near him and no man dared. Anyone who shared his company ended up in an argument at least; anyone who shared his bed found only coldness and anger and rejection.

Two months later, Cathbad the druid went in search of the King. He found Conor drinking at his table, his face, as always, black with unspoken passion and thoughts of the wrongs that had been done to him by Naisi. Cathbad looked at the King for a long time, but Conor would not meet his gaze. Cathbad thought of the divisions at court and in the province caused by the quarrel, and remembered Conor when he had been at peace with himself and his Champions. Cathbad was the only man who could make Conor do what had to be done.

'Enough!' cried the druid, and took the goblet from his hand. Conor started up with surprise and would have struck at him, but Cathbad brought his staff down on the King's head and Conor fell to the ground. The druid had the King carried to the steam lodge, where he was kept for three days and three nights. When he emerged the King was sober and his mind had cleared. He asked Cathbad what he should do.

'Call off your dogs,' said the druid. 'Receive your loyal friend Usna, whom you have refused to see these two years. Accept that Naisi and Deirdre have made their choice, and that Deirdre would rather live in poverty and exile than be your wife. Heal the wounds in your kingdom, as only you have the power to do.'

Conor looked at him. 'Do you know where they are?'

Cathbad shook his head. 'But if you announce an amnesty, they will hear of it. They will accept your protection and return home.'

Conor realized that he could see clearly for the first time in two years, and resolved to do as Cathbad advised him.

When the sons of Usna heard that Conor had publicly proclaimed his forgiveness, had reconciled himself with their father and offered them his protection, they were overjoyed. The brothers danced with happiness on the sands around the small fishing cottage that had been their home for almost a year. Naisi turned smiling to Deirdre and saw that she was sitting apart from them and that a tear was rolling down her cheek. He knelt beside her and asked her gently why she was not happy.

She looked at him with eyes filled with love and sorrow. 'Because I do not believe in his forgiveness,' she said. 'He bears us a grudge, and the thing that was taken from him has never been returned. Why should he forgive so easily? I do not feel confident under his protection, I feel threatened by it.'

All three brothers tried to persuade Deirdre, but she was adamant. She would not go to Conor, nor would she let Naisi go. Naisi had never known her be so obdurate, and was beginning to have second thoughts himself, when Ardan had an idea.

'I know what to do,' he said. 'We'll ask Fergus to give us his protection and escort us home. He is a man of his word. If he agrees to escort us there will be nothing to fear.'

The brothers agreed that it was a good plan. Deirdre argued against it, but when all the men agreed that they would feel secure if Fergus came to escort them, with Dubtach their friend and Cormac the son of Conor, both of whom had been in the Boys' Troop with all three of them, she found it hard to stand against them. Eventually she stood up, holding her hands apart to show her acceptance. She embraced them one after the other, as if she were saying farewell before a long and dangerous journey.

'We will go then,' she said, 'although I do not trust the King. But you are determined to go, and I would rather be in danger with you than safe and separated from your company. And if the good men that you mention are prepared to come and protect us, perhaps it may all yet come well.' And she tried to smile, because they talked happily of going home, and Naisi spoke soft words of comfort to her, but her eyes were always full of sorrow from that day forward.

Ardan went to Emain Macha alone and announced to Conor that he and his brothers were willing to return with Deirdre and accept his protection. Conor embraced Ardan with every sign of goodwill and forgiveness, speaking of the valour of the sons of Usna and the high regard he held them in. He did not, however, speak of Deirdre. The next day, Conor called together Fergus, Dubtach, his own son Cormac and a number of others that Ardan had asked for, and requested them to accompany Ardan to where Naisi, Deirdre and Ainle were waiting. The escort set off the next day, led by Fergus and loudly welcoming the coming of harmony again between Ulstermen and the return of the mighty warriors from the house of Usna.

Ardan's brothers greeted him heartily when the escort reached the agreed meeting place, and Fergus gave the sons of Usna his protection and assurances of the King's good faith. That night there was a celebration around the campfire, and in the darkness and merrymaking none of them noticed Calum mac Fachtna slip away and gallop back through the dark to report to Conor what had happened and what he had seen.

'Well?' asked Conor. His voice was quiet but urgent and his body bent forward like a hook. 'They told me she was grown fat with child-bearing. They said her face was plain and lined from working outdoors in the wind and rain. They described to me her skin and hair, grown coarse with rough living, her hands red and chapped with gutting fish, her eyes dull with poverty. Is it so? I want to believe what they said to me, although I suspect that they told me those things so that my loss would be easier to bear. You have seen her? Do not lie to me.'

Calum nodded, but said nothing.

Conor saw his uncertainty and knew the truth. He jumped from his throne and seized Calum by the hair, forcing him against the wall. The King put his sword against Calum's neck hard enough to break the skin and let his blood flow and said, 'I swear I will kill you if you lie to me. Speak!'

Calum closed his eyes. 'She is as slim as an arrow and still childless. Age has thickened only her hair and has made a beautiful woman of a girl. Rough living has untamed her movements so that every action has the grace of dancing and no man can take his eyes from her body, and yet when she is still every man continues to watch her, filled with the sense of lying calm in a lover's arms. Being near her made me feel like a man, and made me feel that being a man was a good thing to be, and that I was the best of men. I know that every other man felt as I did. Her dark eyes shine at you from a clear and peaceful place, and her skin is as soft as a gosling's throat and glows as gold in firelight. She is the most beautiful woman I ever hope to see.'

For a moment, Conor looked as if he would kill Calum, then he released him with an oath and flung himself back in his chair. Conor felt his passion rising once again and he fought it down and clung to his good intentions, hoping that when he saw her again his rage would have gone and he would only feel happiness at her return.

It was as if he was two men in one body. One Conor hoped that the old feelings were gone, yearned to have peace, wanted to be a King to his people again. The other Conor saw only Deirdre, thought only of Deirdre, and made arrangements to do what was necessary to get what he wanted.

Messengers were sent to a number of chiefs along the way that the escort would pass. All these chiefs issued invitations to Fergus to come to their ale-feasts. Fergus was under a geis never to refuse an invitation, and it was not one he found it onerous to observe. So he left the escort, taking Dubtach with him. Normally, Fergus's departure would not have mattered, for they could have waited for his return, but the sons of Usna had sworn that the first food that they would eat in Ulster would be Conor's. This was a compliment, intended to show their eagerness to get to their host's castle, but now it meant that they could not wait for the three weeks or more that Fergus and

Dubtach might be occupied at feasting. So they were forced to ride on with the remainder of the escort.

Conor the King stood on the walls of Emain Macha and watched them arrive, from the moment that he saw a plume of dust rising like a small tree on the horizon until they arrived at the gate below him. Usna ran out to greet his sons, and for a moment all was movement below the King as Naisi and his brothers embraced their father. As they shouted and clapped each other on the back, the small, dark, still figure who stood in the chariot behind them looked up at the King. On her face was an anxious, questioning look, wanting but not daring to hope.

As Conor gazed down at her he knew that Calum had not lied to him. The intervening years had, although he would not have believed it possible, made her even more beautiful. The sadness and pleading in her eyes passed by him in the overwhelming passion that gripped him as he looked at her. Her beauty rushed over Conor like a wave over flat sand to a place deep inside him, and a darkness flowed back out from that place through his body and into his mind, and his desire to do right and to honour his promises drowned in a moment beneath it. Deirdre saw the effect that her face had upon him, and the pleading expression on her face disappeared. She knew that their fate was already written.

Conor feasted with them, but it is said that he never looked at Deirdre after the moment she arrived, not even when he toasted their return. That night Ardan and Ainle were slaughtered while sleeping in their beds. Naisi was awake but he was unarmed when Eoghan cut him down without speaking a word. Deirdre was dragged off his dying body and brought to Conor's rooms with Naisi's blood still warm on her nightdress. His hands were clean. Eoghan mac Durtacht and his kinsmen did the killing, for a blood-feud that went back longer than anyone could remember. But Conor knew. Eoghan wouldn't have done it without Conor's knowledge, without his protection. The blood-feud between Eoghan and Usna was proscribed, and even if it hadn't been so, they were all under Conor's roof. He did nothing to stop it. It took place in his house, they were all under his protection, he was the King. The blame could only lie in one place. Even if he had known nothing about it, the fact that he did nothing to Eoghan, let him return home, the fact that he kept Deirdre beside him, made it a crime. The King allowed a guest to be killed under his roof, did nothing to prevent it, did nothing to avenge it. Then took the murdered guest's wife prisoner for himself.

He did all those things. Fergus told us, and the other men told the same story. Conor had committed the gravest sin an Ulsterman could do. He was anathema.

And we went back to him.

# 31

Owen and I knew that we had to return to Emain, if only to find out who was still alive and who dead. Fergus agreed in a gruff way that we should go. He had sons that he wanted news of, but was too proud to send for word of them. He took us aside, out of hearing of any of the Connaughtmen, and spoke urgently.

'Go quickly and spread the news of what is happening here. My quarrel is with Conor and his kin, not with Ulster. I would not see my country destroyed or ruled by Connaught, her wealth taken and her people enslaved. I march with them to fight Conor, but I will slow their preparations and progress as much as I can. If Ulster intends to surrender, I will give her time to hide her gold. If Ulster will fight, I will give her some little time to prepare. Do not delay, Maeve will march immediately and her army will move quickly despite anything I can do.' He walked away without waiting for a reply.

After watching Maeve's army gather and start marching, Owen and I drove fast towards Emain Macha, filled with trepidation. Fergus had told us what to expect, but we knew that only seeing it for ourselves would tell us how bad it really was. Fergus's story of returning to Emain Macha with Dubtach, the guilty silence, his demand to see Deirdre denied, his realization of what had taken place and challenge to Conor over Naisi's death, of harsh words exchanged, swords drawn, sides taken, battle joined, Emain Macha burnt to the ground, half its Champions gone, some of them dead, killed by friends, many more gone to live and fight with Ulster's enemies, and the knowledge that Conor still had Deirdre and the sons of Usna were dead and that therefore peace was impossible, all of this filled our minds as we drove back. We alternated between furious but useless debates and total silence.

I preferred the silence. Most of the time Owen wanted to talk. I let him rattle on, while I retreated behind my thoughts. Owen liked to set up possible scenarios and debate them. I thought that this was pointless, partly because we didn't know enough of the facts, partly because events would have moved on by the time that we returned. I knew enough about royal power struggles to know that perhaps only one thing is certain: the man who goes into the situation with a fixed point of view is lost. The survivor is the man who is open to any possibility and course of action. Survival is adaptation. I know that. Owen was trying to make up his mind before knowing what was happening. He wanted to decide whether we should stay or leave. He was even trying to bring morality into it. I have seen what morals can do to people. The important thing is to find out what you want to do as things change, and then reassess with every change in the currents and winds that surround you. If you try to make a stand that you aren't prepared for then you will get flattened or swept away. I wasn't ready to leave Emain yet. I wanted to see what Emain would be like without half its Champions. I wanted to see if Conor was just another Menelaus ready to ruin his kingdom and pull all the rest of us down too for a darker Helen, or if he was still grinning like a wolf looking up from a kill, and knew what he was doing.

Most of all, I wanted to be there when Cuchullain got back. I wanted to see him, and the woman who stood silently beside him.

We arrived back early in the morning. The new sun was still reflecting off the morning frost and the air was clear and still.

The tired horses pulled the chariot over the last hill with a freshened step, the smell of home in their nostrils. They pulled at the reins, but I made them stop. I heard Owen gasp as we saw what was left of Emain.

The walls were blackened with smoke and a huge hole had been bitten out of one side. The great keep was destroyed, and with it the banqueting hall and the stables. The great gates were charred by fire but still standing. From where we stood it looked as if some of it could be saved, but there was no way of being sure. We could see figures wandering amongst the ruin, but they were too far away for us to see who they were.

As we rode towards what remained of the castle, we began to see evidence of a vicious battle. Broken chariots lay where they had come to rest, smashed like toys from a child's fist. Some still had dead horses under them. Broken spears littered the ground like reeds on a riverbank after a flood. Arrows stuck up from the ground everywhere. The earth was marked deeply by curved scars where chariot wheels had dug in as they turned too sharply. Many men's feet, stamping down for grip in the press of battle, had left their imprints all over the soft turf. In places, the outline of a man could be seen in the earth where he had fallen and been trodden on by men still fighting, pressing the corpse into the soft earth. There were no bodies left for us, but in places blood could still be seen on the grass and in the holes left by horses' hooves where the dew had not yet washed it off. Great fat carrion crows waddled about the field, looking for more of the feast. As we drove past a dead horse tangled with the wreck of a chariot, a flock of them were startled by us and burst upwards from its distended stomach in a black shrieking mass, their wings colliding with each other in their haste, slime and gore from the dead animal dripping from their beaks and making their heads shine dully.

Owen was pale, and I thought he was going to be sick. 'Death has been here,' he murmured quietly. 'The air still moves from the beat of his wings.'

I was not feeling too steady myself. I circled the chariot in front of the main gate and stopped. We stepped down off the boards, and I immediately stumbled, like a sailor setting foot on dry land for the first time in many months. As I caught myself on the chariot edge to prevent myself falling, I heard a shriek of delight. 'Look out!' said Owen.

I turned round and was sent reeling as Ulinn landed on my back like a child saying hello to an old school-friend. We collapsed in a tangle of arms and legs onto the ground, both of us asking a hundred questions at the same time. Owen watched without speaking, still pale, a wan smile on his face. Eventually Ulinn managed to disentangle herself from me and embraced him too. Then she was crying, and Owen was crying, and I would have laughed at their foolishness but some dust had got into my eye when she and I were rolling about on the ground and I was having trouble getting it out and it made my eyes water more than I would have thought possible.

Half an hour later we were sitting in a small room in a cottage near the ruined keep. A jug of beer was in front of us and Ulinn was pressed up warm against my side, so at least two things were all right in the world. It was starting to sound as though not much else was.

'So where is Conor?' asked Owen. Ulinn flicked back a lock of hair and looked as if she was going to spit.

'Gone to stay with his friend Eoghan, the bastard who killed Naisi.' She did spit then, as if both names were too much for her. 'Conor says he's going to rebuild Emain, but we haven't seen anything of that yet. He's probably too busy with Deirdre at the moment to think of anything else.'

A picture of Deirdre and Naisi as they first met fell into my mind. Naisi in the river, almost naked, and Deirdre on the bank, lovely as the dawn. I also remembered seeing – no, I suppose I was spying on them, although it hadn't felt like it – them on my bed the day they left Emain. I could still see the way the firelight glowed on their skin, and how she stroked his face. I was still having trouble believing that the three brothers were dead, all that rumbustious life just snuffed out, never mind accepting that Deirdre was a prisoner of Conor's. Conor was my friend. Naisi had been my friend. What was I supposed to do?

'Where is Cuchullain?'

Ulinn shrugged. 'Still in Muirthemne, as far as anyone knows. I don't know if anyone has sent a message to him yet.'

'Why would they?' I said. 'The sons of Usna were not his family. Their death would not be his concern.'

Ulinn sat up stiffly and looked at me with a surprised frown, pulling away slightly as she did so. 'Don't you think that this is perhaps something that goes beyond family? When a King breaks the law of hospitality, kills men who are under his protection, lies to those who serve him, picks a fight with men who have served him all their lives, and steals a woman who does not love him?' Her sarcasm was an obvious rebuke, but I couldn't explain my mixed feelings. Conor had perhaps behaved as badly as a man can, but I wanted to hear the story from his mouth. If I was to take sides against him, I wanted to see his face before I crossed the Rubicon.

'Cuchullain is Conor's kinsman. I don't think . . .'

Ulinn looked at me with something approaching contempt. 'You think it's all right, don't you? You think he should be allowed to get away with it!' In the face of her incredulity I had to make some sort of reply.

'I just think we shouldn't move too—'

She didn't wait for me to finish. She banged her mug down onto the table so hard that brown liquid jumped out like a startled animal and splashed down my shirt. I thought she was going to throw it in my face. The words that came instead felt much the same.

'I have misjudged you! I thought you were the sort of man who— Well, I was wrong. Keep your precious Conor then, and much joy may he bring you!'

I should perhaps mention that she slapped me across the cheek, if a closed fist counts as a slap. It pitched me right off my stool and over backwards. My head hit the wall and an ill-tuned harp started playing in my head. I was so dazed that I didn't even see the jug she aimed at my head, and only heard it smash against the wall beside me. A shard cut my cheek. I still have the scar.

I knew that my stance on Conor's behaviour was indefensible and probably misconceived. Nevertheless I did not feel that I could just walk away. I still wanted to know if he was Menelaus or Conor. I wanted to see him before I made up my mind.

'Don't you think you're behaving like an idiot?'

I had forgotten that Owen was there. I reached out an arm, which he grabbed and hauled me upright. I prodded at my jaw with gentle fingers. It felt broken, but I had never broken it before so there was hope that I might be mistaken. It hurt like Zeus with a hangover.

'An idiot? Oh, I don't know. I've upset a good friend and have allied myself with a man who appears to have behaved despicably. I've a sore jaw and I'm covered in beer. Does that make me an idiot?' Owen nodded. Suddenly I wasn't able to go on thinking everything was going to be all right. I sat down like a sack of sawdust falling off a cart.

'Owen? It's all fallen apart. What are we going to do?'

He looked serious. He loved it when I asked his advice. 'You said it yourself,' he said. 'We have to see Conor.'

It was as simple (and as complicated) as that. We got back into the chariot and rode to the castle where he was camped. His men stopped us at the edge of the field as we approached. They made us dismount, searched us thoroughly (despite Owen's indignant protests) and walked us to the King. I knew almost all of them, some well, but they were unfriendly and watchful, suspicious of everything. I had seen that look on men's faces at times of turmoil in Rome. Men who feel that they have made a choice which they are not sure is the right one are always on the lookout for men who are not as committed as they are. Such men are enemies until they are proved friends. We were such men.

The King was sat on a heavy plain wood chair. He looked dreadful. When he had sent me to Maeve's court he had been the man of action, in his prime, full of energy and life, confident and able to sum people up in a glance. Now he looked drawn, pale, empty. His body slumped in the chair, making him graceless. I had never seen him graceless before. Only his eyes burnt bright, as if he had a fever or had not slept for a long time.

I did not know what sort of reception we would get. I suppose I thought we would be welcomed. After all, we had already been at Maeve's court, and we had left it, not stayed with the Exiles. I thought that that would show our bona fides. One look at Conor told us it did not. He looked up from his chair and his sick eyes burnt with suspicion and uncertainty. This was not Menelaus, but it was not Conor either. In a few weeks he had become someone else.

He looked around him and scowled. 'Clear the room!' he shouted. I turned gratefully to go. 'Not you two,' he said, more softly, and motioned to us to sit down. People scuttled away, probably glad of the chance to escape. The atmosphere was heavy with recent events, and Conor looked ready to strike out at anyone who got in his way. We sat opposite him, and he looked at us from under heavy brows, waiting until we were alone. The door closed behind the last of them, and a heavy silence fell. Owen and I made the same uncomfortable shift in our chairs at the same moment. Conor smiled. It was not a pleasant sight. That much of the wolf remained in this man I hardly recognized.

'So,' he said, 'you came back.' I paused for a few moments before replying. Directness seemed best. He didn't look in the mood to be played with.

'Yes, as you see. Did you think we wouldn't?'

He threw back his head and laughed, a short, barking sound. It seemed to unblock something in him, and he sat up straight. 'Why not?' he mused. 'A bard, who I can't touch anyway, and a piece of German driftwood. Or are you Roman today? Neither of you have to be loyal to me, you have no family, no ties. You can come and go as you please.'

We all knew that this was not true. At least, there was some truth in it in theory. In practice he could have us killed in a moment. He knew that bards across Ulster and in Maeve's castle would be composing poems about him as we spoke. He had broken the laws of hospitality. It could perhaps theoretically be worse, but no-one had ever thought of something else that bad yet. Therefore killing a bard that no-one had heard of would not make things worse for him, much, and killing me would not even ripple the surface of society. We were not in a good position. Owen spoke up. I hoped he wouldn't antagonize Conor, which is what Owen speaking up usually meant.

'We came back because we met Fergus mac Roth and the others at Maeve's castle.'

Conor nodded slowly. 'Yes. And?' Owen looked staunch. I tried to look supportive without looking committed. After all, I wasn't sure what he was going to say.

'The stories that were told about what had happened here seemed . . . coloured, by the emotions of recent events. We came back to see what really happened.' It sounded good. In Owen's case it was probably even true. The truth, after all, was supposed to be his job. Conor made a languid gesture. He looked as if he didn't care very much. Suddenly, I felt anger. I fought it down. Conor looked at me, and he knew. He arched an eyebrow, inviting me to speak. I asked my questions.

'Did you have Naisi killed?'

He hesitated a beat. 'I . . . allowed it.'

'And his brothers too?'

No hesitation. 'Yes.'

'And you took Deirdre, against her will?'

'It isn't as simple as that.'

I looked into his eyes. It was like looking into a deep well at midnight. Still, dark, unmoving.

'The question is as simple as that.'

He looked back, his gaze flicked across at Owen and then back to me again, and then away. He looked confused. I could not remember ever seeing him like this. Owen looked at Conor and then at me, and stood up.

'I will leave you to talk,' he said formally, and left so swiftly that I could not protest. After he had gone I was glad. Conor's demeanour changed. He leant forward in his chair until he was only an arm's length away with his hands clasped together and he looked at the floor as he spoke. His voice was a soft

258

monotone, and the words came in a rush, as if he was afraid that if he stopped he wouldn't be able to begin again. Sometimes I had to lean forward until our heads almost touched in order to be able to hear him.

'I stood on the wall over the gate,' he said, without looking up. 'Leary, I saw her look up at me. I had so many good intentions. I promised Cathbad, I promised myself, I promised Fergus, nothing was going to happen, nothing, I swore it. Then,' and his voice dropped even lower, 'then she looked up at me and I was deaf and blind except for her, I couldn't hear the birds, I couldn't see the bright sun, I knew nothing except her. She filled me up, Leary, she filled me up so that I felt whole. And while I was feeling like this, another part of me was saying that she was mine, that I had risked the prophecy and agreed to take her as a wife to help my people, that I had waited for her, that she had been stolen from me, and worse, stolen by the sons of a man who had done my father wrong, and I felt everything in me collapsing, and I thought that my mind would snap, and somehow I sat through that meal while they laughed at me and told of how I had tried to catch them and how they had avoided me, and she spent the whole night looking at him, and I couldn't feel anything, not love, not passion, not hate or pain, I couldn't even feel myself breathing.' His voice was a whisper. 'When Eoghan came to me late that night with the plan to kill him, I didn't say anything, I didn't do anything. I didn't say yes to him, but I didn't stop it. I could have, but I didn't. I felt nothing, I couldn't speak. When they killed him, I felt nothing. When they brought her to me, I felt nothing. Since the day he died we have slept in the same bed, eaten the same food, breathed the same air, and I know that I love her more than I love life, or Ulster, or the Gods, and yet I feel nothing except emptiness, because before, when I was without her, I could always feel that one day she would be mine, that she would want me, even love me, that she had been stolen and that when she was returned to me everything would be all right, but now, now that I have her, now that I have no rivals, I look at her and I know that she hates me, and nothing that I do pleases her, and when we lie close beside each other I look into her eyes and I see only winter cold surrounded by famine and no matter how close I pull her to me she lies still under me and the pleasure I take is more painful to me than the agony I felt when she was with Naisi. So I have gained nothing and lost what I had, and by getting what I wanted I have now not got anything I need.' For the first time he looked up at me. 'I do not want your answer, or your pity, or your judgement. I just want you to know.'

With that he sank his head into his hands, and his back moved up and down with his sobbing breath.

I watched him for a moment, wondering what to do, when I became aware of a commotion outside. I jumped up, fearing the worst. Owen had told me that no King had ever been assassinated in Ulster. However, things were taking a distinctly Roman turn, and I knew from experience that assassins do not usually scruple to kill others in the room with their intended victim.

The door opened, and Cuchullain walked in. He looked a lot older, and he had grown, although he was still slim and smaller than most men. He stood at the door, waiting for Conor to look up. Eventually he did. The King looked mildly surprised.

'Cuchullain? You here too? Have I you with me?'

Cuchullain nodded. 'Of course. You are my kinsman, and my King. I have sworn loyalty—'

'Loyalty!' spat Conor. 'What do Ulstermen know of loyalty? They have joined our enemies in Connaught. Will they help that hell-bitch invade, do you think, is that their plan?'

I took Cuchullain by the arm and out of the room. Conor's head was sunk into his hands again as I closed the door behind us.

'Leary! You've become fat!' He prodded my stomach.

I bridled. 'No I haven't, you've become rude. How much do you know?'

Cuchullain shrugged. 'Naisi dead, Deirdre with Conor, Fergus and half of the Champions deserted to Connaught, Emain Macha in ruins. Is that all of it?' He was completely calm. It was infuriating.

'Isn't that enough?'

He seemed amused. I realized I didn't know him any more, not as I had done. 'Quite a lot of goings-on, it seems. I'm sorry I missed it all.'

'And?'

He looked puzzled. 'And what?'

He could still exasperate me, that hadn't changed. 'Don't be stupid! Are you still with Conor, or against him?'

Cuchullain looked serious. 'I told you. I swore loyalty to him, as we all did. What is the point of loyalty, if you can put it on and take it off like a cloak?'

'Even if the one you have sworn to no longer deserves it?'

'Is that what you think?'

'I want to know what *you* think.'

'I've told you.'

'You are Conor's, then.'

'I have said so.'

'Against Fergus?'

'No, not against Fergus. Fergus is my friend.'

'But Fergus is not Conor's friend. He stays with Maeve, in her castle.'

'Then if he marches against Ulster, I will fight him. I defend Ulster against anyone who attacks her. But Fergus is still not my enemy.' It was an attractive idea. He wasn't against anyone, just not for all of them. I wondered if it would last long when Fergus led Maeve's army over the passes into Ulster, and Cuchullain stood in his way.

'And you?'

'Me?'

He looked at me with casual intensity.

'Are you Conor's man?'

I shrugged. 'I'm here.'

Me, Conor's man? I was Cuchullain's charioteer.

# 32

I have seen many armies on the march. I saw the Seventeenth Legion, the Indomitable, leave to fight the Scythians. I saw my tribe returning from helping Arminius to annihilate Varus and his three legions. I have seen armies of grim-faced Iberians; as a boy I ran beside ill-disciplined hordes of painted Gaulish auxiliaries; I have seen every kind of military movement. Of all these, three stick in my mind.

I remember best the army that my father was part of. His group started at our village. Twenty men set out with my father at their head, to be joined almost immediately by similar groups and individuals from other villages near by. By the end of the day they were perhaps two hundred strong. The next day, more small groups joined them, until they were nearly four hundred, and then they met another group the same size as their own. They knew that, all over the land, the same scene was being enacted. Like rain that falls in drops, gathering to become pools which fill and then spill over in rivulets, which grow to streams, which meet and merge and flow on until they form mighty rivers and surge forward down to the sea, our men gathered together as they advanced to the meeting point. We did not have time for forming columns or any use for orders of march. If a group met an obstacle, it would part and go round it. If a knot of men met a tree fallen in their path, some went left, some right, some over it, rejoining as a group on the far side. So the army of the Celts flowed over the landscape without disturbance, leaving little trace of their passing except the black circles of their night fires in the clearings of the forest.

I also remember seeing Tiberius's army on the march to subdue some tribes of my people who did not accept the treaty that the rest of us had submitted to. It was thus a punitive expedition, intended to show those who were to be subdued that there was no point in resistance, and to confirm the impression in the minds of those whose subdued lands the Romans marched through not that they had submitted too easily, more that they had given in to the inevitable. To this end, the Romans did not flow over the country like water, they went through it like a starving burglar goes through a rich man's larder, picking up everything of value in a controlled frenzy, careless of the signs of his presence. Tiberius sent out scouts to find where the food was, and then marched towards it. No Celtic nonsense about going through the forest like trickling water. If something was in the way of the legions, they knocked it down. If it was too big to knock down, they cut through it, or climbed over it, or built bridges and viaducts across it, just to show that they had considered it, measured it and, inexorably and utterly, defeated it. Wherever they went, they left a trail. The aim was simple. Advance with all speed to be sure, but leave a road behind with engineers to maintain it, and build and fortify supply depots, and leave stations at intervals for changing horses. And garrisons, everywhere leave garrisons, like the intersection points of a spider's web, so that there is always support within clear sight. And above all else, fear ambush. Make sure that the forest is cut back for a bowshot on either side. No Roman feels safe marching in shadow; he will destroy a wood rather than risk walking while overlooked by trees. Since Romulus, long before the vain idiot Quintilius Varus marched twenty thousand of Augustus's crack troops into the great dark forest at the heart of my land, where they were cut to pieces and filled with arrows by men carrying light arms and armour half the weight of their own, Romans have always feared to fight on ground not of their own choosing. Since Varus, sensible precaution had become a superstitious compulsion. The Roman army went through the land like fire on rails, burning a straight path before it and a wide swathe either side.

The army of Maeve and Ailell was both like and unlike these others. We rode out and watched from a nearby hill, out of arrow range. Maeve didn't mind us seeing it, we knew that. She wanted the news to travel. Her army was huge by Gaelic standards, but Tiberius's had been bigger. Owen said that the normal way that the army would have formed would have been close to the way that my father's army started out with a small core of men and gathered numbers to itself as it marched. However, Maeve had gathered all the chiefs together for the Counting, and she had no intention of letting any of them go home and have second thoughts on seeing their wives and children. So the whole army started together.

The numbers were swollen by men of Leinster who joined partly because of an old alliance that most people had forgotten about, but mostly for spoils and the hell of it. The Connaught-men did not much like them and did not trust them, but were not going to turn away help. Furthermore, they were huge, battle-scarred men who feared nothing and no-one and fought as you or I would breathe, naturally and without thinking. They were renowned as such ferocious fighters that Ailell insisted that their group be split up between his own companies, a dozen here, fifty there. Cuchullain commented approvingly at this even though he knew it made things harder for us; it would prevent the Leinstermen gaining elite status, and it would stiffen the resolve of the Connaughtmen to have such men beside them. It would also force the two groups to rely on each other. Apparently – or so the gossip went – Maeve wanted the Leinstermen as a sort of Praetorian Guard for herself, but Ailell had drawn the line at that. It was one thing for her occasionally to pick out a well-muscled young soldier for her bed when she felt like it. It was quite another to have a horde of potential lovers guarding her bedchamber. You could see his point.

When the chief of the Gauls summoned the tribes to arms, the last man to arrive at the muster point was arrested and tortured to death in front of the whole army before it set out to war. Partly as a sacrifice, partly to encourage promptness. It wasn't necessary here. Most people were more frightened of Maeve than they were of dying anyway.

Then it struck me for the first time. Ferdia was a Leinsterman. He was down there somewhere too, near Maeve, bound by loyalty to his chief.

As we watched the column march towards Ulster, a rider came out towards us under a flag of truce. I realized with a shock that it was Ailell. I tried to imagine a Roman governor riding out alone to meet three fighting men whose land he was in the process of invading, and failed. He greeted us as if we were all meeting to go hunting together. Cuchullain treated him the same way, but didn't say who he was. He didn't want Ailell to know his name. Owen sat on his horse, saluted but said nothing for once. I reckoned they were both mad, but I went with the majority.

We looked down on the thick winding whip of men setting out towards Ulster. We watched in silence for a long time. Then Ailell spoke.

'You see this?'

Cuchullain nodded agreement. Ailell spoke urgently.

'I want you to ride on ahead of the army. Go to Conor with all speed, convince him of the futility of trying to oppose us, tell him that there need not be slaughter.'

Cuchullain and I exchanged a glance. Cuchullain spoke formally. 'What must Conor the Great King do to earn this peace?'

Ailell looked weary, and his voice sounded old and care-worn. 'Tell him we must of course have tribute. Cattle, slaves, gold. Tell him that our demands will not be unreasonable.' He smiled. 'Oh, yes. And we will require the Bull of Cooley.'

'And if he refuses?'

Ailell swept an extended arm from right to left in a wide arc, encompassing the length of the huge column. 'As you see,' he said. 'You know the Queen's mood and intent. We will take what we want back to Connaught, and you will not stop us. But it will not end when Connaught leaves. There are those with us, Leinstermen and bandits, who have no quarrel with Ulster but simply seek plunder. They will not leave when we do. They will stay and burn and rape your country until they are driven out, which will take time and many deaths, many burnt houses, many cattle driven off and slaves taken. All this can be avoided. If Conor agrees to what I ask, then Ulster's borders will not be crossed. We can avoid slaughter, we can spare your lands from fire and anger, and this quarrel will end here.' He paused for effect, and drew himself up. 'But if you resist, you will be crushed, your women will be taken, your men will have their heel-sinews cut before they are taken as slaves, your children will grow up not knowing their parents, your houses will be burnt, your crops taken, your fields left dead and useless.' He paused again, searching our faces for a reaction. Cuchullain looked as though Ailell was talking about the weather. I hoped my face wasn't reflecting the feeling I had in my stomach. Ailell went on. 'I am not making threats, I am stating facts. This is your reality. It is the future of Ulster, soon, unless you can persuade Conor to submit. I do not know if this weakness, this curse of Macha that the Daughters of Calatin screech of is real or not.' I winced and felt my skin move at the mention of their name. Ailell studied my reaction, but could not understand it. He went on. 'It does not matter if a weakness is amongst the men of Ulster. If it is, you are doomed already. If it is not, just look round you. You cannot stand against us, and many will die for nothing.' He smiled. 'Fergus is a good friend to you and Ulster. He has slowed us down in every way he can think of short of turning round and attacking us.' Ailell looked at his vast army. 'But you can see that it does not matter. A few days here or there will make no difference to the future. Ulster will fall. Tell Conor.'

Cuchullain and I were still for a moment, and then we saluted

Ailell in silence. He wheeled his horse around and rode away. The three of us did the same, and rode in silence for a short distance before Cuchullain spoke.

'Why did he do that, do you think?'

'He is doing his best,' I said. Cuchullain looked surprised.

'What do you mean? He is our enemy.'

'I can think of worse men – and women – to have as an enemy. He's trying to stop this going any further than it has to.'

Owen looked grim. 'I never would have thought that Maeve's husband would turn out to be a coward,' he shouted.

The horses' hooves drummed three times before I replied. 'Is that what you think he is? Because he wants to stop a lot of innocent people getting killed, that makes him a coward? Is that all you can see?'

Cuchullain leant forward to help the horse go faster. 'That is the way it is.'

'Horseshit,' I growled. I didn't want to talk to him. At that moment Ailell felt more my friend than Cuchullain or Owen would ever be. Ailell wanted to stop the war. Of course, I knew enough about Conor to be sure that he would spit in their faces and die before giving in, and his men would gladly die beside him. Still, Ailell had tried, and he was more concerned with saving lives than with pride. I respected that.

We cantered away from the great army. We rode in silence for a long while. The night came and went. At dawn Cuchullain turned west towards his own land. He intended to make sure that Emer was safe before coming to Emain Macha.

Emain looked defenceless as we walked the exhausted horses up the hill towards the remains of the great castle. The dawn broke over the hill and shone on the brown walls, a dark jagged broken tooth on the horizon. There were a couple of figures guarding the ramparts. We waved to them and saw them move along the walls to the point nearest to our arrival. I called up to them to pour us a drink, and we did our best to hurry towards them. As Owen and I got off the horses and hobbled up to the gate, clapping each other on the shoulder and grinning like idiots, promising ourselves a bath and a drink before we spoke a word to Conor or anyone else, and thinking ourselves very fine fellows, two arrows hissed into the ground a man's length from my foot, which is too close by about the width of the Forum by my reckoning. I stopped abruptly and looked up. I could not see the archer's face; the sun was rising behind them.

'What in Hades are you playing at?' I yelled.

'Perhaps Emain has been taken by the enemy!' whispered Owen.

'Perhaps your head is a turnip!' I snarled at him. 'How can they have taken it when we left before them and have been riding flat out in a straight line away from them? We'd have chariot tracks up our backs if they'd overtaken us!'

'No need to be so bloody insulting! If it hasn't been taken by the enemy then perhaps as you're so clever you can tell me why they're shooting at us?'

He had a point. I shouted at the walls again. 'Don't shoot! We're friends!'

'Your personal life is no concern of mine!' a voice said from the top of the walls.

Owen took up the call. 'We are messengers, we bring news for the King. And I am a bard and my friend here is—' Slowly, I put out an arm to stop him. I knew the voice from the walls, and it wasn't a man's.

'Ulinn?'

There was a pause, then a figure leant over the battlements. I was right. Her red hair tumbled about her shoulders and curled around the quiver of arrows on her back. The sun was getting higher, and I could now see her face. I could also see the arrow notched in a drawn bow and aimed at my heart.

'What's going on?'

Ulinn spat sideways, a gesture I had seen Conall perform many times. I felt a pang at the thought of them together.

'The great Champions of Ulster are lying in bed like women in labour, so the women of Ulster have taken on the men's job. One job is keeping out Ulster's enemies. That's what I'm doing.'

'But we aren't Ulster's enemies!' Owen sounded quite indignant. I saw her turn to spit again.

268

'You have been with Maeve.'

'On Conor's instructions! Ask him, if you don't believe us. Anyway, I thought you had left Conor's camp?'

She shrugged. 'I have. This is Ulster's camp. Conor just happens to be in it. As soon as Maeve is sent packing I'll be off again.'

I felt another pang. 'It's good to see you. Can we come in?'

The bowstring slackened. 'Yes.' I must have looked hopeful because her expression darkened. 'Don't. Nothing's changed.'

There was a pause while orders were shouted and bolts drawn, then one side of the great wooden gates swung open. I looked round. Cuchullain was standing a little way off, looking at the ruined walls. Owen and I went in through the gate without waiting for him.

The courtyard would normally have been a cockpit of noise, full of animals and people going about their business. It was almost deserted. A dozen women were practising with bows at the far end. Others were sword-fighting near to us. The sword-master was an old man. The pains of Macha were hardest for those who were most useful in the defence of Ulster. His eyes narrowed and his lips tightened when he moved, but he was able to instruct the women. Apart from him there was not a grown man anywhere.

Ulinn came down the steps towards us, her face grim. 'There isn't a man who's any use in a fight left in the castle,' she said. 'You three are the first men we've seen on their feet for a week.' I suspect I may have smiled at the thought of being the only fit man around, but stopped when she growled at me. 'Don't think we're delighted to see you,' she said. She looked at us doubtfully. 'A charioteer and a bard. Unless there are a lot more like you – or preferably much better – we're all done for soon enough.'

I knew it wasn't the time to argue with her. 'Where is the King?'

She looked cheerful for the first time. 'In his chambers. His pains are the worst of all of them. Cathbad says they will be worse and last longer than before.'

Owen and I headed for the King's rooms, with Ulinn just behind us. Along every corridor we heard the cries of men in pain. Passing Buchal's room I heard him groan and call out for water. A woman came out carrying a jug and pushed past me unsmiling. I remembered a day that I saw Buchal laughing as a boar-tusk slash in his leg that I could have lost my hand in was roughly sewn up by a drunken soldier using sack-thread and a fisherman's needle. If Buchal was crying out in pain, there was nothing imaginary about it.

'They won't dismiss women's birth-pains so lightly next time,' said Ulinn, grinning happily. Owen and I both swallowed and kept going.

Conor's door was open. I could see directly in to where his bed stood. On it was the naked King, writhing like a trapped adder as the pains ripped through him. Two women tried to cover him with a bearskin but he kicked it off again.

'The King will see you now,' murmured Ulinn drily, looking at him with a mixture of exasperation and satisfaction before walking away. As we approached, the pain abated slightly, and Conor fell back on the bed exhausted. His breath rasped in his throat. He was drenched in sweat and smelt as if he had not washed for a week. His eyes opened slightly. He beckoned me close with urgent fingers. 'It is true then? Maeve marches on us?' I nodded. A shadow of pain crossed a face already dark with it. 'Then we will all die,' he said. His back arched off the bed again in agony. I tried to help, but there was nothing I could do. The pain seemed to go on for ever, and then, just as it seemed that his body could not bear it any more, he fell back onto the bed with a cry of exhaustion. I guessed his question.

'The armies of Connaught are marching, but Maeve has sacrificed speed for numbers. They will be at the Pass in three days, perhaps less.'

He grabbed hold of my shirt and pulled me close. I could smell his sour fever, his desperation. 'Cathbad says that the pains will pass in twenty more days,' he said, his breath fetid. 'Is there a way that they can be delayed?'

I shrugged, not knowing an answer. 'Fergus marches with

270

them but his loyalty is divided. He will slow them perhaps,' I said. 'And the size of their force makes for slow marching. Cuchullain will be here soon and—'

'Cuchullain? What can one man do?'

'What he can,' said a soft voice. I turned. Cuchullain stood in the doorway. None of us had heard him come in. I saw a movement behind him and realized that he had brought Emer to Emain Macha for safety. My heart banged against the inside of my chest so forcefully I was sure others would hear it.

'Come on,' Cuchullain said. 'We must hurry.' I turned to the King, but another spasm hit him at that instant and there was nothing more to say or do. I stood and followed Cuchullain, vaguely aware of Owen trotting after us. I looked around but Emer had gone. It was no time to be mooning after another man's wife, and yet I felt a pang that she had not stayed to greet me. I pretended it hadn't happened.

'Where are we going?' I asked.

'To Iraird Cuillenn,' said Cuchullain, grimly. 'The Connaught-men have to go through the Pass. If we meet them there then there is a chance. If they go through the Pass before we arrive, then they will spill into Ulster's lap like wine from a cup and there will be no stopping them.'

I didn't ask how we were going to stop them. I have always been good at not worrying about the future when there is a problem to hand. Get there, then worry. Besides, I didn't want to think about it too much. I was sure that we were going to die at Iraird Cuillenn.

# 33

When we slept that night – briefly, badly – I had another dream.
My third visit from the Daughters. I didn't remember them
coming to me, but when I woke I had the now-familiar smell of
unwashed skin and sour milk on my body, and I remembered
the first morning when I woke after a dream and I stood under
a waterfall and scrubbed my skin with sand until it bled to get
that same smell from me. Their footprints were in the sand
of my mind as sure as their nails had scored lines on my
skin. They wanted me to see what was happening, wanted me to
know that Ailell sat with Maeve outside a cave high above
their camp, and that our deaths were foretold. It amused them,
I felt their pleasure on me. While I slept they showed me
what happened many miles away as if I walked beside Ailell
himself.

Ailell pushed the heavy canvas flap aside and walked straight
into Maeve's tent. He was already talking as he entered.

'I must speak with you. There is talk in the camp of leaving.
The Leinstermen—'

He stopped. She was not there. Several slaves were trimming
the wicks of the lamps, which cast a golden glow on the rich silks

of her bed. Ailell saw with a muted pang that the bedclothes were disordered on both sides, neither by him.

'Where is the Queen?'

The slave women knelt in front of him and bent their heads. 'She left no message.'

'Damn! If she returns, inform me at once!' They nodded without looking up. Ailell turned on his heel and strode out of the tent. He grabbed the shoulder of the guard at the entrance, pulling him round. 'Where did she go?'

The guard was a heavy man, thick-set, with a curling black beard to his waist. Ailell recognized him as a veteran, one of those who had fought for Maeve as long as Ailell had fought with her. He was Eoin mac Gonall. Ailell didn't know Eoin well, though he had a vague memory that he had got to know Eoin's daughter quite intimately one drunken night. Now that he thought about it, the resemblance was quite unmistakable.

'Eoin, I have to speak with the Queen. You must have some idea of where she went. I don't care who she's with. I must speak with her.'

Eoin looked at Ailell ponderously for a few moments.

'You and I have not spoken.'

'Understood. I do not know you. We have never talked together, ever. I have only ever seen you once in this life, several Beltanes ago and you were ten spear-throws away, upwind, with your back to me and it was dark. Now, where is she?'

Eoin smiled, a process distinguished more by the time it took to get from start to finish than by its beauty, then looked around over each shoulder in order to make sure that they were not overheard. 'She took her box, carried by two servants, and headed over that way.' He pointed with his spear. Ailell looked. The twilight was just enough to show him a small rocky hill not far off.

He put his hand on Eoin's shoulder. 'Thank you. I shall remember this.'

The stout man shrugged dismissively. 'Don't. What is there to remember about a conversation that never took place with a man you never spoke to?'

Despite his agitation, Ailell smiled.

The pony picked its way carefully between the jagged boulders strewn around the foot of the hill. Ailell fretted, but he could hardly see where he was going, and so let the animal make its own way. One of the men of his escort cursed as his mount went under a thorn-bush so that a branch caught him in the middle and almost sent him sprawling. The other men laughed and Ailell rounded on them angrily.

'Shut up! I'll kill the next man who makes a sound!'

Ailell turned to face forwards again and his pony stumbled, dropping down onto its knees and pitching him over its head before he could react. He landed with a metallic crash as his breastplate hit a boulder, driving the breath out of his body with a sound that echoed round the hillside.

Ailell's escorts sat in dignified silence, looking steadily anywhere but at their King, and waited for him to get up. He stood, breathing with difficulty, daring someone to laugh. There was not a sound except the creaking of leather and the wind to carry it away. Ailell took hold of the reins again, resisting the impulse to bash the pony's head against a rock. 'Dismount,' he snarled. 'We walk from here.'

One man was left with the horses at the bottom of the hill while the rest scampered up the slope after Ailell, who was hurrying ahead, eager to find Maeve as well as angry at his fall. Halfway up the slope, a light became visible ahead of them. Ailell gestured to his men to wait.

'We should come with you. It might not be safe,' protested the nearest guard, a tall man with thick moustaches reaching his collarbones.

'Don't worry,' said Ailell. 'If it is the enemy, I do not fear them. If, as I suspect, it is the Queen, I am very afraid, but nothing you can do can save me.'

The guard grinned sympathetically and leant on his spear. Ailell went on alone.

Maeve was sitting on a rock just inside the entrance to a small cave, looking inwards. The slaves had just finished building a fire further inside the cave and were coming out as Ailell appeared over the rim of the hill. One of them called a warning to the Queen, but Maeve only chuckled without looking back. 'It's all right. It must be my husband. No-one else could make so much noise while trying to creep up on someone.'

Ailell waved the slaves away and brushed past them, bending almost double to avoid the low ceiling, then sat beside Maeve.

'What on earth are you doing?' Maeve smiled at him in a way he wasn't sure that he liked, then leant forward, and lifted the hinged lid of a small oaken box beside her foot. Ailell recognized it and froze. 'Should I stay?'

Maeve shrugged. 'Why not? You might learn something. Do you remember Calatin?'

Ailell thought for a minute. 'Yes. A kinsman of Forgall. Didn't he die in Ulster?'

Maeve nodded assent. 'Yes.' She looked at the open box. 'I thought we'd invite his family round.'

Ailell didn't understand, but he knew enough not to pursue matters. When Maeve was in this mood, things usually became plain soon enough. He sat back and waited. Maeve watched in silence. Nothing happened. He could hear his blood pounding in his head from the climb and his mouth was dry. The shadows in the cave moved as the fire pushed them from side to side, and he could see pictures in the flames and on the walls. It seemed to him that it was suddenly very cold. He turned to Maeve and saw that she was leaning forward, looking into the flames. They flickered and turned blood-red.

'Yesss? You have disssturbed usss again. What isss it you want?' The voice came from nowhere, hissing malevolently like water dripped on hot stone.

Ailell jumped so violently that his head collided with the roof of the cave, throwing him back down again onto his back. His eyes wouldn't focus. Pain flooded his mind. He cursed silently as his hands felt wet blood in his hair. Maeve paid no attention.

'Daughter of Calatin, tell me of what will happen in the battles to come.' She used a tone that Ailell had not heard from her before.

The sibilant voice was silent for a few moments, and then

Ailell jumped again, ducking this time as he did so. A girl perhaps twelve or thirteen years old appeared in front of them. He was sure she had not been in the cave before, nor had she walked past him, but now she stood just an arm's length away. Her face was thin, the bones unnaturally sharp. Red hair streamed to her waist and a green dress covered her body. She had the eyes of an old woman. An old woman who has seen everything, known much and done more.

When she spoke Ailell could still just hear the sibilance, so faint that he felt perhaps he was imagining it, but knew he was not. Her tones became like a child's song. She closed her eyes and rolled her head as she prophesied.

'I see your armies crimson and carmine. I see them through a red cloud, through a fog of blood.'

Maeve shrugged. 'That is not prophecy. We are fighting a war, we expect blood and we will know death. Tell me more.'

'I see an army through the red mist of blood, Connaughtmen with their heads lowered, their spirit broken.'

Maeve sat upright in surprise and anger. 'But that is impossible! Conor and the men of Ulster are in their beds, writhing like women in labour! How then can you say my armies will be beaten and bloody? Look again.' There was a pause. Ailell felt a drop of sweat run down his back.

'I see your armies crimson and carmine.'

Maeve stood up and walked to the edge of the cave, talking to herself. 'What does it mean? There are no Ulster Champions left to perform this bloodshed.' She turned back and sat again. 'Is some natural disaster about to happen? Will a mountain fall on us? How will this blood be shed?'

The slight pause came again. Ailell saw the girl's eyes roll up and backwards into her skull, and he shivered. When she spoke again, the sibilance was more marked. 'I see a youth performing great deeds. I see many deep wounds on him, although his skin is like a girl's and his beard is not yet grown. His body is marked with sword- and spear-cuts at every point so that he bleeds without stopping, and yet still he stands defiant before you. A hero-light shines around his head and victory is on his forehead, and he grows and changes shape, twisting into something unearthly. His face is modest, his eyes clear, his clothes rich with gold and silk, and yet he wears them lightly. He is slim like a boy, but he is more than a dragon in battle. His name is . . .'

She paused for a moment, as if stretching for a thought just out of reach. Maeve leant forward, her face eager. 'Yes? What is his name?'

'Cullan the Iron-smith's Hound. I do not know what that means. From Muirthemne. He is armed for battle. Soon he will fall on your armies like an eagle, and men will fall in rows of hundreds before him. Their blood will stain the ground and their cries will be heard in Connaught. Many women will cry over the torn bodies he leaves behind, and many tribes will seek new leaders after he has passed their battle-station. The Hound of the Forge will cut down men as the sickle cuts through corn, and few will remain untouched by his anger.'

'But will Cuchullain die?'

The pause was even longer. Ailell watched in fascination as the girl swayed and seemed about to fall.

'He will die.'

'In battle?'

'Yes . . . I cannot . . .'

'When? When?'

The girl crumpled to the ground. Ailell blinked, and then she was gone. Only the voice remained. 'We cannot ssee . . . the fog surrounds usss . . . it is not given for usss to sssseeee.'

Maeve swore and sat down abruptly.

'Will I die?' she asked, quietly.

The voice answered straight away. 'You will return to Connaught, although many of thossse with you will not.'

Ailell felt that a concerned glance from his wife towards him would have been nice at that point, but it didn't happen. Maeve leant back against the wall of the cave and looked at the roof. She breathed out, a long slow breath. Then her gaze came down and landed on Ailell's face. He knew that whatever expression he put onto his face was going to be the wrong one. There was a slight pause. He didn't move. It made no difference. She flew at him as if pushed by giant hands.

'Imbecile! Pig-fucker! Dog-breath!'

He caught her as her weight knocked him backwards. His hands held her hips. He felt the warmth of her, and for a moment hoped that one of her swings of mood might be taking place. Then he saw her contorted face, ugly in its frustration above him, and twisted away as she spat at him.

'You are not a man! You are dried fat on a filthy plate that a dog would not lick! Why must I drag you around like a stone? Why do you not leave me and give me hope? Why?'

Ailell knew that there was nothing to say. He fended off her blows as best he could, and waited. Eventually the storm moved off slightly. She stopped hitting him and beat her hands against the wall. From the floor he could see her face twisted with tears. He waited. She did not move. Gradually her breathing returned to normal. Ailell, moving very slowly and quietly, picked up the box and closed the lid. He carried it to the mouth of the cave and sat down with his back to her. After ten minutes or so had passed, he heard her cough and spit twice. Her footsteps came up behind him and stopped. He concentrated on remaining still. Then he felt a hand on his shoulder.

'Come,' she said. 'The Daughters of Calatin have spoken. We have much to do.'

He looked up at her. 'Were those women always like that?'

Maeve looked faraway. 'When Calatin died, his wife was pregnant. She mourned him for a month and then died giving birth, cursing Cuchullain with her last breath.' She smiled. 'Her pain made her daughters old before they were born. Their bodies were already wrinkled, their minds alive. They lived only to carry out their mother's dying words.'

'Did they always look like . . . ?', Ailell faltered.

'Always three in one, but not as they are now. When they finished studying, their teacher offered them a gift. Most people choose to hide their grief and hatred. They chose to change their appearance so that anyone could see what was in their hearts.'

'They chose to be monsters?'

278

Maeve nodded. 'They chose to be honest.'

'But the girl, I saw her . . .' Ailell's voice trailed off.

'A disguise. It amuses them sometimes to take on other shapes. Their natural form is three in one.' She took a deep breath. 'They were born only a few years ago, and yet they are older than you or I, with a power we can only guess at. Do not call them monsters unless you call us all monsters. They simply allow others to see it.'

Ailell hesitated, then looked up at her. 'Do we stop, or go on?'

There was great distance in her eyes and an urgency to her voice. 'We march,' she said. 'We march, and we burn, and we take everything they have. By the time we leave, win or lose, Ulster's wealth will be safely on its way to Connaught.' Her hand dropped to her sword. 'And when we meet Cuchullain, we go around him if we can, or if not then we attack and overwhelm him. He is only one and we are an army, with many Champions amongst our forces, including half the Heroes of the Red Branch, and the Leinstermen, including Cuchullain's own training partner, Ferdia. Ulster's Champions, the ones who remain to defend her, are in their beds screaming in pain. Those who are with us do not suffer because they do not defend Ulster, as the curse foretold. The Daughters of Calatin may be mistaken. We are committed. We go on.'

Ailell looked at her for a long moment. She was gazing out over the countryside, her golden hair blackened by night and burnished by the moon. Her mind was already at the first meeting with Cuchullain. He took a deep breath.

'Very well. We go on.'

As I rasped myself with a hard brush until blood seeped through the raw skin, I knew that the day might be my last.

# 34

We drove the chariot like never before, leaving Owen and his tired horse far behind us.

The Pass of Iraird Cuillenn is the gate from Connaught to Ulster, and the only alternative is a long march around it. It is a narrow defile, perhaps a mile long, with a deep stream running down the centre of it from Ulster towards the Connaught side. On one side are steep hills, and on the other a wide and treacherous marsh over which nothing heavier than a dragonfly can pass safely. Bards sang stories of ancient invasions of Ulster from the Connaught side, and they all had one thing in common. So long as Iraird Cuillenn was held, Ulster was safe. As soon as the Connaughtmen broke through, they would be able to spread out onto the central plain of Ulster like warm honey poured from a jug onto a plate. Generations of tacticians and common sense both said the same thing. If Cuchullain were to make a stand, it had to be at the Pass.

He stood beside me in the chariot, staring west while the wind whipped tears from the corners of his unblinking eyes, as if he could drag our destination closer by the force of his will. He didn't need to urge me to hurry. I drove like a man chased by the Eumenides, calling to the horses for greater and greater effort. The Grey of Macha and the Black Sanglain leant into the breeze and pulled the chariot apparently without effort, skimming past boulders and hillsides close enough to reach out and touch them, frightening me until I was all fear, like a bowstring drawn to within a moment of breaking, and then I went past fear and started to laugh because I no longer cared. When whatever happens is going to result in your death you are free. In the interval between that realization and its fulfilment, you become what people call brave. For a little while anyway. I didn't want to die, and my only real hope was for us to get to the Pass first. I believed that Cuchullain could do almost anything, but even Ulster's greatest Champion could not hope to hold up the march of an army tens of thousands strong advancing on a broad front. We had to reach Iraird Cuillenn before Maeve, or the war was over before it started.

As our chariot carried us in a thundercloud of pounding hooves and swirling dust away from Emain Macha across the central plain of the province, we met a thin stream of women and children coming the other way, running from the forward raiding parties that Maeve had sent out to harry the Ulstermen and pillage their farms to bring back supplies for her army. To begin with, we tried to wave cheerfully and make light of the situation – which, certainly in my own case, was far from what I really felt – but every refugee called to us with anger and pain on their faces, every one had a story to tell, which Cuchullain listened to with courtesy, while I fretted with the need to hurry onwards. We heard of wives dragging their groaning men to barns, or to clumps of bracken, anywhere, hiding them from the Connaughtmen, turning away from the sight of their burning farms and their precious cattle being driven off. Stories were told of women taking swords and defending their families and cattle against the invaders, beating at them until they could no longer lift their arms to strike a blow, and I watched tears run down the teller's cheeks as she told us of the laughter of Maeve's men as these women were slaughtered and their bodies thrown into their burning homes. We heard how some of the men, less badly affected by the weakness than others, had managed to resist, and even gain a few small successes before retreating to the hills, but they were too few to be worth paying any attention to.

Cuchullain and I listened to their stories. I heard the grief in their voices. We watched as the fighting men of Ulster were taken past us writhing like eels on the bottom of flat carts, or tied to their horses, groaning with pain and unable even to guide the reins. Cuchullain's brow darkened and he swore an oath under his breath. I sang to the horses, and we galloped forwards to the enemy. I was feeling unlike I had ever felt before. For the first time in my life, I was starting to feel that something was important enough to die for, and that frightened me more than anything else. I resolved to watch myself closely, for I felt that at any moment I was likely to get myself killed doing something heroic and utterly futile.

There was one more story that we stopped to hear and which neither Cuchullain nor I fretted to get finished so that we could be on our way. We met one of Cullan the smith's boatmen, the same Cullan whose hound Setanta killed. He recognized us and flung himself at Cuchullain's feet. Owen heard his story too. I tended not to listen terribly closely (or even stay near by) when Owen sang, but I still remember the song he created that day.

> Cullan the Iron-smith's castle is grass and ashes
> Smoke rises from the sleeping quarters
> No living thing stirs inside.
> The rain falls on Cullan's table
> Through a blackened Hall with broken rafters
> The roof burnt off and open to the sky.
> The men and women who laughed and danced
> Enslaved, their Champions stripped and dead.
> The walls stand nowhere higher than a child's boot.
> Cuchullain's Hound, the castle's defence
> Lies by the corpse of Cullan the smith
> Outside the blood-blackened gate,
> The lives of seven times seven of Maeve's men
> On its lips, and seven more on its feet

> A hundred arrows gathered in its sides.
> Even as it died, the dog drew blood
> From the arm of a man who approached its master
> And the men of Connaught feared to approach it
> Thinking it enchanted, and would not believe it dead
> Until its head was cut from its body.

Some things that you hear pass you by, and some strike home. When my legion fought the Scythians, we were told stories about how they would split your prick along its length like a cucumber and then drip hot tar into the cut so that you wouldn't bleed to death. Even though we knew that such stories were often just rumours, that particular one made me swear to myself that no Scythian was ever going to capture me. Further, many of us had friends who had been captured, and stories like that made us fight all the harder to get them back. Perhaps our centurions made the rumours up for that reason.

At the story of the death of Cullan and of the dog he had trained, Cuchullain's brow darkened further, and his frown became something terrible, and a great writhing vein stood out in his forehead like a live snake under his skin, and he reached past me and spoke directly to the horses in a language like nothing I understood, but the horses knew his words and put their ears back and seemed to be refreshed. They leapt forward as if they had rested for a day and a night, and every man, woman and child fleeing from Maeve's army saw us go past them, headlong towards the spear-points of the oncoming army, and they sang to their children that the only Champion of the Red Branch who was still able to fight, and the greatest of them, was riding straight into the mouth of the enemy on a cloud of smoke shot through by lightning. They told those they met of how Cuchullain's chariot was pulled by two huge horses, one grey and one black, with dark fire whirling in their eyes, and how great sheets of foam dropped from their mouths to lather their shining chests, and they told of flames jumping high from the ground where the horses' massive hooves struck stone, and they spoke of how the Champion was driven by a giant blond charioteer who guided the horses with a touch of his rod left or right, needing neither bit nor whip to make them understand his intention, and especially they told with hope in their voices of how Cuchullain the Champion of Champions stood strong and ready armed beside his giant charioteer, leaning forward with eager intensity as if to climb over the front of the chariot to reach his enemy the sooner, with his cloak behind him lifted and whipped by the moving air like the wing of a huge white and crimson bird, his face pushing into the wind as the prow of a boat cuts through water, as his chariot flew past trees, hills and rivers on the way to the Pass of Iraird Cuillenn.

Owen making history again. Well, I liked the bit about me.

Cuchullain and I arrived at the Pass in the afternoon of the third day. The ground was still smooth, unmarked by chariot wheels. We knew that we were in time. By the hoofmarks on the soft earth, lightly armed skirmishing parties had passed through but no more. We could see the main body of the invading army camped on the Connaught side of the Pass. Wiser leaders would have driven through the Pass without pausing.

'They could have gone straight through,' I said. 'We could not have stopped them.'

Cuchullain stood on his toes in the chariot, his whole body tense. 'Perhaps Fergus had a hand in it,' he said with a grin of satisfaction. 'Maeve would not have stopped without good reason.'

Cuchullain unhitched the horses from the chariot and patted their steaming flanks, then led them forward to see their enemy's camp, so that they knew that their efforts had not been in vain. The horses smashed their teeth against their bits and stamped their feet at the sight. Cuchullain laughed and let them loose to graze, promising them plenty of fighting later. His eyes were wide with excitement and he had that disconnected air about him that made me wonder if he knew I was there or not. I took the horses away quietly to the stream and washed the foam off them, then rubbed them down with dry grass. When I got back he had arranged his weapons around the chariot so that they were within easy reach, and he was sitting down on his haunches, watching Maeve's army. Owen was sitting beside him. The bard's horse was tied to a tree, its whole body shaking with fatigue.

For once, I was genuinely glad to see Owen, even though I knew his motives were more than just friendship. He had many stories still to tell, and listened carefully to what I had to say about our journey. As I spoke, I could see his mind working on the events as a sculptor works on marble. By the time we had finished, it was growing dark. The three of us sat together, eating dried meat so that we made no smoke, and waited.

The Connaughtmen didn't know we were there. They must have assumed that we would be coming, of course, but they didn't know for certain. They sent out patrols to find us and report back. Some found us, but none of them got the chance to report their success. Some we caught looking for Ulstermen lying defenceless in their beds. Others were found while stealing cattle. They were mostly scavengers, irregulars, almost useless in battle but the scourge of an invaded country. We killed them all. Cuchullain took their heads as trophies. I wanted Cuchullain to let some of the Connaughtmen go to return and spread fear amongst the enemy, but he laughed and said they would fear him soon enough in any case, and that rumours would start quickly when men left in good health in the morning and failed to come home by nightfall.

'A man who defeats many opponents may be reported a fearsome warrior, but he is still a man. A man who makes opponents disappear without trace may seem to be more than just mortal.' Cuchullain was getting pompous. I wondered if he had been quoting Julius Caesar, then remembered that he couldn't read and there were no books in Ulster anyway.

Cuchullain then had an idea of his own, and we caught a horse that had belonged to one of the men that he had killed, and tied all of Cuchullain's rapidly expanding collection of heads by their hair to the saddle. As night fell, we sent the horse galloping down the hill into the enemy camp. There was a shout, then another, and soon a great commotion, and many torches burnt throughout the night. I do not think that the men of Connaught slept well after seeing a horse gallop past with fifty or so of their comrades' heads bouncing against its flanks.

Cuchullain and I camped at a ford which was the only point at which the river that ran through the Pass of Iraird Cuillenn could be crossed by chariot. He asked me to stand watch for a few hours, and lay down to sleep. As night became dawn he woke, and we harnessed the horses to the chariot and put on our finest armour and, taking every arrow that we had, we rode down upon Maeve's army like an eagle swooping from a mountain-top. I didn't think it was a good idea to expose ourselves in this way, but Cuchullain was determined to put the fear of Zeus (or Laeg, or anyone who might be around) into them. I knew that the only way we could survive was speed and surprise, and I made the Grey and the Sanglain race faster than they ever ran before. I drove us around the Connaught army three times with the light of their campfires reflecting from our shields, and we showered them with arrows and slingstones fired into the dark, and they say that each time we went round Cuchullain killed thirty times three, either in full combat with those who saw him and were prepared to come and meet him, or else with arrow and javelin and sword as men ran past us in fear and confusion from the havoc we created.

Then we went back to our camp and I stood watch, but I was so tired that my thoughts seemed to swim like quicksilver, running away from me as I tried to make sense of them, rushing back like waves up a beach to form and re-form faster than I could control them while Cuchullain slept.

Ailell realized the damage that had been caused by this attack, and he ordered his men to withdraw and regroup further away, with their backs to a rock face and behind an easily defensible frontal redoubt, in order to repair their equipment and bandage their wounds. Maeve then descended on him in a rage, cursing him and all his men as cowards, driving them with harsh words up to the Pass where Cuchullain waited for them. Cuchullain rode his chariot straight towards them, splitting the attacking force in two and knocking Ailell off his horse. Ailell's Champions grouped around him to prevent Cuchullain killing him, but he didn't follow up the attack. Instead he charged the foot-soldiers again, intent on frightening them as much as possible. Many fled in fear at the sight of the battle madness which warped his entire frame. They say that it made his body writhe and his limbs exchange places with each other and the hair on his head stand upright and a thick dark fountain of blood spout upwards from his forehead to fall as a red curtain in front of his opponent's eyes. Many men died under his wheels, and many more fell under the hooves and teeth of Cuchullain's horses which slashed and tore their way through the throng. Those who did not flee were overwhelmed by the ferocity of his onslaught and were forced to fall back in front of him, leaving many dead behind them, and no amount of curses or bribery or cajolery by Maeve could get them back up the hill that day.

That night Cuchullain attacked again as he had the previous night, and again he threw the hundred hosts of Connaught into disarray and slew many and disabled more, and the next day an army attacked Cuchullain's camp, but he was waiting for them and was not where they sought him, and he attacked them from above with arrows and javelins, driving them back, and then pursued them, picking off fleeing men around the edges until he was within bowshot of the army.

This was repeated for two more nights, and each time Cuchullain killed many, and each time his reputation grew until the soldiers of Maeve's army began to think of him as a devil not a man, but Cuchullain knew that while he could create much confusion even he could not fight an army for ever alone, and so when Ailell persuaded Maeve to ask for a parley Cuchullain agreed to it gladly.

When we went to the parley the next day every man I could see was backing away and looking at Cuchullain as if he were likely to burst into flames at any moment. He stood before the hundred hosts of Connaught with only his charioteer for an ally. His head was held high and proud. His armour gleamed in the afternoon sun, which caught the white- and red-gold chasing on his breastplate and flashed from it into the eyes of the Connaughtmen so that the light seemed to blaze from his body.

His long black hair fell loose around his shoulders, and a gentle breeze curled one dark strand around his great ash spear like the arm of a child around her father's neck.

We looked across the dusty space between us. Maeve stood in her chariot in front of the thousands that she had led to Ulster's gates, and she glared at the lone man who stood in her way. He was easily in range of her arrows. The flag of truce fluttered over him or he would be dead already. I looked at Maeve and then at Cuchullain, and tried to see what she saw. He was looking at her with the shade of a smile on his face. His limbs were slim, pale-skinned and with only the finest down of dark hair. White scars like frost on glass covered those areas which were not defended by armour, but his face was untouched by wounds or blemishes, and his skin was as clear as a girl's. His face was beardless, and his calm eyes looked directly back at her. There was no air of excitement or tension about him, no sense that he was appraising his enemy or the size of his task. He stood patiently, waiting for something to happen. Beside him stood his charioteer, whom Maeve no doubt recognized as the young not-Ulsterman who had come with the talentless bard to spy on her. No doubt she noticed as well that he was tall and blond, the physical opposite of his master. I fancy we made an interesting couple. As a fine judge of such matters herself, Maeve would have no doubt also noticed how the tall charioteer held the reins with an almost insolent ease and grace considering the size and mettle of the horses that he controlled.

Maeve and Ailell rode forward in their separate chariots, stopping a spear's throw from where Cuchullain and I stood. The Champion watched them without expression, and then looked beyond, at the whole of their army drawn up behind them. He made a movement with his head that most people would not have noticed. I clicked my tongue softly and the two great horses walked smoothly forward together in step, pulling the chariot as easily as if it were made of straw. We moved forward without haste, stopping when we were within calling distance of the King and Queen. I noticed a small brown head peering round the side of Maeve's chariot. It looked up at us with curiosity, and then its ears went back and it started to growl. Maeve looked down at her dog and a swift affectionate smile passed across her face.

The Champion saluted his opponents, and they replied formally. Cuchullain spoke first, as he was the man on his own territory. 'You seem to have lost some men,' he said.

Ailell smiled. 'I do not like to lose anyone,' he replied. 'But, as you can see, we are many. We can lose a few more and still survive.' He turned round, indicating his army, which covered the valley and the surrounding hills on every side. Cuchullain looked serious and paused for a long time as he looked, as if he were counting them. Then he shrugged.

'You are many, but you are not unnumbered. If I kill a hundred of you every day, one day there will be none left. Then what will you do?' Maeve shifted impatiently in her chariot.

'What makes you so sure that we will not kill you?' she spat.

Cuchullain nodded, as if considering her words seriously. 'No man can be sure of that. But I do not think it is my time to die just yet. Besides, I am prepared to take that risk. I am at home. I have nowhere else to go. How long do you think your men will be willing to stay here with you if your campaign goes on like this?'

Ailell looked at Cuchullain. I saw respect on his face. We all knew that the huge army that had marched from Connaught was held together by two things: loyalty and loot. The Connaughtmen had sworn themselves to their King and Queen. The Leinstermen had no loyalty except to themselves and surprisingly little of that. The mercenaries from Alba and a dozen other places were there because they were paid to be there. The slaves faced us because they hoped for freedom or death. However, plunder united them all. They did not care about Maeve's quarrel or the Bull of Cooley. As long as the army advanced, as long as slaves were taken and streams of captured cattle flowed back to Connaught, the army's cohesion would not be tested. However, if the army had to remain where it was, taking embarrassing losses and making no gains, eventually either they would lose faith in the power of Maeve and Ailell to win or else the food would run out. At that point, anything could happen, and Ailell had no way of knowing what it would be. It was not a question that he would have wished to see put to the test.

'This is not a good situation for either of us,' said Ailell. His wife's fierce glance was ignored. 'Perhaps a better way can be found.' Cuchullain smiled at his apparent openness.

'Indeed? What way is that? You must know that only your journey home will please me.'

Both Ailell and Cuchullain knew that the present situation could not go on indefinitely. Even if Cuchullain continued to hold up the army as he had been doing, he was only one man. He could be bypassed. It was a long way into Ulster bypassing the Pass, but it could be done. In the meantime, Cuchullain would surely eventually be overwhelmed. Ailell's problem was one of time. There was no guarantee that the weakness which afflicted the fighting men of Ulster would last for ever, and when it ended the triumphant invading army would be attacked from all sides by men fighting with a strong sense of grievance and on their own territory. Cuchullain knew this, which is why he was playing for time. Ailell played his strongest card.

'I suggest that we allow you to stay here, at the ford. We will send a Champion to meet you each day. For as long as the fight lasts, we shall advance. If you are killed, obviously we march on. If our Champion is defeated, then we stop at the moment of his death and wait until the next day and the start of the next fight before continuing. Is that fair?'

There was a moment of silence while Cuchullain considered, and then he smiled and nodded his assent. 'I agree,' he said. 'It is fair. Although the fighting will not be pretty, as I shall have to kill your men as quickly as possible.'

Ailell permitted himself a small smile in return. 'Then our Champion will meet you here at daybreak,' he said, saluting Cuchullain and turning his chariot away. Cuchullain did the same, and drove back up the hill to an outcrop of rocks. I stood beside him.

We were too far away to hear what was said between the King and Queen, but Fergus told us later.

In moments, Maeve's chariot was beside her husband's.

'What did you do that for?' she hissed. 'You have given away our advantage in numbers, and for what?'

'To save the alliance, and to kill Cuchullain who I would rather were my friend, not my enemy,' replied Ailell in a flat low voice. 'Now shut up. Not these words, not now, not here.' He turned his horse away.

Maeve snorted in disgust. 'My men will march around him and into Ulster, whatever you say,' she said, but Ailell was already moving away. She pulled on the reins and wheeled her chariot viciously around, taking the little dog that sat between her feet by surprise. It lost its balance and was flung out. Maeve looked out anxiously as it landed on the ground and was about to jump down to help it, but it stood up again uninjured, shook the dust off itself in an aggrieved sort of way and trotted back towards her.

Maeve looked back up the slope to where Cuchullain stood. 'Does your mother know you, Ulsterman?' she cried, her voice as harsh as a gull's cry in the wind. 'Has she said goodbye to her son?'

Cuchullain looked grimly back at her without replying. In his hand was a sling, and in the sling was a flat stone. His hand suddenly jerked back, the sling flickered around his head twice and then his wrist flexed and the stone flew from the sling faster than a thought. Maeve reached for her shield, but the stone was not meant for her. As the lap-dog sat poised to jump back up into the chariot, the stone hit its head with a crack that carried to Ailell and made him pause and look back. When he saw what had happened he turned his chariot instantly and lashed his horses back towards where Maeve stood.

She looked down in horror at the dog's crumpled corpse with its brains spilt onto the ground next to it.

'NO!' Her scream reached to the very back of the army so that not a man failed to hear it.

'That is for the death of the Hound of Cullan,' said Cuchullain softly. 'Now we start even.'

As he spoke, Maeve was thrashing her startled horses towards him. They galloped forward until they came up against the rocks and then stamped their feet and reared up, unable to go further. After a few moments Maeve saw through her fury that there was no point in beating the horses. With a scream of frustration she jumped from the chariot, flung off her cloak and ran towards where Cuchullain stood. He stepped calmly down from his chariot and I passed him his sword. As she reached him she raised her sword and brought it down at his head. Cuchullain lifted his sword in front of his face and the two weapons met in a shower of sparks. In a moment Maeve had slashed down once more, only for him to block it again. She flailed at him in a frenzy, making no attempt to defend herself, lashing at him with words while her sword rained blows at him from every direction. Her sword was more than half the height of a man, but in her rage she lifted it like a reed, striking at him from whatever position the weapon found itself after the previous blow. Cuchullain refused to give ground, meeting her strokes with his own but making no attempt to carry the fight back to her. She realized that he was not trying to injure her and this discourtesy doubled her efforts. The swords flew in great circles around them and clashed with the sound of hammers on an anvil. Three times she broke his guard and wounded him, but not deeply enough to give her an advantage, and still he stood his ground without pressing his attack home, blocking her blows with both hands wrapped tight around the pommel.

The ferocity of her assault could not have been maintained by anyone for long. Running towards her, Ailell could see that tiredness was already slowing her down, and he knew that soon only her anger would keep her going, until she was forced to stop with exhaustion, shamed and humiliated. Ailell did not pause, but threw himself at her as she raised the sword for one last effort. She almost broke his grip on her wrist, but he held on, and she was forced to step back. He did not let go until she relaxed, dropping the point of the sword onto the ground, her breath coming in deep hoarse gasps, thickened by tears.

'I will never . . . forgive you . . . for this!' she rasped. I was not sure to which of them she was speaking. She looked at Cuchullain with hate in her eyes and then turned away, walking slowly back down the hill. Ailell turned to Cuchullain, and their eyes met. For a moment I felt that there was an understanding between them. Then Cuchullain spoke.

'It is not too late for you to leave, even now.'

Ailell smiled and shook his head. 'It is,' he replied simply. 'Too late for all of us.' He saluted his opponent. 'Until tomorrow.' Cuchullain saluted back, but did not speak. He watched as Ailell made his way back to his wife, who sat on the ground with silent tears flowing down her face, falling onto the still-warm corpse of a small brown and white dog.

# 35

Early in the morning of the first day of the truce Maeve sent for Fraech mac Fidaig, a Champion who had recently shared her bed. I know this because he appeared at the ford. I know what she said to him because the Daughters of Calatin visited me and showed me Maeve in her tent and what was planned for us. I was let see what happened elsewhere, and the price was an unquiet mind and the sour yellow skin of a sick old man.

Maeve looked up as Fraech entered.

'Fraech, the boy is a nuisance. Go and get rid of him for me.'

Fraech set off with nine companions and found Cuchullain bathing in the stream. 'Will you yield?' he shouted.

'I will not.'

'Then we must fight.' Fraech turned back to his friends. 'I'll attack him in the water. Ulstermen aren't good in water.' He stripped off his clothes and waded towards Cuchullain.

'If you come any closer I shall have to kill you,' said Cuchullain. Fraech kept moving. 'Very well then. Choose your style of combat.'

'Each to keep one arm around the other,' said Fraech, and gripped Cuchullain swiftly round the waist and tried to throw him.

They grappled for a long time in the water. Then Fraech slipped and went under. Cuchullain held him there for a few moments then pulled him up. 'Now,' he said. 'Will you let me spare you?'

Fraech looked into Cuchullain's face and shook his head. 'I would not have it said that I was given quarter.'

Cuchullain looked at him with understanding, and shortly afterwards handed Fraech's dead body back to his friends with respect and honour.

On the second day, Cuchullain killed the Champion Orlam, a son of Maeve and Ailell, but spared his charioteer on condition that the man did exactly as he was told. Cuchullain took Orlam's head and tied it to the charioteer's back.

'Go back to the camp and don't stop until you have reached the centre. If you stop or deviate then you'll be hiding from my sling.'

Orlam's charioteer walked to the camp with Orlam's head, but when he saw Maeve and Ailell at the edge of the camp coming to meet him he took the head and set it at their feet and explained what Cuchullain had told him to do. When he had finished, they heard a shout, and turned to see Cuchullain on the hillside, whirling his sling. A stone flew between the King and Queen and smashed the man's head.

Maeve did not wait for the third day but sent three more Champions against Cuchullain, one after another. Cuchullain killed them all, but the third fought well for an hour before he died, and Cuchullain fell asleep exhausted immediately after the fight, even before I finished staunching his wounds.

When Cuchullain woke and returned to his camp, he was set upon by the three sons of Graech and their charioteers, who preferred personal dishonour to the damage that Cuchullain was doing to the honour of Connaught. Cuchullain killed them all, although he took a deep wound in his sword arm. From that moment he swore that if he saw Maeve or Ailell he would sling a stone at them, in memory of the dishonourable attacks by their men. In this way he killed a squirrel that Maeve was feeding, a pet bird that was perched upon her shoulder, and a number of other small animals that followed her as pets. Maeve fell into a fury each time this happened, and sent her Champions to fight Cuchullain in ever-larger groups. Sometimes they refused to fight him except one at a time, sometimes they were less principled and all attacked him at once. It made no difference: he killed them all, but at great cost.

I slept, and as the Daughters circled around me I saw how Maeve used Ferdia.

On the ninth morning, Maeve sent for Ferdia, who was eating with the Leinstermen. She had to send for him three times before he came.

The tent flap pushed back and Ferdia entered Maeve's tent. They looked at each other for a few moments. Ferdia folded his arms, making his bone armour creak. 'You want me to fight Cuchullain,' he said.

'Yes.'

'I cannot.'

'Will not?'

'Indeed, will not. He is my brother.'

Maeve smiled. 'He was a comrade when you trained together, years ago. That's all.'

'No matter. We are still friends.'

'You haven't seen him since.'

'Do your friendships have a time limit?'

Maeve shifted her ground. 'He fights for Conor.'

Ferdia looked uneasy. 'Conor is his lord. He is sworn to him.'

Maeve leant backwards in her chair. 'Sworn to a man who has broken the laws of hospitality, who split his kingdom for a girl who doesn't even want him, and who now moans and squats like a woman at Emain Macha? Would you keep an oath to a man like that?'

Ferdia shrugged. 'Cuchullain would.'

'Then he is a fool.'

'Perhaps. He is still my friend, and I will not fight him.'

Maeve stood up and walked to the tent entrance, not looking

at him. 'I will give you Finavir. My daughter, and so my friend-ship.' She saw him shake his head. 'You have always admired her.'

Ferdia smiled without humour. 'True enough. But does she admire me?'

'Finavir and all the land and cattle you want. I offer you great honour.'

Ferdia picked at a fingernail. 'I am not so honoured. Does Finavir know that you have promised her to every Champion who has gone up that hill? In the camp, they are saying that to be offered Finavir is a death sentence.'

Maeve swung round on him angrily. 'Enough! Will you go for honour alone?'

Ferdia looked at her for a long moment. 'My honour is my own affair. You cannot talk to me of honour when your men march into Ulster every day, ignoring the promise you made with Cuchullain only to march while he fought.'

She flushed a deep red. 'Ailell's promise, not mine.'

He folded his arms. 'I have sworn to follow you. I will fight beside your Munstermen who a year ago were the enemies of Leinster and are still not our friends. I will fight with my kinsmen against my friends, I will fight with you against Ulster, but I will not fight Cuchullain. I do not want Finavir, I have no need of your land, my honour is my own. No, I will not go.'

Maeve shouted a command. Ferdia stepped back and reached for his sword as men started to come in through the flap, then dropped his hand as he saw that they were unarmed. They stood in a line in front of him.

Maeve gestured to them. 'Do you know who these men are?'

Ferdia shook his head, as if trying to clear it. 'Some of them. They are bards.'

Maeve smiled. 'Tell the great Ferdia what you will do tomorrow.'

A short, dark man stepped forward. 'Tomorrow I ride to Leinster. On the way I will compose a satire on Ferdia, the coward who would not fight for his Queen.'

Ferdia stuttered with anger. 'This . . . you are not my Queen!'

297

Another stepped forward. 'Tomorrow I go to Munster, to sing a satire on Ferdia, who rejected the fair Finavir, whose hand any man would die for, because he knew he could not satisfy her.'

Ferdia gestured feebly, but a third bard started talking immediately. 'I also go to Munster, to tell of the traitor Ferdia, who ran from the battle because he could not bear to strike a blow at his lover, Cuchullain.'

Another opened his mouth to speak, but Maeve cut him off with a gesture. Ferdia's face was pale, and his gaze moved wildly about the tent.

'They will satirize you for a hundred years if I tell them to,' she said softly. 'They will do nothing else for the rest of their lives but sing about you in every village in Ireland. They will sing the name of dishonourable Ferdia, the coward, the impotent, the pederast.' She leant close to him and whispered. 'Every man will know the name of Ferdia, it will be remembered long after the name of Cuchullain is forgotten. You should be grateful.'

Ferdia had gone deathly white. Maeve waited.

'It is not just,' he whispered.

'The choice is yours.'

'It is not just.'

Maeve said nothing, then turned to the bards to dismiss them. Ferdia caught her arm. 'Wait!' There was a long pause, then his shoulders drooped and he seemed to crumple. 'I . . . I . . . I will go. I will do your will. There, you have it.'

Maeve smiled and waved the bards out of the tent. Then she turned and picked up two goblets of wine. She offered one to Ferdia, who held it as if it were about to explode. 'You'll win, don't worry,' she said, lifting the goblet. 'And the offer of Finavir and the land still stands. I am a woman of my word.'

Ferdia looked at her. His wrist turned slowly and the wine fell untouched to the floor. 'And I am a man of mine,' he said, so quietly she hardly heard it. He turned and walked out of the tent. Maeve watched as he left, then raised the wine to her lips. Her tongue darted into it several times, then she pressed the rim against her bottom lip and smiled.

\*　　\*　　\*

And I woke, and knew the pleasure that the Daughters of Calatin felt, and knew that this was the fight they had been waiting for, and how much it pleased them to show me that it was coming.

# 36

I had not seen Ferdia for a long time. I had forgotten how big he was. He stood on the bank of the stream like a statue of a (much taller) Augustus, one imperial hand on the shaft of his great spear, the point aimed square to the heavens, the other holding a shield the height of a normal man, slung easily and loosely by his side. The sun was high above him so that his red hair was shot through with light, dazzling us and surrounding his head with fire. He stepped down to the shallows, his horn jerkin making its faint grating noise, like insects on a hot night. His face was dark, serious.

Then he grinned. His smile was always like a door opening outwards to let the day into a dark room.

'It's good to see you, Cuchullain.'

Cuchullain looked at him gravely. 'Of all the men I knew I would have to face, I did not prepare to meet you.'

'All the better for me then,' laughed Ferdia. 'Why not?'

'I did not think that you would come.'

Ferdia gave a little shrug, and his smile looked less easy. 'I had to come. I hoped I would not find you here.'

Cuchullain's expression did not change. 'You know I have

sworn to be here until this is over. Did you seriously think that I would not be where I promised?'

A slight pause. 'No. I knew you would be here to face me.'

'Yes.' Cuchullain's face suddenly flooded dark with feeling. I knew that he had not really believed, could not believe even now the evidence of his eyes, that Ferdia had come against him. 'What did they offer you that you needed so badly that you would try to kill me for it?' he asked bitterly. 'Was it Finavir? They offered her to everyone else.' He spat the name of Maeve's daughter from his mouth like a piece of rancid fruit. 'Many men have died here with her face in their minds and her name on their lips.'

Ferdia shrugged. 'It was a matter of honour,' he said. 'In my position, you would have come too.' I thought he seemed unsure, almost embarrassed.

Bitterness and resignation mingled in Cuchullain's soft voice. 'I would not. Not against you. Never against you.' He opened his hand across the water. 'You would kill me for Maeve's daughter and the honour of Connaught, what there is left of it? Is this honourable, Ferdia? By coming here you are saying that one of us must die. Is that honourable for a brother?'

Ferdia was stung. 'Honour? Was it honourable when Conor stole Deirdre and burnt the Red Branch house? Was it honourable of him to connive and deceive, to break his word and kill Naisi and his brothers and Fergus's son when he had offered them hospitality? Is it honourable to call such a man your King? I came against you today it is true, but it is your standing here as Conor's Champion that provokes the fight.' He lowered his voice, made it sound reasonable. 'Leave now, under my protection. This quarrel is not with you. Your lands will not be harmed, and we will come together as friends again one day.'

Cuchullain smiled a hard, wry smile. 'That is not worthy of you. How did I provoke the fight? I do not attack Connaught's Champions, they attack me. Ulster does not invade Connaught, Connaught invades Ulster. Ulster does not covet Maeve's bull, but Maeve invades Ulster to take the Bull of Cooley. Whatever quarrel the Ulster Exiles have with Conor, how does that quarrel give Connaughtmen cause to invade Conor's kingdom? Cause to burn Ulster's crops, kill her people, take their wealth? Is that for honour too? Or is it perhaps the whim and blood-lust and pride of a witch-Queen that drives you to satisfy her greed?' He paused slightly. 'And yours too, perhaps?' He gestured around him. 'All Ulster lies helpless. Your troops burn my country and make slaves of my kinsmen as we speak.' (I saw Ferdia's eyes flicker as Cuchullain's gesture included him with the Connaughtmen.) 'The Great King and the warriors of the Red Branch lie on their beds unable to move. You would have me leave my post for your friendship, when there is not one man left in Ulster to lift a sword to take my place?' Cuchullain spread his hands wide and his voice became intense in a plea for understanding. 'Even if it were not so, even if there were another Champion to take my place, and even if I cared nothing for my own honour, even if I would leave and allow another to fight you because I would not be your death, do you think I could leave Ulster to fight without me?' His voice rose in weariness and pain. 'No, you must be the one to leave, for I am at home. I have nowhere to go.'

'You know I cannot leave.'

'Then we must fight.'

Ferdia shrugged. 'So be it,' he said.

There was a silence. They had nothing left to say to each other, made dumb enemies by honour. I thought of all those Roman heroes from the dim past who died for honour. Rome remembered them in school and in statues, but didn't want to be like them any more. Ferdia and Cuchullain were figures from Rome's past, like Aeneas and Horatius. Tiberius would have loved them. Or he would have loved the idea of them.

Cuchullain walked to the bank. They faced each other across the water.

'So,' said Cuchullain. 'How shall we start?'

Ferdia lifted his javelins, the small spears used to demonstrate skill, accurate as arrows in a Champion's hands. 'Do you remember how Skiatha taught us to use these?'

'Of course. What terms?'

They were going to fight formally. All Cuchullain's other fights at the ford had been rush and hack until the opponent was dead so that Maeve's armies must stop marching. This was to be more like a dance. I had never seen it, but Owen had often told me how it was done. Romans did this sort of thing on the Field of Mars, I saw it done by my brothers in Germany, we did it for Tiberius as training, but with sticks and a way out, never with spears and no retreating. This was real stupidity, as opposed to the pretend stupidity we played at in training. The idea was to stand still and be impossibly brave as spears rained down on you. They said it took courage. I think it takes less of a brain than I've got, as I could see a spear taking my head off in no time. I often think that what we call bravery is just lack of imagination. If someone is shaking with fear and still stands his ground, that's brave. Puffing your chest out and refusing to consider the possibility of dying isn't brave, it's just unthinking. I wouldn't do it. Still, I was quite prepared to watch other people do it. This was like watching the two best gladiators in the world choose which exhibition they would put on that day.

Ferdia named his terms. 'The small shields only. The feet to remain still.' I knew that both of them would rather die than break the rules. Me, I would rather die than submit to such a fool arrangement, but then that's why I'm a charioteer, not a Champion.

Nodding his agreement, Cuchullain lifted his shield and paused. He spoke quietly, without hope.

'I would not be your death, brother.'

Ferdia looked at him, then spoke so softly his voice barely carried across the stream. 'I know,' he said. And hurled his first spear with all his strength straight at Cuchullain's chest.

For half an hour the earth was pierced a hundred times as the javelins flew back and forth. A very few were wide of the mark, and their target did not have to move. Most were accurate. They tried not to use their shields, to show their courage and disdain, but it was often necessary to defend themselves. Not moving the feet meant no jumping either, so a spear aimed at the belly had to be blocked. It was not enough just to stop the spear, it had to be stopped on the middle of the shield. If the spear missed the heavy iron boss at the shield's centre then it might stick in the wood, dragging the shield down, leaving the body uncovered for long enough to get the next throw in the vitals.

As fast as the spears bounced off the shields Ferdia's charioteer or I would pounce on them, making sure that there was always one ready for the next throw. Cuchullain's hand would come back, I would slap the spear into it, he would hurl it almost faster than the eye could follow, and we would watch, admiring Ferdia's skill as he knocked it aside without shifting his feet. Then I would wait with Cuchullain while Ferdia was given his spear, he would throw it, and we would avoid it, Cuchullain by swaying away from it, me by doing the same or by flinging myself headlong, whichever was appropriate. Then the dance would begin again.

Given the chance, they would perform Feats, particularly the Feats of Catching and of the Spider Throw. They would not only avoid the spear, they would attempt to catch it as it flew past them, or throw it back from impossible positions. Always they watched, their eyes locked together like two men knife-fighting with their wrists tied together. I don't believe that either of them relaxed their gaze for a moment, not because they feared treachery, but because that was how they had been trained. I could hear Fergus's voice again, shouting at the Boys' Troop as they practised the Feats of the Thrown Apple and the Feat of Walking On Knives, ringing over and over again across the grass to where I was lounging beneath an oak tree and enjoying watching other people working. 'To drop the gaze is the same as to drop the guard. It is the act of a beaten man.' Not bad advice to a Champion, but of somewhat less use to a warrior like me. I had other methods. Fergus probably hadn't ever heard of dropping one's gaze to get someone to relax and lower their guard so that you can perform the Feat of Disembowelling Them Just When They Least Expect It.

After a time, all the small spears were lost or else broken, blunted and shivered to nothing on the iron and brass shields.

Such was their skill that neither man had suffered a scratch, even when demonstrating their Feats. I was tired and hot. The showing off left a sour taste in my mouth. Feats were supposed to awe the opponent, to demonstrate the ease with which you could defeat his best efforts, and to show your own fearlessness and skill. These two were watching each other with the critical eye of a training-ground instructor. If the Feat were not perfect, the other would attempt to perform the same, better. If it were well done, that would be acknowledged with a nod, and then a greater Feat attempted. They were fighting to kill each other, and yet treated it like a contest on the training field. For a true Roman it would have been incomprehensible, and enough of me was Roman to find it annoying. Fights are there to be won, quickly, economically, cleanly. They are a means to an end. For Ferdia and Cuchullain, for all their race – and, I suppose, my own, a long time ago for me – it was an art form. Celts did not sculpt, or draw, or build, but they made Death their Muse, war their stage and combat their drama. A Roman would have thought it ridiculous to try to impress an opponent by flighting perfect spear-throws at him and acknowledging his skill in deflecting them. A Roman would have been busy digging lines of high defensive earthworks to shelter behind and organizing a troop of crack swordsmen to cross further downstream to circle round and take his opponent from the rear, while seeing to it that a few dozen Parthians laid down a barrage of arrows and spears to make the enemy keep his head covered and con-centrating on what was happening in front of him. That's what a Roman would have been doing. Rome has seen too many deaths, has killed too many men and women in order to create and enforce the Pax Romana to see war in terms of anything but a business, a business to be pursued as economically as possible. This Celtic bravado, turning war into something simultaneously deadly serious and light-hearted, both an exact science and a subjective art, this was madness.

And yet, and yet. I admit there was a part of me that thrilled to it. Sometimes the waste seemed wonderful, almost justified the pain. Sometimes it made you feel that this way of death was what life was made for. If nothing else, I could see how easy it was for old men to send young men to war.

'This is play for women and boys, not men,' said Cuchullain contemptuously, looking at the splintered spears around him. 'Shall we try with the battle lances?'

Ferdia nodded, and picked up his great spear. It was a head taller than himself, as thick as my wrist, and it was almost as much as his charioteer could do to lift it. Ferdia held it carelessly in one hand. They stepped into the stream, circling each other, jabbing underarm with the spear-points, testing each other.

I watched for a few minutes. Something was wrong. They were thrusting at each other like . . . yes, like gladiators in a fixed contest, where the winner was pre-arranged. I realized that they had partnered each other so often in the past that they were, consciously or unconsciously, slipping into a practised routine of jab, feint, parry. Cuchullain once told me that Skiatha said that watching them fight was like watching two hands locked together, each trying to clasp tighter than the other. I saw what she meant. This was not fighting, it was an exhibition. It could go on all day, and meanwhile the armies of Connaught marched around us and burnt our homes. My home, Cuchullain's home. Emer's home.

It was time for me to do something extremely foolish.

'Cuchullain!'

They stopped. Cuchullain dropped his guard and turned to me, turning his back on Ferdia, who wiped the sweat from his brow and waited, rested his weight on his spear. I almost laughed. A Roman would not have done either thing. He would never turn his back on an enemy, nor would he be slow to split the head of a man foolish enough to do it for him.

'What?'

I did not bother to get up from where I sat beside the horses as they grazed on the riverbank, but lay back and looked at a piece of grass with which I had been pretending to pick my teeth. I chose my words carefully and I did not look at him as I spoke. This was doubly insulting to him. Cuchullain was touchy about being insulted. I hoped he would let me get the words out before he killed me.

'I was admiring the display very much, but I was just wondering one thing.'

Cuchullain looked amazed. 'What?'

I took a deep breath. 'Is Cuchullain content to play pretty war-games with his friend the traitor, while the armies of Connaught burn their way towards his castle and the wife who believes that he is defending her?'

Cuchullain's cheeks drained of colour except for a high point on the bones, and he fingered his spear.

'What do you mean?' He knew well enough what I meant. He wanted me to say it. I was taking my life in my hands – given a straight choice, I had no confidence that Cuchullain would rather kill Ferdia before me – but I knew that this fight was no fight, that it was going nowhere. I stood up on the riverbank and looked at him with all the scorn I could muster. His fury was intimidating. I didn't try to defend myself. There was no point. I tried to remember if Owen had ever told me about whether a Champion was allowed to kill his charioteer. I took a deep breath.

'The Hound of Ulster is soft as a woman – no! Why should the brave women of Ulster suffer comparison with Cuchullain, the great Hero who plays games with his bum-partner while his enemies burn a path across the province he is sworn to protect? The women of Ulster prefer to fight like wild animals and die gladly rather than stand aside and watch while a crowd of wall-eyed inbreds from Connaught take an arrow's length of land or a single starving calf from Emain Macha. Cuchullain is not a woman! To call him that would be a compliment to him and an insult to women! The women of Ulster love their land, they love their people. They do not fear death if it means they die protecting their children and their land. They take arms! Indeed, they are armed now, and they rest in their homes tending the wounds they got fighting the invader, trusting that Cuchullain the so-called Great Champion will buy them the time they need to allow their menfolk to recover. How would they feel to know that the Great Champion is more interested in playing girls' games with his friend the traitor?'

Ferdia lifted his sword at the insult. Cuchullain was twitching with fury, and I knew I had gone too far. The light was dancing around his brow like fire round a ship's mast, and the vein the size of an ox-whip stood out in his forehead. I was dead anyway. Might as well carry on. 'But what does the Great Hero do? He plays pat-me-pat-you with his smiling bum-friend while his bum-friend's real friends go and take the Great Hero's cattle and fuck his wife and piss on her afterwards!' His spear drew back, trembling. His eyes burnt into me. I raised my arm and my voice. I was going to miss living, I had always enjoyed it. 'Do you think that Ferdia cares for the fight? He is here to keep you busy! You think he is your friend. It might have been so one day.' I leant towards him, roaring my scorn across the stream. His arm was fully back. I closed my eyes. 'Perhaps he tells the truth when he says he does not want to kill you, but he does not mind using your friendship against you, in the service of his real friends and masters!'

For a moment, I thought Cuchullain had thrown the spear. I braced myself. Then Ferdia saved me. Cuchullain heard Ferdia move through the water in his fury to get at me, and held out an arm to prevent him.

'You will not pass me,' he said, in a voice cracking as if he could not get his breath.

Without meaning to, I had saved myself, or perhaps the less stupid part of me knew what it was doing and arranged events. In provoking Cuchullain I had also provoked Ferdia, and Cuchullain had not forgotten why he stood in the ford. His spear was across Ferdia's chest. Ferdia protested, and then saw how it was. Cuchullain was in control again. A seed of doubt was in his mind, and that was all that was needed. He could not really believe it, but nor could he get rid of it. And the core of it was the truth. As I spoke, as Cuchullain and Ferdia fought, Maeve's men burnt our houses and took our cattle.

I relaxed slightly. I felt a warm stream run down my leg.

'He lies!' hissed Ferdia. 'If Maeve breaks faith, it is none of my doing. I would never betray you.' And then, more softly, pleading. 'He lies, Cuchullain.' Then flat, toneless. 'He lies.'

Cuchullain lifted his spear, ready for the fight. 'It does not matter.'

I knew that I had done a great thing and a terrible thing. I had shown Cuchullain his destiny: the Saviour of Ulster, the greatest Hero of them all, the conqueror of Ferdia and all the armies of Connaught. But at what cost? I had made him doubt his brother. I felt that he would never forgive me for that. I never really forgave myself. But what else could I do? He was going to get himself killed, and then all of us were as good as dead. And meantime Maeve's men were spilling across Ulster, not just the ones who were sneaking into Ulster in breach of Ailell's word, but the main body, marching as agreed while the fight lasted. Only he could stop them, and he had to be made to do it. I only wish it had not been me who had to make him, or Ferdia who stood in front of him.

And now Ferdia's charioteer was on his feet, yelling imprecations and insults at Cuchullain (some of which I noted for later use) until the two Heroes turned on each other with wild oaths of frustration and lashed out with their swords. They could not attack us; very well, they would attack each other.

Nevertheless, I could see that they still enjoyed the fight, admired each other's swordplay, refused to take advantage if either of them stumbled, allowed the other to retrieve his arms if they were dropped. And when dusk fell, they threw aside their arms and embraced, walking together onto the Ulster side, followed by Ferdia's charioteer bringing food. The four of us shared our food on the one bank, and both of them were scrupulous in ensuring that the healing herbs that each had brought were shared out equally. The charioteer and I shared the watch, while the two Heroes slept on opposite sides of the same fire.

They were still brothers, for all that I had placed a worm at the centre of their friendship. I knew they were grasping at the short time left before one of them died. They had accepted the inevitable, and neither would be deflected from it, but nor would they waste the time remaining. Ferdia's charioteer and I hardly spoke at all while we ate, but the two Champions laughed and told stories and reminded each other of shared adventures.

I would have liked to be Ferdia's friend. I would have liked to be Cuchullain's friend in the way that Ferdia was.

I would have liked very much not to feel that everything was about to go terribly wrong.

# 37

The next day the dew lay heavy on them when they woke. They moved slowly, their joints stiff, wounds aching. I felt tired myself, and I had not spent all the previous day fighting my friend who was trying to kill me, so I could only imagine how it was for them. The light behind the hills grew brighter, the stars slipped away and vanished one by one. Ferdia and his charioteer crossed the stream to be ready for dawn. The Heroes did not look at each other until they were ready for the fight.

The sun struck the stream waters and they were ready. Cuchullain's fingers were cold, and he fumbled his sword as he reached for it, knocking it to the ground. An Ulsterman would have called that a bad omen.

Omens and prophecies haunted Cuchullain. Cuchullain was to save Ulster. That much Cathbad had told us. His exploits were to be sung for ever. That much we knew. What we – what I – did not know was if Cuchullain was to live past this day. His deeds were already legend. For all we knew, holding up Maeve's armies for as long as he had done might already be enough to save Ulster. He could die today and still fulfil the prophecy. He was to save Ulster, but the prophecy had not mentioned whether or not he might die in the attempt, or whether Ferdia was to be his death or some other. The prophecy gave him a sort of invulnerability before its conditions were fulfilled. Now they had been, and it seemed to me that he was very vulnerable. And, of course, one should not discount the possibility that that old fart Cathbad had got it plain wrong – that he had read the entrails upside down or was making it all up as he went along.

I looked across the river and wondered. I wanted Cuchullain to win and live, and yet . . . It was just that Ferdia was such a grand warrior, so full of life, he seemed immortal. He had fought Cuchullain to a standstill, parried as he advanced, chased him when he fell back. He knew all his tricks, could match all the Feats that mattered. Cuchullain had often told me that Ferdia was the only man who could meet him and seriously hope to win. The only thing that separated them was the Gae Bolga. Ferdia had no such weapon. But the Gae Bolga lay unused in a saddlebag. Cuchullain would never use it in a straight fight, certainly not against Ferdia. He would beat him head to head or fail. No special arms or magic. Win fair or die.

The two men were whacking lustily at each other in the centre of the ford when I heard hooves behind me. I knew who it was without looking round.

'Hello, Owen,' I said. Owen looped his reins around a branch and scuttled across and down the bank to sit beside me. He was almost rubbing his hands with glee, he looked like a man with a good bet on a dog-fight and a promise afterwards.

'How is the Great King?' I asked. My spirits fell with his face.

'Not well. The sickness is still on them. Every man is still in his bed. Cathbad says that Conor's treachery may make Macha's curse last twice as long as before.' Things were getting even worse.

'And the armies of Connaught?'

'They advance daily. While Ferdia lives they march. Our men are powerless to stop them.'

'A shame bards cannot fight.' I cursed myself. That was unfair. Owen looked sideways at me.

'We are forbidden,' he said. 'Unlike charioteers.'

That was fair enough. We were both outsiders.

312

The ring of metal on metal, brass-bound shield on shield, rang across the water. Owen and I watched silently while the sun passed overhead and started to descend. They fought without stopping. Their feet churned the stream until the water was dark with earth, and their search for purchase as they strained against each other dug a hole in the stream-bed almost as deep as their knees. Blood streamed from every limb, from heads, from hands, from every exposed place. Neither had yet managed to land a crucial blow, but the combined buffeting and loss of blood would have finished off lesser men hours before. I heard Owen muttering beside me. He was perched on a rock and looking to the sky, murmuring to himself, his hands strumming an invisible instrument. I nudged him, hard, making him topple onto one side.

'What the hell are you doing?'

'Composing the song that will tell the story of this day.'

'Shouldn't you be watching what actually happens and composing later?'

Owen looked at me with a peculiarly infuriating smile. 'Oh no,' he said. 'You still haven't got it, have you? I'm not going to just tell people what happened, not just relate what we see today. I want them to *feel* it.' His hands started to writhe together in the air. 'I want them to *be* here, to feel what it was like to be Cuchullain, to be Ferdia, to be us. I want the sun, and blood and the trees and the grass. Otherwise I might as well say that "Ferdia hit Cuchullain who hit him back." Don't you see?'

'Don't patronize me, you horse's arse,' I growled.

A particularly loud clang interrupted our bickering. Both Heroes had landed a mighty blow simultaneously on the other's helmet, and the impact had thrown them both backwards into the water. Both were now splashing about in the murky stream, trying to stand up. Their heads must have been ringing like dropped metal pots; neither knew which way to face. I looked indignantly at Owen, who took the hint. He gestured at the sun, which was getting low, although the light was still adequate.

'Enough!' he shouted.

The bard's word was obviously welcome. The two clambered

with difficulty up their respective banks, clumsily pushing away their faithful charioteers' well-meant attempts to help.

That night, although they were both solicitous in the sending over and sharing of the food and medicinal herbs, they slept separately. Something had changed. They had fought each other to a standstill. Both had taken a dozen wounds any one of which could have stopped an ordinary man, and they were still fighting. However, they fought like condemned men, by reflex, without thought. It could not go on. One way or another, tomorrow would see an end.

The night was cold. I couldn't sleep. The Champions had taken herbal draughts to help them rest and try to repair the ravages of the day, but still Cuchullain moaned and thrashed in his sleep. Once he cried out. It could have been the name of his wife.

Owen had wandered off, unable to rest. We had run out of conversation, so he decided to be on his own. He had his song to write. He would be back by dawn.

The dawn broke like the day before, cold, dew-damp, with the first ray of sunlight slanting through the trees, making the bark glow golden and silver. I slipped off the tree I was leant dozing against and staggered, grunting with surprise. Cuchullain was instantly awake. He sat up and grimaced in pain. We both looked across the stream. Ferdia was standing ready. Cuchullain cursed me, and threw off his blanket. I tried to help him get ready but he looked at me with a wildness in his eye that made me stand away from him. I don't think he knew who I was. I went to one side and climbed a rock so that I could watch.

Within a few minutes the two of them stood facing each other. There was a pause. They both knew that today would decide the fight. Cuchullain rapped his spear shaft once against his helmet as a mark of respect. Ferdia did likewise. As his arm lifted, his cloak opened, and from where I stood I could see a huge flat rock against his stomach, bound up with straps and held on by his body armour. Ferdia had come prepared. I thought to warn Cuchullain, but they were already wading towards the centre of the stream. Besides, what could I warn him about? That Ferdia was carrying a heavy weight tied to his middle?

The first attack from each of them came from high overhead, and the two swords bit into the shield edges and slid off each other with a metallic snarl. Their shields crashed together like two wooden waves, and the fight was on again.

They dropped their exhaustion and wound-stiffness as if they had rested for weeks. Cuchullain was everywhere, one moment solidly planted on the stream-bed trading blows with Ferdia shield-boss to boss, the next moment performing the Salmon-Leap with a flick of his waist, landing behind Ferdia and slashing at his unguarded back. But Ferdia was almost as quick, as determined and as lethal. The fight rocked back and forth. Their legs were streaked with blood like red wax running down candles, colouring the water which broiled around their feet. Cuchullain was faster, more athletic, but Ferdia was stronger and defended himself with skill and imagination, and neither of them could gain a decisive advantage. The sun rose high in the sky, and it looked as if they would hack and hew all day until there was nothing left of either of them but two sword arms, each still slashing at the other.

A large black crow flew in a circle overhead. I saw it out of the corner of my eye. When I turned to look at it, it was gone.

What happened next was confused and very fast. I saw some of it myself, Cuchullain once told me a little more, and Owen coloured in the picture later. I have heard it and relived it so often I am no longer sure which piece comes from which source, what is true and what is imaginary. Sometimes I think about it and try and make sense of it. Mostly I do not think about it at all, in case my head should ache.

Cuchullain stumbled. Caught by the momentum of a heavy blow from Ferdia, he dropped onto one knee, falling sideways so that his sword hand had to go into the water to support him. Ferdia seized his chance. With a roar he flung himself at Cuchullain and the two of them crashed into the water, setting up a curtain of spray. In a moment Ferdia was up, kneeling on Cuchullain's back, using the full weight of his stone-wrapped body, pushing Cuchullain's face into the stream-bed with both his great hands. I saw Cuchullain drowning, his hands thrashing

315

beside Ferdia's legs, his feet pounding on the river-bottom and flailing the water to foam. Ferdia was inexorable. His face was mottled red with the effort, his arm-muscles bulged until I thought they must burst, but he kept Cuchullain's face in the water, grinding it into the gravel.

It was utterly quiet. Even the running water was silent. I watched, but couldn't speak. Cuchullain had stopped moving. Ferdia still held him down, concentrating every particle of himself into a single effort, arms locked straight, mouthing silent obscenities that he did not have the breath to shout. Still grinding Cuchullain's face into the gravel, still holding his head under the water, fingers tangled in his dark hair. Then, slowly, tentatively, Ferdia realized that Cuchullain was no longer moving. He relaxed his effort very slightly, not really believing it.

The light flickered and changed, as if something enormous had passed overhead at great speed. For the briefest moment, I felt sure that the earth shook. Ferdia trembled, his eyes widened, and he took a great gulp of air, letting out a shout. Then he pushed down, hard.

The stream seemed to erupt, as if something had exploded under the surface of the earth directly below them. A great fountain of angry water shot straight upwards, obscuring the two men. The stream boiled into steaming eddies and currents, slapping into Ferdia as if great snakes thrashed in the water all around him.

Something fractured, slipped.

I felt as though a minute of my life had been stolen from me. I blinked, and looked at my raised arm. I had thrown the Gae Bolga into the water, as if in answer to a silent request. It was floating downstream towards Cuchullain's outstretched motionless hand. Ferdia had not seen me throw it. He was totally focused on holding Cuchullain's head in the water. When the Gae Bolga floated between Cuchullain's fingers I saw the great spear shiver, as if it shook with pleasure. Cuchullain's fingers closed around the rough shaft.

Then he moved.

Ferdia felt him tremble. With an oath he sprang back, almost in time, but his cloak hampered him and he was lost.

Cuchullain rose from the water as if he had dived upwards from inside the earth. His face was a ruin of torn flesh. A jagged light shone around his head, and it seemed that blue fire flowed up from the earth to turn him into something writhing and inhuman. In the same movement he spun round, knocking Ferdia's arms away, and then thrust the Gae Bolga hard and low, angled upward into Ferdia's body. The great spear burst past Ferdia's guard and smashed into the flat stone that covered his vitals. The stone shattered from the centre in a dozen silver cracks that flew to its edges with the sound of fat thrown onto hot metal. The spear flew through the smashed stone and pierced the horn jerkin underneath, diving deep into Ferdia's belly with a hiss of delight.

Everything stopped.

A bright light blazed for a long moment inside Ferdia, turning him transparent as if he were just skin stretched on a frame so that the sun shone through him and silhouetted his bones, like a thorn bush at the instant of being struck by lightning, and during that flaring paralysis I saw the spear writhe its way through every part of him. The ten thousand bones tore through him in a moment, embracing his body like pointed ivy, sinking into his soft joints like sharp fish-hooks, dragging and tearing at his flesh. The great stone that he wore for protection fell in pieces at his feet and the straps hung loose around him as he stumbled forward, clutching for air. His innards coiled at his feet. He screamed. The sound still rings in a part of me yet.

Cuchullain caught him as he collapsed forwards, and the two of them fell together and lay in the water like lovers. I moved to help them. Owen caught my arm and held me back. Holding Ferdia out of the water with one hand, Cuchullain called at me. 'A cloak!'

I threw it to him, and he caught it and wrapped it round Ferdia so that his torn belly was hidden. Then he splashed water onto Ferdia's forehead and gently washed the blood out of his eyes. Ferdia coughed twice and looked up at Cuchullain, unable to speak. Cuchullain dipped his fingertips into the water and dabbed a little on Ferdia's tongue with a finger to cool him. He picked his friend up like a bride and carried him to the far side. I watched Ferdia's golden hair hang limp around Cuchullain's arm like a shawl. The last shadows of the day started to lengthen across us all.

Ferdia's hand came up slowly and almost touched Cuchullain's face. He spoke, his voice a rustle of autumn wind through leaves.

'Take me . . . across. I would like to die . . . on the . . . on the Ulster side.'

Cuchullain hesitated, then turned without speaking and splashed across to where Owen and I stood. We stepped out of the way, and he put Ferdia down gently on the wet grass. He cradled Ferdia's head. He was not yet dead, but his lips were grey and the shadow of Charon's cloak was on his face.

Ferdia tried to smile but the pain pulled his lips back into a grimace. Cuchullain opened his mouth to speak but no sound came. Tears cut ragged white streaks through the dirt on his face. Ferdia reached out and touched Cuchullain's face again, gestured helplessly at the damage the river-bed had caused, made a sound that could have been laughter or blood bubbling in his throat. I knelt down beside Cuchullain and looked into Ferdia's eyes. They were ash-white, colourless. The sockets writhed and coiled, full of the pale bones of the Gae Bolga, intertwined like filaments of frost on iron.

Ferdia's head slipped back. Cuchullain pulled it back up again. A thin trickle of blood came from the corner of Ferdia's slack mouth.

Cuchullain stood up, his head bowed.

I heard a noise behind me. I spun round. Two boys were peering through the trees at us. They were Connaughtmen. The light was poor; if they had not made a sound they might not have been spotted. I started to wave them away but then Cuchullain saw them. For a second, his eyes became impossibly wide, then he grasped his sword and ran at them. They turned and fled. I hurled myself after Cuchullain. I breasted the hill and had a panoramic view of Maeve's army. It was a shock; I had forgotten how large it was. I saw Cuchullain catch up with the two boys, come up behind them as they ran shoulder to shoulder. For a few steps he ran just behind them, then he raised his fist and hit both of them, left then right. The boys crashed forward to the ground. Cuchullain pulled one on top of the other and put his foot on them, his sword-point at the top one's throat. They lay still. I could see the top boy's chest heaving with the effort of breathing.

Cuchullain was about a third of the way down the hill, on a lip, a sheep-track round the side. I saw him stand still for a few moments. Then he put back his head and screamed. The sound ran through my brain like the first time I realized that one day I would die. A wave of light from the camp in front of us made me flinch. Every man in the army had turned towards us at the same time. The thousands of white faces reflecting firelight were like a human lightning-flash. The faces watched Cuchullain on the hill. They saw his sword arm high against the sky, and then they saw the sword descend. They saw him bend down and lift the severed heads, saw him hold the trophies high, saw him turn away like a discus thrower and then uncoil and hurl them high and deep into the heart of the camp. I watched the heads bounce towards Maeve's tent and disappear. Cuchullain turned and came back towards me. I saw that his face was the colour of old bones, streaked with the blood that the upraised heads had dripped onto him. He stood and looked up at me.

'What?' I didn't know what he wanted.

'They were no danger.' His voice was hoarse, an old man's rasp. 'They were just boys. Say it.'

I shook my head slightly, and took his sword from him. As he loosened his fingers he stumbled, as if a puppeteer had released his strings. His shoulders sagged and his head dropped. I took his arm and we walked back to our camp. Just before we reached the final bend in the path, he turned to me. His eyes were wet with tears, his voice thick and dull.

'It isn't real, is it? I didn't kill him. He's over there. Safe. He's safe, isn't he?'

I put my arm around him to hold him up. We walked back towards Ferdia's body.

# 38

Cuchullain looked lifeless. He was utterly exhausted. His light had gone out. He sat cross-legged beside his dead friend, with his head drooping and his back bent like an old bow. He didn't look up when he spoke.

'Cut my spear from him, Leary. I must have my weapon.' I looked at Ferdia, lying grey and cold with the Gae Bolga in his gut, and I felt my own stomach heave.

'I cannot.'

'You must. I did not use it this long while, because I did not want to take an unfair advantage against any man, and now I have used it for the first time to kill my friend.' He looked towards the Connaught army. 'She sent him. Maeve made him come. He would not have come against me if they had not made him do it. They made me kill him.' I had never heard his voice so cold, passionless. It was more frightening than his anger. 'Now no-one is safe. I will use the spear that they made me use on Ferdia on any man who gets in my way until Maeve is dead or I no longer have strength or life to lift it. Cut it free for me.'

I knelt in front of him. He looked through me as if I were still water, through and on to the horizon. His eyes were dead, grey stone and wet dust. His face had gone slack, without expression, without life. For the first time ever, he looked old, small, and tired beyond endurance.

'Very well. I will if you move away. I cannot do it if you watch.'

After what seemed a very long time he started to stand up. When I tried to help him he stopped moving, and did not start again until I let go. Slowly, painfully, he stood up and limped away alone. I pushed the spear through Ferdia's body, washed it free of his blood, then put it in a saddlebag wrapped in kid-leather. I covered Ferdia with a blanket.

Then I went behind a bush and vomited until bright blood spotted the bile on the ground under me.

'It was all a game to him. Life was just a game. That's why he was always laughing.'

'What?' I was on my knees, washing out the sour taste from my mouth and splashing water onto my neck.

'He knew that you understood him.'

That was not Cuchullain's voice, it was deeper and more rounded, and it wasn't talking to me. It was familiar. I turned round. Cuchullain was leaning against a tree. The tallest man I have ever seen stood in front of him, dressed in armour that shone dull red and silver in the setting sun. His hair was gold, and his spear was taller than myself. In his other hand he carried a small leather sack.

Cuchullain put his hand on the stranger's arm. 'I didn't want this.'

The stranger nodded. 'I know,' he said. I recognized the way he spoke.

It was my father's voice.

'It was just a game, all this, before he came, the others, it was just sport. I am trained in ways they have not dreamt of, only Ferdia . . .' Cuchullain gestured with his hand, a movement without meaning. 'I would have let them live, all they had to do was walk away, although none of them did, but they could have, I wouldn't have killed them.' His voice broke. 'Only Ferdia. Only he could not walk away. All the others could have lived, had they chosen to, but not him. And we were brothers. Why do brothers have to kill each other?'

Cuchullain was talking to the stranger as a boy would to his teacher. He wanted a reply. The stranger took his hand and looked into his eyes.

'He knew,' said the stranger. 'What was the last thing he said?'

' "Play the game to the end," ' called a voice. It was Owen. He had appeared from Zeus knew where. I didn't see him witnessing the end of the fight, but that wasn't surprising, I had been busy watching the men in the stream. The stranger looked at Owen, and for a moment Owen looked almost embarrassed. 'He said, "Play the game to the end," ' repeated Owen, in a quieter, more diffident voice.

'A Hero's words.'

'No, that's not right. He didn't say that. He said he wanted to die in Ulster,' I whispered hoarsely, standing closer to them now, a great pressure expanding in my chest, listening to my father's voice. They did not look at me. I don't think they heard me. Cuchullain looked at the stranger and then seemed to crumple, falling to his knees at the stranger's feet. I rushed towards Cuchullain and was relieved to see him open his eyes. His voice was flat and hollow.

'I have fought all day. I have fought every day since I came here. I have not slept lying down for what feels like a year. There is not an oak-leaf's width of skin on me that is not bleeding. I cannot lift my sword, let alone defend the ford. I cannot even wear my clothes when I sleep, for they press on me so painfully, and if I put on my breastplate I must stuff it with grass to stop it touching me and brace it with hazel-twigs away from me or I cannot bear the pain.' Cuchullain looked up at the stranger. 'I must fight, for Ulster is undefended, but if I fight again now I will die, and Ulster will be lost.'

The stranger shook his head. 'You must rest,' he said softly. 'I have herbs and medicines, and you will get better quickly, but you must rest.'

'But if I sleep who will guard the ford?'

The stranger looked at me properly for the first time. 'Leary and I, of course.' I nodded. I didn't know what he wanted, but whatever it was I wanted it too.

Cuchullain lay back on the ground, close to unconsciousness. 'Who are you?' he asked.

'I am Laeg,' the stranger said quietly. 'I knew your mother once.' He pulled a blanket over Cuchullain and put the leather sack beside him. In it I could see bottles and medicine jars. We arranged him as comfortably as possible on a soft bank of grass. Laeg prepared Zeus knew what in a cup, a mixture from a dozen different phials, bottles and packets, stirred it up and poured it down Cuchullain's throat. He swallowed, and at once seemed to relax, as if he lay on deep fresh snow and settled into it.

'He will sleep now.'

I could believe that. If I were Cuchullain I would have slept for a month.

'What will we do?'

He looked at me. His eyes were silver, like Cuchullain's. He put a hand on my shoulder. 'You will go and get what help you can. Maeve has broken the agreement. Her troops are marching into Ulster now. The men of Ulster are still laid low, but that will not last much longer. You must try to rouse them, try to muster what defence you can. I will continue here, in Cuchullain's place.'

'But should I not stay with you . . . ?' I knew he was right, but I didn't want to leave Cuchullain. I didn't want to leave the stranger's voice. He smiled.

'Don't worry. Cuchullain will be well by the time you return. And I will still be here. You and I will speak again.'

There was nothing else to say. Owen and I harnessed Cuchullain's horses, Owen on the Sanglain and me on the Grey, and drove the chariot into Ulster.

Laeg had told the truth. I could see the tracks of Maeve's armies through the uncollected harvest. We passed the buildings that they had burnt while Cuchullain fought, believing them safe. They had taken the long route around Iraird Cuillenn, bypassing the ford that Cuchullain defended, outflanking it. They could attack him from both sides now if they wished, but seemed to be contenting themselves with plundering everything they came across. Several times Maeve's patrols spotted me, but the Grey and the Sanglain were too fast for them to catch the chariot in a straight race and we reached Muirthemne unscathed. There was a man at the gate. He was leaning against the gatepost, his face creased with pain, but he was on his feet. It was Sualdam, Cuchullain's father. One of them anyway.

'Where is Cuchullain?' His voice sounded unexpectedly old. I looked at him. His face was lined and his hair was thin and grey, plastered by sweat to his head. That was why he was recovering faster than the fighting men. He was not much use in a battle any more, so the pains were not as bad.

I jumped out of the chariot and helped him to sit down. 'Resting. He has held the Pass, but Maeve has broken the agreement and is advancing towards us. I have come to try and rally a force to hold them up until Cuchullain recovers.' Owen watered the horses while I explained quickly what had happened, about the death of Ferdia, and the stranger who fought in Cuchullain's place.

'I do not know what will happen when the next Champion comes to fight Cuchullain and realizes it isn't him,' I said.

Sualdam grinned, showing good teeth. 'Maeve broke the agreement first, not Cuchullain. She cannot complain now if he changes the rules as well. Anyway, if your stranger kills Maeve's Champion, who is going to tell her that it wasn't Cuchullain that did it?' He let out a cackle of laughter. Then his face grew serious. 'But you are right, we must think of what may happen. It would be better if you returned as soon as possible.'

'But who will rouse the Champions from their beds?'

He stood up straight and took a deep breath. 'I will. If I can stand, then they can. Give me one of the horses, and I will ride through the castles of the Champions until I reach the King himself, and I will not leave off shouting and cursing them until they get up and follow me to help you.'

I was worried for Sualdam, but worried too about Cuchullain, and I allowed myself to be persuaded. I gave Sualdam the Black Sanglain to ride, and he galloped off towards Emain Macha. I called after him to beware of Maeve's men, but the old man seemed to have thrown off his pains completely and he didn't stop, just leant back and shouted that as far as he was concerned Maeve's men could do something painful and anatomically impossible. I was not too concerned. He was a wily old man, and had been a fine warrior, and the Sanglain was as good as any horse Maeve had, probably better. Sualdam might even survive.

'I'll be back soon!' a voice yelled from behind me, and I watched Owen's figure recede into the distance after Sualdam. I didn't even bother trying to call Owen back. He wasn't going to miss the confrontation between Sualdam and the warriors at Emain, and if I had been him I'd have wanted to see it too.

I saddled the Grey of Macha and made my way back to the Pass, dodging Maeve's patrols on the way. This meant several detours. I was on one of these when I rounded the bottom of a hill and met a column of men coming the other way. I was caught, exposed and well within bowshot. I pulled my head into my shoulders like an Anthropophagus, ducked down low and raised my crop ready to make the horse gallop like he'd never galloped before.

'Leary! Don't go! It's us!' I was so surprised that I swung round and almost fell off. The voice belonged to Mordach, Conor's youngest son. I watched as a group of boys ran up to me, Mordach at their head. They were all from the Boys' Troop. They clustered around me, faces bright with excitement under the dust of marching. Mordach took hold of my foot as if to assure himself I was solid.

'Leary! I thought it was you.'

I looked down at him. 'What in Hades are you lot doing here?'

Mordach grinned. 'We were out training and we met Sualdam, and he said that Cuchullain was in danger. We came to see if we could help.'

I looked at them. The oldest in the Boys' Troop was fifteen, and many of them were a lot younger. I shook my head and tried to think like an adult.

'It would be better if you went home. Cuchullain is being taken care of, and Maeve's men are everywhere.'

I was a fool. I spoke to them as if they were Roman Senators' sons practising mock battles in the Palatine Gardens. These boys had fought battles. Some of them had already killed more men than I ever wanted to. Mordach looked up at me, and I saw his jaw set. He looked very much like his father. 'We are not children.'

Yes, you are, I thought, but children of a different sort. I smiled at him. 'I am sorry. Please forgive me. I know well the courage and reputation of the Boys' Troop.' Mordach looked pleased. 'Is this all there are of you?'

Mordach gestured beyond the fifty or so boys surrounding him. 'The rest of the Boys' Troop is a half-hour away. We split up, it is easier to keep hidden that way.'

I nodded agreement. At that moment, a large group of boys came trotting round the edge of a small wood perhaps a mile away.

'There they are!'

They joined us. There were perhaps three hundred of them. Mostly Kings' sons – 'King' being a title like 'Chief' in Ulster, which is why Conor was the 'Great King' – with a sprinkling of other lower-born boys who for various reasons had been allowed to join as well. They were well trained, eager to fight, armed to the ears, and horribly young. They also obeyed no-one but their trainer, and he was no doubt prostrate with pains at that moment. It looked as though they had elected Mordach their leader. There was no point in trying to persuade them to go home. I tried to think how they could best be used.

'I suggest that you spread yourselves amongst the rocks at the Ulster side of Iraird Cuillenn. If the Connaughtmen haven't tried it already, they will attack Cuchullain from the rear eventually.' (I saw no point in telling them about Laeg. The danger was the same either way.) 'If they come, fill them full of arrows.'

Mordach thought for a moment and saw the sense of my suggestion.

'Very well,' he said. 'We will follow you back to Iraird Cuillenn, and then we will defend you and Cuchullain from surprise. You will call us if you need us on the other side of the Pass.'

I smiled at him. 'You can bet on it.' We set off towards Iraird Cuillenn. I was quite pleased with myself. My plan was quite a good one. It needed doing, and it might stop all of them getting killed.

It might have done.

We were almost at the Pass when we heard horses' hooves battering the dried earth behind us. The Connaughtmen had come to catch Cuchullain between forefinger and thumb. We were in the open without cover. I looked down a gentle slope at the chariots rushing towards us, close enough for me to see their body paint, close enough to count the heads bouncing around their chariot rims, and I realized we were done for. I turned to Mordach, feeling that I ought to take control, so I shouted, 'Run!' He stood his ground and grasped my arm, unsheathing his sword with the other hand. He brought the flat of it down on the Grey of Macha's backside. The horse leapt forward with a startled cry and galloped off towards Iraird Cuillenn. Mordach shoved me after him.

'Take half and run for the rocks! We will hold them here!'

He didn't wait for me to argue. With a practised signal he split the Troop in two with a wave of his arm. Half of the boys turned and ran towards the rocks, the other half wheeled to face the oncoming chariots, leaving me standing like an idiot in the middle. Mordach waved frantically at me to go to the rocks with the other boys. Suddenly I found strength and sprinted after them. I reached the first line of boulders and turned to see what was happening.

Mordach formed his boys into three squares, in rows like Romans. Their spears pointed outwards. They stood and waited for the yelling Connaughtmen to arrive.

I stood up and watched as the first chariots crashed into the front line of the Boys' Troop. The boys' bodies and spears brought many of the horses down. This unseated the men in the chariots so that they were easily killed by the boys behind. I saw Mordach duck under a sword that scythed towards him at shoulder height. He slashed at a chariot that skimmed past the outside of the square. The horse came to a stumbling halt and the driver was thrown to the ground where he lay without moving. Mordach turned and rallied his troops, bringing them forward and forming them up into a tight group. He turned to them, waved his sword over his head, and then hurled himself and the remaining boys downhill in a headlong charge at the Connaught foot-soldiers running up to support the chariot attack. The two groups crashed together with a grating metallic scream. For a moment the Boys' Troop had the advantage, but more and more Connaughtmen arrived to join in, and soon it was clear that Mordach would not escape. I saw his fair hair once as he leapt high to bring his sword crashing down two-handed on an opponent, then lost sight of him in the melee. The ground was heaped with dead Connaughtmen, but there were too many of them. The fight parted for a moment, and I saw Mordach on one knee, back to back with another boy, surrounded by enemies. I saw him clubbed to the ground, and then the melee closed up again and he was gone. The fight came to a stuttering halt. None of the Boys' Troop was still standing. We watched, as the Connaughtmen walked around, finishing off the wounded. I stepped forward, unable to stand still, pulling at my sword, but a small hand held me by the wrist and pulled it back. I turned to see a child's serious face looking up at me, a sharp sword in his other hand. It was the boy with the broken shoulder from Skiatha's island.

'They knew why they were fighting. They died for Ulster. Do not try to help them if it will mean that Cuchullain falls.' I stood irresolute for a moment, and then realized that they were all dead. I drew my sword and waited.

The Connaughtmen regrouped. There were more of them than us, but not many. They did not attack, there was no need. They settled down to bind their wounds and wait for reinforcements.

An hour later their comrades arrived. My force had by then elected a new leader, and he split the group in half, the same tactic that Mordach had used. The boys that grouped around the new leader seemed very few. He saluted us and then turned to face the attack. As the Connaughtmen came towards us he charged them with his Troop behind him. The two waves collided and broke up into small conflicts. I watched as the Connaughtmen cut down the boys one by one, and felt that my chest would burst. I knew that when it came to our turn I was going to fight those men until they were all dead or I was.

It was dark when the fighting stopped. The remaining boys knew that in the morning there would be a final attack. They sat around talking quietly and sharpening their weapons. I sat to one side, unable to join in. I felt that I should have been helping to stiffen their resolve, or better still trying to save them, but instead they were calmly sitting around discussing the next day's battle and I was unable to do anything except hug my own uselessness. That night it seemed more important to me not to let these boys down than to escape. For the only time in my life I forgot about living and thought only about dying well.

The sun rose early. The attack came at dawn, as we knew it would. I lined up with the last of the boys. As the Connaughtmen charged, I turned to look back at the Pass behind us.

Laeg stood in the light of the sun, signalling me to come back.

I hesitated, turned back to face the charge, then looked back again. I did not know what to do. Then the same boy who had held me back from helping Mordach looked up at me again, his soft urgent voice trembling with excitement.

'Go back, Leary! Go back and help Cuchullain! We will slow these cattle-thieves down, and by the time they have recovered you will deal with them easily.'

'But I cannot . . .'

The boy's face seemed to glow. 'Go! Remember our names when you tell the bards the story of this day!' As he spoke, every boy uttered a shrill cry, a yell of defiance and excitement, and as one the group flung itself forward, leaving me standing in indecision. I watched as if paralysed as the boys attacked the enemy, killing more often than they were killed, but dying too quickly just the same. I saw the fury of both charges dissipate, and the fight become a series of duels. Then I saw the two sides part for a moment, as if by mutual consent in order to draw breath. I saw the boy who had told me to defend Cuchullain standing at the front of them, his sword arm dangling bloody and useless, a knife in his left hand.

He looked across at me. His good arm lifted slightly in salute.

The two sides crashed together again, screaming defiance at each other. I stood still, unable to move, trembling as if I was plague-stricken, crying silently without tears. A hand appeared on my shoulder. My father's voice spoke to me.

'Come, Leary, it will soon be over.'

I gestured helplessly towards the fight. As if released by his touch, the tears began streaming down my face. Laeg nodded. 'They are doing this for Cuchullain. We must not let them down.'

Laeg led me like a ghost from the battlefield. I looked back only once. The grass was strewn with corpses, frozen in every possible position, as if a giant hand had hurled them down like dice. Many of them were too small to be men. The Boys' Troop no longer existed.

We ran back to the ford. I shouted with relief. Cuchullain was standing by a tree, dressed only in a cloak. He was covered with cuts and scars, but the grey of fatigue had lifted and his face was alive again. I had feared that the killing of Ferdia had finished off something inside him too. Now he looked like something of his old self. He listened while I told him about meeting Sualdam, and the defence of the Pass by the Boys' Troop. His face clouded and a dark light flickered around him as I told him how the Troop had bought him time with their lives. He swore an oath to all his Gods and reached for his weapons. His anger was real. Mordach had been in the Troop as a small boy when Cuchullain joined it, and there were other comrades of his lying silent in the long grass outside the Pass, their lives ended before they had really begun.

We helped him arm himself. I harnessed the Grey of Macha to a chariot abandoned by the Connaughtmen and Laeg brought his weapons. Cuchullain took particular care to bring every weapon he had, and to dress in the finest clothes we had brought. I bound knives to the wheels and the front and every other part of the chariot until it looked like a metal hedgehog. I piled arrows and slingstones and javelins into the chariot until there was hardly room for the two of us. As I stepped back to admire my handiwork, I saw Laeg and Cuchullain with their hands on each other's shoulders, saying goodbye. My heart slipped sideways, and without care for my dignity I ran to Laeg and took his hand. He smiled at me.

'Don't go,' I said.

'Cuchullain is better now. You do not need me any more.'

'I do. I will.'

'Then I will be here when you need me,' he said, and turned and walked away towards the rising sun. I held tight to his hand but it slipped through mine like gossamer. I watched until I could see him no longer and the sun burnt my vision white. Cuchullain turned me round and made me walk to the chariot. We climbed in and I took the reins. Cuchullain started speaking. Not to me.

'Because you have invaded Ulster. Because you have attacked my home. Because you have killed my friends and burnt their houses. Because you have made me kill my friend.' He took a breath, and his voice lowered. 'Because you have caused the death of the Boys' Troop. Because of all these things, and much more, I swear that I will not cease to hound you until either you leave Ulster in shame or I am dead. No invader is safe from me, not until my head is separated from my body.' He turned to me. 'Drive to the Connaughtmen.'

'Which direction?'

Cuchullain smiled. His eyes were cold. I saw the light of battle flickering around his head. 'We are surrounded,' he said, 'so it hardly matters.'

331

As I touched the horse's flanks and we raced across the gentle hills that stood between us and the plain where we knew Maeve to be, Laeg's voice sounded all around me and Mordach's face filled my mind.

# 39

The storytellers have a particular liking for the scene when Sualdam arrived at Emain Macha. I have heard it many times, told in many different ways.

Sualdam left three different groups of Connaughtmen exhausted in his wake, yet when he pulled Cuchullain's horse up in front of the walls of Emain Macha the Black Sanglain was as fresh as when they had begun riding and his tail was held as high as the old man's beard. The horse's coat shone wet in the sun. Sualdam had discarded most of the horse's ornaments to lighten the load as he rode, leaving only a silver armoured head-guard and the medals on the reins. He stood up in the stirrups and bawled at the castle walls.

'Wake up, men of Ulster! Cuchullain is alone and needs your help!'

He waited. There was no sound in return except the cawing of crows. Sualdam rode up to the gate and kicked it open, then rode across to the door of the Banquet Hall and went directly in without dismounting. He shouted up into the great arched roof, so that his voice boomed around the Hall and carried to every corner of the building.

'Is there no-one here to help Cuchullain? Are all the Heroes sleeping in Emain Macha? Are there only cowards here? What is the matter? Are—'

Cathbad appeared at a side entrance. His eyes were red, and his body was bent sideways with pain.

'Stop shouting, you old fool,' he said in a hoarse voice. 'You know very well what is wrong. There is nothing to do but wait. Cuchullain must fend for himself.'

Sualdam looked at him scornfully. 'Don't you think I am suffering too? But I have still managed to ride halfway across Ulster dodging Maeve's soldiers to fetch help! Perhaps the Champions of Ulster have come to accept their pain, perhaps they will accept Cuchullain's death as the price of a few more hours' peace, but I will not!'

Sualdam wheeled the horse round and goaded it to kick out at a pile of armour. The Sanglain's great hooves lashed out twice, knocking the shields every way. They flew through the air like coins thrown by a rich man for street-urchins to fight over and crashed to the floor and against the wall with a noise that ran through the castle and back.

Cathbad was furious. 'Do you think that doing that will help, apart from waking everyone?'

Sualdam glared at him. 'If it wakes everyone, then at least I am not wasting my time!'

The druid grimaced. 'You have made your point. Now go. The Champions will fight when they are well again.'

'So, the Champions lie in bed like mewling children crying for warm milk, while my son bleeds his life away for Ulster? The Champions snore and stuff themselves and snore some more, while the Boys' Troop lies cold and still on the plain of Iraird Cuillenn? Not while I breathe!'

A soft hoarse voice came from behind Sualdam. 'What is all the noise? What has happened to the Boys' Troop?' Sualdam turned on his horse to see Conor, bent over like an old man and holding onto a spear to keep upright. Sualdam drew himself up in the saddle, and the iron on the Sanglain's hooves struck sparks off the stone floor as it felt his impatience.

'The Boys' Troop is fighting Maeve's men while we talk. They go to defend Cuchullain, and they are sure to meet Maeve's soldiers. I passed them as I rode here and their minds were set.'

'Then you do not know what has happened to them?'

'I know that they went to defend Cuchullain. I know that the Connaughtmen were in front of them and behind them. We both know that they would never surrender.' Sualdam paused meaningfully. 'Yes,' he said softly, 'I think I know what has happened to them.'

Conor said nothing for a few moments. 'And Cuchullain?'

Sualdam swallowed, and his shoulders slumped like an old man's. 'He was alive when I left Leary, but his wounds cover him like a red cloak. Maeve has broken the bargain that she struck with him, and her troops are burning every house between here and Iraird Cuillenn. Even if he is alive, Cuchullain can barely defend himself, let alone stop her armies. If the Boys' Troop is no more then he may be dead already.'

Conor groaned, and tried to stand straight. A spasm of pain cut deep lines down his face and he gave up the struggle. 'As you see,' he said wryly, 'we are not much help to him at the moment.'

Conall appeared beside the King, his hair wild and unbrushed, his long beard matted like red moss. The pains had stripped his pride from him, and he had lain for days in a bed stiff with his own sweat. Sualdam saw him and shouted, making the horse rear up.

'Conall of the Victories! Did they not call you that once?'

Conall bristled. 'They still do.'

'Did you and Cuchullain not swear to avenge each other, whoever died first?'

Conall nodded, and then bent over in pain. It was some moments before he could reply. 'We did.'

'Then it is time to leave your bed and fulfil your vow.' Conall looked at him wildly.

'Is Cuchullain dead?'

'If not, he is near to it.'

Conall tried to walk forward, then gestured helplessly to Conor and Cathbad, hoping for understanding, moaned in pain and sank onto one knee like a supplicant. 'I cannot,' he said, the sound a croaking parody of his normal voice.

Sualdam shouted a wordless noise of frustration and jerked furiously at the reins. The Black Sanglain, accustomed to Leary's gentle handling, whinnied in pain and pawed at the stone floor. Sualdam reached behind his back, grasped his spear and waved it wildly around his head. 'Then I shall go back alone and tell Cuchullain I have failed. I will tell him that Ulster still sleeps, and then we will die together!' he shouted, and pulled the horse around to face the door. As he did so, he lost control of the spear, and the butt end came down and cracked across the animal's soft nose. It reared up, arching its back so that Sualdam left the saddle with a curse and had to grasp the pommel to stay on the horse's back. The horse twisted left, kicking out and throwing its head up. The armoured top of its skull hit the bottom of Sualdam's shield with a loud crack. The sharp top edge went up under Sualdam's chin-guard as he came back down to land on the saddle and sliced through his neck like a sword. Sualdam's head fell off backwards, rolled across the floor and came to rest at Conor's feet. He glanced down at it and saw that Sualdam's lips were still moving. Conor and Conall then had to jump back quickly away from the frightened horse as Sualdam's body swayed sideways and back, a thin fountain of blood pumping from its neck, then slid slowly off the horse's back and hit the floor with a crash. The horse turned and galloped out of the door.

All three men looked at the headless body. No-one spoke. Conor braced himself with his spear and dropped his other hand from his stomach. Very slowly, he stood up straight. He leant briefly against the wall, wiping greasy sweat from his face, a thread of blood running down his chin from his bitten bottom lip, then stood away from the support. Conall and Cathbad hesitated, then drew themselves as erect as they could. They followed Conor as he walked out of the Hall. Conor kicked a footstool in front of him and it came to rest against a moss-covered rain-butt brimming with water. He stood on the stool and then stepped into the barrel. For a few moments he disappeared under the water, then he burst upwards through the whirling surface. Water streamed down his face. He waited for a few moments until it had gone, then spoke.

'Wake everyone,' said Conor, his voice low and commanding. 'Wake them all. We leave in an hour.'

It was said that the pains of Macha left every Ulsterman at that moment.

As the Champions of Emain Macha rode west behind Conor's chariot their spirits rose. By the time they reached Maeve's armies they had gathered men from every castle, every village, every farm. Many of their women rode beside them. The two armies met on the Plain of Muirthemne, and the greatest battle that Ireland ever saw was fought there. There were no tactics, no manoeuvres, no reserves. Each army attacked the other completely, head on, like two flood-swollen rivers meeting in a gorge. The bodies of men lay piled in strewn heaps like turf ready for drying, shored up by the carcasses of horses and spliced together with the smashed remnants of blood-spattered chariots. Others lay alone, scattered like the first autumn leaves, so close together that those still alive stumbled over them as they advanced and retreated, or slipped on the purple grass to land beside them. Dead men covered the plain, trampled like hailstones under the horses' feet.

The battle swung one way then the other, then back again. Parts of the battlefield would sometimes become still for a few moments as if by unspoken agreement while exhausted men paused from fighting each other and fought instead to drag the air into their scorched lungs. Then they would fall upon each other again with screams and curses.

Cuchullain and I came upon the battle from a ridge overlooking the plain. We had met a large group of Connaughtmen who were detached from the main army. Maybe they were lost or late, maybe raiders, maybe deserters. It didn't matter. Cuchullain drove straight at them. Many died; the rest fled back towards the safety of their brothers. We rode after them, letting them take us to where Maeve was camped. It didn't take long. Soon

337

the breeze brought the metal chime of violent death and the sharp stink of fear and fresh blood and trampled grass to us. Cuchullain smiled. His dark hair blew back like a crow's wing gliding on warm air, and the sun reflected off the armour and jewels he wore so that he shone like a mirror. The chariot bristled with outward-pointing spears and sharp knives were attached to the wheels. The Grey of Macha pawed at the ground, the hair on its back pricking upwards into a ridge with anticipation. Then we heard hooves batter the ground and turned to see the Black Sanglain galloping riderless towards us.

'Where is Sualdam?' I asked, holding the stallion's bridle and speaking softly to the trembling horse, my breath stroking its nose and quietening it. Cuchullain saw spots of blood on the saddle.

'There is another death to put on Maeve's account,' he said. 'Put the black beside the grey and we will start exacting some payment.'

At that moment, a chariot broke off from the part of the battle nearest us, dragging itself away in a lame circle like a bird with a broken wing. It had a smashed wheel. The horse was in a frenzy, kicking backwards at the damaged chariot until the traces broke and it could gallop free. The charioteer was dead, slumped over the front of the chariot. His Champion jumped free as the horse's hooves smashed the wood in front of him, and stood watching for a moment, shaking his head. Then he turned to rejoin the battle on foot.

Cuchullain drew a javelin from the quiver at the side of his chariot, stepped past me as I put the Sanglain in the chariot harness, and hurled the spear at the man below us. It flew higher than an arrow and hissed down just over the man's shoulder, making him jump backwards. I looked at Cuchullain, surprised.

'You missed.'

Cuchullain stood and watched as the man realized where the spear had come from and whirled to face us. His red beard jutted towards us as he threw his head back at the sight of Cuchullain.

'Cuchullain!' The sound was like a bull's mating roar.

'Conall!' Cuchullain raised an arm in greeting. Conall made frantic motions of his sword arm, inviting Cuchullain to join him. Cuchullain acknowledged the invitation. He stepped forward and stood in full view of the battle, watching.

Those nearest Conall heard his shout, and some of them took it up. In what seemed like a few moments the whole battlefield knew. The Ulstermen shouted it and their sword arms rose and fell with new energy, but the Connaught army whispered it to each other like schoolboys or said nothing but glanced over their shoulders.

'Ready?' asked Cuchullain.

'Ready,' I said, giving the harness a final tug and patting the horses' flanks. Cuchullain jumped into the chariot beside me.

'Attack,' he said.

'Where?'

'Anywhere,' said Cuchullain. 'But watch out for arrows. I don't want to die before we even get there. There are scores to be settled.'

I flexed the reins and the horses jerked forward and galloped down the ridge. A Connaught Champion saw us and urged his chariot forward. Cuchullain ducked his whirling sword and thrust a spear through him as we passed. 'Circle!' he yelled. I dragged us around on one wheel and Cuchullain knocked the other charioteer to the ground with the back of his fist. He caught the reins and threw them to Conall, who jumped in with a huge grin of pleasure on his face.

'Where is Maeve?' shouted Cuchullain, hacking at a soldier who was trying to grab at his horses. Conall leant over and brought his sword down on the man's head. Cuchullain drew an arm back and hurled a spear directly at Conall, whose eyes widened as the spear hissed over his shoulder into the throat of a man poised to attack him from behind. Conall spun in the chariot and heaved the dead body off the platform.

'The bitch is there,' he said, pointing towards the sun with his dripping sword. 'The King is sworn to chase her out of Ulster today or die in the hunt.'

'Get yourself a charioteer and follow us,' shouted Cuchullain.

'We are going hunting with the King.' I slapped my hand on the horses, and Cuchullain's chariot raced at the Connaughtmen, the knives in its wheels spinning round and catching the sunlight, making a flickering hole of death in the air as it hurtled towards them.

# 40

The Ulstermen killed many thousands that day, and left many of their own on the field as well. The attack that Cuchullain led was the beginning of the retreat to Connaught, a long slow funeral train that left dead men marking every yard of the road. We harried Maeve's men unceasingly. Cuchullain gave them no peace to make camp. He set fire to the tents that they pitched, he cut down the Champions who came to face him, he hurled stones and fired his arrows into the centre of the army and circled them and made them change direction so often that soon all they wanted to do was get out of Ulster as quickly as possible. The heads around Cuchullain's chariot were bunched like mussels on a rock at the tide-line. The men of Ulster gathered up much of the gold that Maeve had plundered in her advance and her men had thrown aside to speed their retreat, and they recaptured many of the stolen cattle that her drovers were taking to Connaught. By the time Maeve's army crossed Connaught's border and Cuchullain ceased tormenting them the army was a tenth of its original size. Many had been killed; many others left quietly in the night to go home without honour but alive.

The Ulster Champions returned to their castles in triumph,

and there was feasting and laughter. The divisions that had arisen over Conor's treatment of Deirdre were not forgotten, but the fighting and the losses that had been sustained brought a truce. Brother had fought brother, and many of them regretted it. Some of the Exiles chose to return to Ulster and their families rather than go back to Connaught and risk being pitted against their kinsfolk again. Fergus and those nearest to him still stayed away. There was a blood-debt between Fergus and Conor, and if they met it would have to be paid.

There was celebration everywhere. We celebrated the bravery of the men who had died, and especially we remembered the sacrifice of the Boys' Troop. As the days went by, more and more warriors gathered at Emain Macha to tell stories of how they had chased the Connaughtmen out of Ulster, until only Cuchullain remained in pursuit, implacable and unsleeping, ranging across the countryside like a sword jabbing at the entrails of Maeve's retreating army.

Cuchullain and I never caught up with Maeve. Other men did, and most of them died. Her soldiers circled her like bees around the Queen of their hive and defended her steadfastly. We searched every valley on the way, responded to every rumour, but although we caught up with many groups of her men, we never found her. We were several times within a short distance of her, but something always happened to prevent the meeting. A mist would come down, or a chariot wheel would crack, or she would just not be where she had been ten minutes before.

One night I slept standing up in the chariot and dreamt that Maeve was hidden by the Daughters of Calatin and that we would never find her, never get through the mist that surrounded her. I told Cuchullain, made him smell what I smelt so that he would know what I knew. He unwillingly gave up the search.

We rode back to Emain Macha where the celebrations went on for what seemed like weeks. We drank and feasted and loved in an unthinking passion to forget and mend and numb the memory of what had happened to us all. Except that no amount of singing of verses or drinking or warm flesh could bring the Boys' Troop back, or help me to forget the memory of a small hand on mine and a man-child's voice telling me to run away while he stayed to defend my retreat. No amount of boasting from Conall or Buchal or any of a hundred others could hide the fact that Cuchullain was now the greatest Champion of them all. And no victory celebration could hide the fact that Maeve was still alive, and that she now had shame and revenge to add to the reasons she originally had to hate us.

And, perhaps worst of all, the symbol of Ulster's shame was with us in Emain Macha to remind us every day that the King was not a man of his word, perhaps not a King at all. Naisi was dead, and Deirdre was Conor's captive. She was kept by Conor for a full year, and for that time she belonged to him. During that year no-one saw her smile. She ate only enough to keep herself alive and hardly slept. She would sit all day in her rooms staring silently out of the window, unless Conor instructed her differently, in which case she would do his bidding, no more and no less. Conor tried to woo her every day by sending musicians to play for her and women to serve her every need, or he would sit with her and speak pleasantly, but she would always reply the same way, in a voice empty of passion, empty of life.

'Do not try to please me. Nothing that you can do will ever make me laugh or make me want to be with you. You have killed the hope in me and I might as well be dead. You have split your kingdom and set your kinsmen against each other. Everything worthwhile that I was lived in my love for Naisi, and he is gone, by your hand and the hand of Eoghan your cur. I would rather one kiss from Naisi's dead lips, one farewell glance, just the sound of his voice, than to have you and your whole kingdom and all its Heroes and their great deeds here in my hand. There is nothing left in life for me. Do with me as you wish, for I cannot prevent it, but do not try to make me happy. If you had spared Naisi, I would even have been your wife, for his sake. Do not, ever, think for even a heartbeat that anything you do or say or give me could ever make me happy.'

If she had screamed her hatred of him I think he would have known what to do, but her flat voice and indifference was something he didn't understand. Conor became crapulous and bad-tempered. He had the woman he wanted, but she did not want him. One wet morose day, after trying to amuse her all morning, he became angry, and asked her, 'What do you see that you most hate?'

'You,' she said, 'you and Eoghan mac Durtacht.'

'Then live for a year with Eoghan,' he shouted, 'for I have had enough of you.'

'No!' she said, but he laughed, made all the more certain of what he would do. Conor knew that she had sworn that two men alive in the world together would never have her. Naisi was dead; Conor had taken her. To go with Eoghan while Conor still lived would break her vow. But Conor was filled with pain and anger and wanted to hurt and dishonour her, and he shouted that he hoped the broken vow might break her spirit, and he sent for Eoghan to come and take her, though the thought of Deirdre in another man's arms must have torn his heart as badly as her indifference to him.

Conor was surprised at her calm face and how little argument she made about getting into Eoghan's chariot to go with him to his castle, and Conor almost called to stop Eoghan, but the chariot flew away as if Eoghan knew what might happen. He drove his chariot fast, the sooner to have her in his home.

'Do you look forward to being with me?' His voice came back to her on the wind.

'I will never be with two men at once,' she replied, so soft he only just heard it. Eoghan laughed.

'That suits me!' he shouted. 'When you have been once in my bed, you'll never want to go back!' His laugh rang across the fields.

They entered a narrow pass, almost touching in places overhead, as if a mountain had cracked open and left just enough room for a chariot to pass through. Eoghan hardly slowed down, so great was his eagerness, and the wheels of the chariot bounced over boulders so that its sides almost touched the rocky cliffs on either side of it. He laughed again, and glanced back over his shoulder to see if Deirdre was admiring his skill with the chariot.

She looked at him as if he was a very long way distant, and then seemed to sway outwards just as they thundered past a large outcrop of rock. Her head dashed against it, and without a sound she disappeared over the side of the chariot. By the time Eoghan jumped out and reached her, Deirdre of the Sorrows was dead.

And something died in all our hearts that day, as if while she was alive there was something good and pure burning in all of us, and after we let her die all we had left was the cold ashes of the life remaining to us. And I know I am only a shadow of the man I felt that I was while she lived.

# 41

The Daughters of Calatin left me alone for a while and the visions they sent me didn't trouble my sleep. Then, one cold night when the branches on the trees were heavy with snow, they showed me that the troubled peace in Ulster was about to collapse again, and to celebrate this news they left me with a fever that put glacier-water into my bones and sand in my joints. That fever never really left me, I have it still.

As the Daughters of Calatin sucked the warmth from me, they made me watch the Connaught warriors feasting in Maeve's Hall. The great Banqueting Hall was full of them, but it seemed to Maeve that their shouting was too loud, that they were trying too hard to be the men they had been on any one of many similar nights in the past.

Ailell turned to her.

'The men are in good heart.'

She turned to him very slowly and spoke in a monotone. 'The men are shouting loudly because their hearts are full of shame. They fill their cups because they cannot look each other in the eye. They drink to forget. Their boasts are null, their shouts vainglorious, their courage empty. They are hollow men.'

Ailell sat silently, looking at his wife. Her head was supported in her hand, pressing against her chin and slurring her speech. Her hair was dull. He saw the beginnings of loose flesh wattling her neck. She turned to him and he saw the fire in her eyes receding, like the light on a fishing boat putting to sea on a quiet night. Maeve looked old for the first time. She looked as if she did not care. She looked like someone he didn't know.

Ailell had never been so frightened in his life.

All that evening he watched her, as if he had never seen her before. He saw how she drank as if she did not care whether she drank or not, swigging from the cup without paying attention to it, neither for pleasure nor to get drunk but because it was there in front of her. That night, when they went to bed, he watched as she dropped her clothes on the floor and slid into bed without brushing her hair or looking at him to see that she still affected him. He lay awake all night, watching her bundled form beneath the blanket, feeling a cold hand with long nails scraping at his soul.

The next morning she did not get out of bed. When servants brought her food she picked at it then threw it back at them, but aimlessly, without the raucous spirit that normally accompanied her rages.

Ailell watched her for three days and nights, during which she virtually ignored him. When he sat beside her and took her hand, she looked at him with dull eyes. When he spoke to her she looked at him as if he were a stranger, and refused to discuss anything.

On the third night, he sat beside her bed as she slept. The firelight was the only illumination, throwing tall shadows onto the gold-threaded tapestries that hung from every wall. His face was gaunt with worry and exhaustion. He slumped in his seat, feeling his head drooping with sleep. Then he suddenly was aware that something had happened.

The room became cold. He sat up, wondering if the door had opened, but it was firmly closed. A dim light was shining from a corner of the room. He stood and walked over to it. A heavy silver-bound chest was across the corner. A soft blue light shone from inside it through the cracks in the planks. Ailell gingerly lifted the heavy lid.

Inside it was a smaller box. Ailell recognized it immediately. He had seen it the night he followed Maeve up to the cave in the mountainside. It was glowing with an evanescent blue light, pulsing in time with his heart.

'What do you want from usss?'

The voice was from behind him. Ailell jumped, and spun round. The heavy lid of the chest slammed down on his fingers. He pulled his hand out with a silent curse. The girl that had been in the cave was standing in front of him. She was more beautiful than he remembered. He sneaked a look at his crushed hand. Two fingernails were already turning black. Pain flooded up his arm. She reached forward and took his hand. It immediately became lifeless. Ailell felt only an intense coldness. The pain was gone, but the arm hung useless at his side. Her old woman's eyes pinned his gaze to the back of his skull.

'You woke usss. What isss your question?'

Ailell looked at Maeve. She was sleeping restlessly, and turned in the bed, putting a forearm over her head. He gestured at her with his good arm.

'She is ill. I am afraid she will die.'

The girl did not look at Maeve, but moved closer to Ailell. He could not see how she travelled as her feet did not move or touch the ground. He tried not to recoil as she approached. She smelt sickly-sweet, like the warm skin of a freshly killed rabbit. As her full crimson lips moved, he saw black teeth between them.

'She will not die. She hasss much to do. But you, you mussst help usss to help her.'

Ailell looked at his wife and a lump rose in his throat.

'I don't know what you are, but I will do whatever you want, pay any price you ask. Make her well again.'

The girl smiled, showing ruined stumps of teeth.

For three more days, Maeve lay in bed while Ailell's messengers came and went from her castle. Then, on the third night, Ailell came to Maeve's bedroom and pulled the blankets roughly away from her. She whined and tried to pull them back. He ripped them from her hands and threw them on the floor. She curled up into a ball and started to cry.

Ailell had never seen her cry for self-pity before. It made his heart swell until he felt sure it would come bursting out from his chest. He bent down and gently picked her up, holding her as a bridegroom would. She folded her arms around his neck like a sleepy child and relaxed in his arms. Ailell wrapped her in a heavy shawl and carried her carefully out into the courtyard of the castle.

All four sides of the courtyard were blazing with light from braziers and torches. A cold wind brushed past them. A crowd of silent men formed lines along three of the walls in deep ranks. The light danced on their dark armour and made the red ochre in their long beards glow like polished bronze. They waited while Ailell carried Maeve to a circular raised dais in front of the fourth wall. On it was a small chair, in which he placed her gently. Then he stepped to the front of the dais and addressed the men.

'Champions, your Queen waits to hear you.'

He moved aside. A grizzled warrior, his hair grey but still worn in a fighting man's style, stepped forward. He drew his sword, held it high above his head in a salute. Ailell, watching intently, saw her eyes flicker upwards. The old man brought the sword down and reversed it, as if to sheath it again. Then he put both hands on the handle and drove it into the boards at Maeve's feet, where it vibrated like a struck harp-string.

'Lead,' he said gruffly, 'where you will. I will follow.'

He stepped back. Another took his place, saluting, then plunging his sword down beside the first.

'Lead,' he repeated. 'I will follow.'

For the next half-hour, man after man came up to Maeve, saluting then promising his sword, unconditionally. Ailell watched her constantly. The swords stood like metal saplings in front of her, sprouting from the wood at her feet. As the line of men passed, he saw her slowly sit up straight. She nodded to some of the men that she knew, and even looked a couple of the younger ones up and down in frank appraisal. At last, the tribute was finished. Every man present had sworn loyalty to Maeve except one. Ailell walked to the front of the dais and faced his wife. The wind had risen and the braziers burnt with fierce life. He drew his sword and held it high.

'Lead!' he said urgently, and brought the sword down with such force that it broke through the plank and plunged into the ground, where the point hit a large flat stone that struck a single spark that flew up like a comet between them and made the sword vibrate louder than any of the others. The sound made the hairs on Ailell's neck prickle. He leant forward.

'Lead,' he said softly. 'Lead even to hell, we will follow you.'

He looked into her face. Her eyes were alive. Red points were high in both cheeks. She reached out to touch his face. Her head made a tiny movement of acknowledgement and respect that was for him only. Then she stood, stepped forward and threw her arms wide. Every man cheered until he was hoarse to see the Queen restored, standing amongst a garden of unsheathed swords.

I knew why the Daughters of Calatin had shown me this scene. Maeve would come again to Ulster. Not tomorrow, not this summer, but soon.

# 42

Two years passed. The sun rose and set, the crops grew and were cut down. We feasted and hunted and brawled and played, just as we had always done. Time passed, and Deirdre ceased to be real to me, though sometimes a shadow or a sound or a warm breeze would send me back to one of the places where I had stood and watched her. Life went on, except that the wine was spilt, the jug broken. The jug could be mended and new wine poured into it, and life would go on as before, but it could not be the same. It was not as strong, it only looked the same because it was never tested.

And then, after two years of working hard at not minding or caring, the test came.

The room was dark. Heavy tapestries covered every window, and the air was acrid and stale. Conor slumped a bit deeper in his chair, and looked at me over the top of his cup as though it were all my fault. I didn't worry too much about that. He now looked at just about everyone that way.

He took a deep gulp out of what was certainly not his first cup of wine that morning, and came up from it with a scowl for me. He was no longer handsome. His lean features were tending to puffiness, the skin loose and dull, and the dark hair and beard were streaked with grey and hung in rat-tails around his face. When I first met him, he bathed three times a day and he seemed to glow with light. Now he looked and smelt as if he hadn't taken his clothes off for a week.

'What are you looking at?' he snarled. White spittle shot forward and landed near my foot. I hesitated. Conor was no longer the man he had once been, but he was still not a man to cross.

'You sent for me.' It wasn't a question. He looked lost for a moment, and eyes which had once sparkled with life and malice, like a wolf in his prime during the mating season, wandered about the room like a dying old man's. Then he snapped back again to being what was left of himself.

'Yes. Sit down.' I thought of saying something pompous about preferring to stand, and then didn't, partly because I quite wanted to sit and partly because I didn't want to make him angry before he did it for himself anyway.

As I sat, I saw him touch his side with his fingers, and a soft breath hissed through his yellow teeth as if a fist forced it from him. He bit his lip in pain. I waited. He looked at me, and saw that I had seen it.

'Don't worry,' he rasped, 'it's nothing fatal.' He sat back, exhaling loudly, as the pain passed. Then he smiled savagely. 'It's worse than that.'

I didn't know what he was talking about. 'Worse?'

He leant forward, prodding my arm like a drunk telling a dirty story. 'Worse. For Ulster, anyhow.' He prodded me again, and chuckled. 'Shall I tell you the future? Shall I tell you something that I know without anyone telling me?'

I nodded. It seemed sensible. He grinned at me, and leant even closer. I smelt his breath, heavy and fetid like an old dog's after a large meal.

'Maeve is planning to invade us again.'

I shrugged. 'No doubt. But the day she will actually do it is a long way off.'

He shook his head, and the rat-tails wagged across his dark face. 'Not later, not soon. Now.'

'Now?'

He nodded. 'She is already moving towards us.' He sank back into his chair again, and drained his cup, following it with a desultory belch. He waved the empty cup at me. 'Know how I know?' I shrugged, and then his face knotted tight with pain, and I knew, and cursed myself for a fool. He moaned, bending forward until his chest touched his knees, and a hand reached out and grasped my sleeve so tightly that the blood left my arm. The pain receded slightly, and he breathed again. 'That bitch Macha reminding us of our misdemeanours,' he said, and chuckled, before doubling up again. This pain was so bad that he rolled off the chair and fell to the ground before I could stop him. I knelt helplessly beside him. He writhed on the floor, his face contorted as if he looked into bright light, hissing words at me between the waves of pain.

'She never . . . forgets . . . to remind me . . . us . . . when we are in . . . danger. At the time . . . of . . . of greatest . . . weakness . . . she said. Trust me . . . Maeve is coming!'

The pain ebbed, and he lay curled up on the floor, the acrid smell of his sweat hanging in the air around me.

So. The pains of Macha again. I had always known that Maeve would return, but not so soon. It was only two years since Cuchullain had chased and harried her army out of Ulster and down into Connaught, searching for the Queen in every valley and behind every tree, but never catching up with her. It was said that the Daughters of Calatin saved her from him and brought her home. I believed that, for otherwise Cuchullain would surely have found her.

I lifted Conor up and laid him on his bed. I went in search of a druid. I eventually found one skulking in the kitchens. He cringed and wailed at me that Ulster was doomed. I relieved my own unspoken apprehension by taking him by the scruff of the neck and kicking him along the corridors all the way to the King's rooms. I pointed at the crumpled body on the bed.

'Give him something for the pain. Make him sleep. And you might give him a wash as well.' I waited until he stopped looking at me mutinously and began to reach into his bag and pull things out of it, then turned to go. Conor's voice, surprisingly strong, called out to me. I turned and went back to him, ignoring the druid slouching at the bedside with a bad grace as he crushed something foul into powder with a stone pestle.

Conor looked up at me. His eyes looked a little clearer, and his voice more like the one I remembered. He reached up and gripped my sleeve.

'Go to Connaught,' he said. I laughed.

'Do you think I can persuade her to turn back? I doubt that.'

'No, you are right, she will not turn back. Nothing will deflect her. You must go to Connaught. Do what you can to slow her down. Then find Fergus and his men, and tell them to come back. Tell them that Ulster's future lies in their hands. Tell them that I will go into exile, tell them I am dead, tell them anything, but do not let them fight for Maeve. Even if they will not fight for Ulster, make them see that they cannot fight for Maeve against their homeland.' His voice cracked with the urgency of the message.

'And will you?' I looked down at him, and saw a shadow of the man I had once known. 'Will you really go into exile? Do you want me to lie to them?'

He swallowed. 'No lie,' he said softly. 'I will not stay in Emain Macha if Fergus comes home. Tell him that. Ulster is his, I will not stand in his way. Tell him that Conor is already the man who split the House of the Red Branch in two, but he would not be the man who brought its walls down. Tell Fergus that I will die fighting Ulster's enemies, or if Ulster is saved and I am not killed then I will no longer be Ulster's King.' His grip tightened. 'I accept his will, whatever that is, even if it means my death. Tell him that. Tell him!'

I suppose I could have ignored him. After all, he wasn't in a position to force me to do anything, and those remaining men who were loyal to him were in as bad a state as he was. On the other hand, I didn't want to see Maeve burn Emain Macha to the ground while I watched, and I didn't want Cuchullain defending the Pass again. Besides, it was spring. Perfect weather for chariot driving. And this time I didn't have to take Owen.

There is something different about passing through a land that fears that it is preparing for war. Perhaps it is the shortage of young men, and the crops that lie rotting in the fields because there is no-one to harvest them. Perhaps it is the suspicion with which people greet you, wondering if you are a friend or an enemy. Perhaps it is the tension that stiffens and lines the faces of the women who remain, wondering if their brothers, sisters, husbands, daughters, will come home again. A sense of suppressed feeling, made up of excitement, fear and self-imposed discipline. I had passed this way to Connaught twice before. The first time no-one spoke much, but I soon learnt that was normal. The second time, there were only rumours of Maeve's invasion, and while they were worried, the men were still with them.

This time they knew. I looked into their faces and saw in them the faces of my countrymen in Germany, waiting for the tribes to come back, waiting for their loved ones to come home after the defeat by Tiberius. Many of them waited till their deaths.

I was still two days' drive from Maeve's castle when a patrol arrived at the house where I had asked for hospitality and got me out of bed and into my chariot without even a cup of milk for breakfast. When I complained, the patrol leader, a grizzled one-eyed veteran, fingered his sword and muttered something under his breath that I was glad I didn't quite catch. I decided that I had made my point. I drove the whole day with them as a silent escort.

Everywhere around us was in a fever of preparation. Several times we passed men cutting down trees for spears and arrows. Twice we overtook long columns of well-armed soldiers, marching in the same direction as ourselves. Every house was salting game and laying down stores, a sure sign that there would not be men around to hunt for meat in the winter.

We camped by a stream. I sat with my back to a tree and ate separately from them. A guard was posted beside me, or maybe just a sentry, for I don't think they thought I would try to escape. Amazingly, he turned out not to be a full-blooded Connaught-man, and actually got bored with standing there with nothing to do. We started talking.

'You know horses,' he said.

'Yes,' I replied. 'Do you?'

He spent the next two hours telling me about his horse at home. I encouraged him, and managed to slip in a few questions about what might be waiting for me at Maeve's castle. The more he told me, the deeper my heart sank.

We arrived at midday. The sun was hot, and I wiped the sweat from my eyes so that I could see properly. Ignoring the escort trotting around me, I reined in my horse as we crested the last hill before sweeping down the broad road that led to Maeve's heart. The plain surrounding the castle was covered in tents so that the grass underneath was almost invisible. The smoke from a thousand campfires turned the sky grey and made my eyes water. My spirits, already low, hit the ground at my feet. The sheer size of the army was daunting enough, but also it meant that the invasion was imminent. No castle, not even the Queen of Connaught's, could hope to feed that many people at once for long. They would have to march soon or starve.

My mission was futile. In the unlikely event of my managing to even find Fergus and his few hundred men amongst the crowd, and the even lesser likelihood that they would listen, forgive all and come back, this army would probably not even notice that they had gone.

The one-eyed veteran led me to the Great Hall, which was seething with activity. Messengers crossed the floor every few moments. At the centre of it all sat the Queen. As I entered, despite the bustle around her and the distance, she looked up, saw me, and smiled. I was taken to an anteroom, and given water and wine. I had used both by the time she came into the room.

Maeve motioned me to wait. I felt like a small animal shut in a cage with a she-wolf. She went across the room and reached behind a curtain. She came out with a brass-bound box. She put it beside a chair, which she then sat on. She looked up at me and smiled again, motioning me to sit. 'I thought we would meet again,' she said.

I had hoped we wouldn't. She looked younger than I remembered. She was dressed for war, unadorned, just a thin gold crown holding her hair away from her face. A long sword hung low from a leather belt. The metal was dull and pitted by enemy shields and skulls. A tool, not an ornament.

'You have come to take Fergus away from me. You are to spy on my army, and report back to Conor, is it not so?'

I gulped. I suppose my mission was transparent enough. I had, it seemed, nothing to lose. 'Yes.'

She made a generous gesture. 'Take them, if they want to go. And walk all you want amongst my armies. Talk to them. Count them, if you want.'

'Why?' She smiled again. I was becoming very worried about all this smiling.

'Because I want you to go back and tell Conor what is in store for him, so that he knows that this time when he sees my armies coming over the hill towards Ulster his kingdom will be scattered like dry leaves in the wind.' She watched me for a few moments.

'Ulster defeated you once. It may do so again. Why are you so sure this time?' I hoped I looked and sounded more confident than I felt.

She threw back her head and laughed, a full, honest laugh. 'Because this time we have learnt from our mistakes. Because this time I have allies. Because . . . oh yes, because of a friend, good friends. Of yours too.'

'Friends? You mean Fergus?'

She patted the box beside her with a long-fingered hand. 'Oh yes,' she said again, 'friends. Not Fergus, no. Other friends. Friends who know.' The last sibilant stretched into a hiss, and I knew who she meant. A dead cold went through my veins. She sat back in her chair. 'The defenders of Ulster are stricken with the weakness of Macha. There is nothing to stop us. How many warriors can you muster?' She waited a few moments for me to reply. I didn't. We both knew that the answer was 'one'. One warrior not lying clutching his belly, and his charioteer, some old men past their best, and a bard or two. We didn't even have the Boys' Troop any more. She pushed on. 'Go, if you wish. Walk amongst my men, find out who my allies are. Or stay here, and I will save you the trouble.' She sat up again, her brow furrowed, and ticked the list off on her fingers. 'I have sent messengers throughout Ireland, to Albany, and to the islands, offering a share of the glory to anyone who has a wish to march with us. Honour or plunder, either is a good reason.' Her eyes looked into me like an iron auger drilling into old clay. 'Every man in Ireland who owes Cuchullain a death, that man rides with me. Every man who owes Conor a death, he also rides with me. Laegaid, King of Munster, son of Curoi, King before him and killed by Cuchullain, has brought the fighting men of Munster to make war on Ulster. Erc, King of Meath, whose father Cuchullain also killed, is here too, with all his men. The King of Leinster is here, not with just a raiding party as last time but with every man who owes him allegiance. There are chiefs from every corner of Ireland and beyond, some with ten men, some with a thousand. There are warriors from Albany too, and men with them from the far north, men who fear nothing, men who know pain as a friend and treat death as an adventure.'

She paused to let her words flow around me. Then she went on. 'There are also many here who are here just for plunder, men without honour, who wish to benefit from being on the winning side. I owe them nothing, but I will use them. They do not fight like men, but they will help us.' She looked at me in the way that Tiberius did sometimes, when he told me about some of the things that people do to each other in war, straightforward, unapologetic. 'I will bring them with my armies to Ulster and I will let them loose without orders except to take what they want and destroy the rest, and they will burn the buildings and fields of Ulster. They will take everything of value and make the rest their latrine.'

She leant forward, fixing me with her eyes like a beetle pinned to a table with a stiletto. 'These men are worthless, the scum on the tide of war, but they are useful to me. They are not my army. There are also many others here, men and women of honour, who wish nothing for themselves from this war. They live only to see Cuchullain and Conor die before they do. They will march with me, driving straight and without stopping to Emain Macha, and Cuchullain will die and Conor will be food for crows.' She laughed. 'You see? I tell you my strategy. There is no need for me to pretend. We march to Emain Macha, where we will kill Conor and Cuchullain. You cannot prevent it. Go back and tell Conor that his days are counted.' Her face was flushed and her eyes gleamed but she was in complete control of herself. The wildness in her was still there, but under harness. I feared that new control in her more than I once feared the fury that preceded it. I tried to look unconcerned.

'And what if Cuchullain stops you until the men of Ulster put off their weakness, as he did last time?' I couldn't even raise the bravado that my question needed to sound convincing. I don't think it would have worked anyway.

'As I said, we have learnt.' She leant forward and picked up a cup of wine, tipping it so that the wine spilt out onto the dark wooden table, forming a rough circle. She spilt another circle near by.

'This is Ulster, this, Connaught,' she said, pointing at the pools on the table. She put a finger into the Connaught wine, and drove the point of it along the dark grain of the wood into Ulster's underbelly. 'Erc will take the men of Meath by the shortest route, to the Pass of Iraird Cuillenn, where Cuchullain will be waiting for us as before. There Erc and his men will stay, and they will attack Cuchullain every day until he dies or withdraws.' She looked across the room. 'And there will be no nonsense about single combats this time. If Cuchullain withdraws, they advance through the Pass and invade Ulster. If he attacks, they will withdraw and draw him out of position. If he waits and defends the Pass they will camp and remain, keeping him there.' She drew another, wider line of liquid to the right of the first, joining the Ulster wine further along its border. 'Fergus, if he stays with me, and Laegaid and the army of Leinster, will swing round and attack from the east. If Cuchullain comes to meet them, Erc will be through the Pass and looking at a straight march to Emain Macha. If Cuchullain stays where he is, then Laegaid will send half his army to attack Cuchullain from the rear and then take the other half and advance as quickly as possible to meet Ailell coming down from the north.' She enjoyed my look of surprise. 'Oh yes,' she said softly. She drew another, wider curve of wine, up past the western edge of Ulster, and then down in an inverted hook into its heart. 'Ailell is already marching. By the time Laegaid reaches your border, Ailell will have driven down through Ulster and cut it in half.'

I could not speak. If Ailell was already on the move then it meant two things. Cuchullain and Ulster were in the jaws of a trap, and the enormous army I had seen camped outside Maeve's castle was only a part of her forces. I gazed at the map on the table and the wine that was Ulster, its edges scarred by three lines. There was a slight dip in the surface of the table. The wine was flowing slowly away from Ulster to Connaught.

She pronounced her sentence.

'Your King is helpless and has lost the respect of his people. Your Champions are unable to ride, unable to fight. They will die in their beds if we choose. Ulster is almost ours, and we have not yet raised a hand.' She paused, to let me think about that. I had a vision of Conall, his still body pinned to his bed by Connaught spears. 'Your only hope is Cuchullain. With one army we almost defeated him last time. Now I have two armies, and each of them is larger than the one that I took to Ulster two years ago. I have told you this so that you will see that your position is lost. I know you believe Cuchullain to be almost a God, but he is human, he can be killed. Think about that.'

She leant suddenly forward, whispering urgent words into my face. 'Think! Do you suppose that Cuchullain can defeat so many? Do you? Tell me if you do, and I will not laugh. I have seen what he can do, and I know what is possible. I do not believe it possible for him to win against us. Many will die, yes, but he will be one of them. Those who march with me and die will not mind, so long as he is with them. And when Cuchullain falls, the Red Branch is cut down. Emain Macha will be silent and her hearths will be cold, and the ravens will fly through her halls without hindrance.'

I felt as if I was about to be given a life sentence for a crime I had not committed. She sat back in her chair. 'Speak. Do you think that Cuchullain can defeat an army like mine?'

No, I didn't. He would die trying, and I would probably die with him. I didn't want either to happen. 'I speak for the King,' I said, trying to sound dignified. 'What do you want?'

She smiled her satisfaction and sat back.

'Not much,' she said.

'What?' shouted Cuchullain. I tried to calm him but he paced in circles around me as if he were a horse that I was training. Emer stood silent in a shadow near by. He scratched his chin agitatedly. 'She wants what?'

'Conor in exile. Fermanagh and Tyrone. Tribute for the next ten summers. And you.'

He stopped circling. 'Me?' I saw Emer start forward then catch herself and become still again.

I nodded. 'You.'

He started again. 'She can't have me. She's a witch bathed in poison and I have sworn to defend Ulster against her. What makes her think I would agree to come to her castle to be humiliated and laughed at?'

I shrugged. 'Because it is the only way to prevent Ulster being destroyed?'

'I'd rather die.'

I nodded. 'That is the alternative she mentioned.' Out of the corner of my eye I saw Emer move again, gliding silently forward until she stood near him.

'Is this what you believe I should do?' I didn't know what to say. He looked at me without expression for a few moments. 'I don't fear death,' he said. It was a statement of fact. I didn't react. 'You find that strange.'

I frowned. 'Not strange, for I now know many men who feel the same way. Incomprehensible, yes, but no longer strange.'

A messenger clattered to a halt outside and came into the room, perspiring with some dignity. 'The King wishes to see you,' he said to Cuchullain. He looked at me. 'Both of you.'

As we went from the room Emer moved forward until she walked beside him. Cuchullain turned to say something to her and then closed his mouth. She was a wife walking beside her husband; if you had never seen them before you would still know it. The look they gave each other left a sweet ache in me, proud of them both and yet left alone by what was between them. I watched her as she walked beside him and my chest moved inside as if I was falling.

Conor had managed to prop himself up against the wall beside his bed, and he was drinking like a thirsty horse to keep the pain under control. 'So,' he growled. 'My only walking Champion comes to see me at last.' Conor's sarcasm was thick and unwelcoming. It was also unkind and unjust. Cuchullain was all he had left. There is a wantonness, a will to destruction of the self, that possesses the desperate sometimes, when all seems lost. Conor was behaving like a man who has gambled away all but one gold piece and is now standing on a high bridge over a deep river, flicking the coin high up into the air and catching it over the water, to test if it too wants to leave him.

Cuchullain looked at him and his expression deepened into concern, but also something more complex. I realized with a flash of intuition that Cuchullain didn't like Conor very much. In that moment I think I understood Cuchullain's reverence for Conor for the first time. It wasn't Conor himself, or the fact that Conor was the King. It was that he stood for something that Cuchullain thought was important. Cuchullain had given his word to be loyal. To take it back would be dishonourable. Just because Conor had behaved dishonourably did not mean that Cuchullain's word could be withdrawn. It was irrelevant what Conor did. It was one for the philosophers. No doubt one of those Forum Greeks could have turned the fire of his logic on Cuchullain's position and burnt it to a wisp of smoke, and even I could see that if you always deal in absolutes then you are going to end up in some very strange places, but there was a simple, bull-nosed simplicity to it that I liked. Cuchullain didn't have a devious particle in his body, so whatever he did was done out of

362

a wish to be true to himself. His word was his bond. That was his beginning and his end and all of the story.

'So,' said Conor, twisting the stem of his cup between thumb and forefinger. 'What shall I ask you to do?'

Cuchullain stood almost to attention. 'Leary tells me that Maeve has asked for me for a plaything as the price of the peace.'

'It is one of the . . . options . . . she has sent to us.' Conor drank deeply, and then spoke through a fog in his throat. 'And how does my Champion feel about that idea?'

Everyone in the room knew the answer to that. 'If I ever go to Maeve's castle, it will be as a corpse or in a glamour, for I will never go willingly.'

Conor nodded in an exaggeratedly thoughtful way. 'Yes. Somehow I thought you'd say that. Well, better get ready then, I suppose, eh?' To our astonishment, he turned to a servant who stood in the corner. 'Dinner. For a celebration. Wine, food. Now.' The startled servant nodded and scuttled from the room.

Cuchullain was annoyed. 'What is this? We must prepare to fight, at once. Leary and I must . . .'

Conor calmed Cuchullain with a gesture. 'It's all right, don't worry. You must eat. There will be plenty of time and opportunity for fighting. I have a plan, don't worry.' With that, he stood up off the bed with some difficulty, drained the last of his wine, and shuffled like a cheerful old man towards the Great Hall, where already sounds of food preparation could be heard. Cuchullain whispered in my ear.

'Go with him. I'll be there once I've checked the weapons and horses. We leave immediately after dinner.' I hesitated for a moment, and then went after Conor. As I caught up with him he took my arm and held me still beside him waiting. After a few seconds he turned round and saw that Cuchullain was gone from the room. He nodded to himself, as if something had been confirmed.

'I thought he'd not take that well,' he chuckled. 'Go to the Hall, I will be there in a short while.' With that, he beckoned to Emer and shuffled off down a corridor. I opened my mouth to speak to her but she shook her head and followed the King without a word.

I was at a loss, so I did what I was told. I walked into the Hall, and stopped in surprise. The Hall was full of people. They were dressed in their finest clothes, covered in jewels, and they all appeared to be having a wonderful time. Food was being brought in, piled high on huge platters, new arrivals were appearing all the time, and the wine was flowing like springtime Fermanagh rain.

They seemed to be expecting me. I realized that I knew most of them. I noticed too that they were mostly women, with a sprinkling of bards and druids. A few old soldiers were there, wincing in occasional discomfort behind their smiles, and a few youngsters too close to their mother's milk to be any use, but there were no Champions. No Conor either.

It didn't take long before I was joining in the fun, as I've never felt that there is such a thing as an inappropriate time for a party, and what more suitable time for one than when things are uncertain and probably about to get dangerous? Raise the spirits, forget the troubles, open the bottle. As the great and pompous Julius once said, 'Between the certainty that disaster is travelling towards you and its arrival, you may as well have a drink.' Actually, that might not have been Julius. But it is still a good idea.

Unless, of course, you are the Hound of Ulster. Cuchullain came in with a distracted look on his face, and didn't seem at first to register what was going on. He came over to me and looked at the visible strip of my face between the almost-touching breasts of the women who were perched on each of my knees, and said, 'The horses are—' before fully taking in the situation. He looked as if someone had raised a fist to hit him, and his hand was on his sword pommel before he got a hold of himself. One of the women stood up and pressed herself against him. He ducked under her arms and reached for my hand, pulling me out from under them.

'What's going on?' he hissed.

I shrugged. 'They were here when I arrived. It's nothing to do with me. The wine is good though.' I took a gulp, to prove my point, and then offered it to him. He looked as if he might knock it to the ground with annoyance, and then a small hand reached through the crook of his elbow, and another hand came to rest on his shoulder, and in what seemed like no time Cuchullain was surrounded by women smiling and offering him wine and much more. He tried to shrug them off.

'I am sorry, but . . .'

They looked disconsolate, and upbraided him for his ill-manners. They had him there, of course. He couldn't refuse their hospitality, or at least had to pretend to accept it. One of the major benefits of being a Champion was that people were constantly offering you hospitality, and you were honour bound to accept just about all of it. Cuchullain sometimes found this a disadvantage, but that put him in a tiny minority. 'We eat, then we leave,' he hissed to me, as he chewed on a piece of meat that a solicitous hand was pushing into his mouth. The owner of the hand then took a mouthful of wine and pretended that she was a jug and Cuchullain's mouth the cup, and I lost his attention.

Determined as he was to get going as soon as possible, even Cuchullain was not entirely averse to the idea of a lot of attractive women making a huge fuss of him, and he was soon persuaded to take a drink or two without assistance, undo his clothing a little, have another chicken leg, tell a few stories, loosen up a bit. I needed no such persuasion, and my enjoyment was heightened by the thought that this might well be the last party I ever went to. Eventually I couldn't take being pawed at any longer, and I grabbed the wrist of my new best friend, whose name was Naimh, and we went off giggling together in search of somewhere quiet.

Once through the doorway we met Emer and Conor. His arm was over her shoulders. Conor stared at me through a curtain of pain and indicated Emer with a jerk of his head. 'I must get myself a wife,' he breathed. 'Useful to lean on at times like this. I had to borrow Cuchullain's.' Emer looked tired, but she still shone a light into every dark place in me. She gave me a wry glance. Conor saw Naimh trying to look inconspicuous, and leered at us through his pain in a way that was almost comradely. 'Having fun?'

I lifted my cup to him. 'Not a bad party.'

Emer smiled sadly. 'Is Cuchullain enjoying it as much as you?' I didn't know what to say, and started to burble something about hospitality and obligations and his eagerness to get away (some of it true) when she reached up and put a finger to my lips. It tasted sweet.

'It's all right,' she said, in a low voice. 'I would rather have him here safe with one of my friends in his lap than cold and alone on some battlefield.'

My heart seemed to fall a great distance. 'He will never be alone while I am alive.' I couldn't take my eyes from her. I was close enough to see the fair hairs that wisped loose under her ears. I could smell cinnamon on her breath. I drew it deep into my lungs like a bear inhaling the first day of spring.

Conor reached out and rested his hand on my forearm. The skin of his palm was hot and dry and I could smell the sour sweat of his pain, but his grip was firm. 'Go. Be sure that Cuchullain doesn't find you for as long as possible.'

I finally began to understand. 'You want to delay him?'

Emer nodded. 'If he goes alone to meet Maeve, he will die. We must keep him here until the other Champions can go with him.'

'Most of Ulster will be overrun by the time that happens.'

Conor opened his mouth and then bit his lip in pain. It was a few seconds before he could speak. The words whistled in his throat. 'He cannot win on his own. We cannot hope to defeat Maeve without him. We have no alternative. We must let her think that she has won. We will keep Cuchullain out of the battle until Conall and the others are fit to fight with him, and then we will attack Maeve together, and we may win. It is the only chance we have.'

Conor seemed to have grown since I had seen him earlier that day. It was as if thinking about Ulster instead of feeling sorry for himself had turned him back into a King again, from the self-pitying drunkard who had killed the thing he loved the most. Just then another spasm knocked him down and sideways, so that he could stand up only by leaning against a wall. He tried to smile, and waved away our attempts to help. He slid down the wall until he sat on the floor, holding the pain tight to his body and waiting for it to pass. Naimh left to fetch him more wine.

Emer stood close to me. I looked at her in a way that I had never felt able to before. She was all around me, she filled me. For years I had never allowed myself to think of her as anything else but my friend's wife. Now, for the first time, I admitted to myself how I felt. I was surrounded by her, intensely aware of the sheen of oil that made her skin glow in the torchlight. I looked down into her eyes. Her breasts, loose beneath the light dress she wore, were close enough that if I took a deep breath my chest would touch her. I wanted to slide my fingers into her thick hair where it rose from her forehead and gently bend her head back until I could press my lips against hers. I shuddered, and she sensed it.

She put a soft hand against my cheek. Unable to stop myself, I reached up to take her wrist and pressed my face against it. She looked into my eyes. 'We must do everything that we can to protect him,' she said. The hot river that ran through me slowed and cooled. Her voice was still kind, but there was a strength of purpose that I had not heard before. Her fingertips fluttered against my cheek. 'This is not a time for thinking of ourselves. We must keep him here, safe, until there is a chance that we can win.' She let her hand slip down until her palm pressed against my chest, a gesture both intimate and final. 'We all know that he must die, one day. I am ready for that. I am prepared for his death, I have been so since the day I met him, but not like this. I do not want to see him die, but most of all I do not wish to see him die uselessly. Help me protect him from that.' I could only just speak.

'I will do all I can.'

'I know.' She looked up at me and gave me a smile that closed a fist around my heart. 'I never had him entirely to myself. Even when we were together he was always somewhere else. And now he will be taken away from me.' She lifted an eyebrow. 'And they call me fortunate.'

Conor levered himself upright against the wall again, and stood beside Emer, his face grey with pain. He gestured towards Naimh, standing quietly near by. I hadn't heard her come back. 'Take your friend here, find somewhere very quiet where no-one – especially not Cuchullain – will think of looking for you, and don't come out until you have to.' He smiled. 'Take food!' I looked at Naimh, and for a moment I could not remember seeing her before. She smiled back shyly. I looked at Conor, who waved us away, and then at Emer. She turned back towards the Hall as we walked away. We rounded a corner in the corridor, and Naimh stopped and looked at me. 'I watched you and Emer. I saw the way things are,' she said. 'I will not object if you have changed your mind.' I looked at her. I didn't speak for a moment. Then I reached out and undid the lace that held her dress together. It slipped over her shoulders and down to the floor.

We found a room, and we made love for what seemed like a day, moving so slowly that sometimes we stopped altogether and just watched each other. When it finished it was like falling from a cliff-face, flying down for ever. The warmth that Emer had stirred in me flowed sweetly into her, and we fell asleep with our arms around each other.

I had been drinking, it was a strange time, and I might have eaten a few too many oysters. Whatever the reason, I had a dream. I thought I was awake but there was a girl in the room and the door hadn't opened. She had long red hair, and wore a thin cotton dress and no shoes. When she walked, her feet didn't move in steps, but shimmered, as if they dissolved their contact with the ground and then re-established it further along. Her face was pale, almost bloodless, and her eyes glowed a soft red with sadness.

Naimh moaned softly in her sleep. I sat up in bed, trying not to wake her. The girl watched me silently. 'Who are you?' I said.

I shivered. The room seemed very cold. She suddenly smiled and her teeth were black behind pale lips.

'We meet . . . again . . . Leary.' The spaces between her words were sudden inhalations which hissed between her teeth.

'I don't remember . . .'

She smiled again. 'Oh yes, we have met. Most certainly. More than just met, much more than that.' In the young girl's face the twisted black smile was that of an old wolf watching a sick animal. Smiling at me as though she recognized me, as though I had been often to her room before. 'Do you not remember the nightsss . . . when we came to you? You were mossst . . . enthusiasssstic.' Then there was no need for me to search my memories, because she showed me. The girl disappeared, and in her place was something which writhed and hissed as it clawed its way onto the bed and up the blanket towards me. A twisted, misshapen torso, bent out of almost all resemblance to humanity, with three heads and six arms, and it climbed up my body and hands clawed at my back and lips felt for my groin and suddenly the familiar dank smell of old meat and sour milk surrounded me. Suddenly my mind was filled with them, I knew them as well as myself. I knew what they had done, where they had been, and why they would win.

It felt my recognition and chuckled. The monster slobbered and hissed its way back onto the floor, and changed back into the girl. I could feel where her cold skin had touched mine. I would never feel clean again. 'We are . . . the Daughtersss of Calatin. You remember usss now.' I shivered with cold and fear. She moved closer to the bedside. 'Cuchullain . . . killed our father . . . before we were born. In our mother'sss . . . womb, we felt it . . . we knew hisss death. We felt . . . our mother'sss pain, until the moment we were born. We felt her dying as we came into the world.' She looked at me. The black eyes were a reptile's, cold and unblinking. 'Can you pity . . . usss?'

Zeus, no. I could smell starvation on her breath. I flinched further away from her. 'Yes, I can pity you,' I said. 'No child should lose a father and a mother.' She grinned, and leant her

369

head to one side as if her neck were broken. Her voice became high and grating, a parody of a coquette's lilt.

'True. But no matter. Soon Cuchullain will . . . die, and we can ressst.' She poked a sharp finger with a black bitten nail at me. 'We have ssshown you what will happen, what . . . waits for you. Will you die . . . with him?'

What was my alternative? I had a nasty feeling I was going to be a sacrifice. 'Must Cuchullain die?' I asked.

Her head flopped forward, and the smell of her carried to me like a damp grave. 'Oh yesss,' she said. 'Oh yesss.'

'Then I will die with him.' I meant it. I never thought I'd say it, but better to face Maeve's army in the day with just Cuchullain than be stuck in this dark bedroom with a monster.

She jolted upright as if I'd slapped her, making her limbs flail outwards like a child's puppet, and then she glided towards me. She leant over the bed. Naimh moved in her sleep. The woman looked at her and grinned, showing me rotten teeth at close range. Every bone in my body felt as though it were made of ice. 'Was ssshe asss good . . . asss us?' The monster stood up straight, reached to her throat, and loosed the cord, just as I had done to Naimh a short while before. Her dress fell around her ankles.

Her breasts were wrinkled and dry as mermaid's purses on the sand, and her grey body was withered and covered with weeping sores. She laughed, holding her breasts in her hands and offering them to me. Then she stepped forward and pulled my face into her belly. I screamed and recoiled, pushing her away. She laughed, thrusting her hips at me like a dancer, and then kicked her dress up at my head. It fell over me before I could rouse myself enough to stop it. The salt and damp earth smell of death surrounded me. The dress clung to my head and arms as if it were wet. I struggled desperately to get it off. Then I felt her hands on me, and I lashed out, heard her cry of pain and alarm, and realized that something had changed. I pulled the blanket off my head without resistance. Naimh was lying on the floor, clutching her shoulder.

'What— Are you all right?' I looked around. The Daughters of Calatin were gone.

370

'Yes, I think so,' said Naimh, levering herself painfully back onto the bed, 'but do you usually thrash around hitting people and then throwing them out of bed?'

I held her close, and she laughed and almost immediately went back to sleep. I lay there for hours, with my arms around her and my eyes open, waiting for the sunlight to fall on me and force the cold from my bones.

# 43

When I eventually made it back to the Banqueting Hall the party was obviously not long finished. There were women asleep in every part of the room; curled up in corners, stretched out under tables, sprawled on chairs, and, in one corner (by a chair), under a table sprawled on a stretched-out druid. Cuchullain was asleep. He was slumped in the cup-shaped chair, his head hanging back as if his spine were broken, his mouth slack and open. He looked dead drunk. I had never seen him like that before, in fact I don't think he ever had been. One of the few women still awake walked past, sipping at a cup of water and holding her head. I stopped her.

'How did you get him to drink so much?'

She smiled and shook her head. A look of pain crossed her face.

'We didn't,' she said. 'Emer put a sleeping potion in his cup, enough for two ordinary men, and it had no effect. He drank three of them before it made any difference to him at all. Laeg knows how many it took to put him to sleep.'

I grinned. 'And what about all of you? Can you keep up with him?'

She gestured to the archway which led to the sleeping quarters at Emain Macha. 'Fortunately, we are taking turns.' She walked away.

As she did so, a group of fresh-faced women came quietly into the Hall and separated, going to each of the sleeping figures around the Hall and waking them. The new arrivals took their places at the table, and waited, talking softly to each other. I smiled. When Cuchullain woke, there would be plenty of attractive company ready to start the party again. Conor and Emer were doing their work well. Every day that Cuchullain spent at Emain Macha was a day nearer the time when the Ulster Champions would be able to fight beside him.

Cuchullain's eyes opened wide, as if he were startled, and then closed again as the light hit them. He opened them a second time, more cautiously. Someone smoothed his hair back and sat in his lap. Someone else passed him a cup. Someone else started to rub his shoulders. I stepped back behind a pillar. He half stood, swayed, then fell back behind the gentle hands of those around him. I saw Emer behind a doorway at the other side of the Hall, signalling to one of the women nearest me. She went forward, carrying bread, honey and water. Cuchullain fell on them ravenously. The women beside him dipped their fingers in the honey and licked it off, waiting.

He wiped his mouth with his hand and stood properly. 'Where is Leary? We must go. There is a long journey ahead of us.'

Emer made frantic signals at me to stay out of sight. I stepped back further, making sure that I could still see him. The women crowded around him, charming him to stay, promising to fetch me, offering him food, drink and a lot more besides. He pushed them gently away. He was about to say more when the door to the Hall blew open and flew back, hitting the wall with a crash that made everyone jump. A black shadow flew in and up into the rafters. The wind came in behind it, tossing a tumbling mass of grass, twigs, puffballs, acorns and dust across the floor. One of the women ran to close the door.

'Stay behind me!' roared Cuchullain, drawing his sword and running after her.

Everyone was struck immobile for a few moments with the

suddenness and ferocity of his shout. In a second, while we stood open-mouthed watching him, Cuchullain had scooped up the woman who had gone to close the door, pushed her behind him, kicked the door closed and was hacking and hewing at the twigs and dust as if it were an enemy.

I ran towards him. As I ran, I saw a rail of sunlight glance off his sword, cutting through the dust like a torch through dark, and as it did I saw for a moment what he saw, heard what he heard. A dozen men were attacking him; outside was the sound of hundreds more shouting battle-cries and struggling to get in. I heard the hiss of the Daughters of Calatin laughing at us. Then the light shifted, my eyes went back to normal, and there was just puffballs and dust.

'Get back, Leary,' Cuchullain shouted. 'Find me a shield!'

I stood in front of him, my arms outstretched, my hands empty. I tried to speak calmly. 'There is nothing to fight. There isn't anyone else here. It's an illusion. See? I'm not being harmed.' His eyes narrowed with bewilderment. He saw armed men fighting all around me, and I was strolling through them, unarmed and unconcerned. My usual dedicated concern for my own safety added to the force of my argument. Cuchullain knew I wouldn't risk myself just to impress him. He lowered his sword slightly. His face was a picture of puzzlement. I almost laughed, but his bewilderment was more pitiful than amusing.

'Leary . . . what is it?' He stepped forward and looked over my shoulder. The dust suddenly settled, and the illusion no longer affected him. 'What is happening?'

For the first time ever since I first met him, I took him in my arms and held him close to me. 'Don't worry. They sent a vision to disturb you.'

'Who?'

'The Daughters of Calatin.'

'Calatin? I killed him. What have his daughters got to do with it?' He didn't know what I was talking about. He broke my embrace in a distracted sort of way and went to get a cup of wine, draining it in one swallow. He had never done that before.

I would have noticed. Then he threw himself onto a chair and was immediately asleep.

Conor appeared at my elbow. He was standing straight, although the lines at the corners of his mouth betrayed the pain that sawed at him. 'What happened? The Daughters of Calatin?' I nodded. 'Cathbad said that they were back in Ireland.' I shuddered as I remembered how the knowledge of them had flooded my mind.

'Their power is growing,' I said. Conor looked concerned. 'Now they can control nature. They made him see an attacking army with a few dried-up leaves. Or perhaps he is tired and sees assassins in the shadows. Maybe the wine is bad.'

Conor looked stern. 'We must put him where Calatin's daughters cannot find him.' I didn't reply. The Daughters of Calatin could find anyone anywhere.

A shriek rang out above us. I looked up and saw a raven in the rafters. I reached for a bow, but it was already swooping down past us and out through a window. Conor looked at its retreating shadow. 'Where that damn bird cannot find him,' he growled.

I watched them carry Cuchullain, still unconscious, to a litter dragged behind a chariot. I asked Owen where he was being taken. I didn't recognize the reply. 'Glenn-na-Bodhar?'

'It means the Deaf Valley.'

'So?'

'It is said that if you stood inside it and the whole of Ireland were to gather outside it and shout your name, you would not hear them.'

I could see that somewhere remote and secluded would be easier to protect Cuchullain in than Emain Macha, or his own castle. Perhaps the Daughters of Calatin might not find us there for a few days, enough to get Conall and a few of the others back on their feet and ready to fight. Perhaps. Anything had to be better than sitting around at Emain Macha, feeding Cuchullain sleeping powders and hoping that the Champions would recover before Maeve arrived. We grabbed a few essentials, threw them onto the backs of horses and into chariots, and everyone who was well enough to get into a chariot or ride a horse headed for the Deaf Valley, dragging Cuchullain behind us on his litter. That meant leaving most of the Champions behind in their beds. I was worried, and wanted to take them with us. When conquering armies enter the enemy's home blood usually gets spilt, and in the absence of proper opposition the blood of the prostrate and defenceless will do very well. Owen assured me that, in Ireland, even someone like Maeve respected certain proprieties. I remembered what Maeve had said about her booty-hunting irregulars, but we couldn't take them, so there it was. We left them and galloped for the Deaf Valley. Conor managed to get onto his horse, but could only bear to let it trot after us. He arrived many hours later.

Glenn-na-Bodhar turned out to be a good place for a relaxing break from the business of living. If I had to go somewhere and pretend for a while that everything was all right, when in reality everything was all wrong and my house was probably being burnt down as I thought about it, then the Deaf Valley would do very well to pretend in. It was green, warm, sheltered, and, yes, very quiet. For two days nothing happened. Cuchullain drank enough of the druid's special drink to keep him happy, and everyone took it in turns to make sure that he never got bored.

Then I saw a raven in a tree. Cuchullain saw ghosts when ravens appeared. This time I got an arrow off after it, and for a charioteer I thought I was remarkably close, but the raven just gave me a raucous jeer and swung away over the hill. The next morning, at dawn, the Daughters of Calatin arrived.

Cuchullain woke with a start, reaching for his sword. I held his arm still. His head whirled from right to left, his expression wild. 'Let me go! Don't you hear it?'

I heard nothing. 'There is nothing, it is just the wind . . .' And then, far far away, I did hear it. From the expression on Cuchullain's face, mayhem and confusion surrounded us, whirling all around us, whereas I could only hear it if I relaxed and stayed perfectly still. It was over the horizon in the distance, small sounds heard on the other side of a lake on a hot day. The sounds in his head were so loud that I could hear them too.

Cuchullain snatched his hand away from me. 'It isn't my fault if everyone is deaf except me!' he shouted, and picked up his weapons. 'Will you drive me? I must stop them!' By now everyone else was awake, and they clustered around us, talking quickly, soothingly. I held his arms.

'Look, everyone is here . . . no-one is harmed . . . I am here . . . we are safe . . . no-one is in danger . . .'

'But I hear them . . . I see them! There!' He pointed. A swirl of dust, leaves, twigs, sprigs of clover, bits of plants, the same trick that had affected him before, was wheeling towards us. Cuchullain pushed through the crowd, sword upraised, trying to defend us against it, but Owen was faster. I saw what he intended and flung myself at Cuchullain. 'Watch!' I shouted in his face, and the noise held him still for a second. In that time, Owen was into the wind and the dust, and it was all around him. He laughed amidst the flying twigs, capering as if he were at a dance. 'See?' I shouted. 'There is no danger!' Owen continued dancing, as if he hadn't a worry in the world. Cuchullain relaxed slightly, his face dubious. Suddenly Owen brought his hands to his face and bent away from us, as if wasps attacked him, and I felt the muscles in Cuchullain's arms tense. Then they relaxed as Owen came upright again and started to dance once more, more slowly, his hands by his sides. He stopped and stood still, as if waiting. Then he looked up at us. 'I'm alive!' he shouted. The wind stopped, and the dust and twigs settled around him like a carpet.

Cuchullain watched, his eyes narrowed, incredulous. 'You see?' I said, trying to mix sympathy with command, still holding him, shaking him a little with each word. 'No harm has come to him. It is a glamour that they are putting on you, to drive us all mad and to get you killed. Go back, go back and sleep. Your time to fight will come soon enough.' Cuchullain shook his head, and allowed himself to be led away, covering his head with his arms. The evidence of his ears and what he saw were in conflict, and he looked like a man on the edge of madness. I wasn't sure how much more of this he could stand. There comes a point where a man will fight just to escape his own mind.

Owen was still standing below us. I waited. He stood still. I walked down the hill and called to him. 'Well done. He's all right now.'

'Leary?' His back was to me, but I knew something was wrong. His voice was strained and quiet, quite unlike his normal excited babble.

'What is it?'

'Where is Cuchullain?'

'He's gone back to the camp. What's the matter with you?'

'Could you . . . ?' He put out a hand sideways to me, but his body stayed still, uncertain, like a man standing on ice, not knowing which way was safe.

'What is it? What's wrong?' I walked quickly towards him. He turned to me as I took his hand. His eyes were full of dust. Blood mixed with tears welled out of them and seeped down his cheeks.

'Leary, I can't see,' he whispered.

'What . . . ?'

'I was dancing and . . . I danced, and then the dust and sticks seemed to whirl up around my head like insects, stinging my eyes.' He put both palms against my chest. 'It hurt. I had to turn away. I almost shouted for help. Did Cuchullain see?'

I shook my head. 'No,' I said. Owen smiled. 'Good,' he said. 'Would you take me somewhere so that I can wash my eyes?'

# 44

We weren't trying to hide any more. The Daughters of Calatin knew where we were, and they would be back. Of course, it was possible that they might give up their tricks with the leaves and sticks and just lead Maeve's armies to where we were hiding, but Conor didn't think that was likely and nor did I. (Not that I was asked.) Maeve knew she had time to play with us before finishing Cuchullain off.

Conor looked around the valley. 'Things could be worse,' he said. No-one else would have. 'There's only one way into this place, and it's easily guarded. Cuchullain could hold it alone for a long time before they got in, and he's got us to help him this time.' But no Laeg to help him this time, I thought. Never a God around when you really need one. Conor smiled as if what he had said was funny. 'I suppose if Maeve is ready to lose half her army to get in here, then we're dead, but . . .' He suddenly gasped with pain, and bent double to ease his twisting stomach muscles. By now we were so used to it happening that no-one did anything but wait as if nothing unusual were taking place until he could resume. After a few seconds he slowly straightened up again, took another swig of wine and carried on talking. 'If the bitch doesn't care how many men she loses, then we'll not last long, but I think she wants Cuchullain dead with as little fuss as possible, then her armies can run all over Ulster like rats across a mill floor. She'll let Calatin's daughters do the hard work for her if she can.'

His voice was steady and unslurred. Since the invasion started Conor had become King again. He drank steadily to kill the pain – they all did – but he hadn't been drunk for days. His hair and beard were groomed and untangled, and (to everyone's relief) he had started bathing again. His eyes were almost clear and his thoughts were quick. He had gained a few lines – we all had – but he looked well. Even his sardonic wolf's grin was back. I felt the strength in him again, and I was glad. Whatever he had done in the past, Ulster needed him strong now more than ever. If anyone could plot and scheme his way out of our situation, Conor could.

As dramatically as Conor was now recovered, Cuchullain had changed for the worse. His hair was unkempt, his skin dull, his clothes dirty. He was drinking a great deal, something he never did, and there was a dullness in his eyes that I had never seen there before. The druid still fed him the sleeping medicine at intervals, but all it seemed to do was make him glower and drink more wine. I sat down beside him. He looked at me and frowned, said nothing, drained his cup. 'You've had enough,' I said. 'Why do you drink so much?'

He scowled. 'Everyone here drinks.'

'But they have Macha's pains, they drink to control the spasms. You don't have them.'

'You all keep me here while Ulster burns. Don't expect me to be happy about it.'

I tried being reasonable. 'You know why that is. There's no point in you charging out on your own and getting killed. We need to delay until the other Champions have recovered and can come to help you.' I paused. From his expression I could tell that reasonable wasn't working.

'Even if I cared nothing for my name,' he snarled, 'which I do, the name which, even as we speak, is being satirized all across Ireland, even if I didn't care about that, I care for my land, my house, my cattle. Maeve has them in her hand like toys, to play with as she chooses. Should I accept that too?'

'You'll get it back,' I murmured, 'all of it. You'll see.'

He turned his red eyes away from me, and someone silently poured wine into his cup. He took a listless gulp, and turned the cup-stem slowly between his fingers. He looked utterly filled up with misery. He didn't care whether he lived or died. Of course, the massive amounts of sleeping draught that he had taken over the last few days, an amount that would have killed anyone else (or so the druid swore), were probably not improving his temper, but the inactivity and uncertainty put in his mind by the visions that the Daughters of Calatin sent him, added to the knowledge that Ulster was invaded and we were doing nothing to defend it, all combined to make him feel a stranger to himself. Cuchullain lived to fight. If he wasn't allowed to do that, he didn't know what to do. He would rather go out and fight visions than stay with us and do nothing. Even Emer couldn't talk to him. She sat a little way off, looking miserable.

I left him with a sense of relief, and a sense of guilt for my relief, and then gave up feeling anything and went to find Owen. The bard was sitting up against an old tree stump, gazing outwards over the river that ran down the centre of the valley. He heard me come, and tilted his head slightly.

'Leary?'

'It's me.'

He gestured to the wide band of cloth around his head. Damp patches marked his eyes where the druids had washed them clear of dust and twigs before filling the raw sockets with a poultice of herbs and then binding the green mess to his face with the cloth. 'They say I'll probably be able to see a little, once this thing is taken off.' I could still remember the sight of him standing in front of me with blood running down his cheeks, asking if Cuchullain was watching him, unable to see any of us, silently enduring the pain because he didn't want Cuchullain to know what had happened. I felt my eyelids prick with tears and cleared my throat gruffly.

'You don't need to be able to see to get your hand onto your balls, and that's all you'll ever need,' I growled. 'At least now you can't play that stupid harp.' He chuckled, and swung an arm at me, missing by a foot.

'Insult me now, while you can,' he said. 'You'll pay, when I get this thing off.' A shout came from further up the valley, towards the entrance. I swung round. Owen half-turned. 'What is it?' he asked.

I saw a man scrambling up the valley from the direction of the entrance, trailed by one of the women who had been on guard. She ran lightly behind him, her spear-point never further than a foot from his shoulder-blades. I saw Cuchullain turn lazily towards him, then leap to his feet. 'Ronan!'

'Cuchullain!'

The man ran panting up the hillside and threw himself on the ground in front of Cuchullain, his mud-splashed hands clutching at Cuchullain's ankles, trying to gasp out a message. Cuchullain lifted the man up, one hand on each shoulder, and waited. I recognized him as one of Cuchullain's freedmen. His eyes were wild and rimmed with the red of fatigue. 'Castledealgan is burnt . . . Muirthemne is taken. Cattle. Slaves. Maeve drives her chariot unhindered through your fields.' He swallowed, and then choked. Someone brought him water, he began to catch his breath, and we listened in silence. It was about as bad as it could be. Everything valuable had either been burnt or was on its way out of Ulster. Slaves were being taken in their hundreds. The homes of the Champions were ashes. Emain Macha was no more than a bleak hill covered in smoking rubble, nothing higher than a man's hip on any part of it.

I looked at Emer. She looked as if she had been struck across the face. Her eyes were fixed on Cuchullain. He turned to Conor. 'Do not order me to stay,' he said quietly, 'for I would not have our last meeting be a disagreement.' Conor and Cuchullain locked their gaze for a few moments, and then Conor made an almost imperceptible movement. Cuchullain turned to me. A vein stood out in his throat, pulsing like a dying snake. His eyes were bright.

'Bring the chariot, harness the horses, load every arrow and spear you can find. We have Connaughtmen to kill.' He looked properly awake and suddenly sober for the first time in days. I thought about protesting, but he wasn't listening. I went to do as he said, while he went to the river to bathe. I harnessed the horses and loaded the chariot with weapons. I had almost finished when I turned round and then, startled, dropped most of the armful of arrows that I was carrying. Emer stood with rigid arms by her sides under the horse's heavy neck.

'He's going to die,' she said.

'Not if I can help it,' I said, hardly recognizing my own voice. 'None of us will die today. Terrible idea. After all, I'll be there too. I'll be driving him. If they get him, they'll get me too, and I don't want that at all.' She stood within a kiss's reach. There was a stone in my chest, pressing down. I couldn't breathe properly. A coil of fair hair moved across her face, and my hand came up to push it back again so naturally that I only realized what it was doing at the last moment and converted the gesture to waving away an insect that flew between us.

A small muscle jerked like a snared animal at the base of her neck. 'We have always looked after him, you and I. Is there anything I can do to stop him?' Her soft voice trickled down my back like warm lover's sweat. I shook my head, mute. She let a fleeting shadow cross her face, and then squared her shoulders and let out a long breath. 'Then I shall not try. He will not see me unhappy.' She turned without pausing and walked away. I watched the small figure leave me and go over the hill and down to the river to where her husband was washing, surrounded by a discreetly admiring crowd of women. My heart felt as though it was full of warm wine, which rose into my throat and forced me to swallow.

I wondered if Cuchullain knew I loved his wife.

I piled the chariot high with every weapon I could find, then brought the horses round and put them in the chariot yoke. I checked the girths and tried to put on the harness. The Grey stamped at me in a way he had never done before and refused the bridle, ducking his head and then throwing it up and away from the harness, so that I had to lean backwards quickly to avoid being knocked over. I spoke softly to him, as I always did. He hesitated several times, then slowly bent his neck and allowed me to put the bridle over his head. As I pulled the last strap tight, a large drop fell from his eye and splashed onto my arm. It was red, like blood. I lifted his head up in alarm and looked for where it had come from. There was no injury that I could see, but two more large red tears rose from all around the eye-socket and rolled out onto the ground. I waited for a few minutes, thinking about unharnessing him and finding a replacement, but the bleeding seemed to have stopped.

His partner, the Black Sanglain, was trembling and skittish, and I drove the loaded chariot back with an uneasy hand.

Cuchullain was standing by the river, and Emer was helping him dress. As I drove the chariot over the rise which led to the river, the sun came out. A curtain of light drew back across the ground, and showed me Cuchullain the Champion.

His armour was white, dazzling in the light, like sparkling water in summer evening sun. Emer had washed his dark hair and twisted it into a rope which hung over his left shoulder. A further pile of weapons was beside him. As I pulled up in front of him he grinned at me in a way that I hadn't seen for weeks. I saluted him back, smiled at Emer once, then tried not to look at her again.

'Throw these on too,' he said, pointing to the weapons. 'We have a lot of killing to do today.'

I smiled, and pointed to the huge bundle of spears that I had already put in beside me. 'The chariot will collapse.'

Cuchullain shook his head. 'Not this one,' he replied. I loaded them up. The chariot axle bent like a bow. The druid picked up three spears that were lying on the ground, and handed them to me. I laughed, and gestured to the pile behind us.

'Don't you think we've got enough?'

The druid beckoned me close and dropped his voice so that only I could hear him. 'Look after them well.' He put a hand on my arm. 'Each of them will kill a King today.' Cuchullain brushed past him as he stepped onto the chariot. He heard the last sentence and paused.

'Only three Kings?' he asked. 'There are more than that in Maeve's army. Still, I suppose there's always tomorrow as well.' He turned to me and shouted so that everyone could hear. 'Maybe we'll manage to get a Queen as well, eh?' He jumped up beside me, glittering. Emer held a goblet of wine up to him. He laughed, toasting her with it. He raised it to his lips, then paused, his expression puzzled. 'Is this wine?' he asked.

'Of course,' she replied. I looked over his shoulder. The cup was full of a red liquid, thicker and deeper than wine. He passed it back to Emer who looked at it, dipped her finger into it and dabbed the end of her finger onto her tongue. She nodded, sipped at it, and offered it to him again. 'Good,' she said.

As she passed it up and Cuchullain took the cup the light altered and I saw the wine seem to change colour and grow thicker. Cuchullain saw it too. He passed it gently back to her without raising it to his lips. She took it again, puzzled. As she looked into the cup, the light moved and the wine became paler again. Wordlessly, uncomprehending, she sipped at it, waited for the taste, and then handed it back to him, her eyes perceptibly wider but still calm. She knew something was wrong, but had no idea what.

Cuchullain took the cup and looked into it. He paused for a moment, then raised it in a toast to everyone around him, and put the cup to his lips. He tossed the wine down in one movement, then passed the cup to me as he wiped his mouth. He glanced at the back of his hand briefly then quickly put it down by his side, where it was out of sight to anyone outside the chariot.

I could see a bright red smear across the back of his hand, as if he had cut himself.

Emer put her hand on the chariot rim, and he bent to kiss it, but I could tell he was impatient to go. I wanted to feel her touch once more, but the horses were growing impatient and the chariot jerked forward just as my hand moved forward to press hers goodbye. I half-turned, trying to laugh, and waved. She wasn't looking at me.

We drove through the mouth of the valley. Standing outside it was the man who had delivered the bad news that had brought Cuchullain back to life. As we passed, Cuchullain shouted cheerfully at him, and he waved a salute. As we raced away from him, I glanced back. The man had gone. Nothing was there, except an old crow wheeling away towards the horizon.

Cuchullain looked at the road in silence for a few minutes. I drove carefully, not wanting to tire the horses. Then he spoke.

'I want you to protect her when I'm not here any more.'

My heart thumped like a club beating on an oak door. I held the reins tighter. 'Who?'

'Emer. She will be safe with you. Take care of her for me.'

Whatever I said would be admitting too much. 'You're not going to die. You'll see us all underground.'

He turned his head slightly towards me. 'I shall not be here tomorrow.' He paused and his voice was suddenly soft. 'Going will be easier if I know that you will be here. There is no-one in whose hands I would rather leave her.'

I hesitated. 'You can trust me.'

He smiled at the horizon and reached out a thin hand to rest on my shoulder. 'I always have,' he said.

We drove on. At the first ford, there was a woman in the shallow centre of the stream, washing clothes. The white cloth swirled around her legs in the water like mermaid's arms reaching out to us. Cuchullain called out as we drove past. 'We'll try not to splash you!' he shouted, and laughed too loud. She turned towards us. Her face was white, as if the sun had never shone on it. She said nothing, looked at us for a few moments, then turned back to her work.

'You wash your clothes very carefully!' shouted Cuchullain.

She stood up and faced us again. 'Not my clothes,' she said. 'Not mine. Cuchullain's clothes.' She held up a shirt. It was stained all down one side with blood and was slashed open and ragged from chest to hip.

I didn't know what to say. Cuchullain looked at me and laughed at my expression. 'Don't worry,' he said. 'I don't believe in omens either.'

He said it so clearly and turned away so quickly that I had no idea if he was joking or not. I hoped . . . I don't know what. I was plain terrified. We were both almost certainly going to die, we were surrounded by omens and portents of the exact sort that I always maintained I didn't believe in, and Cuchullain – who did believe, or so I thought – was laughing like an idiot and urging the horses on, as if he couldn't get there fast enough. I looked at the pale woman. She suddenly smiled, showing me black teeth. Cuchullain banged his spear on the chariot floor with impatience, and I flicked the reins to make the horses drag us out of the stream.

The next corner was sharp, and as we rounded it I almost had to turn the chariot back on itself. As we came straight again, I smelt woodsmoke, and wondered with a pang of fear if Maeve's men were camping near by. A woman's sharp voice called to us. 'Cuchullain!' I couldn't see anyone. I had a feeling that, whatever happened, it was not going to make me feel better.

'I am Cuchullain. Who calls me?'

'We do. Come and eat with us.' We moved a few yards forward and saw them, sitting around a fire just off the track. I was right about not feeling better. There were three of them, they were dressed in rags, they each looked about seven hundred and ninety years old, and I knew they wished us nothing but harm. They were squatting around a tired-looking fire, over which was an ill-made spit. On the spit was the half-cooked carcass of a dog. I would have liked to have been able to fool myself that the animal was a small calf or a pig, but they had left the dog's head on so that we could be sure what it was.

'Oh shit,' I said.

'Come and eat with us,' said the crone nearest us, beckoning us over with both skinny arms. She picked up a stick and prodded at the blackened meat. Hot fat ran down into the fire, making the flames burn up around it and bringing an acrid smell of burning flesh to us. The horses shifted uneasily, and for a moment I considered giving them their heads. One of the women must have realized my thoughts, because she jumped up and hurried to stand in front of us. The rags she wore parted as

387

she lifted an arm in salute to us, and her withered breasts hung down like empty coin-purses.

'Eat with us, Cuchullain.'

'I cannot,' he replied. I heard something strange in his voice, and turned to look at him. His eyes were fixed on the fire as if it was Charon's gate.

She put her hands on her hips and spoke scornfully. 'Champions were not always so arrogant!' She stepped forward, and her sisters came and stood next to her. 'They said Cuchullain was not proud. Is Cuchullain so great now that he will only eat the finest food off silver plate? Is plain food in the company of the poor no longer good enough for him? Do the laws of hospitality mean nothing any more?' There was a familiar but muted sibilance to her speech. I knew who we were talking to. She made a disdainful gesture.

'You have offered, that is enough,' I said. 'It is not pride that stops him. He does not have to eat.' I found my hand had a spear in it, and lifted it up so that they could see. They paid no attention. The one with the inadequate clothes spat at the horses' feet. The horses were nervous enough already, and they jerked away from her. Cuchullain caught me by the wrist as I made to jump down and push her away.

'No, that is not the reason,' he said. 'I am forbidden. It is a geis.'

I lost my temper. 'This is ridiculous! You are the Champion of Ulster, of the whole of Ireland. Why are you wasting time arguing with this dried-up old bat? There are whole armies out there to disagree with!'

He looked at me with a sad smile. 'Hospitality is an obligation. You should know that by now.' The colour had left his face completely. Cullan had put a geis on him. Offering Cuchullain roast dog was like serving wolf-meat to Romulus and Remus, like carving a man a slice of his own child. To Cuchullain, breaking a geis was a sin against the Gods; worse, a sin against himself. But, of course, hospitality was a sacred obligation to all Ulstermen, and a Champion never refused. It was one of the things that made him a Champion. We were on the horns of a social dilemma while Maeve burnt Ulster. The old hag still blocked our way. I picked up the whip. Cuchullain prevented me again. He held out a hand in supplication. 'Will you release me from this obligation?'

She stood back from the horses and waved us on. 'Go!' she shouted. 'Go, and take our cursssesss with you! We will tell many a bard about this day and they will sssing about the great pride of Cuchullain, who was too mighty to ssshare food with ordinary people!'

The hiss in her voice was the same as on the night she came to the bed I shared with Naimh. I didn't need telling twice. I flicked the reins and the chariot lurched forward. Cuchullain reached over and pulled the reins back sharply. The horses reared up and the chariot stopped.

'Wait,' he said, and got down from the back of the chariot.

'You can't be going to let them blackmail you like that!' I shouted. 'It's obvious what they're trying to do, they . . .' He walked forward. 'Cuchullain! Don't! I know who they are, they . . .'

He raised a hand to stop me. 'It's all right,' he said. 'I already know who they are. It's all right.' He paused and set his shoulders. 'Really,' he said. 'It doesn't matter.'

'It does! You . . .'

Then it was done. He stepped forward to the fire, grasped the nearest hind leg of the dog with his left hand and tore it off. The fat on the meat was still bubbling as he raised it to his mouth. He grinned at the three women and then sank his teeth into the meat. The women laughed wildly. His arm fell by his side and the meat dropped from his limp fingers to the ground. With his right hand he picked up a burning branch and whirled it around his head, sending a shower of burning wood and sparks over them. They screamed as the fire touched them. Then there was a bright light which forced me to close my eyes and shield my face with my arm, and when I could open them again, the women, the fire and the dog were gone.

Cuchullain got back into the chariot. His left arm hung loose by his side, and his foot dragged as he walked as if the muscles in his leg had withered. I looked at him with horror. 'Are you all right? Why did you . . . ?'

He looked calmer. He smiled at me. 'Yes, my friend, I'm all right. Let's go on.' His voice was soft, resigned. No more shouting about killing Connaughtmen, no more desperate need to get to the battle. Just, 'Let's go on.' I spoke to the horses, and they trotted slowly forward. As I drove, I watched from the corner of my eye as he took his left hand in his right, lifted it and then let it go. It dropped as if every bone was broken and every muscle severed. Cuchullain had used it to eat dog. The dog was his symbol. The goodness was bound to go from the arm that had desecrated his symbol. I knew that I could spend all day telling Cuchullain that there was nothing wrong with him, but it wouldn't make a difference. He had eaten dog. His shield-arm was gone.

We drove in silence for a while. The sun was shining, and the first spring flowers were showing through the banks on either side of us. I could hear the insects humming at the thought of the season to come, and, despite our position, I found myself in reverie, almost asleep. I remembered spring in Italy, where the insects hummed and flew and fought all day. This feeling was the same.

The insects were loud, much too loud. I snapped back to wakefulness. I looked at Cuchullain. He was standing straight, as if propped up, looking forward like a statue.

The insects were no longer with us. Instead we were surrounded by the sound of men. I could hear shouted orders, wheel rims shrieking as they ground against the hard earth, the high whine of metal rubbing against metal, the crack of hooves on flint, and the hundred other sounds that marching men make. I looked around. We were surrounded by trees, closely packed together. We could see nothing of them, and yet there were men all around us.

Cuchullain looked at me. 'Connaughtmen?' he asked, lifting an eyebrow. I shrugged. 'Not Ulstermen at any rate.' Ulstermen were all at home groaning in their beds. Marching men, from anywhere, were enemies. Cuchullain smiled, and picked up a handful of light spears. He propped them against the side of the chariot and held them there with his foot. He took out his slingshot and hung a large bag of brain-balls around his neck, where he could reach them easily. I knew I wouldn't have much time for fighting, but balanced a few spears near by, just in case.

'Ready?' he asked.

I nodded. 'Which way?'

He held his dead arm up with the other hand and laughed as he used it to point out over the horses. 'Forward. Let them find us.'

# 45

The last time the Daughters of Calatin visited me the vision they gave me cost me the warm marrow from my bones. I felt them inside me, their thin hard fingers around my heart. And I could do nothing but lie still and watch the dream they sent me.

Maeve drummed impatient fingers on the arm of her chair. Ailell sat beside her, his stillness in contrast to her agitation.

The room was cold. The silver-bound box sat in a corner, and the red-haired woman, the same that Ailell had met in the cave the first time they marched on Ulster, stood in front of them. Her head was bowed, and she spoke to the floor.

'You have called usss again. What isss your wisssh?'

'Where is Cuchullain?'

The red-haired woman lifted her head and tilted it, as if listening for something, and looked at Maeve through pale eyes rimmed with red. 'We have brought him out of the Valley of the Deaf. Cuchullain isss now coming to you, he and the charioteer from the sssea. Already they have fought with the King of Leinster in the foressst to the north of here, and your allies lie still amongst the treesss like the red leavesss of autumn.'

Maeve clasped her hands together and leant forward in her eagerness. 'Will he die today?'

There was a pause. The red-haired woman hesitated, and then raised her hand, as if trying to pull a curtain to one side.

'It isss . . . not given to usss to sssee.'

Maeve sat back in her chair. Ailell looked sardonic. 'What exactly is it given to you to see then?' he asked. The red-haired woman gave Ailell a nasty glance that made him shift uncomfortably. Then she smiled. Ailell saw black teeth.

'He has three ssspearsss.'

Ailell raised an eyebrow. 'Only three? We'll soon kill him if he only has three.'

'Shut up!' snapped Maeve. 'Go on. What three spears?'

The woman looked beyond them and her eyes turned blank. 'Three ssspearsss. Three ssspearsss that will kill three Kingsss.'

Ailell laughed awkwardly. 'Any particular three, or just the first three that happen to be passing?'

Maeve rounded on him. 'If you don't shut up I'll kill you before Cuchullain has the chance!'

'The Kingsss here are many. Which ones ssshall die here today isss . . .' (she paused, and smiled at Maeve coquettishly) '. . . in your handsss.'

Maeve pulled her hands to her breast, as if clutching a gift. The red-haired woman's body seemed to become insubstantial, and she glided to the back of the room into shadow. Ailell did his best to look contrite. 'What does it mean?' he asked. Maeve was intent on her thoughts, concentrating in her excitement too much to bother abusing him for a fool.

'It means that I can move against him, and he will die, or I can do nothing, and take what comes.'

'But what must you do?'

Maeve turned and faced him with a wilful look on her face. Ailell felt a pang of recognition. It was the same expression she had worn the first time she refused to marry him. 'Find me three druids,' she said.

'Any particular druids?' he asked.

Maeve smiled grimly. 'Any three that I don't like.'

393

As Maeve spoke the vision faded and the Daughters left me for the last time. They never sent me another vision, never again shared my bed. But since then I never sleep without wondering, and there is a cold inside me that never leaves.

Cuchullain and I drew the chariot to a halt by a stream. Both of us were too tired to speak. The horses, steam rising from their bodies, ducked their heads into the water, splashing it from side to side, as they drank greedily. Cuchullain stepped down from the chariot and limped into the stream until it was swirling around his knees. He splashed water into his face with his right hand and shook his head like a dog to remove the drops. Then he plunged his sword arm into the water, rubbing it against his calf to wash the blood off. When that was done as well as he could, he laid his useless left arm in the water and bathed a deep wound in the shoulder. I pulled the horses' heads away, so that they could not fill themselves with water and be unable to gallop. Cuchullain splashed past me and sat on a rock in the shallows. I wound the reins around my hand and knelt beside Cuchullain. He looked at my reflection in the water beside his. He smiled wryly at my concerned face.

'This arm hurts,' said Cuchullain. 'It's bad enough having a dead arm I can't use to hold a shield, but you'd think that at least if I can't use it then I wouldn't be able to feel any pain from it. Doesn't seem fair, does it?' He went back to washing the blood off his shoulder with slow movements of his fingers.

I didn't reply, but went on watching him bathe. The light danced around Cuchullain's forehead, and all morning he had seemed monstrous as he fought, twisting his body into impossible shapes as he slashed at his enemies. He was different today. Normally when he fought he became an animal designed for slaughter, slashing and hacking in a battle-thirst that only killing could slake. There was a calm about him now that was new. His frenzy was controlled, as if he was saving his strength. Not that Cuchullain saving his strength made much difference to the men of Maeve's armies, who lay strewn on the ground in every direction. I leant back against the bank of the stream. The muscles in my arms and back ached with pulling at the reins and warding off blows. We drove all morning, and everywhere we met Maeve's men, and everywhere we fought them and killed and killed again, until suddenly there was a lull, as if there was no-one left prepared to come and meet us, and Maeve's armies stood off from us in the midday heat, waiting.

Cuchullain finished washing, and drank from his cupped hand. He stood up heavily and adjusted his armour. Then he walked slowly back to the chariot, dragging his left leg as if a weight were attached to it, and clambered in like an old man.

I walked the thirsty horses away from the stream to stop them pulling back towards it, and we breasted the top of a small hill. Maeve's armies were spread out in front of us like a fan. The plain was covered with men. The Queen rode at their head. When they looked up and saw Cuchullain's chariot they were suddenly silent. I looked out over them, the thousands of men, and could hear nothing but the wind flapping their banners and the stamping of horses' feet. Then Maeve drew her sword, and every man in the army did so too, metal swords rasping against metal scabbards, ripping the silence like a sheet of linen.

'What shall we do now?' I asked. A parley trumpet sounded before Cuchullain could reply. We waited. A small group of men broke ranks from the front of the army and ran up to us. Maeve's chariot came forward more slowly, and stopped just within hearing distance. 'I wonder what they want,' mused Cuchullain.

'Perhaps they want you to fight them one at a time again,' I said. He smiled.

'Laegaid, son of Curoi,' said Cuchullain to the closest of the men in front of him. 'I did not expect to see you here. Has your mother's bed lost its charms?'

Laegaid stepped forward angrily. 'Placed against the prospect of bedding your wife, after which our whole army will take a turn with her, yes,' he replied. 'Will you surrender?' I recognized him as the young stallion that Owen and I had upset the night Maeve called us to her. I laughed at the memory. Laegaid rounded on me furiously. 'What is it that amuses you?'

I looked at him with a smile. 'Why, you do. And the memory of one night in Maeve's castle two years ago.'

Laegaid blushed scarlet, and shouted at Cuchullain. 'Surrender!'

'To you?'

'Yes.'

'Not today.'

'Then when?'

Cuchullain laughed scornfully. 'Not until your mouth and your backside change places so that the smell of your breath improves.'

Laegaid glowered and moved slightly to one side. There was a small commotion behind him, and then a druid stepped forward. His face glowed red as if he were drunk, and he stood like a blustering prize-fighter, except that prize-fighters don't usually sway like fat reeds in the wind.

'Give me one of your spears!' he shouted.

Cuchullain looked at the druid as if he were a very small animal roaring impossibly loudly. He spat languidly to one side, then leant on the chariot rim.

'Why?'

'I claim it as a gift. Either give it to me or I shall make a satire on you.'

I put one hand on Cuchullain's shoulder. 'Tremble,' I said earnestly. The druid bridled, and pointed at me furiously.

'I shall make one on you too!' I did my best to look stricken.

'No need for that,' said Cuchullain mildly. 'I am sure that the satire you would write would devastate my reputation entirely, and I would not have that.'

The druid looked surprised. 'Then you will give the spear to me?'

'Of course.'

The druid stepped forward with a relieved smile. Cuchullain picked up one of the three spears and hurled it straight at him. It passed through the druid's neck, killing him instantly and the three men standing behind him.

'How do you like your gift?' asked Cuchullain.

396

Laegaid bent down and pulled the spear free, then in a sudden movement flung it back at Cuchullain. In his haste, the spear was not aimed true. It missed Cuchullain but caught his faithful charioteer high in the chest.

I felt as if a giant had punched me. I stumbled and fell, dropping into the well of the chariot. Cuchullain knelt beside me.

'I am sorry,' Cuchullain whispered. 'It was meant for me. Shall I pull it out?'

I shook my head slowly. I could see my reflection on his breastplate. Pink foam moved on my lips as my breath passed over them. 'No. It's the only thing holding me together. Go on, I'll be all right.'

Then everything went black.

# 46

Cuchullain stood astride his friend and faced Laegaid.

'Now you have only one arm and no charioteer. Will you surrender?'

Cuchullain wound the reins around his waist and shook his head. Another druid stepped forward. 'I claim a spear,' he shouted.

'I have given more than enough gifts today,' said Cuchullain, 'and they have already cost me too much.'

The druid sneered at him. 'You are not honourable. The bards of Ireland will sing of your closed fist!'

'That they will not!' shouted Cuchullain, and hurled the second spear so hard that it passed through the druid and killed the three men standing behind him. Cuchullain's face twisted with rage as he watched Laegaid pick the spear up and prepare to throw it back. The Champion drew himself up to his full height. Laegaid faltered as he threw, and the spear went sideways and plunged deep into the side of the Grey of Macha. The horse screamed in pain and dropped onto one knee. As it struggled up again the blood surged across and down the horse's flank. Cuchullain jumped down by its side.

'Don't worry, old friend,' he said softly. 'Go and find a better place.'

Cuchullain's sword slashed at the harness, and both horses were free. The Grey cantered awkwardly away, the spear hanging low from its side. The Black Sanglain whinnied softly and trotted after him.

A third druid walked forward. He stepped over the bodies of the two that had gone before him.

'I too claim a spear.'

Cuchullain reached back into the chariot for the third of the spears. 'Somehow, I guessed you might want one.'

The druid walked almost up to him and Cuchullain knew him for an Exile. An Ulsterman. 'You understand, I promised that I would ask.'

Cuchullain nodded. 'I know. I gather that Maeve has that effect on people.'

The druid did not understand. 'Making promises?'

'Bringing death,' said Cuchullain, and swung his arm forward. The spear went through the druid's throat and out the back of his neck, killing the three men behind him.

Laegaid pulled the spear free with difficulty. It was slippery with blood. He levelled it at Cuchullain like a lance. Cuchullain stood by the chariot with a disdainful expression. Laegaid and he looked into each other's eyes for a second, then Laegaid half-ran, half-fell towards Cuchullain, the spear pointing forward straight at his chest. The Champion waited until the point was an arm's length from his body, then made to dash it aside with his shield, a movement he had made a thousand times to protect himself.

This time his arm was dead and held no shield. It did not move.

The spear drove deep into his side and broke off. The force of Laegaid's charge brought him within reach and Cuchullain's right arm struck at Laegaid's throat like a snake, grasping his windpipe and twisting so that it cracked loud enough to be heard by Maeve in her chariot.

Laegaid fell to the ground, clutching his neck, unable to

breathe. Cuchullain dropped into a kneeling position. He hooked his good arm over the edge of the chariot wheel and watched with a detached expression as his entrails coiled onto the earth in front of him. Maeve rode forward. She saw Cuchullain's wound and smiled. 'So, Ulsterman, your death is come.'

Cuchullain looked up at her. 'Not long before yours, I trust,' he rasped.

Ailell jumped down from his chariot and walked to Cuchullain. His face was grim. 'I do not glory in this,' he said. 'Is there anything I can do for you?'

Cuchullain looked at him gratefully and gestured to the stream. 'I would like to go and drink. If you will wait for me here, I shall . . . return shortly.' His voice was almost a whisper.

Maeve scowled. 'What if you do not return?'

Cuchullain smiled. 'Then you will know where to find me.' He knelt down, opening his cloak around himself in a circle, and pulled back everything that had fallen from him so that he could pick it up like a woman clutching a child to her breast. He stood up almost straight, and said to Ailell, 'Remember, if I do not come back, you must come and look for me.' He smiled. 'I shall not go far.' Ailell nodded his agreement, and Cuchullain limped slowly off towards the stream with the sound of Maeve's voice behind him rising in anger at Ailell.

He reached the stream just out of sight and knelt to drink, holding the cloak close to his chest. Then he stood and looked around. Near by he saw what he wanted. He moved slowly to where a post had been driven deep into the ground, all that remained of a bridge built many years before. He sat at the base of it. With difficulty, he undid his belt and looped it around the post and himself, then stood leaning back against it. A shock of pain went through him, and his legs buckled, but the belt round the post held him up. He brought his useless arm round the cloak which held his insides to him and wound the fingers into his straps so that it would not fall away. Then he drew his sword, and waited.

'He is taking too long!'

Ailell looked at Maeve incredulously. 'Too long for what?'

'Too long for me!' She whipped her horse forward.

'Where do you think he has gone?' shouted Ailell with exasperation, but she paid no attention. Ailell ran after her, with Laegaid beside him, the breath whistling through his ruined throat.

They saw Cuchullain hanging slumped against the post, his head fallen forward. He did not move. A dim light seemed to flicker around his temples. His sword arm had dropped, but the hand still held the sword. Maeve stopped her chariot once she could see that he had not tried to escape. Laegaid ran past her, a sword in his hand.

Ailell shouted to him. 'Don't, there's no need, he's already . . .'

Laegaid paid no attention. He wanted a trophy to pay for his ruined voice. He slashed at Cuchullain's wrist before he had even come properly to a halt. Cuchullain's grip was still firm. Laegaid's sword severed the hand from Cuchullain's arm, but the fingers did not release the sword. The force of Laegaid's blow spun Cuchullain's sword up in a circle, flashing light off the shining waters of the stream. The sharp edge of the sword caught Laegaid on his wrist, and his own hand and sword joined Cuchullain's on the ground. For a moment, the cut was so clean that Laegaid did not realize what had happened, and he whirled in triumph, raising his sword arm above his head. He looked up in puzzlement to see his blood shoot like a fountain from the end of his arm, and then he felt the pain of the loss of his hand.

'Shut that noise, for Laeg's sake,' ordered Maeve, as Laegaid fell to his knees, faint and crying out with the pain. 'Cut off his head.' Laegaid looked up in horror, but Maeve was not talking to him any more. She pointed with her sword at Cuchullain's dead body. The light had vanished from his brow. He looked small, almost a boy, and his skin was hairless and fair. Ailell stepped quietly in front of her. The sharp point of her sword almost pricked the soft flesh between his eyes.

'No-one touches him. No-one touches his head.'

Maeve paused for a moment. Their soldiers shifted nervously, not sure what to do. She pulled her cloak back with one swift movement, jumped down off her chariot and walked determinedly past him. 'By Laeg, I'll do it myself!'

Her sword was raised high and about to come down on Cuchullain's neck when Ailell caught and held her wrist. She tried to force it down despite his grip, but she was off-balance, and the effort twisted her round so that she almost fell. The sword dropped from her deadened fingers. She thrust her face into her husband's. 'What is the matter with you?' she hissed.

Ailell looked stolidly at her, but his voice was determined. 'He was always honourable, even when we broke our agreement with him every day. He stays as he is.'

Maeve laughed. 'You think he would not have had your head for his chariot rim? Thrown your brain-ball at me from his sling?' She pushed past him and got back into her chariot. 'If only your brain were big enough to be worth the throwing!'

Ailell did not reply, but watched silently as she swung the horses round and churned the soft earth into waves with her chariot wheels as she galloped away. Ailell bent and tied a leather strap tight around Laegaid's arm so that the bleeding stopped. He turned to the nearest of his men. 'Take him to the druids. Let them see if they can save him.'

A captain gestured to Cuchullain. 'What should we do with the Ulsterman?'

Ailell glanced back at the dead body, and a shadow seemed to settle over it. The raven sat on the top of the post supporting Cuchullain and three shadows writhed and danced around his head. Ailell turned away. 'Cover his head so that the birds won't get his eyes.'

'Is that all?'

'That's all he'll need. His friends will find him soon enough.'

Ailell turned, and suddenly he thought that a great black cloud came hurtling over the bank towards them. His men shouted and lifted their swords to defend themselves, but Ailell didn't move. He stood still, waiting.

The Black Sanglain collided with him chest to chest and Ailell was flung sideways, his head snapping back as he landed heavily amongst the rocks in the shallows of the stream. He lay still, face down in the water. His men ran to help him, but the horse turned and was amongst them, his sharp hooves flying like long knives tied to whirling chariot wheels and his teeth tearing angry rents in their bodies. When at last they rescued the King he was almost drowned.

Men said that three Kings died from three spears that day: the Grey of Macha, who was the King of Horses; Leary, the King of Charioteers; and Cuchullain, the greatest Champion of them all.

# 47

Conall knelt in the water by Cuchullain's feet and Cuchullain's blood swirled around his legs and was carried down the stream. Conall bowed his head so that no-one could see his face. The other Champions stood back and waited. Eventually he stood up. He walked back to his chariot, his face grim but composed, and drove off in the direction of Maeve's army. The others helped to cut Cuchullain's body down and laid him on a bier. They took him to Emer at Muirthemne, and then set off after Conall.

Conall took something of Cuchullain with him that day, and it was said that he swelled into a hideous monster who led the Champions of Ulster into the midst of Maeve's army, raining killing blows onto the Connaughtmen without feeling his own wounds or tiring, until the Connaughtmen finally broke and fled in front of them. Fergus and the Exiles stood aside from Maeve's army and refused to fight for either side. They stood on a hillside and watched as Conall killed seven Kings that day, and soldiers beyond counting, and he chased and harried the Connaughtmen in their retreat without resting, until the only men left in Ulster who had not been born there were lying still on the cold ground, and their comrades were deep in their own province, bathing their wounds in quiet places far from harm's path. This Conall did in Cuchullain's memory, as he had sworn.

When the Connaughtmen were defeated, Conall led the Champions of the Red Branch back to the ruins of Emain Macha. There they found that Emer had ordered a deep tomb to be built for Cuchullain, with his wealth placed in it, and Ogham stones with his name and lineage cut into them. Emer stood next to Cuchullain's body at the entrance to the grave and looked around her. Every man and woman who could walk or ride had come to hear her funeral song. She turned her back on them and lifted her arms through their silence. Her voice rose and flew along the valleys, soared over the trees, raced along the shores.

'I was soft wax and you pressed warm inside me;
Marked and sealed our opening and closing.
Now the waiting is over and you have gone.
Do not hurry away;
I would not stay long alone.

You held the warm spiced wine of our love
Cupped in the palms of your hands;
Now your fingers are stiff and cold.
Red pools on the earth
Mark where your life is spilt.

Harbour of my happiness and shelter of my soul,
You flew fast as thought, along dawn's silver river,
Across dark forests, down passes of grey stone and heather
That lead to plains of contest and bloodshed
Where Ulster's fighting men shout your name to each other
Then raise their reddened arms and fall to battle again.

You were the iron that bound their shields,
You were the hand that steadied their reins,
You were the shadow that flew between them and their fears,
Stood the watch for them in the hour before dawn.

405

You were the horizons of my sight, my heart's breath.
You were my dreamtime, pressed warm against my back.
Now, greycold and closed, your face waits my end,
I watch your brow's fire dwindle, flare once and scatter;
It brushes past my heart and is gone.

Your name and mine will for ever be one word.
Our last breaths embrace then cool upon your cheek.
Better this damp earth and your cold fire
Than the warm arms of summer without your touch.
Better to end our short tune together
Than stay alone to listen while poets sing your song.'

There was a long silence, as if every man and woman there no longer breathed. Then she lowered her arms. Emer watched as his body was carried into the tomb. She waited until the bearers had come out again, then went in herself. She lay down beside Cuchullain, and pressed her lips against his. She filled herself with his cold breath, then breathed her last into his body.

Conall stepped into the tomb, and stood watching them, as if waiting for something. Then he bowed, and left them. The great stone was rolled across the entrance, and the tomb was closed for all time.

# 48

The spear didn't kill me, although it did finish the King of Charioteers. Driving horses was the only thing I was ever any good at, and after the spear split my chest I couldn't do that any more. Or perhaps the third King wasn't me, maybe it was Ailell, who died in every important sense that day except for the fact that his heart kept beating. Or perhaps it's just a sad world where you can't even rely on prophecies any more.

I lay on the ground for a long time, ignored in the rush to see Cuchullain die, and then lay there again for another longer time while everyone decided to chase off after Maeve. It would have been nice if someone had thought to check that I was actually dead.

I should say that if it wasn't for Owen I probably would be. He came calling out for me, almost blind and in pain, staggering like a drunken man amongst the corpses and broken equipment. When I heard his voice I tried to shout and felt a fire light in my chest. I felt his hand on my shoulder and then I must have lost consciousness.

When I woke it was like the first time I came to Ulster, gazing up at the roof and thinking how comfortable I was. Then I moved a fraction and felt as though there was molten iron running through my veins.

Owen and Ulinn sat with me for a month until I could move, and then they bullied me into something like walking. I suppose I owe them both my life. Ulinn and I spoke long into the night of what had happened. She seemed to have forgiven me. I was going to ask her to stay, even to marry me. One day without warning she kissed my cheek and walked out of our lives. I called after her, but she just waved without turning round. She never came back.

Owen and I were left alone. History went on around us and occasionally someone stopped on their journey and told us what was happening. Conall and some of the other Champions tried to keep things going in Ulster, and for a while it seemed that everything might be all right, but then there was an argument and all the Champions left Emain Macha for their own castles, and instead of Ulster being one large kingdom it became a lot of small chiefdoms, strong enough to hold onto what they had, but unable to expand.

Conor, true to his word, went into exile, bequeathing Fergus the poisoned chalice of a kingdom divided. Fergus died within two years, sad and worn out by the hopeless task of trying to keep Ulster together, and the few Exiles who still remained in Connaught never came home. The Connaughtmen came again the following summer, just old-fashioned cattle-raiding, not an invasion force, and were surprised to meet almost no resistance. They pushed on into Ulster, expecting a trap to shut on them any moment. There was no trap. The Connaughtmen took what they wanted and went home. Two weeks later every man who could lift a sword was heading for the Ulster border, although Maeve was not with them. Conall gathered all the men he could find and went to meet them. They say that as Conall stood at the head of his small army, facing a Connaught force many times larger, Conor the old King, returned from exile, rode up to them and asked humbly if he could join them. There were men there that he had wronged, even to the extent of causing the death of people they loved, but it is said that every man welcomed him, and he took his place amongst them. They say Conall turned to his small army as if he were about to give a speech before the charge. They obviously didn't know Conall if they thought he would talk when he could fight instead. For a few moments he hesitated, then he smiled without speaking, looped a brain-ball into his sling and flung it at the nearest Connaughtman, breaking the man's head and throwing him off his horse. Then the men of Ulster cheered and charged behind him into the heart of the huge enemy army.

Many Connaughtmen died before the battle was over. When it finished, there was not a single Ulster Champion left alive. Conall, Buchal, Conor, a hundred others, all were dead. The Red Branch was no more, and I had lost the best companions I could have hoped for. Back at Emain Macha we braced ourselves for an invasion that never came. News filtered slowly through from Connaught. Maeve was no longer the Warrior Queen. Ailell lay unmoving on their bed with his eyes open, his mouth slack, one side of his head soft as new bread. He never spoke again after the Black Sanglain knocked him down in the river beside Cuchullain's body. It was said that Maeve shut herself up in her castle, feeding her half-dead husband with a spoon and talking only to spirits. Perhaps with him almost dead she realized what it was she had when he was alive. Perhaps the spirits she spoke to were the Daughters of Calatin, who, with Cuchullain dead, had no purpose, and waited for death by keeping the Queen company. They no longer bother me with their visions, and I sleep as well as an old man can.

Ulster is no more. Robbers roam across the countryside but everything of value has been looted and we are now too poor to be worth bothering about. It seems that no-one even thinks us worth conquering, so there is no law, no government, no authority. It won't last. A land that has no-one in charge is like a room with no joists at the centre of a house; eventually everything around it will fall inward into the empty space. It's quite fun for the moment, although I'm sure things will get nasty sooner or later. I shan't be here to see it.

The glory of Ulster had died when the Exiles left for

Connaught. Only Cuchullain had stood between Ulster and destruction. With him gone, there was nothing to keep it together.

Meanwhile, Owen and I have some small local fame because we knew the Champion of Champions, and so we are looked after in a desultory sort of a way. We'll live till we die. Meanwhile, we tell each other stories, stories about things that really happened. Things that happened to us when we weren't even there. We sit here, an old blind bard and an old lame charioteer, and sometimes we talk about the old days, and sometimes – more frequently now – we don't. Most days we don't even argue any more.

Telling stories isn't as easy as I thought it would be.

# Historical Note

Readers interested in finding out more information about the Celts now have a wide choice of texts to choose from. I was brought up on Nora Chadwick and Frank Delaney, and while their work has since been built on by others, they offer a combination of scholarship and entertainment that still holds at least one small boy enthralled.

The source material for *Hound* is the Irish epic *Tain Bo Cuailnge*, or 'The Cattle Raid of Cooley', perhaps best known as 'The Tain'. If there is a more lyrical and exciting translation of this adventure than Thomas Kinsella's then I'd like to read it. Anyone remotely familiar with 'The Tain' will see immediately that I have taken substantial liberties with almost every aspect of the story, except, I hope, its spirit. If I have trodden on your dreams, *mea maxima culpa*.